Praise for
The White Rose

"Incisive and urbane . . . it harks back to the gender confusions of Shakespeare's comedies while adding some surprising contemporary twists . . . a roman à clef, a sendup of gossip columnists and Manhattan strivers and a paean to professional fulfillment. Korelitz's characters—charming, idealistic and contradictory—are what make *The White Rose* so appealing . . . This novel represents a significant step forward."

—*The New York Times Book Review*

"Korelitz is a strong writer . . . capable of descriptions that are hers alone."

—*Washington Post*

"Korelitz is alert both to New York's social geometry and to the melancholy that underlies the glittering surface of her novel."

—*The New Yorker*

"Juicy Fun."

—*Entertainment Weekly*

A "lighthearted novel . . . Based on a comic opera, *The White Rose* naturally ends with everything put right . . . Great comic plots persuade us that coincidence is not random chance but destiny."

—*The Boston Sunday Globe*

JEAN HANFF KORELITZ

The White Rose

miramax books

HYPERION

NEW YORK

ISBN 1-4013-5986-8

COPYRIGHT © 2004 JEAN HANFF KORELITZ

10 9 8 7 6 5 4 3 2 1

PRINTED IN THE UNITED STATES OF AMERICA

FOR INFORMATION ADDRESS:
HYPERION
77 WEST 66TH STREET
NEW YORK, NEW YORK 10023-6298

FOR PAUL MULDOON

THE WHITE ROSE

Act I

CHAPTER ONE

Right Now

I N A BED AT THE CENTER OF THE UNIVERSE, a man is inside a woman he loves and they are moving, the bed is moving, the apartment is moving, the island of Manhattan is moving. There is a bowl of roses on the bedside table, fat white Boule de Neige—his own—chosen for her, and right off the truck, in the blue hours of the morning, this very morning. Now it's late afternoon and outside, Park Avenue is clogged with strident, resentful cabs, but Marian—her name is Marian—feels oddly becalmed, borne aloft in the safe familiarity of her city and her bed, even as the angry horns float up and through her bedroom window, even as this wild pounding (his hips and her heart weirdly in tandem) moves her roughly against the sheet—a top note of friction, but good friction. This pounding—there is no other word for it, thinks Marian, but how odd. Pounded into submission? Pounded into sweetness? She smiles, her eyes closed against his neck. How odd a way to change a thing from something hard to something soft, as she is most certainly being made into something soft, into a sweet soft thing, tight between him and the sheet. Sweet butter, for example. And what is that thing they pound into butter? Is it milk? Is it cream?

"Yes," says Oliver, as if in confirmation, and she laughs into his soft dark hair.

And then, quite suddenly, he stops, and Marian has one of those moments, those rare and otherworldly moments, when a person can see herself as if she were not herself at all but someone else, looking at her, and she sees (greedy, not knowing how long it will last) through the scrim of all this ambient affection, and all this situational lust, herself: white shoulder, white breast, dark nipple, fleshy. And—much to her own surprise—she is absolutely ravishing. Possibly, she appraises, almost coolly, the most ravishing woman who ever breathed. How dull of her never to have seen it, for all these years of mirror scrutiny and social unease, all these years secure in her twin designations of smart and plain. What a waste, never to have noticed her own loveliness, for surely men have longed for her since she put away roller skates. Surely someone will again before they put her in the ground. But never before, nor ever again, as much as right now.

Oliver moves again. It is a relief and a sadness.

"Sweetheart," he says, though not distinctly.

From far below, a howl of enraged traffic drifts into the open window, and it occurs to Marian that she is inhabiting the moment of her greatest happiness. Never mind the reasons she should not be in this particular bed with this particular man—and there are many reasons, and they are very good reasons. Right now, right now: in her life, in this bed, with Oliver and the roses and the noise and the dusk of a Manhattan day in October. And she sees, as if she were falling from her own open window, her life flash not back from the end nor forward from the beginning but both of these at once, the ends racing for the middle, for this moment at the heart of her life, so that in the instant before she smacks to the last of consciousness, this is what she will see: herself and him, inside, in motion, in love, and then she will know that her life was actually a good life, with sweetness and pounding and car horns and the smell of him, Oliver, who looks at her that very instant and says what he says, which is: "I love you."

Marian, in answer, in restraint, shifts a bit. This has the unintended effect of letting him sink—incredibly—even deeper inside.

"I love you," Oliver says again.

There is the faintest pause, barely longer than a breath. Then she says, "You don't have to say that. You shouldn't say that." And she moves again. She is not uncomfortable, precisely. But she wants to move.

"Why not? *I love you*." She hears impatience in his voice. He has decided to take offense at this, in the way only a man can do.

"You'll know others," she says, her eyes on the roses. "You're young."

"Marian," Oliver says. "Marian. Look at me."

Marian turns. She does not want to look at him. She wants to look at the wall of her bedroom, which is taking the full hit of October light on a plaster painted six times with ever deepening greens. Like—she remembers Marshall saying, once, between coats four and five—"living in a goddamned terrarium." But perhaps that's not untrue, she thinks now: her burrowing instinct. Earth mother, that's her! Can you be an earth mother and childless?

The sheets rustle. He is waiting for his answer, the angry young man.

But she is losing herself, too. There is something dizzying in the smell of him, she thinks, shutting her eyes tight and feeling him move. The smell where neck meets shoulder, back of knee, palm of hand: clean and hard, talc and tough, the animal scent of purest desire. Either that or the bed is rocking, or the building, which is not so very tall, but they are nearly at the top of it, and the beguiling of those impatient cars and screeching brakes, or his hips, which, being narrow (or more likely her own being wide) fit so neatly between her thighs and move so cunningly, or...there's that smell again, Marian thinks. She wants to stop what she is doing, what they are doing, and just *smell* him. *Hold still! I must smell!* And she imagines herself slipping him over and onto his belly, immobilizing him with a well-placed knee, and leaning over him, nose to ear, nose to nape.

And then, quite suddenly, she remembers the way Caroline used to smell Oliver's hair when he was a little boy—with a whispered *"My luvvie,"* and a kiss to his chubby, little-boy cheek—and it's all over.

How small? How young? Having no children of her own, she has never been good at ages. Did he wear diapers? My God! (*"My luvvie…"* She concentrates: little boy, curly brown hair, corduroy pants, a grubby stuffed bunny clutched in a grubby fist, and Caroline, her hair gamine short, worn short those early years in Greenwich, when? After college, certainly. After Marian left Yale? Before New York? The math? The math?) *My God!*

"Marian," he is crooning, and though she is now too miserable to let go herself, she is also too generous to hinder him, so she follows him with her hips and sounds, making herself hollow (*vessel*, Marian thinks grimly, *old gourd, old girl*) until he is rattling, like a death rattle. Little-death rattle. This breaks her misery and actually makes her laugh, though only for the briefest instant.

"Sweetheart," moans Oliver, misunderstanding. There is a mist of sweat between them.

Marian closes her eyes. She holds the moment even as it slips from her, even as he slips from her, but Oliver's elation lingers.

"Mmm," she offers, noncommittally. She knows he loves her. And the terrible thing is, she has never not wanted him to love her. Not from the first and never since. He keeps throwing her golden apples, and she keeps stopping to pick them up. She will never have enough apples, she thinks.

"I want to tell everyone," Oliver says, avoiding eye contact.

"Oh?" She says evenly. "And who constitutes 'everyone'?"

"Well," he considers, "the Upper East Side. Upper East and Upper West. SoHo. The West Village. Brooklyn Heights and Park Slope. Those people who move to Brooklyn, they're so defensive, aren't they? And Hastings-on-Hudson, and Montclair. They get very offended if people leave them out. Also the New Haven Line, or else I could never go home again. The Hamptons, of course. Or should I say, 'the East End' like the rest of you reverse snobs?"

Marian thwacks him.

"I figure an ad in the *Ascendant* should cover it. I'd just put it in the shop ad, it wouldn't cost me any more! It could say, *The Calla Lilies Are in Bloom Again at The White Rose. Order some today. And incidentally I am in love with Marian Kahn. That's right,* the *Marian Kahn...author of* Lady Charlotte Wilcox*! Maybe I should do a special: Get a free pink paperback with any order of pink callas over $50.* What do you think?"

"I think that's shocking." She shakes her head, indulging him. "My book, a freebie for a lousy fifty bucks? Make it at least a hundred."

"Writers," he says, and rolls his eyes. "God, the ego of writers."

Marian laughs. She hadn't seen it right away, this Puckish side of him, not in their serious, panicky, and reverent first months, and not often since, but it's there. Oliver, for the most part, is a serious man, broody even, given to silences and careful speech, but now, very occasionally, a streak of playfulness turns itself to the light, and when it does, Marian finds herself disinclined to resist. In what she stubbornly considers her real life, levity is rare and abandon pretty much unheard of. She loves to laugh with Oliver. She loves to feel her body against his, both of them shaking with laughter. So long as he doesn't go too far.

"Besides," he says now, "why not bring in the fans? I'm a small-business owner. I'm supposed to be keeping my eye on the bottom line."

"And just how," Marian says, "is invoking a woman who's been dead two hundred years going to increase your sales of calla lilies?"

"Not *her* fans, silly," says Oliver, nudging her shoulder with his forehead. "*Your* fans. You have fans."

"I teach history, Oliver. She was a wild adventuress whose boyfriend wore a dress. She has fans."

He winces. "I forgot about the dress. I wish you hadn't reminded me."

"Oh?" she says archly. "And what do you have against a man in a dress?"

"Well, nothing. I mean, to each his own. But honestly, what kind of self-respecting heterosexual guy goes around in a skirt?"

"Hmm," she says. "How about a heterosexual guy whose vengeful wife and creditors would like nothing better than to find him and drag him back to England? She had the money, you know. The wife," Marian says. "Besides, I think Charlotte liked it."

Oliver turns to her. "You're suggesting she was of the Sapphic persuasion?"

"Oh, don't be so small-minded, Oliver! I'm suggesting that his willingness to masquerade was a sign of his devotion, which she would have liked. And maybe it was a little bit titillating as well."

He makes a face. "Titillating."

"Sure. Why not? You're traveling through Europe with your 'girl-friend.' You walk down the street, sit out in some public place surrounded by your countrymen abroad, half of whom have heard the scandalous story of your elopement and are dying to know where you are... and in addition to getting away with it—which is quite an aphrodisiac itself—you know that under that dress is the man who's going to take you back to the inn and make love to you."

Oliver considers this. "And this scenario would be appealing to any woman."

"I can see its appeal," Marian tells him. "Beyond that, I make no assumptions."

"Interesting," he says. His hand materializes, softly, at her breast, which he kisses. "And I thought I knew all about you."

Marian closes her eyes. "You know enough," she says.

"Sometimes," Oliver says with a grin, his face to her neck, "I try to remember how I used to think of you. When I first read your book. Or when my mom would talk about you. But I can't. I can only see you as I see you now."

"Now," Marian says, echoing him. This is promising. *Now*, she can handle. Only *then*—the one in the past and the one in the future—gives her pause.

"But did I tell you?" He perks up, lifting his head and looking slyly at her. "I remembered you the other day."

She frowns. "Remembered me? When?"

"I think it was you. You tell me. It was in Greenwich, in the back-yard. I was with Billy Pastor, so that would have been sixth grade, because he pissed me off the next year and we were never friends after that. My mom and Henry were having a party. A cookout."

"Big steaks," she says, her voice thin.

"Right. All the men stood around all night drinking G and Ts and acting like they were total hunter-gatherers, not suits on the train. And there was this woman on a log, smoking a cigarette, in this wild dress with purple squiggles on it."

Marian swallows. "Marimekko," she says.

"What?"

"Marimekko. From Finland. Very chic in the seventies. Never mind."

"And it was you!" He crows in conclusion. "I remembered, the other night on the subway. Man, you were beautiful."

"Yeah," she says with a sigh. "I were."

"You *are*." He nudges her. "You're not tricking me into that."

She looks at him. "What were you doing looking at women when you were in sixth grade?"

"No." Oliver laughs. "I wasn't looking. It was just...just a filed memory, you know? And suddenly it came back to me."

"On the subway."

"Yeah, on the subway. I had you all over my fingers. It did some-thing to my brain."

"Oliver!"

"Oh," he says, grinning. "Do that again. Blush again! From now on I'm going to leave your trail all over the IRT."

"God, you would," Marian says, repelled and elated.

"I would. I will," he teases.

"You're foul," she says, laughing.

"But I clean up so nicely."

"Foul. I'll tell your mother."

It has slipped. She hadn't been thinking. Now it is out there, in the world, between them. His mother is her oldest friend—not her great-est, not her best friend, but certainly her oldest. An old girl's oldest...that meant older than many, many. Caroline, who had white-blond hair and hated Miss Fokine's dancing lessons as fiercely as Marian had, so so long ago. Marian will not tell Oliver's mother. Marian is terrified of Oliver's mother being told.

"Why not?" he says, his voice soft, but steely soft. "I'll tell her myself. She has to know sometime."

Marian shivers. And then, quite suddenly, she is on the point of tears. Where have they come from? Queued up behind the eyelids, they threaten to course like obedient soldiers, pouring from the trenches. "No, you wouldn't. You can't! Oliver, you can't!"

But now he is sulking. He is off on his own stamp, his little performance piece: *I am a man! I deserve! I'm entitled!* Amazing how they all have this same soliloquy, in the end.

"Why shouldn't I tell her? Why shouldn't I tell everyone? What's so terrible if I tell?"

"Tell," Marian says, testing the word. At the tail of the *l*, a sudden hit of iron.

One of his arms slithers beneath her back, forcing her into an arch not quite comfortable, but she can live with it for a while. From across the apartment, she hears the purr of her office phone, and pictures it, for a moment, down the corridor, across the living room, and through the dining room, hooking around her kitchen with its cool Portuguese tiles and into the maid's room that serves as her temple to Lady Charlotte Wilcox—the now very famous Lady Charlotte Wilcox—a sleek black phone with its little light blinking. She turns toward Oliver.

He is so lovely, she thinks again, and not only the part of him that she can see, nor even what she feels: the heat from him, the sweet frictions of his fingers and tongue. It's his kindness, his goodness, the as yet undiscovered depths of his introspections and generosities. He is that sought-after thing: the good person, the good kid, the nice guy. That he is also passionate and smart and crushingly romantic seems almost beside the point. He is so good she dares not waste her time regretting that the situation is impossible. There will be time later for that, Marian thinks, desperate to clear even a wisp of preemptive sadness from her thoughts. *Not now. Later. Not now.*

"There's nothing that has to be hidden here," Oliver says. "I want everyone to know! I want your doorman to know. I want my customers to know! I want Pete at the Pink Teacup to know! Why not? Don't I love you? Am I not of sound mind?"

"Yes," she says, clutching at him. "I mean, no. *Please.*" Even to herself she sounds frantic. "Caroline would be devastated."

"She'll get over it. She'll want me to be happy."

"Not happy with me. Not happy with somebody her own age. And your father!"

"You mean," he says coolly, "my stepfather."

"Yes. Oliver, please think. This is wonderful. This is... I'm..." She shakes her head in pure frustration. "I'm so happy. This year... I wouldn't have missed it for anything."

"Missed it!" he says.

"Please, we need to keep it private. Oliver, promise me!"

"I won't." He crosses his arms in classic petulance. "You misunderstand me, Marian. This is for good with me. I mean, this is *it*, you know? So I want to be with you now and I want to be with you next year. I want to be with you in twenty years. I want to be with you in thirty years."

The thought of herself in thirty years fills her with total horror. Reflexively, she pulls up the sheets.

"Too late," he says smugly. "I've seen it."

"And what about Marshall?" Marian says. "Doesn't he have a say?"

"He had one," Oliver says. "But he blew it. Besides, what's he doing right now? He'd rather go off to some hut and shoot things than stay home and be with you."

"Oliver. You know that's not fair." She swings her legs over the side of the bed, still holding the sheet across herself but prepared to make her getaway. "It's a corporate retreat."

"I've never understood the appeal of shooting things," Oliver muses. "I think it's an I'm-a-man-and-I'm-getting-old thing."

Marian turns abruptly. "Well, perhaps when you're getting old, you'll understand it better."

He recoils. "Marian."

"Look. I'm sorry. But there's no point attacking Marshall. His life is a very big house with lots of rooms and I don't go into all of them. I'm happy with that." She softens. "After all, I wouldn't want him in all of my rooms, either, would I?"

Oliver, looking hard but not quite fierce, says nothing.

"But look how we're wasting the moment, Oliver. We're here. He's there. When have we ever had this?"

"And what," he says archly, "is *this*?"

The very question, thinks Marian. She would like him to be quiet now, and kiss her.

Marian considers him as if seeing him for the first time: man on the street, man through a restaurant window, man with flowers. There is a bloom on him that breaks her heart, and hair so richly brown it makes her think of fertile earth. Each cheek bears a brushstroke of pink, fading at the jaw line, as if he has just come in from a run on some spiky peak in New Hampshire. Oliver is twenty-six, elated, connected, utterly alive. She is forty-eight.

Again, that purr as the phone makes its transapartment statement. It can be nothing important enough to wrest her from her bed, her lover, even her petulant lover. Increasingly, these past months, it has been Lady Charlotte groupies on the line, wanting to touch her telephonic hem, so to speak, so much so it now seems to Marian that it's time to change the number altogether. She holds her breath: the phone stops.

"I'm not trying to ruin things," he says suddenly. "Believe me, that's the last thing I want. But I want more, and I don't see why we shouldn't have it. And don't—"

She has begun to speak, but he continues, "Don't try to tell me it's for me, because it isn't. I'd marry you today if I could. I have no problem with the age thing, you know I don't. I only mention it because I don't want to ignore that it's problematic for you."

"I appreciate that," Marian says carefully. "That's very sensitive of you. But I'm asking you to do nothing for the moment. I just need some...stillness, I guess. I need to be still. Let's give ourselves some time." Please, she adds to herself, since she is not deluding herself about the rest of it.

"How much time?" Oliver says.

"Until..." Marian smiles, considering. "Until my rose is ready."

He smiles. "You mean Lady Charlotte's rose."

"Of course."

"A rose to order: pompous, overblown, and...what was the rest of it?"

"Pompous, overblown, and incapable of regret. That's what I asked for, I seem to recall," says Marian, laughing. "Surely that can't be too difficult."

"Difficult? It's a serious challenge! But it might take time. I may not get it on the first try, you know."

"Then I will wait," Marian says, and they kiss.

Kissing him is her favorite thing. Kissing him is a thing she can do for hours. Oliver is a kisser of spectacular abilities, because he—alone, she believes, of his gender—has grasped the secret power of a kiss that does not necessarily lead to activities more genital. In other words, he can kiss for the sake of kissing, and a woman need not fear kissing him if she is not prepared to have sex immediately afterward. Marshall, it occurs to her even as she luxuriates in Oliver's tongue, Oliver's slightly overbitten front teeth, has never quite gleaned this fact, though she doesn't hold it against him. Most men, after all, offered kisses as they might offer invitations to join a board: if you accepted, you'd better be prepared to come up with the goods. Marshall, a man of his generation (*their* generation, she reminds herself), had better things in mind than the meeting of lips, even the interplay of tongues: they were in it for fucking, pure and simple. Not that fucking didn't have its place.

But Oliver...well, Oliver likes to kiss. Just now, indeed, he is holding her head, fingertips light on her jaw, lifting it, adjusting it, and her mouth is full of him and her thoughts are full of him, until she is almost helpless to keep herself from taking those demure above-the-shoulder hands and placing them decisively *below* the shoulder so that she can disprove her own point about kissing for kissing's sake as quickly as possible. But before she can do that, there is a rude buzzing sound from the kitchen.

"Drat," Marian says, pulling back.

"Oh, let it go," says Oliver, his voice dreamy.

"Can't." She sits up. "It's downstairs. The doorman knows I'm here."

"So?" He leans back on his elbow. "If it's a delivery he'll take it."

Marian gets out of bed, wrapping the sheet around herself like a lady on a Grecian urn. "Mr. Stern," she informs him, "I live in this building. I have lived in this building for fourteen years. These doormen know far too much about my life, and I know virtually nothing about theirs. It is a strange and strained state of affairs that requires a highly choreographed dance involving all participants, and an inordinate amount of courtesy. And part of that courtesy, my young man, is answering the house phone when it buzzes."

"Okay!" He puts up his hands and grins. "Answer! Answer!"

"Also random chats about the weather, cooing over baby pictures, superficial commentary about city politics, and a working knowledge of the championship prospects of major New York sports teams. I do not refrain from answering the house phone when he knows I'm upstairs and then expect the departure of my young and lovely friend in due course to pass without some salacious interest. Do you follow me?"

"Like a slave," Oliver laughs. "Now hurry up and answer the phone."

Marian does. She trails her sheet through the apartment, hearing the house phone sound its angry buzz a second time as she pads over the dark wooden floors. In the dining room her mail from yesterday is piled on the long oak table: magazines, catalogues, bills, a fat manila envelope of Charlotte reviews, from Italy this time, forwarded by another satisfied publisher. Also a box from Hammacher Schlemmer, another of Marshall's gadgets to be fussed over, perplexed by, and ultimately consigned to molder with its gadget cousins in the hall closet. "All right!" she hisses to herself as the house phone blasts anew.

"I'm here!" She reaches the kitchen and snatches it up. "Sorry, Hector. I was working, didn't hear the phone."

"Mrs. Kahn? It's Hector downstairs? I try to stop him."

Marian goes cold. Her sheet slips in her grip. Irrationally, she thinks of Marshall up there in Nova Scotia. He is up there, isn't he?

"What is it, Hector?"

"He coming up. He say he your cousin. He insist! He say you expecting him, he your cousin! Mr. Barton Ox he say he name is."

Ox?

Oh no. Oh no no no, Marian shakes her head. And it's her own bloody fault: the idiot said he was coming to town and she'd failed to head him off. And now he's here, on his way up. And she is in the kitchen holding a sheet over her breasts. And there is a naked man in her bed.

"Thank you, Hector!" Marian yelps. "That's fine!" And she hangs up the phone and tears back to the bedroom, letting her sheet fall behind her on the rug. "Oh shit!" she is muttering. "Oh very much shit."

"Hmm?" Oliver is in the bathroom. Water runs into the sink.

"Oliver!" Marian hisses. "You've got to get out of here! My cretin of a cousin is coming upstairs. I completely forgot he was coming to the city, and now he's in the elevator."

"Why's he a cretin?" Oliver asks with interest.

"Not now!" She is fumbling with her bra strap. It springs from her fingers once, twice. "Shit!"

"Calm down, sweetheart. I'll just leave."

"You can't leave. I mean, you have to leave, but you can't leave. You can't go out the front door, you have to go out the back door. You have to go *now*."

"But I have no clothes on," Oliver says wickedly. "Have you thought how that will look?"

"Where are your clothes?" Marian asks frantically, but even as she does, two things happen: she knows where his clothes are—they're where her own clothes of the afternoon are, deposited all over the living room as she and Oliver had moved from chair to rug to sofa hours earlier—and the doorbell rings.

"Oh shit!"

"So why's he a cretin again?" says Oliver.

"Go!" She swats him and opens a bureau drawer, snatching out a black cashmere sweater. "And be quiet. Get your clothes, go into my office, *quietly*, and when you're dressed, go out the back and take the service elevator down. I'll... I'll call you when he's gone. I'll call you at the shop."

"Will you have dinner with me?"

The doorbell rings again. Twice, this time.

"Sure, of course. Just... Oliver, please, just scram."

But he insists on kissing her once more, catching her head as it emerges from the neck of her sweater, and even amid her panic she feels the briefest rush as he clutches her. Then he pads nakedly away, refusing, like any man, to be hurried. Marian yanks open the drawer of her dresser and takes the top pair of pants. Black, like the sweater. She'll look funereal, but she is already dressed and moving toward the door. And yet there is something... something nagging her, and not the now-enraged rings of the bell. It's something about... no, not the clothes. (As she moves past the living room she can see that Oliver has picked up her own as well as his—sweet of him.) Not the doorman, not even her cousin, who is the last person she wishes to see, it's something about...

"Hi!"

Marian flings open the door, and a fleshy index finger is lifted away from the buzzer.

"Oh, Barton! What a treat!" She gushes. And then it comes to her.

It's the service elevator. Which is broken and awaiting repair, and not going anywhere.

CHAPTER TWO

A Ridiculous Man

T HEY DIDN'T WANT TO LET ME COME UP!" he says indignantly. "Can you imagine that?"

Barton's face is a veritable purple, Marian thinks. She offers a kiss with minimal contact to his sweaty right cheek.

"Oh," he pauses in his rant to smear the cheek against hers. "I said, 'Of course I'm going up! I'm her cousin!'"

"We've had some trouble with people who've read the book…," Marian says lamely.

"Yes, yes." He waves his thick hand dismissively. It occurs to Marian that he does not know which book she means. Does he even know she has written a book?

"So they're very careful, you see. Once we had a whole busload from Indiana down in the lobby. Luckily we were out at the beach that day, but the other tenants were not happy."

"What?" He seems to be looking around worriedly. "Can I get something to drink?"

She takes his coat, which is heavy tweed, and drapes it across her arm. "Come on into the living room. Come tell me all the news."

Marian turns on a lamp. The day has turned its corner into dusk. She strains to hear some sound in the kitchen, in the maid's room–office, and beyond. Surely he can't still be getting dressed? "What will you have?"

"Oh," he says, considering. "Maybe some bourbon. You have bourbon?"

"It's in the kitchen. Give me a sec." And she takes off, moving quickly in her bare feet across the hallway and dining room. When she gets to her office she finds Oliver lounging on the daybed. He is wearing a pair of boxer shorts. Only a pair of boxer shorts.

"Did you know your elevator is broken?" he says casually.

"No! I mean, yes. Yes, I did, but I forgot. Oliver, where are your pants?"

He appears to consider this very seriously. "Maybe under the sofa?"

"Oh no! You forgot them?"

Oliver shrugs, but he is clearly enjoying himself. "I didn't forget them. I missed them. I was in a hurry."

Her own clothes from earlier, she notes, are piled at the foot of the daybed.

"I have to go. I have to get him a drink. Look, just stay here, okay?"

He grins at her. At the sight of his little overbite, she melts a bit. "Where would I go?" Oliver says mildly. "I'm in a compromised position. I'll just amuse myself in here."

"Fine," she says, distracted. "But quietly."

Marian dashes into the little bathroom next to her office, flushes the toilet and loudly shuts the door. Then she grabs a glass, scoops up some ice from the icemaker in her freezer, and scoots back to the living room, where the bourbon has been all along. "Sorry!" she says gaily. "Had to pee!"

Barton looks up. "What?"

She crosses the living room to the bar, flicks open the door, locates the bourbon and pours. "You're looking good. It's so nice to see you in town. You never come down anymore, do you? But you should have called."

You really should have called, she thinks.

"Oh, the phone," Barton says bitterly. "It just rang and rang. Then that message machine. I refuse to speak to a machine! I'm not a machine, I won't speak to one! Besides, I knew you were here. Why didn't you pick up?"

"I was working," Marian says lamely. "Sometimes when I'm working I don't answer the phone."

Does he know what I mean by work? she wonders. And why is she defending herself? Marian goes to the bar, before the window. The light outside is going and she feels the day slipping from her hands. Though perhaps, she thinks longingly, it can still be salvaged. Perhaps Barton will drink his drink and go away and there will be more time. On top of the bar, massed in a silver pitcher, are more flowers from Oliver: roses, but strange roses, white with pink at the tips. Oliver has a thing for roses, and these are lush, lovely, and greedy for attention.

"I finally decided, I'll just go upstairs," he continues, as if he has not heard her speak. "And they wouldn't let me come up!"

Then he is off again, on the doorman and his impudence. "I told the man I was your cousin, but he said..."

Poor Hector, Marian thinks with a sigh. This will require a tip. A big tip.

Barton drinks his bourbon. He has put on weight, mostly in the neck, but the effect—she observes with irritation—is actually not to his detriment. Barton has always managed solid good looks in spite of his corpulence. Moreover, having now attained the age at which his comportment—prematurely middle-aged—is more or less appropriate, he looks like nothing so much as a captain of industry. This is odd, because Barton has never had anything to do with industry. In fact he has never, to her knowledge, had any sort of job, let alone a job likely to pay what a captain of industry might expect to be paid. In fact, it occurs to her now, Barton can't possibly have much remaining wealth at all. Whatever money his side of the family once had must now be much dissipated by his generation of one. The final generation, Marian imagines, since he has never shown the slightest inclination to procreate. And that, she supposes, is no bad thing.

"Didn't you get my letter?" he says, accusatory.

His letter? She got it: *Coming to NY Oct. 9/10, will call.* On a heavy cream-colored card with a pen-and-ink drawing of his house near Rhinebeck on the front. The house had a name—*The Retreat*—also rendered in said drawing. And a date, likewise inscribed: *c. 1830.* And a provenance, ditto: *The Home of Henry Wharton Danvers, 1804–1878.*

He is a ridiculous man. He has been for years. Before that, he'd been a ridiculous boy.

"I got it," she says merrily, pouring some seltzer into a glass for herself. "I was looking forward to seeing you. When shall we get together?"

Tomorrow, Marian is thinking. I can do tomorrow. A drink somewhere. Not here. Maybe the Cos Club. Her precious weekend with Oliver, and she has to have drinks with her visiting cousin at the Cos Club!

He looks at her as if she is insane. "We're...together...now." He speaks deliberately, as if she is a child. Not only a child, but a backward child.

"Well..." She thinks of Oliver in his boxer shorts, and then, as if on cue, there is a distinct rustle from the direction of the kitchen. Barton does not seem to notice. The ice in his highball glass tinkles.

"So don't you want to know what it's all about?" He leans forward, extending the glass toward her.

What it's all about? Marian thinks. She hadn't known there was an *it*. Where was the *it* in *Coming to NY Oct. 9/10, will call*?

"Of course! I can't wait!" She takes his glass. "Tell me."

"I'm getting married."

There's a definite fumble at this point as Marian grapples with the highball glass, which somehow is prevented from falling on the Aubusson while nonetheless bathing her hands with seltzer. She stands still for a moment, barely gripping the glass between wet palms. Barton getting married? The very notion is absurd. Barton uttering the phrase *"my wife"*? Barton in bed with a...woman? She wants desperately to laugh, but she manages to muster enough control to sputter, "How wonderful."

Wonderful. As in full of wonder. As in will wonders never cease?

How Marian wishes she were in a position to give full voice to her wonder. In the most delicious of all possible scenarios, she would now be shrieking, YOU CAN'T BE SERIOUS! and WHO CAN YOU POSSIBLY INTEND TO MARRY? and WAIT A MINUTE, I'VE ALWAYS ASSUMED YOU WERE—

"Yes, I'm quite pleased," Barton says, and indeed he is now the picture of pleasure. "She's a fine girl. A lovely girl. Not silly at all."

This seems an odd point of defensiveness, Marian thinks. "Girl?" she manages to say.

"Well, young lady. Of course, she couldn't be old, you know!" he offers cheerfully. "We intend to start a family."

"Family?" Marian thinks she might faint. "You're going to have children?"

"Well," he grins, enjoying her all too obvious state of alarm, "not me of course! *She's* going to have them." Barton looks at her. "I've surprised you, I see."

This is pointless to deny. "I'm very happy for you, Barton," she says, fetching his refill. She is thinking, Don't be such a snob. Maybe it's true there's a mate for everyone. Maybe he's been looking, all this time. Maybe all it ever took was the right woman.

Marian fixes him with an extravagant smile. "So! Don't hold out on me. Who's the...young lady? Do I know her?"

He grins, showing many teeth. "Do you know Kaplan Klein?"

"Well, sure," Marian frowns. She ought to. She and Marshall had had a broker at Kaplan Klein for nearly twenty years. "Does she work for them?"

"Work for them!" He laughs riotously. "Work for them!" He shakes so hard his bourbon sloshes onto his hand. "No, Marian, she doesn't work for them. They work for her!"

"Oh," Marian frowns. "You mean, she's a Kaplan. Or a Klein."

"A Klein. Sophie Klein. Her father is Mort Klein."

Damn, Marian thinks. *Mort Klein.* How like Barton to fall right in the clover. *Mort Klein!*

"Wow," she can't help saying. "Where'd you meet her?"

Barton grins. "I allowed the Hudson Valley Historical Society to hold their fund-raiser at The Retreat. Mort was there. Sought me out. Utterly fixated, you know. On us." Barton chuckles.

Marian sighs. It's not that she doesn't understand him perfectly. She understands him perfectly. Mort Klein's penchant for the first Jewish families of the city is not exactly obscure. But what is there to say about it?

"He knew all about The Retreat, but that's to be expected. It's a very important house, you know."

"Yes," she offers.

"Loves old houses, too. Do you know, he lives in the old Julius Steiner mansion, on Fifth and Ninety-second. He's restored it completely. Right back to 1910. I'm going there myself, this evening."

"Well!" Here Marian must fight to hide her actual envy. The Steiner restoration has been lauded in *Architectural Digest* and offered for various fund-raising events of heady social heights—the New York Historical Society, she seems to recall, and the UJA. She has never been there herself, though.

"But here's a funny thing!" Barton slides his palms over the generous thighs of his trousers. "This guy, all the money in the world, fabulous house, incredible stuff! He bought an entire set of Rosenthal china at Sotheby's, five hundred pieces! Once belonged to Isidore Schwartz. Uses it for breakfast. And the place in Millbrook, you wouldn't believe. He has a vineyard starting up next door. All that, and he talks like a tough from the Bronx."

Which is precisely what he is, thinks Marian. Mort Klein is the ultimate tough from the Bronx. Mort Klein rules the corner, the corner rules the world.

"He's very smart," she says, thinking aloud.

"What?" Barton says gruffly. "Oh, well I suppose he must be. But that voice! I mean, all that money, why not pay for a speech therapist?"

"Maybe he doesn't think there's anything wrong with it."

Barton finds this hysterical. He laughs above and beyond the call of humor. He laughs so long that Marian actually becomes bored. He has been here at least ten minutes, she thinks. How much longer?

Finally, Barton checks himself. "Well. I'd take a refill."

Relieved, in a way, to have something to do, she goes to get it for him. Behind her, on the couch, there is a crunching sound as Barton shifts and resettles his bulk against the raw silk pillows, then, farther off, a distinct answering rustle from the kitchen. Instinctively, Marian fakes a cough.

"I'm sorry!" Her voice is falsely bright. "Change of season! Getting a cold!"

"Is somebody else here?" He is looking over his shoulder.

"Oh..." She is frantically thinking. Should she invent a servant? Or gamble on Oliver's being spooked enough by what's just happened to keep very still for the remainder of this excruciating interview? But before she can choose one of these unenticing options, a well-timed distraction occurs in the form of a ringing telephone in a corner of the living room, for which Marian lunges, taking Barton's glass with her. "Just a sec, Barton. This might be important."

It is important. As she approaches the phone, she sees that the light for the home line is blinking and the light for the office line is steady. Oliver is calling her. She takes a breath.

"Yes!"

"Sorry, sweetheart. I was reaching for something up on the shelf and it fell."

"Oh. Yes, that's fine."

"How long is your cretin going to stay?"

"That's not easy to say."

"Because there's something I've been thinking of doing to you," Oliver says, and Marian, despite herself, feels a brief flash of longing.

"Ah," she says tersely. "Well, I'm not sure what you had in mind."

"Well," he says, "I thought I'd see if you were telling me the truth before. About that thing you found so titillating. And I'm getting a little impatient."

Now this, thinks Marian, is an intriguing statement. Another afternoon, she might chomp on it awhile, and with some pleasure, before answering. But this is not another afternoon.

"And this is in reference to...," she lobs, and the receiver vibrates with his soft laugh.

"I had no idea we were the same size," he says. "Well, the skirt's a bit loose, but the tights are nice and snug. I guess that's why they call them tights, yes?"

He pauses for her response, then, when it doesn't come, he charges on.

"I have to say, it wasn't as hard as I thought it would be. Everything feels so...*soft*. This sweater is so soft, you know. Well," he says gleefully, "of course you know. I just wish I filled it out as nicely as you do. Is this breast envy? Do women get that? And what are you doing with a wig, anyway?"

For a minute the question does not compute. Then she feels her heart begin to pound.

Marian glances at Barton, who seems to be frowning at the painting above the mantelpiece. She is not surprised. The painting is dark, abstract, and difficult. Barton is strictly an ancestral portrait man, himself.

"I want you again," says her lover, from her office, from her clothing.

And then, for the first time in all her forty-eight years, she truly understands the phrase *weak in the knees*. The heavy tumbler slips in her palm.

"I'm sitting here thinking about it."

"Oh," she manages to say. "It's on the left. In the drawer, on the left."

"I love that place under your arm, where the freckle is. I love where your thighs touch. I'm not going to make a big deal about it. If he's such a cretin, he won't notice if you excuse yourself."

Marian stands perfectly still, perfectly firm. She has turned away from her cousin. Outside, in the sliver of open space between two Fifth Avenue towers, she can just spy the glint of setting sun on the Reservoir.

"Hmm?" Oliver prods. "Are you coming?"

She can see the little runners, too. Little bug-sized runners, running around. She used to run around the reservoir, herself, but it proved too hard on her knees, her old knees, her weak knees. They are now very weak, indeed.

"Come on. You can lift my skirt and I'll lift yours."

I'm not wearing a skirt, she nearly says aloud.

There is a rustle from the sofa, gratuitous and clearly impatient. "Look, we'll finish it tomorrow," she hears herself say, and even allows herself a moment of smugness: *I sound good! I sound fine!* "That's enough for right now."

"Marian...," Oliver is crooning. "We'll light a candle under Lady Charlotte's portrait. I'll kiss you in the precise place Lord Satterfield kissed her."

"Yes," she says tightly, no longer amused. "We'll do that tomorrow."

He sighs so audibly she wonders if she is hearing it through the phone or all the way from the office. "Then I'd better just come out," Oliver says suddenly.

Marian gasps. "What? No, that's not necessary."

"Tell him I'm your research assistant. Let's have some fun."

She is about to yell at him, but the light on the phone has already gone out. The phone is silent. Out of breath, Marian replaces the phone and turns around.

"My research assistant," she hears herself say.

His eyes leave the painting and study her. "What?"

"That was... my research assistant."

And now she can't think what to do. Give him his drink? Run for the kitchen? Head for the nearest exit?

"What about her?" he says impatiently, and then there is a new, unmistakable sound from the kitchen. Her office door: shutting. Barton turns around once again.

Marian goes to the bar and clutches at the bottles. She resists, but only barely, the urge to down Barton's bourbon herself.

"Oh, hi!"

The greeting comes from the doorway, though the voice is not exactly familiar. And then the chilling rustle of silk as her cousin rises.

"Hello!"

The second voice is Barton's. A different Barton. A Barton enthralled. She has never heard this Barton's voice before. Marian pivots, drink in hand.

"Oh God," she can't help saying, and very loudly.

Oliver, quite placid, and quite pleased with himself, looks languidly in her direction. He is indeed wearing her clothes, clothes he evidently gathered from the living room floor on his dash for the service elevator: one gray cashmere turtleneck sweater, one camel-colored wool skirt (which hits her at the knees but him decidedly above), one pair of black tights, Marian's shoes—and amid her shock she allows herself the briefest moment of horror at this information: he can fit into her shoes, her feet are as big as a man's!—and...and this is what takes her breath, what she cannot, cannot understand, refuses to accept: her wig.

This, then, is the item that fell from the shelf. She can't even remember which shelf precisely, or when she put it there, years ago, how many years? Diagnosis, surgery, chemotherapy...twelve years. Twelve years ago!

"Hi!" this absurd new Oliver says again.

She wants to hit him. She will never speak to him again.

Barton repeats his equally avid greeting: "Hello! You must be Marian's assistant!"

"Yes," he says affably, as if this scenario is entirely mundane. His voice is not precisely normal, but it is not fake, either. It is breathless, she decides, as if Oliver has exerted himself in walking from the kitchen. "I'm her assistant. I'm Olivia."

Olivia, thinks Marian with astonishment. But of course.

"Well, sit, please!" Barton says enthusiastically. He reaches for Oliver's elbow and force-guides him to the couch. As Oliver sits, he delicately crosses his legs at the knee. He has, Marian notes, great legs. But she knew that.

"Olivia," Marian says quickly, "is one of my graduate students. She's been helping me on the new book." She hustles across the rug and practically hurls the glass into Barton's lap. He chuckles a bit as he takes it, then introduces himself.

"I"—pause for emphasis—"am Barton Ochstein."

"Yes!" says Oliver. "Of course I know that. Marian has told me about you!"

Barton leans forward. "Nothing but the truth, I hope!"

"Nothing but the facts!" says Oliver and giggles, and Marian, slinking dejectedly back to her own sofa across the room, wonders why, if he needs to be a girl, he has to be the giggling type.

But of course, he doesn't need to be a girl—that's the point—and since he isn't a cruel man, there is something else in play here, an attitude not essentially mean but not unwilling to make levity from someone's ignorance, either. It's a quality she hasn't seen in him before, Marian reflects, because he is not like other New Yorkers she has known, many she has known, who will willingly comment on the taxi driver's hygiene or the waitress's intelligence. His kindness, she has always thought, comes from his knowing the inequities of the world, and how fortunate he's been: in his health, his comfort, the love of his family, and the bounty of his education. And perhaps that is why he is willing to make sport of Barton Ochstein, whose privileges outweigh even Oliver's own, and who has made so much less of them than he ought.

Marian watches them in silence for a moment. They are on a wavelength, this absurd couple, chortling in concert, making small, flirtatious touches of neutral body parts. Can Barton actually think Oliver is a girl? Fresh as the memory of his flesh may be, she forces herself to see Oliver with neutral eyes: young female, demurely dressed, clear skin and hairless jaw, flat-chested but also flat-throated, as the turtleneck covers his Adam's apple. His body is lithe and twists with a suppleness she herself has not possessed in some years, his hands are masculine but small. His voice—to her ears—is strained, but perhaps that is because she knows his natural voice. (This voice, she suddenly realizes, is his sexual voice, the voice of his neediness and discovery, the voice of his pleasure. It is *her* voice, it *belongs* to her, and how she resents his using it now, only to make fun.) And while the wig, which she has happily not seen in years, looks a bad fit to her, it might fool someone who cares to be fooled, or just isn't looking.

Barton is looking. He is leering, and she does not know which offends her most: that he is newly affianced, that she has always supposed him to be gay, or that the object of his perfectly evident lust is the object of her own. She watches Barton's hand, at rest on the cushion between them, delicately turn at the wrist until the knuckle presses Oliver's leg. This charade, she thinks, is the worst thing Oliver has ever done, and by far the most dangerous. This is the joke that will drag him into trouble. Only don't, she thinks fervently, let it drag me, too.

"Oh, I know Rhinebeck!" Oliver is saying. "I once had a boyfriend who took me up for the weekend."

"Ah!" Barton's eyes widen.

Marian sits forward. "Don't you need to leave, Olivia?" she asks pointedly.

"No!" Barton says.

"No," Oliver smugly agrees. He sinks back into a cushion. "I have time."

"You..." Her thoughts grasp. "You have a...doctor's appointment, isn't that right?"

"It was canceled," Oliver says languidly.

Barton assumes a look of concern. "A doctor! You're not ill, I hope?"

"Never better," Oliver confirms.

"Don't you have..." Marian searches. "A date?"

"Canceled," he says, leaning back against the cushion.

"Now who would cancel on you?" asks Barton. "Whoever he is, he isn't worth it."

"I couldn't agree more." This is Oliver, shaking his pretty head. "I think he was ashamed to be seen with me. He denied it, of course, but that's what it was. Some people are. Some people," he says, with a little choke, "don't set much stock in living honestly and openly with the person they love. I have nothing to hide," he adds, in case Marian has failed to glean his meaning. She has not failed.

"Nor should you!" says Barton. "We are human creatures, with human needs. If there is love between two people, that is all that matters." He reaches over to touch him, to touch Oliver, on his thigh. Barton's hand, damp from the glass, leaves a damp mark on the soft cashmere skirt, and staring at it Marian suddenly understands that her cousin is quite clear on Olivia's gender. He is not flirting madly with a person he mistakes for a woman. He is flirting madly with a man in women's clothing. Oh Barton, she thinks, equally piteous and pissed off. But she can't seem to take her eyes away from them.

"You are a remarkable young woman," says Barton, and not to Marian. "To have such strength of character, and at your age."

Oliver actually blushes. "Thank you. But I owe that to someone else. Someone who taught me to believe in myself. Do you know who that person is?"

Barton shakes his head, but Marian, with a plummeting feeling, thinks she does.

Oliver gets to his feet and fixes her with a look of such tenderness that in ordinary circumstances she might meet it with open arms. Then he walks to the couch where she is sitting and perches on the armrest, settling one cashmere-clad arm behind her head. "This woman," he says in his breathy voice.

"Oh?" Barton sounds dubious.

"This wonderful woman. She sat down with me and showed me that if I was not myself, truly myself, I was nothing. And that I deserved to be loved for who I was."

"Ah," he mutters. "Yes. Good."

"She changed my life, this woman."

Marian shrugs with embarrassment, but she is experiencing something equally uncomfortable, from his nearness, from the thin strength of his arm, through the cashmere of her sweater and through the cashmere of his, which is also hers.

Barton nods avidly, like a convert in the front row of a revival tent. "Yes!"

Yes indeed, Marian thinks. She can't help glancing to her right, where Oliver's knees peek out from beneath the skirt, crossed in black tights. They are lovely knees, attached to lovely thighs.

"I've spent so much of my life," Oliver says, carefully, "well, cut off, in a sense. All I want is to connect. Like Forster said!" he ends brightly.

"Forster?" Predictably, Barton is dim on Forster.

"He once wrote, 'Only connect…' That's what he craved. Contact with another person. Human touch. Not even bodies, but souls. The people he wrote about lived alongside one another, but they never really looked inside one another." Oliver pauses. "Forster was a very lonely man. I don't want to be lonely," he says, with a catch in his voice.

The catch, Marian realizes, is real. She turns to look at him and he looks frankly back. And there is her Oliver. She would know him anywhere, with his cool gray eyes and the tiny brown mole at his left temple. And then, unbidden, there is a great leap inside her. She wants to reach for him. She wants to put her hand under his skirt. She thinks of her own hands unfastening his bra—an astonishing thought. Is he even wearing a bra? Is he wearing *her* bra? What would it be like to unfasten a bra and slip forward the shoulder straps? she wonders, unable to turn her thoughts aside. She knows the mirror of this, the clumsy hand behind her back, the way her shoulders fall forward, protectively, the hands coming up to cover her breasts in modesty. But how would it feel to reach behind him and flick that latch of hook and elastic? Would he hold the fabric against his chest, unsure about letting go? And what would it be like to pull up a skirt and strip down a pair of tights? Would he cross his legs? Would he…Oh my God…would he open them? She is stunned by the realization that her thighs are pressing together, right now, right this second.

Oliver stares at her, that infuriating half smile still taut across his face, but less certain than a moment earlier. Because he knows, Marian thinks. He knows exactly what she is considering, exactly what she is wanting. Then he moves beside her. The motion is so small, it is more an adjustment than a motion, but it leaves him just perceptibly turned in her direction, and the hand in the lap of his skirt—her skirt—slowly twists, like a card player showing his cards, and lies palm up and open.

Across the room, Barton clears his throat.

God, she is thinking, what will it take to make him go away? What will it take to make him disappear so that she can make love to Olivia?

Perhaps this: the house phone sounds its metallic buzz from the kitchen, and up she leaps, automatically, leaving the two of them in dangerous isolation in the living room, the inadvisability of which occurs to her almost instantly. She is about to rush back, to warn them both in some idiot way not to talk to each other, not to look at each other, when the house phone buzzes again, three short jolts this time, and it gets her attention, as Hector tends to favor the long and languid depression of finger to button. Not Hector?

Snatching it from its hook set in the marble backsplash, Marian cries, "Yes? Hector?"

"Marian?" The voice, not Hector's, chirps. "Oh, super! Are you ready to go? I'm bringing up your mail."

From the living room there is a sudden burst of laughter, and she stands, paralyzed for the moment by her two developing scenarios, numbed by the notion that they are about to collide.

Ready to go? She thinks, blankly. *Ready to go where?*

In her hand, the house phone begins to emit its distinct, I-have-been-disconnected rumble, and she replaces the receiver. She is wasting precious seconds. She can practically hear the elevator whir, the rolling clatter of the door opening on her landing, the muffled chime of the doorbell. She needs to move, *now*.

Laughter. What are they laughing about? What common ground can possibly exist between her conceited, no-longer-quite-certainly-homosexual cousin and her lover in his—or, rather, *her*—stockings and wig? Another precious second passes. It is nearly dark. In ten minutes, the lights will be on in the city. In two minutes, Valerie Annis—who has just elevated herself from tiresome acquaintance to object of utter loathing—will be in her apartment, braying in that barely tolerable voice of hers. How has she come to know such disagreeable people?

"Oliver?" she says faintly.

No one comes. The living room noises continue.

Marian steadies herself. "Olivia?" she calls. "Can I see you, please?"

The elevator whirs. Only a few more flights to go before the door clatter, the ring.

"Olivia?"

"I'm here," Oliver says. He pushes open the kitchen door, lets it swing shut beside him. "He's just asked me to meet him later. Can you believe it? He wants me to come to the Regency, for a drink, at eleven." Oliver grins. "What kind of girl does he think I am?"

"Oliver," she says frantically.

"Don't worry. I said I was busy."

Then, incomprehensively, he is kissing her. She flails at him. The elevator door clatters open on the landing.

"Oliver! I'm…" She shoves him away, "I'm trying to tell you! That's Valerie Annis, she's coming up."

Oliver looks blank. He is a clueless brunette. "Valerie?"

"I told you! That woman with the column!"

"Ah," he nods. "The one my mom refers to as *that cunt*."

Marian stops. "Really?" Caroline is not given to profanity.

"She outed some nice old lady on the board of the ballet. Absolutely no reason, just malicious."

That would be Valerie, Marian thinks.

The doorbell rings.

"Why's she here?" Oliver says.

"God, I have no idea. I haven't seen her since…"

Marian stares at him.

"What?"

"Oh no. I saw her last week at a dinner party. There's a benefit tonight, at the Guggenheim, but I never intended to actually go. I just made a donation."

"Marian," he says, hurt.

"No, honestly, I couldn't tell her *why* I wasn't going, not right in front of Marshall. Maybe she said something about going together. I wasn't listening, I guess. I should have paid attention."

"You were daydreaming about our weekend," he says, floating the notion.

Quite possibly, Marian thinks. Though it's just as likely she'd been tuning out Valerie's drone.

The bell rings again. If a bell can be made to sound testy, this one does.

"Look," she says, pushing him, "just get back in the office, and this time stay there. I'll get rid of her as soon as I can, but this woman is no fool. She'll take one look at you in that wig and we'll be the lead item in a certain salmon-colored weekly." He opens his mouth. "No. Just get in there. Oliver, for once, just do it."

He puts up his hands and goes.

From the living room, she hears an aggrieved "Marian? Where've you gone?"

From the foyer, three short rings.

Oliver closes the door.

"Coming!" she cries, to everyone, and rushes out of the kitchen.

How has it happened? How has she moved from the serene privacy of her lover's arms on a weekend that was meant to have been theirs alone to this wild invasion of people she despises? How has she become someone people feel free to just drop in on? Don't they know she has a book to write? *Aren't they aware that she is trying to get something accomplished?*

Marian reaches the front door and flings it back. She refuses to be effusive in her welcome, but good manners compel a gracious expression to the woman her open door reveals, a brittle blonde with suspicious cheekbones and a black Italian coat so conscientiously understated it reeks of money. She is carrying a wide cardboard box topped by a stack of catalogues. "Valerie," Marian allows.

"You're not wearing that." Valerie Annis frowns.

"What? Oh, Valerie, I am so, so sorry. I completely forgot, and now I just can't walk over with you."

The "walk over" is meant to be a terse reminder. Marian had not, after all, agreed to be Valerie's date for the evening—but merely to "go with her." Besides, she is under no illusions that Valerie wants actual companionship for the evening. Valerie wants, merely, to arrive with Marian, then promptly ditch her to speak with everyone, anyone else.

"You're not skipping out," Valerie says sourly.

"I'm afraid so. Not that they'll miss me. I made a donation," she adds, somewhat defensively.

"Well," Valerie pouts, "I think you might have called."

"I was just about to!" Marian cries. "But then my cousin turned up. Unexpectedly. I apologize. I wouldn't blame you for never speaking to me again!"

I should be so lucky, she thinks.

Valerie scowls, shifting the weight of her burden.

"Oh, let me take that!" Marian says, grabbing it. The catalogues teeter and spread. "I'm going to have such a boring weekend," she tells Valerie, reassuringly. "Marshall's out of town and I'm not doing a thing but working."

"Oh working… don't tell me about it. I'm constantly working! I said to Richard, I said, 'You keep me running around this way, I'll get overexposed, and nobody will tell me anything anymore.' Really, I ought to just put my foot down, Marian. He knows perfectly well I'm the only reason anybody reads his silly paper."

"Hmm," Marian says. Richard is her boss, a venture capitalist who fueled the first online matchmaking service, and whose favorite plaything is the *New York Ascendant*. The two women are still standing in the doorway, though this is rather optimistic on Marian's part.

"Even so, three parties a night! Sometimes more! What does he think I am?"

A Class-A gossip, quite accurately, she thinks. "That is a lot," she agrees.

"What *is* that?" Valerie groans theatrically, and nods at the box in Marian's arms, as if someone had asked her to assume the burden in the first place.

Marian, noting the familiar logo on the return-address label, says, "More Lady Charlotte letters, I suppose. They forward them to me."

"*What, still?* You've got people writing to you *still?* After all this *time?*"

"It's only been a year," she says, offended. "A year since the paperback."

"Oh!" Valerie sweeps past her into the foyer, her green lizard Jimmy Choos clicking smartly on the parquet, probably doing some damage. "Did I tell you I had dinner with Yusuf last week? Just the two of us and some woman he was with. And the bodyguards, of course, but they were at another table. Before his reading at the Y. Unfortunately I couldn't stay for the reading. He said he had read your book."

Marian has just begun wondering at the apparent non sequitur when this last nugget is tossed off.

"Really?" Despite herself, this impresses her. Yusuf Hanif has taken time out from being the subject of international militant hostilities to read her book?

"Poor man." Valerie shrugs off her coat. "So lonely. Imagine what his life must be like, with those bodyguards. I tell you, they looked like longshoremen."

Marian clucks sympathetically. She watches, with resignation, as Valerie slings her coat over one of the foyer chairs.

"Marian," says Barton, who has appeared in the doorway of the living room, pointedly holding his empty glass. "I didn't know you were expecting company."

"I wasn't!" she says brightly. "This is an unexpected..."

"I always try to be unexpected!" Valerie says, clicking across to him with her immaculate hand outstretched. "You must be Marian's cousin! There's certainly a family resemblance."

He takes the hand. "The Warburg chin," he says, seriously. "It's quite distinct."

"Warburg?" she chirps. "As in Warburg?"

Barton looks sharply at Marian. The notion that she has not informed each and every one of her acquaintances of her Our Crowdliness is nothing short of astounding to him. "Certainly," he says fiercely, as if his very manhood has been challenged.

Valerie pivots on the spike of her heel, without letting go of Barton's hand. "Marian," she scolds.

"On my father's side," Marian says, with reluctance. "My father and Barton's mother were brother and sister."

"Well, of course!" Valerie says soothingly. "And where have you been hiding yourself, Mr. Warburg?"

For a minute he looks abashed, but he recovers. "My mother was a Warburg. My father's name was Ochstein. Which is also my name." He has always resented that, Marian thinks. That Marian, a mere female, got the Warburg surname for her very own (and then was so poor a guardian that she traded it for her husband's!) while he, though obsessively attentive to family history, is one name removed from their illustrious mutual ancestor. Marian has sometimes known Barton to refer to himself as Barton Warburg Ochstein, though she knows perfectly well that his middle name is Samuel.

"Well, Mr. Ochstein," Valerie says. "Don't tell me we've met before! I've met many, many people, but I would certainly have remembered you." She has left him and his hand in her wake, now, and moved into the living room. Marian and Barton meekly follow her. "Do you live abroad? Are you in town for this party at the Guggenheim?"

It takes Marian a moment to understand this question. To Valerie and her ilk, charitable events are entirely divorced from the actual causes they benefit. They are parties. With themes. Valerie, more likely than not, has no idea that tonight's very elaborate shindig is meant to fund art programs for inner-city children.

"Not abroad," he responds, sinking again into the soft cushions of the couch. "Only as far as Rhinebeck. My home is The Retreat. It once belonged to Henry Wharton Danvers."

Henry Wharton Danvers? Valerie frowns.

"Surely..." he begins, but she interrupts with gaiety.

"Oh, I'm an utter *moron*! You must understand! That's why my column is so successful. Because people are forever having to explain things to me! They sit me down, and they say, 'Valerie, you're clearly ignorant, my dear, so I'm going to tell you everything.' And they do!"

"Column," Barton says, puzzled.

"In the *New York Ascendant*. I am the Celebrant," she says, solemnly.

"Ah." He is blank. Marian is not surprised: Barton's snobbery is rooted in the past. He has, and this is perhaps to his credit, never been very interested in new money. Except, perhaps, in the rather newsworthy new money of his prospective in-laws.

"You read me," she says smugly.

"I have," says Barton. And now he remembers his glass. "Marian? I've just time for another."

Marian rises.

"Are you off somewhere?" Valerie asks.

"My fiancée's family home. Her father is giving a little dinner tonight."

"You're getting married!" Valerie exclaims. "And to whom?"

"Valerie?" interrupts Marian. "A quick drink?"

"No, darling." She doesn't take her eyes off Barton. She does not want her concentration disturbed.

"Sophie Klein," says Barton, with crudely attempted indifference. "She is the daughter of Mort Klein."

There is silence. The silence is impressive. Even Marian, crouched at the liquor cabinet, can feel it, like pricks along her spine. Finally, the contents of Valerie's lungs are expelled in a rush. "Well, this is...I offer you my congratulations, Mr. Ochstein."

"Barton," he reassures her. "*Please*."

"Barton," replies Valerie. "Well, this is just *lovely*."

"Thank you," says Barton, but it's directed to Marian, as he accepts his drink. "I'm delighted, myself."

"Miss Klein is in the family business?" Valerie asks.

"Oh no. A student. Sophie is at Columbia."

Marian looks at him. The fact that Barton, barely cognizant of her massive best-seller, is also, apparently, unaware that she holds a chair at Columbia should not surprise her, but it does.

"Columbia?" Marian asks, nearly wounded. "Your fiancée is at Columbia?"

"Undergraduate?" Valerie leans in. "That's adorable."

"No, no," he chuckles, enjoying their attention. "Sophie's writing a thesis in the history department."

"That's *my* department," Marian says, and she is shocked to hear it come out a whine.

The others look at her for a perplexed moment, then turn back to each other.

"How fascinating. What about?" Valerie has leaned back against the cushion.

"Oh," he says and waves his hand, "Germany in the forties. She gave me the rundown, but it's very complicated."

Marian sinks onto the opposite couch and sets down her load of mail on the rug. How many people, she reflects, could wield the phrase "Germany in the forties" with the apparent abandon her cousin has just used? The Holocaust, the Shoah, the Third Reich... even the war, yes, but "Germany in the forties"? Does he even know, she wonders, what *happened* in "Germany in the forties"?

Vaguely, and from a not unwelcome distance, she watches them, the two of them, fanning their mutual flame. *Sophie Klein! Daughter of Mort Klein! As in Kaplan Klein!* She hears Barton tell again the story of his meeting with Klein père at The Retreat, *c. 1830*, and his now distinctly offensive appraisal of his future father-in-law's accent. She is happy for them to take up these minutes with their exchange. Minutes spent on each other are minutes Oliver will be forgotten—or in Valerie's case, undiscovered—and minutes that will lend legitimacy when she kicks them out, a prospect now tantalizingly near. Idly, discreetly enough not to break their spell, she nudges the teetering stack of mail with her foot, toppling a cascade of shiny opulence onto the Aubusson—Bloomingdale's, Neiman Marcus, Tiffany. Beneath these is a large envelope from none other than Kaplan Klein, and then the charitable appeals: first the mass mailings with their computer-generated pseudo-handwriting, which she can safely ignore, then the more exclusive supplications, addressed in cool script, for the New York City Ballet, Goddard-Riverside, and Women in Need, to which she will inevitably respond.

"He's not a well man, you know," her cousin says.

"No," Valerie coos, rapt. "I didn't know."

Marian closes her eyes. When she was a child, the solicitations her Irish nanny received daily made even this cacophony of requests seem muted by comparison. Every Catholic mission from Korea to Zimbabwe had had Mary's address, and appeals arrived continually from around the globe, each and every one of them to be answered with a crisp one dollar bill. Marian smiles, remembering the afternoon routine of letter opener, coil of stamps, and stack of bills. How much of Mary's salary had gone into those envelopes? Marian wonders. How many Park Avenue nannies had blown it all that way, between their left-behind siblings in Cavan or Monaghan and those little brown babies, lining up for a shot and a school uniform? Where were those brown babies now, and where were the nannies?

"Marian?"

She looks up. "Hmm?"

"I said," Valerie says, enunciating carefully, "have you?"

"Have I what?" Marian says.

"Been to the Steiner mansion."

"Oh. No."

"No?" says Valerie with disbelief. "You mean, in all this time?"

Marian feels addled. She must have missed something significant amid the superficial nattering on the opposite sofa. "Time since...?"

"Since the restoration. Mort is so generous with the house. I've been to many events there," she says, smugly.

With one pocket full of purloined Beluga and the other hiding a tape recorder, Marian thinks, but she assembles her most gracious smile.

"Oh, you're lucky. I've never been. Is it lovely?"

Valerie turns back to Barton, since this is a question which evidently needn't be answered.

"Now what's happening tonight?" she asks.

He shrugs his meaty shoulders. "Haven't the faintest. Some sort of family dinner. They have it every Friday. But Sophie and I have an appointment tomorrow with an attorney for the prenuptial."

"Ooh..." Surprisingly, Valerie has found room to lean back still farther. Any more and she'll be supine, Marian thinks. "Aren't you smart. We all have to be so careful today. It's extremely wise to settle financial matters before a marriage."

Oh Barton, thinks Marian, *the time has come to* shut up now.

"I couldn't agree more," he says with a nod. "Where there are assets, there must be clarity. For example, when Mort was last with me at The Retreat, I was telling him about all the work that the estate still requires. There is a significant problem with the original molding on the ground floor, which we are going to have to replace. Now I don't need to tell you that this is fantastically expensive. You've got to find someone who can mill wood on the old machines, and with the kind of intricate original we've got there, this makes the thing doubly challenging. But Mort said at the time, he said to me, 'Barton, this is preservation work of the highest order, and it must be done right. We cannot take the chance of having it bungled, it's too important!' "

"Sure." Valerie nods.

"So clearly he intends to make some contribution to this effort. Not that I'm surprised, given his interest in early architecture, not to mention New York history and the part my family has played in it. Soon to be his daughter's family, I should add. But I do think we will all be more comfortable once these intentions are down in black and white." He finishes with a nod.

Marian looks at him blankly. Does he mean to bill Mort Klein for his restoration costs?

"Barton," Marian says. She can't stop herself. "You're not intending to make your repair bills part of your prenuptial agreement."

He looks at her as if she is mad. "Not at all! Not at all! I mean for it to be a separate matter. Entirely separate."

"Oh." She is relieved. "Well, good."

"A separate document. Quite apart from any arrangements we

might make regarding the marriage. If Mort wishes to contribute to the restoration of an important American home, and he has given every indication that he wishes to do so, then I see no reason we shouldn't put that in writing."

Marian looks at Valerie. Valerie is beaming. Valerie must be wild to get to her laptop, her cell phone.

Barton, misunderstanding, leans forward conspiratorially. "After all, I am making my own gifts in this arrangement, am I not? Over the years I've had many opportunities to marry. I mean, within my own social group. I say this not as a snob, mind you! Marian can tell you that I am a very humble person. I do not call attention to myself or demand special favors because of our family, do I, Marian?"

Oh leave me out of it, she thinks wearily.

"But I do recognize that my family, like any other American family, has always moved in a circle of like-minded people, people with the kind of common history that makes us all feel..." He ponders. He is having an actual reflective moment, Marian thinks. "Comfortable!" Barton says, triumphantly. "Now I am bringing someone into that circle, do you see? And while that is far from an impossible thing—this is America, after all—it is not simple, either. I am, so to speak, standing up for this person. I am vouching for this person, and uniting my own fortunes with those of this person."

Marian wonders whether "this person" refers to his future wife or to Mort Klein. She imagines the two men, for a moment, standing staunchly side by side, with her cousin's great hand around Klein's shoulder. There is, it occurs to Marian, even a slight resemblance between them, notwithstanding the "famous" Warburg chin: a high crown and strong nose, and that certain satisfaction arising from a life lived by principle, even if it is a lousy principle. They're a pair. They are, truly, she sees, made for each other. And isn't it a pity Barton can't marry the father?

Valerie, for once, is speechless.

Barton, Marian thinks, deserves everything the Celebrant is going to do to him.

"You know," she hears herself say, "this is horrible, but I'm going to have to leave you. I need to get ready."

They both look at her.

Ready for what? she knows they are thinking.

She wishes she had taken a moment to answer this question, herself, before speaking up.

"Ready for what?" Valerie asks, as though she is only now noticing Marian as a creature of any independent interest whatsoever.

"Dinner. I'm having dinner with one of my graduate students. A woman," she adds, unnecessarily. "She's in trouble with her thesis. She's writing about the bluestockings, and she hasn't been able to get focused. I said I would take her out to Nicola's and we would talk about it away from the office. It might help," she finishes lamely.

Valerie looks quizzical. "Blue stockings? I didn't know they wore blue stockings in the eighteenth century."

"Oh," says Marian with a hopeful nod. "But they did. And there is so much material."

"Well, it's fine with me," Barton says, plunking down his tumbler on the end table. "Only I could use some advice from you ladies, since I want to send flowers to Sophie. I went into one poky little place on Lexington and all the flowers looked half dead. I couldn't send those."

Valerie shakes her head in mock horror. "Naturally, you couldn't."

"I don't have time to look around. Just tell me where one goes. Who does the best flowers now?" He peers, suddenly, past Marian. To the bar? No—of course, to the flowers. "Who did those?"

Valerie turns, too. The white roses with their strange pink tips, so open, nearly baroque, Marian thinks. Like a still life: *White Roses in Silver Vase with Manhattan Skyline.*

She bites her lip. "The White Rose."

"Ooh!" Valerie gives a little chirp. "Yes! That's it!"

"I can see it's a white rose," Barton says impatiently.

"No, it's the shop," Valerie says. "The shop is called the White Rose. It's a darling place in the Village."

"That's too far," he says dismissively. "I'm hardly going to go all the way down there just for flowers."

"But you needn't," Valerie reassures him. "Just call them. Tell them what you want and how much you want to spend. They'll do something beautiful. Their flowers are so lovely, *everyone* uses them."

Her emphasis on "everyone" has its intended effect. Barton looks back at the flowers, frowning. "What's the name again?" he says.

Marian smiles. Despite her anxiety, she is pleased to hear Oliver's flowers praised. "It's called the White Rose."

And here, quite suddenly, and quite unaccountably, Barton grins with apparent delight. "Yes," says Barton. "That'll do. She'll find that amusing. Do you have the number?" He gets to his feet.

Marian, thrilled at this development, gets to her feet, too.

"No," she lies.

"Perhaps Olivia does. I'd like to say good-bye to her, anyway."

"Good-bye?" Valerie stands, too, but she is not ready to depart just yet. "You mean someone else is here?"

"Just my assistant," Marian says. "Working back in the office. We were working"—*when you interrupted us*, she had been about to say— "earlier this afternoon. Marshall is in Nova Scotia this weekend on one of his board retreats. I try to keep the decks clear when he's away. I usually get a great deal accomplished."

"Well, I'm sorry we've interrupted," Valerie offers, apparently speaking for Barton as well and not sounding sorry at all.

"No, it's fine." It's fine *now*, Marian is thinking. Now it's almost over.

"Where is Olivia?" Barton insists. "I want to say good-bye." He looks knowingly at Valerie. "Absolutely charming girl. Well," he says with a smirk, "not actually a girl, you know."

Valerie, who cannot bear not knowing anything that might precede the phrase "you know," perks right up. "What do you mean?"

"My lips," he says gravely, "are sealed." But he looks at Marian with a pleading expression.

My God, thinks Marian. This man must never be allowed in public.

Valerie looks at Marian. "Well? What is it? You've got a hermaphrodite assistant?"

"No, no," says Marian. "Nothing like that. Just, you know, a cross-dresser. She's one of my students, actually."

Oddly, this comment seems to make all the difference. "Academia!" declares Valerie, giving Barton a conspiratorial glance. "Where would all the oddballs go if we didn't have universities to put them in?"

Marian resists responding. This comment may be the broadest of unbased slanders, but she would rather take it than prolong the visit.

"I'll look up the phone number for you," Marian says. "No need to trouble Olivia."

"But I insist," says Barton. "I must say good-bye. I will not leave without doing that."

"Yes, let's have a look at her," Valerie says, looking around. "Is she a pretty girl at least or one of those bad jokes with a beard?"

"Adorable," Barton says.

"Oh please," Marian says, pleading. "Please don't say anything in front of her. She's very sensitive. She doesn't want people paying attention to her. Just," she looks at Valerie, "try to pretend you don't notice. Promise me, Valerie."

Valerie puts up her hands. "Sweetheart! Of course! You know how good I am at pretending not to know things."

Marian looks from one to the other. Her nerves are shot, she realizes, and there is no fortitude she can summon for another round of Olivia the transvestite assistant, not with Valerie Annis figured into the equation. The Celebrant is no Barton Ochstein, tenant and restorer of The Retreat and prime oaf. The Celebrant wields a scalpel in New York society and holds allegiance to herself, alone. She will take one look at beautiful Oliver in his cashmere turtleneck and pumps, his skirt and wig, and understand that Marian is in love with her oldest friend's twenty-six-year-old son, who is the proprietor of the aforementioned White Rose, and who happens to be in drag. Tasteful drag. Understated drag. But drag.

But what can she do? She wants them out, and then she wants a brandy.

Marian goes to the living room phone and dials her office. It rings in the distance, once, twice.

"Yes?" says Oliver softly.

"Oh…*Olivia*, Mr. Ochstein needs to leave and wants to say good-bye to you. He's also asked me to recommend a good place for flowers to send to his fiancée. Can you find the number of that place I like in the Village?"

There is a pause. "Marian," he warns, his voice low, "are you sure about that?"

"Do you remember what it's called?" she says tersely. "The White Rose? I think I may have their card somewhere. It came with one of the arrangements."

He is silent for a moment. "All right. I have one."

"That's it." She is breathless with strain. "Bring it out and say good-bye, then we can do a bit more before you have to leave." She puts down the phone. Expectantly, the other two turn toward the kitchen.

The office door opens and closes. They hear footfalls, Oliver in unaccustomed heels—just as well they aren't high heels—approaching.

Then he is there, her strangely lovely girl, smiling shyly, with the white business card in one hand. Valerie stares, uncharacteristically silent, her lips pursed in concentration. "Oh," Oliver says. "I didn't know someone else had come."

"I am Valerie Annis," says Valerie, staring.

"It's very nice to meet you," says Oliver politely. "My name is Olivia."

"Olivia…" Valerie shakes hands, but lets the name linger. She is angling for a surname.

"I work with Professor Kahn."

"That must be fascinating."

Oliver smiles but doesn't answer. He has gleaned that Marian wants this cut short. He is helping.

"I understand you have something for me, Olivia," says Barton.

Oliver extends the card.

"And do you approve of this place?" He glances: "The White Rose?"

"Yes, they do very nice work. Professor Kahn gets flowers from them sometimes." His pride is now engaged. Marian watches him look past the group to the roses. His roses. "I think…," he says pointing, "aren't those from the White Rose, Professor Kahn?"

"I think so," she agrees reluctantly.

"Of course, I don't know anything about flowers," Olivia continues with becoming modesty, "but I think they're the most beautiful roses I've ever seen."

Marian gives him a brief look. Brief, but pointed.

"Well, that's quite a recommendation," says Barton. "Perhaps one day someone might send *you* some flowers from the White Rose."

"Oh," Olivia says, "I doubt that."

"We'll see." He raises an eyebrow and nods meaningfully. "I'll tell you what. May I put you in charge of this errand for me? I would like to have some flowers sent to a young lady. Some roses I think. And they must be white."

"Oh," Oliver gives Marian a brief, uncertain look. "Well, I'd be happy to."

"You're very sweet," Barton says. "And, may I say, very charming."

"And very *busy*," Marian says pointedly. "Really, Barton, can't you take care of this yourself?"

"No, no," Oliver smiles. "It's fine. I'm glad to do it."

"Well, I'd be appreciative," Barton purrs. "Next Friday will be fine. I'll write down the address." And he reaches into his jacket for a pen and one of his own cards. Marian watches him write: Sophie Klein, 1109 Fifth Avenue. No apartment number, no zip code. And no instructions about payment, she notes.

"How should Olivia arrange the bill?" Marian says shortly, and he makes a dismissive gesture as he hands over the card.

"Oh. Have it sent to The Retreat. That will be fine."

Fine for you, she thinks. Bills sent to The Retreat probably all disappear into the same black hole of nonpayment. Perhaps this one will even be absorbed by some trumped up "restoration" project to be delineated as part of Barton's prenuptial agreement. Sophie Klein, in other words, will end up paying for her own flowers. Well, thinks Marian, she'd better get used to that.

Barton's hand lingers for an extra moment in Oliver's hand. Then he leaves his card behind. "You'll take care of it for me?"

"I will," Oliver says amiably.

Well, what is she worried about? Marian thinks with resignation. This is a good development for Oliver and his shop, possibly even a great one. It's an expensive order, or will be if somebody actually ends up paying for it, and no bad thing to send a beautiful arrangement to the Steiner mansion, where some of the wealthiest people in the city are likely to admire it, not least Mort Klein himself.

Barton turns to Marian, as if abruptly recalling her presence. "I must go. I'm late for the Kleins. Where is my coat?"

Oliver sets down the card on Marian's coffee table. "I'll get it," he says cheerily, and goes.

"Oh, Barton," Valerie says, finally breaking off the gaze she has fixated on Oliver, "you're going to the Kleins now? I'm going that way. I'll walk with you."

It is an announcement, not a request.

"Fine!" says Barton. He is shrugging his broad shoulders into the coat Oliver holds open. "You can walk me as far as the door."

Valerie flinches a mite at the put-down, but recovers admirably. "Of course. Good-bye, Miss...," she says to Oliver, who has finished helping Barton on with his coat.

"Olivia," he says.

"Well, very nice to meet you. Marian?"

Marian steps forward and kisses one bony cheek, then the other bony cheek. She smells some awful cucumber perfume. She pulls back and smiles with a practiced facsimile of fondness, but Valerie, she notes, is staring frankly at her, without a veneer of sociability. Marian watches as her gaze makes a clockwise sweep, from crown to waist and up again. "Who's doing your color now, Marian?" she asks suddenly.

"My...?"

The question takes a moment to sink in. Either Valerie has forgotten that they are not alone, or she is being cruel. So cruel, Marian thinks, frantically avoiding the eyes of her cousin and her lover.

"We can do better. Whoever you're seeing, I'm going to set you up with my person at Fekkai. He's impossible to get, but I'm going to fix it for you. I want to," she says. "Please, don't say anything. It's done."

"Oh," Marian says, burning.

"And I want to take you up to see Peter Davidoff on Madison. He's the biggest whore, you can't imagine! You tell him, 'I don't like this freckle,' and he says, 'Don't worry, we'll zap it. It's gone!'" She laughs, a glasslike laugh. "His office, everyone you know's in the waiting room! It's what La Côte Basque must have been like in the sixties, only we all know what we're doing there. Who cares! Why look older than we have to?" She looks at Barton. "Isn't that right?"

He frowns, baffled, so Valerie tries Oliver.

"Not that you'll need to worry about that for eons, Olivia. You have lovely skin."

Oliver refuses to thank her aloud. He offers only a half smile.

"Well," Valerie chirps, "must go. Barton?"

"Yes!" He steps forward, and Oliver grabs the door. "Marian," Barton says as Valerie stabs the elevator button, "I will be in touch. I want you to meet Mort. And Sophie, of course."

"Of course," Marian echoes. Her voice sounds flat.

"Good to see you!" Valerie says. "I'm so glad I stopped in. I hope we didn't interfere too badly," she says gaily, as if she and Barton are a couple.

"Not at all," Marian says. Oliver steps back as the elevator door opens. Carlo, the elevator man, doesn't need to see the young man he brought up this morning dressed in women's clothes. "Good-bye," Marian says as they step into the elevator. "Good-bye," as it closes. "Good-bye," as they descend.

And then Oliver is around her, beside her, pressing her arms with his arms, and her face is hot against his face, and he is holding her so tight the strength of his arms is the only thing keeping her from flying to pieces.

"That bitch," he says, swaying and swaying. "That bitch."

CHAPTER THREE

About Time

THERE IS A TIME IN EACH DAY that is neither afternoon nor evening but something breathless in suspension between them, when every particle of the air is briefly infused with fierce, fierce color, one instant so utterly there, then gone. This time occurs frequently, perhaps even daily, but it is easily missed, and feels, as a result, beyond uncommon. It can be missed by looking in the wrong direction, or by being under an umbrella, or by being indoors or at the movies or the Food Emporium at just that instant. To catch it, then, is rare and not a little glorious, which is why Marian always notes it when she does. She remembers, most clearly of all, the first time she noticed it, coming home from the Fokine School of Dance on Seventy-ninth with her hand in Mary's hand, and finding herself on Park Avenue at just that liminal moment to see a sparkle in the sidewalk beneath her school shoes. And she remembers thinking: *I never noticed that before.*

Aubergine Time, she came to call it. ("Aubergine" being a word used by her mother, and meaning a kind of purple, though with exotic overtones.) Aubergine Time passed so quickly that you could barely close your hand around it before it fled between your fingers, and in

Marian's life she had never clutched at more than a hundred. There had been four on the front steps of the Brearley School; one slinking out of the park, shivering beneath the arm of her first boyfriend, Roger Frank, one outside the Fairway on Broadway and Seventy-fifth, a rash of them in and around Gramercy Park, where she and Marshall had spent their first married years, and one a month before today on Commerce Street, while she was racing the length of the block to Oliver's door with her arms full of groceries.

And oddly, at this particular moment, even as Marian wrenches herself away from Oliver—from *Olivia*—and walks to the end of the living room, the two large windows begin to beckon with that uncommon but familiar light, and she thinks (even with all of her rage and encroaching depression and also humiliation, because it had happened in front of Oliver, who knew that she thought it was all true, even if he himself did not): *Oh! It's now!*

It is now. It is right now, on the great glittering ravine of Park Avenue, and she just has time to wish that she were not here inside, even with Oliver, but outside in that light—even looking as terrible as she does with her puffy face. *I love this*, Marian thinks, which is absurd, because she is actually quite miserable. And yet... the spiky buildings, the rising steam over the East River, and the floating specks of light as planes dispersed, poor things, from this very center of the universe, in a sky thick with aubergine, which makes Marian remember, as she always remembers, the white, white shoulders of her mother, seated at a white dressing table by a window flooded with this exact light.

"Marian?" Oliver says. He is still in the hallway.

And then it is over. Fled. The aubergine called back up to the heavens as evening fills its void.

"I did not like that woman," he says.

"She does not expect to be liked," Marian says, turning. "She expects to be reckoned with."

He looks relieved at her apparent recovery.

"What a thrill for her, to find my cousin here. And with his news!"

Oliver frowns. "Why? What's it to her?"

"Well, it's a scoop. It's a big deal, Mort Klein's daughter getting married. Mort Klein may be generous with his house, you see, but not with his private life. I mean, you can see his ballroom if you support the Jewish Museum or the Philharmonic or the Crohn's and Colitis Foundation, but you won't find the family there. They're private people." Marian sinks onto the couch. "People like Valerie don't understand them. What's the point of being private!"

"'For what do we live, but to make sport for our neighbors,' right?"

"Right," Marian says. "Actually," she continues, "I ought to be grateful. If Barton hadn't been here she'd have been a lot more interested in you."

Oliver crosses over and sits beside Marian on the couch. After a moment, he crosses his legs at the knee.

"Good girl," Marian says and laughs. "I thought that was a nice touch, before. Who taught you to do that, anyway?"

"Dustin Hoffman in *Tootsie*," says Oliver.

"Oh, but you're so much prettier than him. I seem to recall some difficulty with five o'clock shadow."

"Well, it's past five o'clock. I might have a bit of a problem," Oliver leans close. "Care to feel?"

Marian reclines, with drama, a hand to her chest. "I couldn't."

He grins. "Scared?"

"Why, no. It's just, you're a very pretty girl."

"And that frightens you?"

"I can't trust myself!"

"How . . . provocative."

His hand, she now observes, is on her knee.

"Mr. Stern!"

"Please," Oliver entreats, "call me Ms."

"I've never!" Marian is laughing.

"Then you ought."

Well, if you put it that way. Proper English is such an aphrodisiac, Marian thinks, letting his weight pin her back against the cushions. She puts her hands on his back and feels the movement of cashmere over his skin and under her hands. She puts her hands under the cashmere and over his skin, which is warm—no, hot. It's hot like his breath against her neck. She can't see much because the long wig has fallen over her face, and there is just room in this diminished range of vision to be persuaded that a woman—indeed, a *beautiful* woman—is on top of her, moving and touching, pinning her to the couch and persuading her that she is no longer in control of herself. A woman is wanting Marian so fiercely that her desire is escaping in sounds of want, in little sighs at Marian's ear. A woman is putting her fingers in Marian's hair and making her want to bring her thighs together, except that the woman is already between her thighs, so she can't. The woman has narrow hips, a flat chest, shiny chestnut hair, and delicate hands. She is not shy, this woman. She doesn't hold back the way Marian herself might, wanting something so badly but only hoping a finger or a tongue will land in precisely the spot she wants it to, or wanting to put her own finger or tongue in some specific location but waiting to see if it might arrive there accidentally, as if in the course of other events. This woman is everywhere, touching beneath Marian's bra, reaching expertly for the zipper of Marian's wool pants, trailing her feathery hair across Marian's bare skin. It's all beyond her. The woman, this beautiful woman, is in charge, and Marian's only choice is whether just to lie here, and let the woman touch her in all of the places that now want touching, or to touch her back in all of the same places.

She could, for example, move her own hands from where they are on the woman's back over her ribs around to the woman's front. To her chest, in other words. She could put her hands on the woman's chest and, well, touch her. Which is not a thing she has ever done before and not a thing she has ever wanted to do, but it is in fact a thing she would like very much to do right now. She would like to see what this woman's breasts feel like and why shouldn't she, since the woman seems very willing and is moving against her in this provocative and yet oddly affectionate way, with one stockinged leg insinuated between Marian's legs. In fact, it now occurs to Marian that quite apart from putting her hands under this woman's sweater and touching her breasts, she could very easily put her hands under the woman's skirt and touch her between the legs. She could do that, and very easily, by lifting up the skirt or merely burrowing beneath it. Simple! Women make it so simple, don't they, wearing skirts. Do they want to be touched all the time? Is that the point of a skirt? She could put her hands under the skirt right now, right this second, without anything to stop her, and get directly at what she wants, whereas she herself is stuck in pants that need unzipping and peeling off—all that work! She hears the scratch of the woman's stockings as her legs move past each other.

"Don't you hate these horrible things?" Oliver complains.

"Yes," Marian says. "I do. All women do."

"Then why not get rid of them?"

"Why not?" She is putting her hands under his sweater. Her sweater. "Get rid of them. Take them off."

"Take them off for me," he teases.

He gets up on his knees and looks down at her in open challenge. Marian slides one hand up under the skirt, experimentally. Then, self-consciously, removes it.

"Chicken," Oliver says and grins.

"I can't. It's too weird."

He kisses her again. The evening crashes down around them. The couch, which is covered with expensive Scalamandré silk, gives a disquieting ping somewhere in the region of her bottom. She puts her hands under Oliver's skirt and, avoiding his crotch, fishes for the waistband. It fights her as she pulls it down.

"Dr. Kahn!" Oliver gasps, theatrically. "What do you think you're doing?"

"Just relax," Marian says, laughing. "I'm not going to hurt you."

He whispers something she doesn't quite hear, and rocks his hips against her, pressing his advantage, and after that, she finds herself both borne away from and then back to the whisper, which was unintelligible but is somehow charged with deeper meaning, so that the farther they travel from it, the more she also returns to it, first idly curious, then aroused, then inescapably anxious, until finally he slips inside her and Marian feels her chest contract in panic.

"What did you say?" she hisses.

"Mmm?" Oliver does not open his eyes. He is deeply inside her, one hand on the small of her back, the other caught in her hair.

"What did you say?" Marian cries. "Before. What did you say when you whispered?"

"What?" He opens his eyes, so reluctant, so knowing what this means, not only to the sex, which is about to wither, but to the evening, which has had too many wrenches already to easily withstand another. "Shh," he tries, optimistically closing his eyes again. He presses his face against hers. "I love you."

"No," Marian insists. "No, you need to tell me. What did you *say*?"

So he stops where he is, which is nowhere she can place, the physical sensations having fled the scene, taking everything of value with them. Even the light, she thinks dully, has gone plain and flat, the Aubergine Time so far in the past it might be embedded in childhood. It is good, Marian thinks, that she can't see Oliver's face very clearly. This is all too pitiful to see clearly. Besides, doesn't she know exactly what there is to see? Isn't she a middle-aged woman on an expensive couch with pants bunched at her ankles under a beautiful boy in a wig?

"It was dumb," says Oliver, her beautiful boy.

"Tell me." She is going to cry. Any second, she is going to cry. She is pathetic.

He pulls the rest of the way back out of her. "I said you can hurt me."

Marian sits up. Her knees snap together. "What?" She is choking back tears now.

Oliver shrugs. "You said, 'I'm not going to hurt you.' And I said, 'You can hurt me.' It's meaningless. We were *playing*, Marian!"

She knows, she knows, but that's all gone, now, and she is sobbing into her hands, because out of the mouth of a babe it has come, this ultimate truth, and she wonders if she actually heard him in the first place and only tried, tried not to give it meaning. *You can hurt me*. She doesn't want that, she doesn't want to hurt him! That is exactly what she has wanted to avoid, from the start. But how can they avoid it?

"Marian," Oliver says softly. He sits back on his heels at the end of the couch. His skirt has come down and covered him. His wig is askew. He gazes at her, helpless and wounded. "Please, why are you crying?"

But she won't say. She is only crying still, and now it feels as if her life is not punctuated by these fits of tears but that her life itself has turned into a long fit of tears, punctuated only by periods in which she forgets that she is a forty-eight-year-old woman terribly in love with a man who does not understand that he is twenty-six and what that means. She curls tightly forward against her knees, gripping them, and wetly, loudly, sloppily sobbing. For the first time all day, including when she was pushing him toward the door, she truly would like him to be gone.

"Marian, can I help?" Oliver says. But of course he can't. Still, she is grateful. A lesser man might have asked, "Are you having your period?" or something equally asinine, but Oliver has not, and a good thing, too, since that might have caused a fresh assault of tears. Marian has not had her period in years.

"Look," she manages to say, finally, between gulps, "I think... maybe it would be a good idea if I had some time to myself right now. It just isn't fair to inflict my presence on anyone else."

She sees but does not hear his sigh.

"Sweetie, I'm just...I just feel done in." Her voice sounds ragged, clumsily patched together. "It's better I'm alone."

"It's better you're with me," he says tersely. "It's better you don't shut me out the minute you think you're not in top form. It's better you figure out that we're in this together, and I am actually capable of understanding what you're going through."

"But you're not," she says. "No one's capable. I mean, really capable of really understanding. We get other people around the edges, maybe, but we don't get inside. We can't."

"I completely disagree." He moves back, putting more space between them, more air. "You think a man can't know a woman? Or is it that a young person can't know an older one?" He waits for a response. "Or just that *I'm* not capable. You think I'm too simple to understand this big"—he shakes his head in frustration—"*soup* of anxiety you're carting around all the time. You think I'm too insensitive to get it. Or just too stupid."

"Oliver," she says, leaning forward, "I would never think such a thing. I wouldn't—" *Love* is the word. *Love* is what she means and wants to say, but won't say. She will not burden him with her love, on top of everything else. "I wouldn't feel what I feel for you if you were either of those things. I meant only that to say 'I know what you're going through' is merely a gesture. We accept that it's the best we can do, but nobody can really know. Look," she tells him, "I know what Charlotte Wilcox ate for dinner on July seventeenth, 1784, but I'll never know how she really felt about anything. How could I? I mean, even if she were here and I could ask her, and even if she tried to articulate it and really wanted me to understand, I still couldn't understand. It's not just my limitation as a historian, it's my limitation as a human being. I can't know, and you can't know," she finishes, but Oliver shakes his head.

"You're wrong. If you gave me a chance, if you weren't afraid to reveal what it is, what is so horrible you can't bear for me to get near it, you might be surprised. This could be something that connects us, but you keep it between us. You make it an obstacle."

She shifts uncomfortably. She would like him to leave now.

"Look," Oliver says, his voice quiet in the near darkness, "I accept that our situation is unusual, but we're not the first couple to have been born so far apart. In this building alone there are probably a dozen men with wives young enough to be their daughters, and nobody bats an eyelash at them."

"That's very different," she snaps.

"It shouldn't be."

"Well, we can agree on that. But it is."

He looks at her. "But think about what matters in a relationship. In a marriage! It's companionship, and friendship. And passion. We have those things. There's longevity in what we have."

"The passion won't last," she says flatly, but he shakes his head.

"I disagree. Or at least, it has just as much chance of lasting as it would if we were both in our twenties."

That's what you think, Marian wants to say.

"Look, maybe this...this haze we're in will burn off, but there's so much between us, of real substance, that when it does"—Oliver, corrects himself—"*if* it does. If it did. There would be something different beneath it. I mean, something of value. Something I'd be happy to live with."

She looks at him with tenderness. "You shouldn't be. You deserve more."

"Oh. *Deserve*," Oliver says dismissively. "I hate that. Everybody *deserves*. It doesn't work like that. We get what we get. Sometimes we get what we go out and make an effort to look for. We don't get what we *deserve*. Besides," he looks at her, "what do you deserve?"

I've had that, she thinks. *I've had my chance.*

What she wanted back then—and yes, more than likely what she'd deserved—was Marshall, who had paid her the compliment of acknowledging her separateness and refrained from putting her on display. Who had treated her with unassailable courtesy, which included conducting his love affairs at such a remove that they truly did not impinge upon her life. Who had also held her hand during chemotherapy, and had not further punished her for the loss of her reproductive organs by leaving her.

"I'm satisfied," Marian hears herself say, and she knows that she is, or at least has been.

"That's not enough," Oliver says.

She closes her eyes. Darkness. The only sound is the traffic far below, the rustle of her own breath. *Go*, she thinks. How much more can she take?

"You're too extraordinary for that to be enough," he says.

"Ah," Marian says, truly weary. "That's where you're wrong. I'm very, very ordinary, and very, very lucky. I'm alive. I'm healthy, so far. I have a stable marriage and wealth and even a career that's given me great satisfaction. And right now I have this, which I'm loving. But I can't have it forever and I wish you would stop talking this way because I want to enjoy it now."

Oliver leans forward, one arm outstretched. Fingers find her face: chin, jaw, ear. "Why not?" he asks, sincerely questioning. "I don't understand: Why *not* forever? Why not take forever if it's offered? And it is, Marian. We'll start from here and we'll just go forward."

"I don't like forward," she says, losing her reserve. "I don't like thinking about it, and I certainly won't be responsible for dragging you down. If you're so empathetic, if you're so sure you understand me, why is this so hard for you to get? I'm forty-eight. If this is the best time of my life—and it is, Oliver, in many ways it is—then where do you think we go from here? I'm not going back to my girlish figure, I can tell you that. I'm not going back to wild abandon. I won't be trekking in Nepal anytime soon, and I'm not going to have any kids. It's a different country I'm going to, do you get that?" She is louder, more shrill than she can remember being, at least with him. "Oliver," Marian says sternly. "Enjoy your youth. Enjoy me, by all means, as much as you want and as often as you want. But please don't humiliate me by trying to make me fit into your life. I won't fit."

"You're afraid to get old," he says with unbearable starkness. She herself has managed to avoid the word "old." "That's all it is. I don't get it. I'm not afraid of it."

"Well, it's a long way off for you." She is harsh.

"No, I mean I'm not afraid of *your* getting old. I know you were beautiful as a young woman. You're beautiful now. I have every reason to believe that when you're an old woman, you'll be beautiful then, so what's the big deal? It's not why I love you today, so why would it matter in the future?"

Marian lurches off the couch, wounded, clutching at her pants. She has never, she thinks wildly, understood the phrase "arrogance of youth" until this moment. Even Valerie Annis did not cut her so deeply. He tries to grab for her as she leans down to yank at the fabric:

"Hey!" It sounds like a bark. She hates him. Then she hates herself for thinking that. "Marian, let's talk about it!"

"Why, so you can patronize me even more?" Marian chokes through new tears. This is getting tiresome. She has always cried too easily. Her classmates at Brearley knew how to achieve the effect: a comment about her looks, her money, her odd pedigree, at once snobbish and deficient with Jewishness. *Warburg weeps again!* she thinks, fumbling with the zipper. She steals a look at him and finds him injured on the couch in his now ridiculous skirt and wig. A wig he stole from her personal cupboards in her personal office. How dare he go into her things! And hasn't he been laughing at her ever since? "You're just being selfish!" she cries. "You're not really interested in understanding. It flatters you to think I might love you so much I would leave my husband and my life and go live with you. Or marry you! But that isn't what you want, really. You want to have your affair with an older woman and then go back to your own life. Which includes things I couldn't give you even if I wanted to."

"No!" He jumps to his feet and makes a grab for her.

"You feed me some line about how it doesn't matter that I'm getting old, but you belittle me by ignoring the fact that it matters to me, and you patronize me by implying that it's because of my vanity. It isn't vanity, Oliver, it's time."

He shakes his head, barely visible. "Time."

"Time! Which is no longer on my side, to quote the music of my youth. I'm losing it, every day. It's running past me, it's going faster than it used to, I swear."

She can just make him out. He is shaking his head.

"No, of course you don't believe me. You're just... you're settling into your life now. You're out of school, so you don't have that artificial calendar anymore that says the year is beginning, it's halfway over, it's ending, and now it's beginning again, so time feels different to you," she barely recognizes her own voice, but she keeps on. "And of course none of your friends are having heart attacks or getting cancer and you all feel like it will go on forever. But it won't. Sometimes I still feel twenty-six and I wonder why I'm so tired and a couple of my friends are dead and everybody else is coloring their hair and getting their eyes done or having injections in their foreheads, and then I remember: *that was twenty years ago*. But it wasn't. I mean, it feels like it wasn't. It feels like..." She trails off. She despises cliché and won't say what it feels like. "You know," Marian hears herself say, "what I hate most of all these days? You're going to think this is absurd."

"I won't," says Oliver, who is straining, she can tell, to understand.

"I hate daylight savings time. I hate having to give up that hour in the spring. I hate setting all the clocks forward. I resent it so much now."

The smallest laugh escapes him. But then he remembers that he is not to think her absurd.

"But you get the hour back, Marian. In the fall."

"Not really." She shakes her head, genuinely saddened. "I never feel it come back. I always feel I've been tricked out of an hour of my life. It all goes so fast." She stands for a moment in the darkness and is grateful for his silence. How she will ever face him again she does not know. She feels ridiculous, painfully neurotic. Ship me off, she thinks, like all of the other middle-aged lady intellectuals who didn't bother having kids to keep themselves sane. Her best book is behind her anyway, so what's the harm?

"Do you want to have your eyes done?" Oliver says, surprisingly. "I mean, is that what you're saying? Because if you do, I wouldn't necessarily like it, and I certainly don't think you need it, but if something like that would make you happy, then I want you to know I'd support it."

This, to her own amazement, lightens everything, and she smiles. "That's sweet. That's lovely of you. But no, I wouldn't do it. I won't try to slow time down, because that's arrogant. And I'm too grateful for what I've had."

"Your health," he says tersely. "Your career. And Marshall. I know, you told me."

"Yes! I am! And I wouldn't...I don't know, get a face-lift or something to try to pretend I'm not as old as I am. And I wouldn't marry a man who's twenty-six to try to pretend I'm not too old to be married to a man who's twenty-six. This might be some kind of important life experience for you, but it doesn't work that way for me."

This she regrets instantly, but of course it is too late, and he is too proud not to take offense.

"Jesus, Marian, how can you say that? You know how I feel about you! Why are you trying to reduce my feelings, which are genuine, to a...a...rite of passage? Is that how you push me away?"

"No," she says, but he is unstoppable.

"I didn't need a sexual awakening from you, and I didn't get one," he says. "I'm with you because I love you and I want to be with you. It isn't about our ages. We're just two people who came together. It's true we didn't start at the same time, but can't we finish together?"

She stares at him, weary. Of course it is right, what he says, essentially right, though there is a certain element of drama, undeniable even to Oliver, connected to falling passionately in love with his mother's childhood friend. She knows—truly, soberly, she knows—that his passion for her is real, that it comes from the planet of all sexual passion and all romantic love. That he loves her and even believes he wants to be with her and marry her. She does not want that love to end on this evening, in this dark, sad, and oddly disconnected scene.

"I could never be with a man who has better legs than I do."

This throws him. He takes a moment to regroup.

"That's not an answer."

"No," Marian says, reaching for his hand. "But it's the best I can do. I'm tired and I'm sad, and I'm worried about what Valerie Annis would do if she found out. Not to mention Marshall. Or your mother. I want to go back to the day we were having, Oliver, but it's gone and I'm just too wrecked right now to pull myself together. So I'm thinking, maybe, if I just hang out by myself for a while, and sleep, and do a little work in the morning, I might be able to get back on track with myself and we can meet tomorrow. We could...I don't know, I could come downtown. We could do something there."

Oliver contemplates. Then one hand comes up to his head and

pulls off the wig. This is a gesture of resignation. "Fine," he says, but not harshly.

"Thank you."

"For what?" There is a note of anger. "For leaving you?"

"For not making it harder than it is. For understanding that it's just an off night, not the whole space-time continuum."

After a moment, he smiles. "Okay."

"Okay," Marian says. Now that it is settled, now that he is leaving, she has lost her bravado, her will to be alone. Suddenly, she finds herself anticipating the vacuum *whoosh* of the front door shutting behind him, the creaking of the elevator gears. *Oliver*, she nearly says. *Don't go.*

Oliver walks over to the other couch, kneels down on the rug, and hunts beneath the fringe for his lost clothing. Then he leaves the room, walking uncomfortably in his hastily pulled-up tights. It is true about his legs, she thinks sadly, watching them crisscross beneath the skirt. They are indeed better than her own: skinny and muscled with fine, smooth knees. Too pretty for her, she thinks. Also too handsome. Christ—had she actually said that about daylight savings time? How sad, Marian thinks. How truly gone I am.

It is going to be a long and unhappy night.

Out in the kitchen, there is a shuffle and then the final click of the office door. Oliver comes back in, dressed in his clothes from the prehistory of that morning. She can barely remember them now: black pullover, olive corduroy pants, the brown leather shoes he inherited from his father and cherishes so much that he will not wear them if it looks like rain. Marian puts on a smile so strained it threatens to break. She forces herself to hug him, then she forces herself to stop.

"Tomorrow," Oliver says.

"Yes." Bravely. "Whatever you want to do."

"I'll have to think about that. I'll have to give that long thought. Long and detailed."

"Good." She is going to cry again, Marian thinks. She would like him to leave before she does. "I'll call you in the morning."

Then, finally, he turns to go. She can breathe, but carefully, knowing he is still near, still close enough to rush back in at the sound she is capable of making. Only a few seconds more. He summons the elevator with a buzz. She counts to three and again to three and once again, and then hears the rumble of gears as the door opens, taking Oliver Stern, whom she does love, and deeply, away.

Marian lets her head fall forward into her hands. The hands, she notes from a distance, are wet, and it takes a long, disconnected moment to understand that she herself has provided—is providing—this moisture. So boring! Marian thinks, pausing in her misery to be miserable about that, too. She is so beneath her own standard, her new standard, of what a woman ought to be at her time of life. This is the curse of history, she thinks, weeping. This is why it is not necessarily a good thing to unearth our betters from the lost sands of lost time: they do not necessarily show us ourselves to best advantage. Indeed, she has acquired the habit of imagining Lady Charlotte as her own personal critic and now conjures her on the other sofa, incongruous and yet unassailably at home on Park Avenue and in the year 1997, with her skirts fanned around her, flicking her tongue in disgust at the blubbering madwoman. Truly mad! Marian laments noisily. Mad to send away her lover in the middle of passion—*idiot, idiot.* Just how many twenty-six-year-old lovers does she believe are waiting to take his place?

Marian gets to her feet. Brandy, she has promised herself, and brandy she will have, in a fine crystal glass in front of the blinking lights of the city. Then, fortified, she will go out into the world and try to do some good thing to redeem herself. Some good thing—she can't imagine what it might be, but there must be something she can do. First brandy. No, first water, to shock her tears into retreat.

The only light in the apartment now comes from the kitchen, in a wedge of illumination that crosses the dining room into the room she occupies. It just reaches the small rectangle of paper Oliver left on the coffee table, and when Marian sees this she stops.

The address from Barton. The address Oliver will need for the flowers. The card to remind him of his commission, and its recipient: Sophie Klein, the fiancée.

This is the moment when Marian understands that she will not be seeing Oliver the following day. This is when she knows that she will be sick, or will say she is sick, and unable to come downtown. This is when she knows that the ground of their affair has shifted beneath her, and at her behest, even though it may be against her will.

Which is why she must make sure Oliver does not leave without the card. She moves quickly, forgetting everything else as she tears through the living room and kitchen and snatches up the house phone. There is a clattering sound from the lobby, as a hand fumbles the button to clear the line, and then Hector's voice, finishing his instructions to a delivery man. "Yes, lobby," he says finally.

"Hector? My guest, the young man who just came down? He left something. Is he in the lobby?"

There is a brief pause. A mumbled consultation. "He's gone. Carlo took him down."

"Can you catch him?"

"Oh...just a minute," says Hector. A muffled sound, like a hand over the mouth of the receiver. "Carlo can see him. He's going after him. Just at the end of the block."

"Oh!" She is thrilled. She is truly so grateful. It is a salvation, to have this piece of evidence gone from her apartment and on its way. "Thank you, Hector! I really appreciate it. Thank Carlo for me."

"I coming up," Hector says.

"I'll wait at the elevator," she tells him, and puts down the receiver.

Then, adjusting her clothing and wiping her hands once more over her face, she exits her own front door to stand in the antechamber and wait.

CHAPTER FOUR

Clos des Fleurs

WHEN OLIVER COMES UP FROM THE SUBWAY on West Fourth there is a fine mist in the night air that seems to come from all directions and is disorienting in its warmth—like, thinks Oliver, a sprayed disinfectant, or the cloud of perfume permanently ambient on the cosmetics floor of Bloomingdale's. He closes his eyes instinctively, but the mist is not unpleasant. Oliver walks north on Sixth Avenue, his hands deep in his jacket pockets. He considers again, and again resists, the notion that he is being sanitized, that the hours of sex and fighting and comedy and grief might be washed from his skin and pass from his thoughts. The truth is, he does not want them gone at all. The truth is that the mess and frustration of his life with Marian—and it is a life, now, despite her terror of admitting it—are part of something that he loves. He doesn't, of course, love her anxieties and self-tormenting, but he knows better than to try to separate the melancholy from her character. He accepts her, in other words. More than that, he wants her.

It isn't, after all, the first time they have turned a corner into such confusion. He remembers one of their early dinners, on a Saturday night at Le Rouge, when she traveled the distance from hilarity to depression in what seemed like a single breath, and could be restrained from leaving the table, the restaurant, and all the elation of their first weeks together, only by his two feet gripping, pincerlike, her ankle under the table. Where it comes from is not a mystery to him. Marian seems programmed to deny herself happiness, and the more she lets pleasure slip past her defenses, the more she seems to beat it back. Since Oliver observes this tendency equally in Marian's relationship with her friends, in her guilt over money, and in her ambivalence toward professional success—which is merited, in her own case, by the most honest of labor—he knows not to take it personally. So the fact that he has just been expelled from her apartment, and from the weekend they had long ago set aside for themselves, does not entirely crush him.

But what a waste, Oliver thinks, echoing Marian's own sentiment from only an hour earlier. What a waste of their weekend, with its absent spouse and its empty apartment and its tender, athletic, glorious commencement. What a waste of this clear night, which might have found them out walking, or holding hands in a movie, or even scouting last-minute cancellations to hear Bobby Short at the Carlyle—he would have loved that, he thinks sadly. And the lost tomorrow, the rare pleasure of waking up with her and falling back asleep, or getting up, or staying in bed...He has experienced these good things just enough to regret their absence. But perhaps, for tomorrow at any rate, there is still a possibility, as Marian said, and he has no reason to disbelieve her, since her moods have a way of shifting back in his direction. They will talk in the morning, and when they do she will say that she wishes she had not needed to be by herself, but hopes they might...soon...

Tomorrow night, then. Afternoon, if he can coax her from her work, but surely by night, and now the reverie unfolds: what they might do tomorrow night. It unfolds even as he walks, like a carpet stretching down the pavement before him: he will cook for her—he is a skilled cook of limited repertoire—and he will buy a really good bottle of wine, taking the advice of the guy at Christopher Street Wines who can't quite tell that Oliver is straight (and is so hopeful that Oliver does not see how to communicate this without hurting the guy's feelings), and then he will talk to Marian and touch Marian and take Marian to bed and be happy.

Oliver, already happy at the prospect of this future happiness, feels himself grin.

Sixth Avenue is roiling with New Yorkers engaged in the business of getting what they need and going home, and the crowd seems universally bent on Balducci's, where Oliver himself is heading. He has not managed to acquire the habit of regular shopping in small, specialized stores. Bread, vegetables, meat, and fish—weren't you supposed to go from shop to shop, making personal connections with your purveyors and supporting family businesses? Instead, he relies far too heavily on Balducci's, though he dislikes its snobbery, its assumption of affluence, the maddening lack of toilet paper and other similarly nonglamorous items. That he nonetheless finds himself doing the bulk of his shopping there signifies a lack of discipline, Oliver thinks.

At the store, he joins a crowd of hypercritical foodies, weighing the merits of basil- or chili-infused oils and upsetting pyramids of exotic teas as they reach for the strategically weight-bearing box they must, above all others, examine. There's a crush two bodies deep at the meat counter, so Oliver takes a number and drifts through the cramped aisles, checking the countdown numeral each time he passes by and accumulating orzo, still-spectacular tomatoes (where they get them he can't imagine), olives, bread, and the aforementioned basil-infused extra virgin olive oil, as well as an expensive prepared beet and chèvre salad for his own dinner tonight and a wooden box of Burdick chocolates, which Marian loves. By the time his number's barked, he has assembled a hearty but elegant menu for the two of them, featuring short ribs, orzo, frisée, and artichokes, to be followed, after a decent interval, by the chocolates. If it's warm, he thinks, ordering the short ribs, they can eat on the roof, though he has a gardener's perpetual regret about the state of his plants. If not, they will eat in the bedroom, which has a table and, just as important, a fireplace. He does not cook for Marian nearly enough, he thinks merrily, maneuvering his basket before him into the chutelike checkout, where the actress or artist or novelist on duty piles his seventy-odd dollars' worth of merchandise into a single bag and extends an elegant hand for his credit card. There are flowers in French tin pots and large steel vats against the door, and he frowns at them, critical but admiring. Here is his real competition, he reflects, signing his name to the slip. Not the little groceries with their well-worn blooms wrapped in patterned plastic, but these exotic stems and bunches tied in raffia, so easy to add to the already obscene contents of the cart. They look good, these flowers, and will last fairly well, it seems to him. That is possibly bad news for the very elegant and very expensive flower shop only a few blocks away, and for his own flowers, Oliver thinks, so much lovelier, so much more deserving than these.

He remembers, then, suddenly and quite viscerally, this very morning, early, with fog over the cobblestones in front of the shop, reaching into the truck while the engine was still running and Bell was hauling out the containers, lifting out those Boule de Neige roses, long-stemmed, dripping, and alive. He had known as soon as he saw them, not only that they were beautiful roses, but that they were the right roses. The exactly perfect roses, for her.

For the lady love, Bell had said then, and laughed, clairvoyant, shaking his dreadlocks.

Now Oliver thinks: *Yes, exactly. For the lady love.*

The cashier hands him his receipt and his credit card.

Then he remembers something else, back before the shopping and the subway and the tears and the sex and the surprising hoot of his pantomime with Barton Ochstein to the moment he was above Marian and inside her and he stopped—stopped still—to look: he remembers how she turned her head away from him, to the side, and how she is self-conscious about her neck, and how she has even admitted that she thinks of having it "done," whatever that means. He can never risk saying that this is ridiculous, but it is ridiculous. There is nothing wrong with her neck, and it does not make her look old as she thinks it does, though he catches her now and then pushing the loose skin this way and that with her fingertips, frowning at a stray reflection. Besides, she isn't old. She isn't even as old as his mother (who isn't old, either) though they were once classmates—Marian so clever they moved her ahead, one year, two years, what does it matter? Besides, what does a young neck look like, anyway?

He looks at the cashier's neck. That is what a young neck looks like.

Oliver hands her the signed receipt, hoists the bag onto his hip, and leans against the door to leave. There are other things he needs, other stops he ought to make before going home, and he rejoins the evening crowd.

A block west on Christopher Street, just past the leather men mannequins of the drag boutique, Transformations, Oliver pushes open the door to Christopher Wines and resignedly notes that his wine-buddy, his would-be friend, is already grinning at him from the merlots. Oliver waves briefly and heads for the aisle where they keep the perfectly respectable but not-for-the-cognoscenti California reds, and there he chooses, purely for its name (Clos des Fleurs) two bottles of middling price, which he takes to the register.

"Nice choice!" says the assistant, sauntering over to him.

"Oh," Oliver says noncommittally. "Is it? I just liked the name."

"Right. You and your flowers."

Have I talked about flowers with this guy? Oliver thinks. Christ, what a jerk I am.

"I guess." Oliver sighs and sets down his grocery bag on a ledge.

"So, is this for a special dinner, or what?"

Oliver shrugs. "Not really." He is wondering if there is another wine store nearby he ought to be patronizing.

"Thirty-six forty-eight with the tax," says the assistant. "So, what are you doing this weekend?"

Oliver hands over his card. "Oh...not much." This is an attempt to avoid conversation, but as he says it Oliver realizes that it sounds downright receptive. Sure enough, the assistant nods eagerly.

"I'm going to a Violet Quill retrospective tomorrow night. At Three Lives. You know the Violet Quill?"

"Um," Oliver says while he signs with a very un-Quillish Bic pen, "no."

"It was a group of writers in the seventies who started meeting in the Village. Most of them became important novelists. Felice Picano. Robert Ferro. Edmund White?" The assistant is frowning now. He has evidently not expected such a level of ignorance. And he is very definitely *not* putting the wine into a bag and handing that bag to Oliver.

Come on, thinks Oliver.

"I'm a writer, you know," he says instead.

"Oh," Oliver says, wild to get away. "I didn't know. Well, it sounds interesting. Have a good time." He makes a grab for the unbagged bottles, and the assistant frowns and tells him to wait. He reaches below the counter and hands Oliver a small paper bag, still folded flat: their romance is over, and moreover it has ended badly. How much simpler, thinks Oliver, it would have been to merely tell the guy many visits ago that he was a poor prospect for a pickup, and spared themselves this. Oliver puts the bottles into the bag. "See you," he says sheepishly.

"Yeah," the man says. "Enjoy yourself."

Now that you've cruelly spurned my advances, thinks Oliver, leaving.

The thing is, it doesn't actually bother Oliver that the guy assumes he's gay. It would have once, Oliver considers, walking now with the wine and groceries each in one hand. There was a time, certainly, in his teens, when he was preoccupied with the subject, a tangent—he thought at the time—to the subject of his medical status. He would have minded it then. Only a few years ago he might have been rattled, even by such an innocuous, friendly proposition. But now, for some reason, he is untroubled. The questioning, Oliver has come to think, has little to do with him, in the end. In his case, it is not a comment on his voice or his mannerisms or his clothing; it is a form of prejudice— occupational prejudice. Because he is a man and he loves flowers. Apparently, only homosexual men are allowed to love flowers.

His response to this is offense on behalf of flowers.

Music is supposed to be the food of love, he knows, but Oliver has never had any special feeling for music. Classical, folk, jazz, or blues—it's all a buzz to him, and more than one girlfriend has shaken her head at his imperviousness. He's not even tone-deaf; he just doesn't care, and would rather have silence. Oliver possesses, as a result, perhaps the smallest collection of music on the island of Manhattan (one CD of Carole King's *Tapestry*, two Devo albums left over from high school, and a cassette tape of *Madame Butterfly* given to him by his stepfather, who adores opera, in a long-ago attempt to make a point of contact between them). For Oliver it has always been flowers, the food not only of love but of life. Flowers to look at, to smell, to be alive with in their brief life spans—they are their own seat of pleasure, endlessly giving. He does not understand people who do not love flowers, or who consider them merely ornamental for the home, like an accent pillow or a Hummel figurine. He does not understand people who assault flowers for their essence, which they rub over their skin like a spoil of war, leaving carcasses of slaughtered blossoms in their wake. He knows that these are extreme, dramatic views, which is why he does not often share them, but it does baffle him that in a world so bereft of pleasure people fail to see that flowers are a part of the solution, that the unlearned lesson of their loveliness bears on the great disconnect between people and other people, between people and the earth, between people and the eternal.

Every now and then, Oliver will catch a glimpse of this passion in someone else, and the recognition will fill him with gratification. He will be in Greenwich, or at the Botanical Garden, or in the flower district, and a woman or a man will catch his eye and they will nod and speak silently in their own language of flowers. Once he smiled at a woman tending the most common of geraniums in her window box on Jane Street. The geraniums were ravishing, and the woman, who was old and spent, was ravishing too, and smiled back. Once it was a man in Central Park who was taking eggshells out of a plastic bag he'd brought from home and placing them tenderly around a bank of daffodils beside Sheep Meadow. And—satisfyingly—sometimes it happened in his own shop, when a person entered and was lit with delight at the same thing that made Oliver so happy when he opened his own door.

He opens his own door now, setting down the shopping bag, hearing the wine bottles clink gently against each other, and then shuts the door behind him with his foot. It is 8:30 and the day has ended with the return of its early fog. The street—which is thinly populated and nearly always empty unless a performance at the Cherry Lane Theatre is beginning, breaking for intermission, or letting out—is very dark and still. Returning his key to his jacket pocket, Oliver's fingers brush the thin card he'd been summoned back to retrieve from Marian's doorman, and it pierces his mood a bit to think of the disagreeable Barton Ochstein, with his heavy hand touching Oliver's thigh through Marian's skirt. The fiancée of a person like Ochstein was hardly likely to care for flowers, herself—beyond, Oliver thought dismissively, the tiresome brand recognition of one dozen sterile blood-red roses in a cheap white cardboard box. Still, he will have to give Ochstein's commission some thought. Because Oliver does not sell ugly flowers, or flowers with their smells removed, or bouquets for the season. He assembles beautiful, living flowers, and he sends them out into the world with hope that they might receive their due in appreciation.

Oliver is aware that he belongs to a distinct occupational segment of his demographic group, set well apart from the officially sanctioned career designations—law, business, medicine—that account for an overwhelming majority of his peers. In addition to this majority, the far smaller yet equally prestigious calling of "artist" in its variant forms, is acknowledged, even afforded bragging rights sometimes exceeding the aforementioned career choices, though only in certain families. Between these extremes, however, there is little in the way of viable career territory. The children of well-to-do Jewish families do not seem to join the police department, become aerobics instructors, drive trucks, or run travel agencies. They are not housekeepers, office managers, landscape designers, or franchise owners. But every now and then, one of them might pop up in an unconventional role, salvaged from suspicion (their parents salvaged from pity) only by the undeniability of a very specific talent.

He imagines the members of his parents' generation at an annual gathering, a holiday open house of sorts, in a venue vast enough to hold the Jewish upper middle class of Manhattan and its more affluent suburbs. In the outer vestibules (the temple grounds, the antechambers to the Holy of Holy) are the younger parents, avidly shaking down the competition on the subjects of SAT scores, GPAs, and, above all, fat letters from the handful of approved colleges. (*Adam Weintraub got in everywhere! Simone Sternbaum was wait-listed at Vassar. Juliane Lieberman doesn't test well. No one can believe Yale took Sarah Gold—just because her older sisters went there and her father is Steven Spielberg's lawyer. It's so unfair!*) Inside, the parents are older, and while there is even more at stake, there is also an air of calm. (Things are now out of their hands, after all—shrugs all around.) Even so, envy courses in myriad subterranean rivers, because here, finally, points are awarded and the children sorted: lawyers to one corner, doctors to another, Wall Street over here, permissible alternate professions (architecture, publishing, academia, journalism, Hollywood, Washington) over there. Then there is a small designated area for the creatives, the artists, the marchers-to-a-different-drummer: the girl dancing with ABT, for example, the two promising novelists, the composer (with a commission already from City Opera! Only twenty-nine!), the girl who won the Yale Series of Younger Poets and teaches at NYU, the *wunderkind* painter who sent his slides right from Harvard and got a show at Andre Emmerich, the guy who directed all the musicals at Fieldston and now does off Broadway.

And then there is the place to which Oliver is directed. It is sparsely populated, indeed.

Hello, hello, these few greet one another. Everyone shakes hands. They are very interesting people in this little corner, and they are glad to meet. One of them might be a chef, for example. And that does not mean a cook! It means a chef—and not only a good chef but a wildly gifted and ambitious chef, already with a well-reviewed and thriving restaurant (probably teeming with his parents' friends and almost certainly on the Upper East Side). Another might have become a carpenter, but that's all right, because he is not remotely like the guy who comes to your apartment and builds your custom cabinets; he is a "master carpenter" (this is a title deriving prestige from having been in use for centuries) whose exquisite furniture is advertised in the back of *Architectural Digest* and who was featured in a recent *New York Times* piece on the new craftsmen. One might have gone to Japan to learn an obscure form of glaze application for a rare type of pottery, which she now produces from her studio in western Connecticut and sells exclusively at Barneys, and which is so exquisite that all three of the Miller sisters registered for her pieces when they were married! Another might be farming in central Virginia, where he raises free-range, cruelty-free veal and has become a rising star in the post–Alice Waters generation of purveyors and an exemplar of the new green entrepreneur. Then again, some of them might do what Oliver has done, opened a shop or a business in which he or she does a very small specialized thing very, very well. Hence, Oliver is not "Oliver the florist" or even "Oliver who owns a flower shop," but "Oliver who opened a darling shop in the West Village and is doing terribly well because he was always so gifted with flowers. Did you see that piece on him in *Elle Decor*?"

They know that their parents are proud of them, but it was a close call—it could have gone either way. These Jewish boys and girls toil in uncharted waters and they have a lot to prove, but they are happy, and feel lucky. They are doing precisely what they want to do—in most cases what they have *always* wanted to do—and even if they suffer a lingering sense that they have missed some important opportunity and will now play catch-up for the rest of their lives, trailing their peers who boast retirement accounts and career prestige, they all know it could have been worse. Because their generation is not all accounted for in this room, large as it is. There are the missing ones, the not-mentioned ones, whose positions are no longer tracked by the chattering moms and dads. There is, for example, Jon Levine, sentenced by mandatory drug laws for selling grass at Wesleyan, still in some prison in Connecticut. There is Dana Friedman, who married a Farrakhan follower and moved to Detroit. There is David Rosengarten, presumed still traveling in Asia, presumed still stoned. And perhaps most fearful of all, there is Steven Nathan, who just failed at everything, who is still searching, who has not settled on the right path. *What's Steven doing? What's Steven up to? How old is Steven now?*

It could have been worse, Oliver thinks, looking around at his place. My place, he likes to remind himself. Where I live. And where the lilies of the field, though plentiful, do not toil, but I do.

Inside, the light of the refrigerator glows blue on the unsold dahlias, bittersweets, and hydrangeas. Branches fill the spaces between the bright tin containers, because the white plastic of the refrigerator has an ugly, deflating quality, and he likes to obscure it. There are large buckets of Black Magic roses, deeply red, and Spicy, the orange rose he prefers. The population of Hocus Pocus red roses has diminished since he left this morning, and this encourages him; Oliver is fond of the variety, which is red with yellow flecks, and he would like to be able to increase his weekly order from the Argentinean supplier. The room is long from side to side and short from front to back, unpolished and dark with age. It's empty, but turning on the overhead light, Oliver notes the general disarray cast in the wake of Bell, who worked until five this afternoon: frayed ribbons on the floor, cut stems of flowers underfoot, and a fat roll of brown wrapping paper left in a puddle of water on the wooden table Oliver uses for arrangements. Tidiness is not one of Bell's attributes. He is not an orderly person in any sense, but rather a juggler of problems. Having spent his first months with Bell obsessing about what his employee had and hadn't done, and whether he had loaded the Tribeca deliveries before heading to the Upper West Side so he wouldn't have to come back to the shop if the traffic was bad, Oliver has learned to back off and breathe deep. If Bell should decide to cross the George Washington Bridge and drive along the river to Nyack for the purpose of surprising an old friend, if he should consider it pleasant to double back ceaselessly to the shop and deliver one arrangement at a time to its destination, if he should spend a long, lazy afternoon talking about rare varieties of orchid with a woman who has happened in off the street and looks unlikely to purchase a single lousy stem...everything still, somehow, and in defiance of all logic, gets done in good time. In fact, since Bell has come to work for him, no customer has ever called to harangue Oliver over the nonappearance of an order, something that was all too common in the pre-Bell era. Oliver does not understand how it all gets accomplished, but it does.

Still...Oliver bends down to gather the scraps of ribbon and paper from the floor. That he lives over the shop is both the delight of his arrangement and its flaw, as he has been known to confuse work and privacy, professional contact and social contact. Disarray belowstairs has a way of rising, he has discovered, like heat, and Oliver has been known to get up in the middle of the night with a compulsion to tidy things in the wrapping area, or to pick through the stems in the refrigerators, plucking a bruised outer petal or removing a spent stem altogether (an activity that inevitably depresses him). He moves quickly now, his bags forgotten by the door, gathering, tossing, cleaning up. The soaked paper may not be salvageable, but he unfurls the roll in an attempt to dry it, anchoring the end with a pair of wire clippers. He pulls three fading dahlias from the water, cuts them midway up the stem, and inserts them in a pale blue old milk of magnesia bottle to take upstairs. Then, noting the unblinking glow of the office answering machine light, he retrieves his bags and unlocks the door to his apartment stairs.

When he first arrived in the city five years earlier, it was with a largely irrelevant degree from Brown and a far more pertinent bequest from his late father, the use of which Oliver had determined in advance and in some detail. This use involved the purchase of a building in which he would live while he established his business, the preemptively named White Rose, and for the first weeks of his city life he walked the neighborhoods, looking for the right building with the right sign affixed—a sign that he imagined would read FOR SALE. His naïveté over matters of real estate, over matters of Manhattan real estate in particular, has given him much retroactive amusement over the past years, and quite rightly, but in fact this method did yield the final result of 22 Commerce Street, even if the sign in question did not read FOR SALE but CONDEMNED BY THE CITY OF NEW YORK.

Oliver remembers the first time he saw it, having passed by the little street many, many times, mooning over a gorgeous, expensive (and, incidentally, fully inhabited) brownstone on Barrow. Commerce Street, after all, is easy to miss, and it goes nowhere that Barrow Street does not, so it was weeks into the steamy summer of 1992 when the emerging crowd of the Saturday matinee caught his eye and made him take what he imagined would be a pointless digression. And there, a few doors up from the Cherry Lane Theatre, was his place: tattered, pink-bricked, the size of a modest suburban home in an older suburb. There were planks of wood in the windows and the front steps had been hacked away (for what? he wondered), and he saw, when he peered into the alley alongside the building, the ominous scurry of a fat city rat.

It was the right place, and he felt first a flood of relief, as if its appearance confirmed every assumption he'd made.

That CONDEMNED sign would mean a delay for his project of many months, so he rented a sterile studio in a new building on Perry Street from which to do battle with the city and gain the abandoned building. There followed months of further delay as he asked permission to make improvements to his newly acquired, formally uninhabitable building. (This was a bureaucracy that only New Yorkers could create, he thought. It featured applications endlessly lost, and paid expeditors who promised to whittle years of roadblocks down to mere seasons. And when his applications were at last approved, he faced the final indignity of another two months wasted before anyone bothered to inform him of the approval.) Additional months passed as he dealt with an entirely different array of Kafkaesque city agencies, this time to obtain a zoning easement so that he could operate a business on the ground floor of his new address. Lastly, there were the months of renovation limbo as he waited in vain for contractors to call him back, contractors to materialize for appointments, contractors to do the work he had finally managed to contract them to do.

All through this period, Oliver's mother, Caroline, rent her garments and phoned regularly to ask, *Was he sure...* and, *Did he understand...* and, *Wouldn't he at least consider...?* Oliver kept his cool. He regretted that his mother did not share his sense of adventure about what he was coaxing from the glorious ruin on Commerce Street, but he wasted no effort trying to convince her. Instead, he placated her with frequent visits to Greenwich and fed her the encouraging news of his growing business, which had indeed taken root in the temporary and unlovely soil of his little Perry Street flat.

Already, Oliver was spending a few mornings a week on West Twenty-eighth Street, arriving early with the other dawn risers of the flower world, poking his fingers and nose into the crates and tubs of inventory as it got hauled off the trucks. The owners of Dutch Line and Fischer & Page got used to the sight of the kid in the old corduroys and fancy leather shoes who turned up in the darkness and stamped his feet for warmth like everyone else, puffing hot breath into the cold, blowing steam off the terrible coffee sold by the only vendor willing to sell it at that hour on that street. He spoke enough to show he knew what he was talking about, but mostly he kept quiet and listened, and he noted how many of the buckets of tulips went to the man with the shop on East Sixty-first, and how many of those buckets were red, how many yellow. He followed the famous—and famously cantankerous—florist from SoHo as he trawled the street and pointed out the white ranunculus and hot pink Daladier he wanted with a gesture so subtle it might have belonged to a bidder at an auction, yet clear enough that his assistant, a slender woman in black, always lifted the right flowers from the water. He watched with raw fascination the huge man who arrived draped in a sort of sheepskin cape and moved among the dealers, chatting, chatting, but never raising an arm, let alone a finger. Yet, when he moved on, the wholesalers would direct that very specific buckets of viburnum and hydrangea be put aside for him. The best buckets, Oliver saw, awed.

He might have apprenticed himself to one of these people, but he was impatient, so he began by dropping into restaurants in the late afternoon, casually introducing himself to managers and sometimes chefs, offering to do their flowers. Most were curt, but Oliver had charm, and often enough he found himself at a bare table with a cup of tea and a couple of serious, nodding men, showing them photographs of flowers and containers and making notes about their color preferences, heights, shapes, and prices. During this period he created his arrangements on a plastic sheet stretched on the floor of his studio, and when they were done he transported them to their destinations in a child's red wagon, the vases wedged tightly and the flowers wrapped against the wind. After the first month, he'd accumulated eight regular clients and a host of sporadic customers. He added office lobbies, doctors' offices, two clothing shops, and an antique store on Bleecker Street. He began to leave business cards beside his arrangements, with the new address optimistically printed and his current phone number. He began to get calls.

All of which made him ever more impatient for his own home.

When the pleasurable part of the day—the mornings on Twenty-eighth Street, the hours working with the flowers, the deliveries—was past, Oliver went to Commerce Street and confronted the creeping pace of his renovation. Termite damage had been revealed in one post, dry rot in a wall, the six-over-nine windows he'd bought by special order from a reproduction glassmaker suffered repetitive delays, meaning that plywood continued to cover the window openings. The upstairs fireplace was declared unusable, then probably unusable, then probably okay, so long as he wasn't intending to actually light fires in it. The missing front steps continued to flummox him; he could not imagine where he might obtain an appropriate replacement. The water ran brown, earthen brown.

Caroline came by as often as she dared. She was in the city fairly often, working with the New York City Ballet Guild and meeting Oliver's stepfather for dinner. She didn't necessarily want Oliver in an antiseptic suburban castle, but the atmosphere of his future home, with its flying plaster and rat droppings, was more than her maternal heart could easily withstand. The choices Oliver was making daily were baffling to her, including the decision to preserve a spectacular crack in one of the original walls, or the failure to install a shower in the bathroom, where Oliver was having the existing fixtures—a worn pedestal sink and a long, rusted, claw-foot tub—reporcelained. She despaired when it at last became clear to her that, having lifted a layer of plywood and two of rotten linoleum from the floors, her son did not intend to recover the original planks, with their scars, knots, and gaps. She assumed an air of quiet martyrdom, bringing carpeting catalogues and samples of fabric for a theoretical couch, proposing paint colors for the bedroom, which Oliver intended to fashion from one end of the open upper floor. Apart from one small victory (a particular green paint he took to so avidly that she was soon begging him to relieve the ubiquity he intended for it with some—any—other color), her failures were comprehensive. When the building was at last ready for furnishings, Oliver rented a U-Haul and went to Brimfield for the May show. He got up at five with the rest of the madmen (the early hours on Twenty-eighth Street were good preparation for this), parked at Quaker Acres, and walked the dewy, muddy fields with a large roll of bills, retracing his steps in the truck that evening to pick up the bed, the vast wooden table for arrangements and the smaller one for dining and the smaller still for his computer, the mismatched chairs, the wardrobes (he had ignored his mother's plea to build closets), the chests, the candle stand nobody wanted because it had been refinished, the trio of luscious still lifes of pansies, a fortuitously discovered edition of *Modern Roses* from the 1970s, and, to his absolute amazement, a three-step block of marble that would prove to fit so perfectly it might have been stolen from his own threshold.

When it was finished, he invited his mother to dinner. He also invited his stepfather, a gesture so magnanimous on his part that it effectively offset Caroline's residual distress. The business was kicking. (He had just done a wedding at the Puck Building, he told them, and one of the guests, a publicist for Ungaro, had called to book him for Fashion Week, which meant at least one huge, slavishly kowtowing delivery to each of the twenty or so opinion makers in the industry. A good gig.) Henry Rosenthal, himself on enforced good behavior that night, seemed actually impressed. Caroline was happy.

Home: check.

Work: check.

But there still was the little matter of his being single. Oliver would have liked to reassure his mother on that point, but anxiety of his own had set him adrift, and he was unprepared to discuss the situation with anyone, especially her. His relationship with Matilda, his girlfriend since sophomore year of college, had been petering out, though she still came to Greenwich with him occasionally and had moved to the city as he had, settling into the Upper East Side postcollegiate den of Rupert Towers, where she shared an apartment with three other initiates in the training program at Morgan Stanley. Matilda had become an aunt in the months after graduation, and now spoke fervently about children. Her intentions were unmistakable, and Oliver, who had never shared with her his own concerns, began to withdraw. He wasn't what she needed now, he explained to her in a final, pained dinner near her apartment (he didn't want her to have to cry through a long taxi ride), but he would always think of her with love, which was true.

Afterward, there was no one. Of course, Matilda had not been anomalous in her desire for children—children someday if not someday soon. Women wanted children—he understood that, and what right did he have to ask a woman to choose? It seemed safer to keep himself to himself, to watch his friends pair off and marry, and not to dwell on what was unavailable to him. Then he had met Marian.

Oliver turns off the light in the shop and goes upstairs, the bag of bottles clinking once, twice against the wall of the narrow stairway. In his apartment, he goes first to the kitchen and puts away the artichokes and frisée, the chocolates and orzo, for his dinner with Marian. He tips the short ribs into a stockpot and opens one of the bottles of wine, covering them by a few inches. Then he puts in some pepper and bashes a couple of garlic cloves, which he adds, and places the whole thing in the refrigerator. The apartment, long like its downstairs twin, is serene, even with the bed unmade and the morning's newspaper on the bathroom floor. His resistance to music and the backwater quality of his street combine to produce a rare silence in a city that's elsewhere frantic with perpetual noise. Oliver, looking around, feels again what he has felt intermittently throughout the day, that he is living the right life, in the right place, with the right people in it. It is a feeling of deep pleasure (and some guilt, because the rest of the world cannot, apparently, be so fortunate), but little security, because while he himself does not fear the future, he knows that Marian does, and he hasn't a clue what to do about that.

CHAPTER FIVE

Who Is Charlotte?

HISTORIANS, AS A RULE, ARE NOT FANCIFUL. They do not speak of inspiration in the way that fiction writers do (or at any rate, in the way that fiction readers speak of it to people who are not fiction writers). No one, for example, has ever asked a historian where he gets his ideas. At least, no one has ever asked Marian that.

Which is not to say that there is never a story. Sometimes, there is a story. Sometimes it's even a haunting one, replete with stray breezes, the slamming of doors, the spontaneous, serendipitous appearance of a new idea. Marian, for instance, has a story about the day she became aware of Lady Charlotte Wilcox, but she has never told it, because no one has ever asked.

Her story began when she walked into the Beinecke Rare Book and Manuscript Library at Yale on a raw March morning some years earlier. She had removed her heavy coat and slung it over her arm, and with her other arm was holding two books from her own library—that is to say, the Nicholas Murray Butler Library at Columbia—to her chest, while simultaneously trying not to spill a take-out latte.

Marian had not been to the Beinecke in years, and if the truth were told, she didn't want to be there now. The day trip was meant to finalize a paper she was scheduled to deliver two weeks hence at a conference of eighteenth-century scholars in Tucson. Marian's subject, well within her habitual stomping ground of the Age of Reason, was the decline of the Society of Merchant Venturers, a happy band of Bristol-based slave traders who only faltered when the Anglican and Methodist churches began to condemn their trade in the late 1770s. She was particularly interested in the family of John Forter, whose six ships made the three-part journey from the Gold Coast to Charleston and back to Bristol hundreds of times, eventually funding the purchase of a great townhouse near the port (now a Lloyd's Bank) and a stately pile near Brund, Derbyshire, called Charleston House (now owned by the National Trust). Manifests of a number of voyages bankrolled by Forter, and the general records of the company, were enshrined in the British Library, but the Beinecke—through a quirk of transatlantic marriage and the Yale-o-philia of one of its alumni descendants—had come into possession of some of the family's personal papers. The official grail of Marian's excursion was a copy of John Forter's will, which was inexplicably absent from the British Library holding, but there was something else, too. There was a stray reference, encountered the previous summer while Marian was doing preliminary work on this paper, in London. It had been bugging her.

The reference occurred in two letters from a Forter ship's captain, one posted from Charleston in April 1762 to his sister in Hertfordshire, the second following some three months later to the same recipient, this time from Bristol. The Charleston letter was a terse grumble. The captain, whose name was (as near as Marian could decipher his signature) George Hartwell, would not be able to take his much anticipated holiday with Anne Beckwith, née Hartwell, because orders had reached him in Charleston compelling a detour to Philadelphia, where he was expected to collect a young lady for the passage to England. Hartwell's crew, the captain wrote, would not mind the digression—Philadelphia was held to be nearly English in its comforts and diversions—but he would miss his sister's company and the hunting he had long been anticipating.

That was the first letter.

The second letter was all about the young lady herself—so sweetly pretty, even with her hair much more plainly arranged than that of the English ladies her age, so witty, so clever with the men, half of them mad in love with her enough that he had had to speak with them severely, for wasn't she scarcely more than a child and entirely alone in the world except for strangers to whom she was bound in Derbyshire?

As in Charleston House near Brund, Derbyshire? Marian wondered.

Marian was intrigued. After all, there wasn't much in the way of west-to-east transatlantic relocation in the 1750s, still less undertaken by a woman. And a young, unaccompanied woman? This, Marian had never encountered. The fact that Hartwell's orders apparently came from John Forter himself was just slightly...interesting.

The young lady did not seem to have a name, Marian had noted at the time, looking up from this document and frowning. She was under the dome of the old British Library, so soaring and noble. She loved it there, loved the fishbowl feel of everyone gathered in their concentric circles of desks, as if all worshiping some central deity, which perhaps they were. Gazing up at the curving vault above her, Marian felt the insubstantial, anonymous, forgotten young lady give a little flutter, like the beating of hopeful wings at her temple. This was an instance of the long dead making a thin but eager claim on the living, a not-unprecedented sensation for her, or for any historian, she supposed. The lost person wanted to be known, and yet there was little to substantiate her claim on awareness. After all, the wisp of the unknown young lady of two and a half centuries before surely had not very much to do with the decline of the Forter family or the Society of Merchant Venturers of Bristol, England, or the Age of Reason and its cultural implications.

Marian shook her head, as if to dislodge the flutter, and went back to her work, readying her paper for the Tucson conference.

But the nameless young woman did not leave her consciousness entirely, and though she would not directly impel Marian's trip to Yale that morning, some six months later, she did come along for the ride, and Marian did wonder, idly, idly, if there might be some additional trace of her in the Forter cache at Yale, some clue to her vague mystery.

So Marian rose that grim gray morning and took a cab to Grand Central and drank terrible coffee aboard the New Haven Line for nearly two hours, but when she arrived, clutching her books and her contraband latte (this, thankfully, from the Starbucks on Chapel Street), the library personnel held her up for a good half hour because one of her two required identifying documents lacked a black-and-white photograph.

"Have a seat," the woman said. She might have been nineteen or twenty, a pasty Midwesterner with four silver studs through the cartilage of her left ear. "And drink your coffee," she said pointedly, as if she were truly a librarian and not an undergraduate doing her work-study job. "You can't take it in, you know."

Marian sighed. She looked at her watch, calculating the lost day. The librarians huddled over her credentials. She drank her coffee and sulked.

There was a bulletin board opposite her bench, just next to the garbage can, and when Marian went to throw away her cup, she remained for a minute or two, scanning the notices, so similar to the ones that papered her own campus: films, plays, speakers, clubs, pleas for rides, queries about used books, bikes for sale. There was a repeated pattern, she noted, stepping back, of bright green sheets of paper with the banal query, "WHO IS CHARLOTTE?" This turned out to be a flyer for a play based on the Somerville and Ross novel *The Real Charlotte*, and Marian, who had long ago read and enjoyed the book, actually took note of the performance dates, which were mostly past. It wouldn't make a bad play, she was thinking when the student called her back.

"Okay," she said. She was filling out Marian's official Beinecke ID form, her head down at the desk, and Marian for the first time noticed the girl's own ID, which had a Yale crest and a gray picture and a name, which was also, oddly enough, Charlotte. This made Marian smile. The juxtaposition of the name, so old-fashioned, and the ear studs gave her a welcome moment of levity.

"Who is Char*lotte*?" Marian heard herself say. She put the emphasis on the second syllable, as in the Somerville and Ross title.

The student looked up, frowning. "What?"

"Who is Char*lotte*?" she repeated. Then she pointed at the many green flyers on the bulletin board.

"Oh. Yeah. But it's *Char*lotte."

"Yes." Marian took her new card. "Thanks. Can I go in?"

"Sure." She pointed. Then she took up her own book, a Mary Daly text, and sat back down at the desk.

Marian climbed the stairs to the Osborne Collection, where the bulk of the eighteenth-century material was ensconced. From the outside, the Beinecke's famous marble walls were sleek and gray, like sheets of snow, but from the inside they appeared almost green, like murky flames or climbing algae. The novelty of this had worn off for Marian years earlier, during the innumerable hours when she had toiled in the Osborne Collection as a Yale graduate student, but the novelty had been replaced by a grudging pleasure in the design: books at the spine of a building encased in stone, with the light of the outside, everyday world trying to poke its way in, and not quite succeeding. The whole thing, Marian thought, was some kind of too-obvious metaphor for academia, as if the architect had laughed at scholars throughout his design's conception, and was still laughing in the stone walls themselves. But the truth was that Marian, like most of her peers, was willing to be ridiculous to the wider world. Scholars know—or ought to know—that they are privileged to lead their lives with their books in their groves of like-minded people. It is a privilege to devote the principal portion of one's waking thoughts to the evolution of the starfish, or to the fate of an artist, dead these long centuries, or to the brief tenure of one particular Ottoman emperor. Anyone who does not feel privileged ought not to be doing it, Marian thought. Anyone incapable of appreciating the rare jolts of delight that can come from finding something out—something wild and obscure, buried in history or chipped from the unknown—ought to be in another line of work.

She was about to get one of those jolts, herself.

Upstairs in the Osborne Collection, she sat down at a terminal and perused the screen. The Forter will, Marian saw to her relief, was indeed accounted for, and she quickly filled out a request and gave it to one of the curators. Then, returning to her chair, she began to browse the collection with reference to the Forter family, fanning forward and backward from the date of the company's demise. Bills of sale for the Bristol property. Letters from Lady Forter. Archival photographs of family portraits (the originals still on the walls at Charleston House). Then she noticed a legal document listed oddly as "Deposition pertaining to matter of Charlotte Wilcox, 14 June 1765."

Who is Charlotte? Marian thought.

She went to the desk and filled out a request for that, too.

The will arrived, brought in its own acid-free box, and was placed before her by the curator, who handled the maneuver as if she were serving an extravagant meal. Marian began making notes: the disposition of property to three of the sons and one daughter, small gifts to an army of servants, the endowment of a memorial dinner at Hertford College, Oxford, to be named the Forter Feast and held each October 8 (the anniversary of John Forter's birth), the horses and kine, the transfer of tenants' rents, the disposition of the living at Brund (which Forter was, evidently, keen to keep from his wife's pious younger brother), and a small house known as Mill Cottage, comprising "four rooms and upstairs two, as well as outbuilding and land," for Charlotte Wilcox, "young lady presently residing at Bristol, known to my family and having no relations nor income."

Who is Charlotte Wilcox? Marian wondered again. Now it was nearly funny. She began to get to her feet. She wanted to see what was holding up that legal document. But even as she did so the curator approached with a second box and placed this, too, on the table. Marian could barely restrain herself. She began to read.

The deposition was created in the office of a Bristol attorney, and neither the constraints of legal idiom nor the formality of eighteenth-century language could mask the rage of its complainant, Lady Forter. It was a rage that leaped from the old wove paper, having crossed an ocean and simmered two hundred years in wait for some person willing to attend to it.

Which is me, thought Marian. And she immediately began writing it all down.

By the time she returned home to the city that night, she knew only these few facts, but there were clues to bring her forward. Eventually, over the following year, Marian would return to the British Library, to Derbyshire, to Bristol, and to points as far north as Newcastle and south as Naples, in avid pursuit of a woman never less than diverting, and quite frequently amazing.

Finally, Marian, like her subject, would come home to Rhinebeck, New York, where in the local public library—a building far humbler than either the British Library, with its grand dome, or the Beinecke, with its laughing marble walls—she would locate the substance of Charlotte Wilcox, and begin to rebuild her out of the past.

This is what she built.

Charlotte Wilcox was not a Forter, not even a distant one, but the surviving child of James Wilcox, a bosom friend of John Forter from their academically undistinguished days at Hertford College, Oxford. Wilcox, a younger son, opted for a career in the army and accepted a commission that soon brought him to the American colonies, where he married a young Englishwoman similarly displaced and took up his post at Fort William Henry, near Lake George. In August 1757, however, the fort came under siege by the French, and when the English surrendered, Iroquois warriors did the dirty work. James Wilcox, most probably, died then and there. Marian never learned the precise fate of his wife and other children, but the survivors of the massacre were few, and Charlotte surfaced in Rhinebeck only several years later, when a letter was written on her behalf to John Forter of Bristol and Brund, Derbyshire. The year after that, the girl was in Philadelphia, awaiting the arrival of the *Hart*, and in May 1762, all of fifteen years old, she went to England to stay with the Forter family at Charleston House.

Only one likeness of Charlotte Wilcox—a drawing by her husband rendered weeks before her death—would survive, so there was no telling how lovely she must have been as a teenager, or how well she might have embodied the qualities Humbert Humbert was to extol two centuries later. It appeared, however, that Charlotte had transfixed her patron within months of joining his household, and that the connection they made was as affectionate as it was lustful. It did not remain hidden for long. Letters (unearthed at Charleston House) flew between Lady Forter and her brother, the Reverend Jonathan Basking-Newton, on a raft of bile, and did not cease until John Forter himself passed away, quite possibly from heart trouble aggravated by the rigors of his love life. This left Charlotte, now seventeen, in some difficulty, for though Forter took pains to provide for her with one of his smaller properties—the Mill Cottage cited in his will—Lady Forter's campaign to prevent this inheritance was nasty, brutish, and long. And successful.

After this information, there was a gap, but when Marian located her subject once again, she was amazed to discover that Charlotte was actually thriving, due to the unquestionable social altitude of the girl's new patroness, Rowena Thomases, duchess of Northumberland. The duchess, possessor of three homes, five sons, and a husband whose vast benevolence was matched only by his vast stupidity, was precisely the kind of woman who might do precisely as she wished, and what she wished was to have this otherwise friendless girl in her presence, constantly. Charlotte would be the duchess's companion for several years.

The duchess was a committed diarist, sparing future generations no detail of her daily irritations and hourly pursuits of pleasure. She was also, as Marian (being a not-unaccomplished scholar of the period) already knew, a hostess of wide and significant acquaintance. Every contemporary personage of note made a pilgrimage to Northumberland House, passing the long evenings in political discussion, literary chatter, and social gossip. Dr. Johnson particularly favored the summer months here, installing himself (and the ever present Bosworth) in the border country to escape the London heat and to watch Capability Brown lay out the gardens. The bluestockings flitted through, buzzing with industry and sniping at one another. Richardson and Fielding came, although naturally not at the same time. And politicians from both sides of the divide undertook the long, dangerous, and greatly uncomfortable journey north.

Charlotte passed safe and formative years in Northumberland, London, and on the Continent with her new friend. She also took the opportunity to hone her skills of observation, and of satire, for it was in Northumberland Charlotte wrote the novel that would prove Marian's single greatest discovery, the pseudonymously published *Helena and Hariette: The Literary Ladies* (1771), a work long known to scholars of the early novel (chiefly due to its cameos of the famous and infamous of its day) but compelling little of their attention. The book had been of no interest at all to scholars of Fielding and Richardson, Defoe and Swift, and when the feminists came along in the 1970s, there were, it had to be said, far bigger fish to fry (Fanny Burney, Ann Radcliffe, and Mary Wollstonecraft alone would keep them busy for years), and only a later generation of academics would be forced to reach down to lesser strata of authorial talent, where *Helena and Hariette* abided. Still, the book had a charm and a lightness of touch that would survive the intervening centuries, and Marian—who would eventually persuade Columbia's library acquisitions committee to procure for her a copy from a rare-book dealer in Leeds—was thrilled by its razor-sharp caricatures and pervasive wit.

By the time it was published, however, Charlotte was gone from Northumberland. She had left the duchess—and the duchess's good graces—and run off to the Continent with a man named Lord Satterfield, inaugurating the period of her life that, two centuries later, would attract so much speculation, censure, and general glee. It was a happy connection, Marian discovered (working from the great cache of letters at the end of the rainbow in Rhinebeck, New York), but it would have been happier had there not been an already existing Lady Satterfield, who was understandably put out by the affair. Lady Satterfield, in allegiance with her husband's debtors (he was an ungifted player of whist) managed to track the couple to Paris, but in Paris, Satterfield's epiphany awaited.

Lord Satterfield was fair and physically slight (this Marian would glean from the Thomas Gainsborough portrait in the National Portrait Gallery), and perhaps that is what inspired him to do what he did next. He and Charlotte remained in Paris for nearly six months, but when they left the city, they left as two women traveling together, with Satterfield's male servant as escort. They went south, naturally enough, to Italy, then Greece, like any English travelers on a grand tour: two young English ladies, quietly prosperous and not very interested in mingling with their countrymen.

Charlotte wrote charmingly of their game, reporting near misses when she and Satterfield strolled in a Roman piazza, not ten feet from Lady Satterfield's brother (sent expressly to hunt them down), and when they shared a boat in Greece with one of the duchess's circle. Even so, legend about them began to filter back to England, and caricatures appeared in some of the London papers, showing Charlotte and Satterfield as milkmaids hand in hand, or else gossiping behind a fan, bosoms pointing to the heavens.

This, naturally, would prove the most infamous period of Charlotte's life, and Marian would be able to count on one hand the interviewers who did not lead with a question related to homosexuality and drag (though their poor preparation often meant they assumed Charlotte to be a cross-dressing lesbian). But the entire subject was a bit of a red herring as far as she was concerned. Marian believed, and would argue, that Satterfield's masquerade had been a practical, strategic move, based on an idea that was already in wide circulation. Paris, after all, had been captivated by its own curiosity, the Chevalier d'Eon, who had recently published his *Lettres, mémoires, et négociations particulières* about his years as a French spy in England, and who alternately wore a dress and his uniform, that of a French dragoon captain. Opinion was divided about whether d'Eon, who, like Satterfield, was slender and short, was a woman who sometimes dressed as a man or a man who sometimes dressed as a woman.

Across the channel, too, an autobiography by the "notorious troublemaker," Charlotte Charke—a cross-dressing English actress—had recently been published, and was much discussed by the duchess and her friends. In other words, Marian would argue, it might as easily have been Charlotte in trousers, had not Satterfield been the more widely recognizable of the pair.

Born to his title, ten years Charlotte's senior, and altogether too well known in the London gambling clubs, Satterfield simply couldn't travel anonymously, and so the burden of drag had fallen to him. Then again, perhaps it was not much of a burden, after all. Italy and Greece would have been jammed with British travelers, but by the time they reached Syria—their final destination and home for nearly two years—the couple must have felt safe. Yet Lord Satterfield did not, evidently, revert to men's clothing. What had begun as a pragmatic course of action might well have evolved into a comfortable habit. The conclusion that he was enjoying himself seemed, to Marian, inescapable. They set up house in Aleppo and lived cheaply and happily until Satterfield died—cholera, Marian thought. He must have been deeply mourned, for nearly one year later Charlotte would write from the same spot about her reluctance to leave his grave were her financial situation not so pressing.

Charlotte's next incarnation was as the consort of a London financier named Morgenthaw—encountered in Rome, secured in Naples, and accompanied back to England in some degree of luxury. For its trade implications as much as its Jewishness, this was a connection that could only have set her farther than ever from her lost associations in Northumberland, but Charlotte would use 3 Queen Square, London—the house she shared with Morgenthaw—as her address for eleven years, and her letters were filled with companionable pleasures, trips to the Continent, and the friendships she formed in the city's merchant classes.

It was now the great age of the Gothic novel, and Charlotte returned to her literary efforts with a suitably spine-tingling tale, set largely in Syria amid dark, malevolent natives. This work, privately published in Bristol (of all places), was entitled *The Terrors of Aleppo* and proved so obscure that even the mighty British Library contained only references to it. It took Marian nearly a year to find a copy, and this—to her amusement—was in the collection at Forter House.

(Clearly, Lady Forter—now in her dotage—had kept up with her former ward and rival.) *The Terrors of Aleppo* (1781) was no match for even its literary predecessor, however. It was a paper-thin tale, more risible than terrifying, of an English girl abducted to Syria by a mad sultan convinced she has wealth enough for a ransom. She escapes the harem with an older woman (revealed as English in the final chapters), setting free the sultan's many prisoners as she goes.

For a time, then, there were no more letters. The homeland of Charlotte's birth was at war with England, and for the period of colonial upheaval there was silence from 3 Queen Square, London. Then, in the aftermath of American independence, she wrote from a new location, and of a new companion. Settled in a village near Exeter, the forty-one-year-old Charlotte was living with Harry Treglown, the freeholder of a small farm in his native village, and a onetime groom to Morgenthaw. (*She ran off with the groom!* Marian would marvel, shaking her head in the musty reading room of the Rhinebeck Historical Society. *At forty!*) At Treglown's farm in the West Country, Charlotte would remain for nine years, caring for her new mate's orphaned nieces and performing the duties of any farm wife. There were no further literary works, if you did not count the letters themselves, which now, at this advanced stage of Charlotte's life, suddenly became lush, textured with description and quite informative about matters agricultural and domestic, as if her American correspondent had asked for specific advice pertaining to cookery, gardening, and animal husbandry.

Charlotte, who had always been a happy person, now found added contentment in domesticity, which her prior social elevations had prevented her from experiencing. She was like the women of Marian's own generation, who leaped off the career or tenure track and suddenly discovered the elation of bread dough, the hypnotic lullaby of knitting needles.

The sweetness of child rearing? thought Marian.

There were twin girls, Mariah and Anne, snatched from a dying mother (Harry Treglown's unfortunate sister) and indifferently fostered until Harry and Charlotte's arrival. In Charlotte's letters, the little girls attained separate characters—smart Anne, sweet, addled

Mariah, who was born second and harder—and grew into jolly, helpful girls. Clearly she loved them, Marian thought. She praised them to
her correspondent, excused them, worried for them. Charlotte's affair
would cool in time, but as long as the girls were at home, she would
not contemplate leaving them. Nine years passed, then Anne married
and took her sister away with her, and Charlotte went away as well.

Away, but where? She was a forty-nine-year-old woman now, without
powerful friends, without funds, without a home. A year would pass
between her departure from Exeter and the arrival of her next letter,
sent from Windermere and containing pages of rapture at the lakes'
loveliness. Then another six months before another letter, this one from
Aberdeen, again rapturous and again without news of any practical matters. It was a mystery of maddening proportions to her biographer, who
knew that women of the late eighteenth century did not pick up and
travel about, especially unaccompanied, merely for the pleasures of
travel (which were dubious at that time) and especially in the country-
side. Yet it appeared that this was precisely Charlotte's endeavor, as if
she had decided to see the country that had (mostly) nourished her, to
discover and admire it, before leaving it for the last time.

In 1799, Charlotte wrote to Rhinebeck from her final British
address, the Fleet debtors' prison in London. She did not provide
specifics about her financial circumstances, nor which of her creditors
had brought about her incarceration, but perhaps this was because she
had more pertinent and far happier news.

She was married. For the first and only time in her life, she had married. And this was no "Fleet marriage," as sham unions or arrangements of legal convenience in that place were sometimes known, but a
love match, and of Charlotte's many such matches, her greatest one.

Her new husband, horse thief by trade and a generation his wife's junior, was an Irishman, giving as his place of birth the city of Portadown in
the county Armagh. He would prove Charlotte's most tender and faithful
companion for the remainder of her life, and follow her briskly to death
in a new country he had never before seen nor thought to visit.

His name was Thomas Wilcox, but this was not the coincidence

Marian first assumed, for the husband—born Thomas Keane—had taken the unusual step of assuming his wife's surname, either on or indeed prior to their marriage. Perhaps there were crimes he hoped to leave behind with his old family name. Perhaps he adored his new wife so much that he sought to join her in this way. Perhaps the two believed their outlook as Wilcoxes was simply more optimistic. Optimism must have been in short supply where they found themselves.

Built in 1197, the Fleet contained mostly debtors and bankrupts at the time of Charlotte's sojourn. The prison was named for a river that flowed outside its walls, and some cells overlooked the street, enabling its three hundred occupants to beg directly from passersby. Some decades after the Wilcoxes left it, Dickens would send his first hero, the boisterous and lighthearted Mr. Pickwick, to the Fleet Prison for a transformative spell, illuminating the "wretched dungeons" and hordes of unfortunates "not possessed of the secret of exactly knowing what to do with themselves." And this place, Marian would marvel, this setting of general despair and lassitude was the one in which Charlotte Wilcox would discover the love of her life.

How they made their escape Marian would not easily discover. Charlotte herself was silent on this issue, and there was nothing in Rhinebeck to explain the circumstances. While the Wilcoxes' combined debt was not vast, neither did the couple possess any funds of their own, nor any obvious friends rich enough or willing to pay. Marian had come to accept the impossibility of answering the question—though it was obviously a frustrating shortfall—when, only by chance, during her last visit to Charleston House, this final bit of information fell into her path.

She had grown unavoidably chummy, over those months, with Serena Makepeace, a local busybody who headed the Friends of Charleston House and served as self-appointed apologist for the Forter family. Marian's habit of breaking from her labors each afternoon to have tea in the National Trust–run tearoom was quickly noted by Mrs. Makepeace, who began to materialize at adjacent tables, noisily turning the pages of her *Daily Mail* and asking how the work was coming. Marian had learned to tolerate Serena Makepeace, but her obsequiousness on the subject of all Forters, past and present, was tiresome. In the eyes of this local devotee, the family attained divine stature as patrons, philanthropists, and humanitarians. (The fact that their fortune was founded on the sale of human beings apparently did not taint Serena Makepeace's esteem.) The character of Charlotte Wilcox—colonial orphan, minor novelist, and ultimate Fleet detainee—did not loom sufficiently large in Forter family history for her name to have made an impression on Mrs. Makepeace, but it was one of Serena's offhand rhapsodies on Forter largesse that nonetheless pointed Marian in the right direction.

Was Marian aware that Charles Forter (the son of Charlotte's first love, John Forter) had taken a keen interest in the poor?

Yes, yes. Marian nodded, mainly to be polite. Charles Forter had, after all, taken up the reins of his father's business with great enthusiasm, milking the slave trade for every possible piece of gold until forced by British law to desist in 1807.

Did she know, continued Serena, that Charles Forter had given several local girls, unmarried girls who were unfortunately with child, cottages on the estate?

No, Marian said, and sighed. How generous.

Did she know that he had written to a local magistrate, requesting that a local thief not be hanged but instead transported to Australia?

Marian did not.

Did she know that he once paid the debt of a poor woman in a London prison, who wanted only to go home to America to die?

Marian sat up. No, she had not known that. She would like to hear more about that.

It had been there all the time, but why would Marian have looked for it in the place it waited to be found? Marian's business was not with Charles Forter but with his parents, and there was no reason at all to think that Charlotte's point of contact with the Forter family had survived the death of Lady Forter in 1784. But Charlotte, quite cannily, had played this final card from the Fleet Prison in the year 1796, writing to Forter *fils* in a tone markedly different from that of her other correspondence. In this letter, which Marian would locate that very afternoon in the papers of Charles Forter (1750–1819), Charlotte gently reminded the great man of who she was and what had been her crime against his mother. She then offered him a false autobiography of such suffering and degradation that Forter could only conclude that Charlotte had been granted her just deserts. Now all she wished, she informed him, was to leave England forever and return to her homeland, much changed though it surely was by its unfortunate severance from the British crown. Forter kindness had brought her here, she humbly wrote. Perhaps Forter kindness would send her home.

He dispatched an attorney with a bank draft within the week, and the Wilcoxes were free to sail.

Charlotte came home with the new century. En route, somewhere on the wide Atlantic Ocean, she and her husband gave each other titles, emerging at New London as Lord Thomas and Lady Charlotte Wilcox. The only word for this was "chutzpah," Marian supposed, but she honored the self-awarded rank in her book's title, because it went to the core of who Charlotte was. From the port, the newly minted Lord and Lady Wilcox made their way to Rhinebeck, to the home of a woman named Alice Farwell, daughter of the man who had sheltered her after the attack on Fort William Henry, so many years before. Alice was Charlotte's contemporary and great friend, and her longtime correspondent. Lady Charlotte would die two years later, and her husband not long afterward.

Who is Charlotte? Marian had wanted to know, and now she knew.

From the Beinecke to the British Library to Brund in Derbyshire, to the great Northumberland House, to the small chamber of records maintained by the National Trust in Exeter, to the tiny museum not far from the site of the Fleet Prison, and finally to the musty local history archive at the public library in Rhinebeck, New York, not ten miles from the home of Henry Wharton Danvers (once) and her own cousin, Barton Ochstein (lately). There was, too, in a cemetery a few miles north in the hamlet of Rhinecliff, a grave, and a headstone, barely legible, bearing the name and dates of this prodigal daughter of the New World, who had fallen so far with such philosophical forbearance. And when Marian found that, she forgot her historian's reserve and actually wept.

Of course, Marian did not set out to write the book that would change her life. She set out to write a small book, primly removed from popular tastes and secure within its academic parameters. After all, Lady Charlotte Wilcox, intriguing as she was, had not affected the eighteenth century in any profound way, or influenced her peers, or made any remarkable discovery, or done any single thing for the first time ever. Marian had begun to write this book, and was in agreement with her publisher that it was to have a print run (circumspect) commensurate with its probable popularity (limited). Luckily, as things turned out, she had not actually signed a contract.

One sticky weekend in the Hamptons, she had gone with Marshall to the home of friends. Not good friends. Not city friends, but Hamptons friends, who hailed one another at the farm stands or from their inert, traffic-impeded cars on Route 27, and met for a single, well-populated meal each summer. Lary and Rorry (Marshall, every year, joked that the husband had given his wife one of his Rs) presented this meal on a grand scale, typically with a cast of sixty or so, a raw bar, and half a dozen Irish lads tending the grill and handing out white sangria. Marian was talking to a woman she knew vaguely when a bright young thing cruised over, clutching multiple glasses. "Oh!" this new person said. "Where'd she go?"

"Hmm?" said Marian's friend. "Suzette? Gone to pee, I think. Oh no, she's over there talking to Rorry. Do you know Marian Kahn?"

The bright young thing grimaced. With all the sangria she held, she couldn't shake hands. "You'll take a glass, I hope."

"I will," Marian said and smiled. She took one, her friend took one, and Marian shook hands with the woman, who turned out to be called Sarabeth Cooper.

"What do you do?" said Sarabeth, in classic Hamptonian style.

"Just a history professor," Marian said. She nearly added: *Sorry.*

"History? History of what?"

Which is how it all began, for it was rare enough that a civilian would even ask, let alone show true interest, as Sarabeth did, drawing forth the long tale of Marian's passion of the moment, an eighteenth-century no-one-in-particular named Charlotte Wilcox, ascertaining that Marian was indeed well along in her biography, encouraging her to ruminate on the many ways women of today might learn from such an unlikely role model, before revealing that she was in fact a literary agent, and there might be something here, you know.

"Oh, but it's already being published," Marian said. "I mean, thanks, but it's all taken care of. Columbia University Press did my last two, and they've agreed—"

"Have you signed a contract?" asked Sarabeth, cutting to the chase.

"No. But—"

"Leave it to me."

What was it that made her agree? Marian would wonder, and not only as she drove home that night, billowy on sangria and—was it possible?—the contemplation of a readership that might actually go beyond the few hundred scholars in her field and the more ambitious of her own students. What was it that had made a historian of her standing, with her tenure and her sweetheart deal for a sabbatical the following year—a sabbatical that would come in handy when her schedule filled with media confetti—suddenly jump the broom into the land of celebrity? With a glass of sangria in her hand, no less.

Sarabeth, a Vassar girl by way of Pittsburgh (where she had spent formative, fame-hungry summers interning at the Warhol Museum), had come to her profession like a light-seeking moth, climbing so rapidly in her first small but chic agency that she was soon taking exploratory calls from people named Binky, Joni, and Mort. Sarabeth demurred. She knew precisely where she wanted to be sitting, and until the seat in question was ready for her, she opted to remain where she was, honing her list like a Josephine Baker assembling her rainbow tribe. By the time her telephone rang—at home, as was only prudent, in the East Village—Sarabeth had a string of writers capable of floating a small institute of higher education, or at least a really A-list party. In due course, and with a feeling of fateful completion, she went into partnership with Roland Saperstein, the most eminent of an earlier generation of literary agents, with the most lauded client list and the best address, a brownstone in Chelsea. The party for their merger took place at the Union Square Café.

Within weeks of meeting Sarabeth, Marian found herself sitting down with editors in high, corner offices all over town. It took one or two of these encounters for Marian to find her rhythm, but she soon discovered an unsuspected fluidity in her historical descriptions, an animated quality in her voice as she interpreted Lady Charlotte, until there was even a sense that Charlotte herself had been conjured and was in attendance, nodding encouragement from the chair in the corner. Marian, Sarabeth, the editors and publicists, all of them moved through a cloud of excitement, with suggestions raining down upon the various coffee tables in the various offices: the biography, sure, but what about those novels? An edition of the letters! What about a sort of pillow book of her wit and wisdom? And what a fabulous part for an actress!

Two hundred years in her undistinguished grave, and Charlotte Wilcox was about to become an industry.

Even now Marian wondered at the chance of it. Had she not met Sarabeth at that overpopulated party. Had she had not, uncharacteristically, allowed her enthusiasm for a project to trump her usual self-effacement. Had her new agent not been the rare person who saw contemporary significance in a figure neither contemporary nor significant…

They had their pick of publishers. The whole world, it suddenly seemed to her, wanted to bring Lady Charlotte Wilcox back to life. Marian let her agent make the decision and went to work recasting her book for a layperson. As she did this, she was gratified to sense the way in which Lady Charlotte seemed to emerge—through the cracks, the letters and novels, the centuries—reconstituting herself as moral compass, self-help guru, and fabulous girlfriend, all at once, her passion for life seemingly untrammeled by the fact that she was dead, and long dead, for that matter. An elaborate publicity campaign was planned and, to Marian's amazement, set in motion, and the services of a media coach were procured to train her in the art of slipping the book's title into virtually every sentence. (This Marian never learned to do properly.) The coach expressed approval of her wardrobe (already media-friendly, with its neutral tones and clean, spare lines) but cajoled her into a major haircut (which, she would later admit, was flattering) and blond highlights (which were not).

At no point during this process did Marian actually believe what they were telling her: that the book was going to be huge. That American women were going to reach back into their own history and embrace Lady Charlotte. That readers would see in her, in her persistent ability to land on her feet and pluck happiness from failure, a model for their own lives. That her version of success was fulfilling and available to all, no matter their circumstances. What Marian thought was that when the book found its way at last into bookstores, readers would remember that they did not like history—that it was too much like school—and opt instead for the latest New Age nonsense or self-proclaimed oracle. She regarded her failure as inevitable and spent much of her time—between media-preparedness lessons, makeover appointments, and actual book writing—preparing her apologies to all concerned.

The advance reviews were good, but what did that mean? Marian had always received positive reviews for her work (her *Triangular Trade: Bristol, the Ivory Coast, and the New World, 1640–1810* had even won a prize from the Historical Association of Great Britain), but she had yet to see a single copy of any of her books on a Barnes and Noble shelf. This time—if one was to be technical about it—was not an exception, for when Marian wandered into the vast bookstore on Broadway and Eighty-first on publication day, her arms laden with Zabars' bags and her heart in her mouth, she saw the stacks of her brand-new volume, the bright pink *Lady Charlotte Wilcox: The Decline and Triumph of an American Adventuress*, piled high on a special table just inside the front door, like a breakwater, forcing the flow from the street to reckon with it.

To Marian's further shock, the pile of books bore, like a flag, a rather remarkable little sign that read: NEW YORK TIMES BEST-SELLER.

She dropped her bags and dug out her cell phone to call Sarabeth.

"I've been trying to reach you," said Sarabeth. "We've had a bit of a development."

It went on like that. Marian did the morning television shows, the afternoon radio shows, and sat down with Dinitia Smith for a flattering (even she had to admit) *New York Times* piece about how a mild-mannered history professor wakes up to find herself on *Oprah*. She began to be contacted by people from her past. She heard from a Camp Pinecliffe bunkmate, ensconced in Shaker Heights with four children and (she eagerly revealed) a sexual addiction. She heard from her old dance teacher at Miss Fokine's, who politely inquired after her weak knees. She heard from Caroline Stern in Greenwich, felt terribly guilty, and set aside the letter to answer. She heard from Valerie Annis, interminably.

She heard from many others as well, their letters forwarded by her publisher by the box load, fans eager to contact the living representative of Lady Charlotte, burning to tell her how the vision of Charlotte at her happiest while in the absolute dregs of English society had altered their lives, lifted their depressions, graced them with the ability to let go of their own suffering. The readers who wrote to Marian clung to Lady Charlotte, admired her, and wept (belatedly) at her passing. They formed clubs to discuss her and—astonishingly—to learn more about the eighteenth century. (They wanted to read the books Lady Charlotte had read, visualize the houses in which she'd lived, and try her recipes for bread and pease soup.) She inspired a song cycle based on her letters. A playwright announced that he was composing a one-woman show about her life. Scores of people informed Marian that they were her descendants—a neat trick given that she had died without biological children. Additional letters and works of fiction by Lady Charlotte—all fraudulent, alas—were discovered with regularity.

After the first months, when Marian strained to answer each letter, singularly and with gratitude, she could not help but find the correspondence burdensome. She developed a tendency to let them stack up in their cardboard boxes, making her small office feel a bit like a warehouse. Marshall, who liked things tidy even in the rooms of the apartment he seldom entered, began suggesting a secretary to deal with the backlog, and Columbia obliged with a work-study student for a time, but even with artfully prewritten responses and a good paper shredder she fell behind. After the foreign editions were published, and correspondence seemed to flow from everywhere, Marian more or less gave up.

The box of new mail that arrived today in the arms of Valerie Annis, in the middle of her already derailed Friday with Oliver, was also bound for the back of Marian's office, where it was fated to rest in baleful accusation for months, probably, before being dealt with. Now, when Marian passes it on her way to the bathroom (where what she has in mind is a long, depressing soak, possibly accompanied by the aforementioned brandy) the sight of it only succeeds in deepening her mood of ineptitude and loss. By this time, she thinks, Oliver is gone, halfway to the subway, probably shaking his beautiful head at the thought of her, and who can blame him? Surely the very notion of them—in bed, in love—is pitiful, and she, for one, intends to feel pity. The weekend is scuttled, with nothing salvaged but a vague promise of dinner the next night. And she did not even kiss him good-bye, Marian thinks miserably.

She turns on the tub faucet and goes to fetch her brandy, pausing to brush her cheek softly against Oliver's roses (this serves only to heighten her misery), then she returns to the bathroom, but as she does, as she is about to pass, once again, the accusatory box of mail, a thought occurs to her. Perhaps she is going about this wrong. Most writers, after all, enjoy hearing from their readers. Most writers can help themselves to the flattery and decline to feel burdened by it. Why shouldn't she? Perhaps, in this box, is just the thing she requires for such a dismal Friday evening. Perhaps she might find something to laugh about in the latest claim of a descent from the noble Wilcox line, or some way to feel pride in Lady Charlotte's life-improving influence. Can't she indulge in a little sycophantic praise without the guilt?

Marian goes to the kitchen for a knife. The box is sealed with brown tape that, when sliced, splits to reveal a thick pile of mail: pink envelopes (to match the pink book jacket? Marian wonders), manila sheaths, white business mailers with dignified return addresses, post-cards of every stripe and even the occasional blue air gram. She helps herself to a wedge of the topmost letters.

In the bathroom, Marian sets down her glass and letters on a ledge and drops her clothes onto the floor, trying to avoid looking through the doorway at the bed, which remains in its earlier, dangerously evocative disarray. Now Oliver is on the subway, Marian thinks, abruptly remembering what he told her, so many hours ago, it seems, about smelling her on his fingertips. She experiences a shock of long-ing, followed by a long ebb of sadness, and then considers the alarm-ing notion that she could call him right now and leave a message at his apartment, telling him to come back. Just then the phone actually rings, saving her.

She steps out of the puddle of her clothing and goes to answer, illogically hopeful though she knows it can't be Oliver and doesn't want to speak to anyone else.

"Hello?" Marian says.

It's Marshall, sounding hale and distant, calling from Nova Scotia. "Marian?"

"Oh, hi! Are you having fun?"

"Yeah. But the bugs, Jesus. And you know that citronella is total crap." Marian sighs. "I'm sorry. I asked at Hammacher Schlemmer."

"It's all right. Ruben brought enough DEET to drown every bug within twenty miles. You know, he shot a deer today."

She closes her eyes. Technically, she has nothing against hunting, but the point of it eludes her. "How's he going to get it home?"

"What? Oh, I don't know. They're cutting it up into steaks or something. We'll pick up an ice chest. Listen, anything happening?"

"Oh…" She thinks quickly. "Well, Barton came down today. I didn't know he was coming but apparently he wrote to me about it. I swear I'm losing my mind."

"He's not after money, is he?" says Marshall.

"No. Well, not ours. But listen, you're going to die: he's getting married."

"That fruit?" Marshall barks. "What, like in Vermont? Do we have to go watch while he marries some guy under a chuppah?"

"No, no! To a girl! He's getting married to Sophie Klein. As in Mort Klein?"

This floors him, even long distance. "You're not serious. Mort Klein's daughter? Why, for Christ's sake, would she marry him?"

Marian sighs. "Love is strange."

"Mort Klein's worth more than a billion!"

"Which would cover a lot of restoration, I'd say."

"Shit, Marian. That's amazing."

She agrees. "So, you're doing lots of corporate bonding?"

Marian hears a grunt. "Yeah, I know it sounds like a bunch of Iron John crap, but the fact is, you go away with someone and you share a toilet with him and sit in a mud hole for a few hours and he becomes a person who is somehow less likely to screw you."

"And vice versa?"

"Well, in theory."

Marian laughs. "That's my Marshall. So what are you all talking about?"

"Oh, the usual. The wives, the kids, the girlfriends."

She breathes evenly.

"Joking!" he says and laughs. "Only two of them have girlfriends."

"Which two?"

She thinks: *You?*

"Hey, I'm not telling. These are my sacred brothers. Secrets revealed in this hunting lodge gotta stay here. But don't fret," he adds, "it's not me, and that's all you need to worry about."

"I wasn't worried," she says, her voice flat.

"Good. I get back on Tuesday. We'll just go to Nicola's, okay?"

"Okay," says Marian. "Unless you want me to cook you up some of the meat."

He pauses. "What meat?"

"The meat! Aren't you up there shooting things?"

"I'll take Nicola's," he laughs. "You okay and everything?"

"I'm okay," she says. And everything.

"Good. See you."

"Yes."

Marian hangs up the phone. Then she looks at it. Then she says to it, to him, "But I am not okay, actually. Actually, I'm in love, and he's twenty-six. Actually, he's Caroline Stern's son, remember? Oliver? Who has the flower shop? I think about him all the time. All I want is to touch him and talk to him and look at him. I love you and I wouldn't leave you, no matter what you've done, but I'm in love with someone else. What's the matter with you, Marshall?"

She sits down on the bed, which is at once the bed of her recent lovemaking with Oliver and the bed of her marriage. Her marital bed. Incredibly, it has never occurred to her before this moment what an additional crime it is, to have brought him here, of all the beds she might have chosen. There is a spot of damp near the pillow that she touches with the back of her hand, and a twisted sheet-end falling over the edge of the mattress. The sheets are from a French hotel she and Marshall once stayed in, so smooth and cool they had ended up purchasing two sets from the gift shop. The other set is out at the beach, and has a small burn hole in one of the pillowcases from when their dryer broke down a few summers back. The nights she has slept in these sheets, in this bed, with her husband—they must number in the thousands. She has never slept here with Oliver but she has done other things, things she never did with her husband.

It seems to Marian that she has been remarkably without introspection in these matters, avoiding the hard topics—shameful for anyone, but for a scholar...inexcusable. How she has managed, these past six months, not to consider herself an adulteress she can't really say, but from the moment she and Oliver began—fell in love, she tells herself—she has evaded most of the self-censure and all of the bitter words: "adultery," "unfaithful," "extramarital," "wanton." *Wanton?* thinks Marian. What is wanton, after all? Immodest? Lustful?

Well, I'm certainly lustful, thinks Marian, conjuring the memory of

Oliver's mouth between her legs, and suffering the attendant jolt of pleasure, then its guilty aftermath.

She has had friends who were unfaithful, Marian reflects. Some discussed their affairs with her, some still don't know that she knows. They were ugly women and beautiful women, newly married and long married to lovely men or utter louts. Some were nonchalant about what they had done, and some were destroyed by it. She knows women whose marriages sailed on, undisturbed, and women who devastated their whole lives, with bitter divorces, distraught children. There seems nothing to unite this group of women, nothing that separates them from the other women she knows, no unifying principle at all, except that she was not one of them. Until now. Until Oliver.

Marian lies back on the bed. It is, for her, a perfect bed, its specific degree of firmness prescribed by the back doctor Marshall consulted some years earlier, and now so familiar to Marian that she finds it difficult to sleep when she is traveling. The damp spot, now close to her face, has a smell of yeast. She closes her eyes, trying to remember the smell of Marshall's semen, and comes up empty. Married two decades, and her husband's most intimate smell is utterly beyond her recollection. *I must hate him*, it occurs to Marian. It's an act of hate, isn't it, to bring a lover to a marriage bed? Yet why should she hate Marshall? What has Marshall ever done to be hated?

Marian, sighing, reviews the list.

What she wants, what she has always wanted, is for Marshall not to find out, so that when it is over with Oliver—as of course it will have to be sometime, soon—Marshall will be there, his future with her unaltered. It is certainly unfair, but she can't help that. She will make up this debt to him as he has made up his own debts to her, with friendship, support, and regard.

Regard, thinks Marian, turning her cheek to the wet patch. It is no match for passion, really. She begins to cry, making the damp spread against her skin. Twenty years with her husband, years of profound challenges and joyful celebrations, and they do not approach that moment this afternoon, in this bed, when he was inside her and moving and she had turned her head to look at his white roses, which are of course still there but of course no longer the same at all.

Marian stops crying by dragging the back of her hand across her eyes. Even more than she wants to vent her sadness, she is tired, especially of crying. She sits up and gets to her feet, then stalks across the room to the bathroom, turning off the tap and easing into the water. It is near scalding, just as she likes it. For the first time in an hour, her mood breaks and slightly lifts. One gulp of brandy and she is very nearly cheerful. The bathroom tiles, gray marble, grow misty with heat, an effect she did not anticipate when she designed the room, but which she enjoys. I am safe, she thinks. As long as I stay here, nothing bad can happen.

Another gulp.

And now, Marian decides, for some entertainment. She picks a letter from the top of the pile, postmarked St. Louis.

Dear Dr. Kahn,
My book group just finished reading *Lady Charlotte*, and we all wanted you to know that we just love your book. We had such an interesting discussion afterward, about how we all grew up with an idea of what kind of shape our lives were going to have, but she must have had no idea. It's a good lesson for a bunch of old biddies like us! (We're in our forties, mostly!) The funny thing is, half of our group didn't want to read the book in the first place. Mostly, we like novels, especially southern novels. But we're glad we did, and we all want to read *Helena and Hariette*, which I read in *USA Today* they are going to publish again. So thanks for your great book, and if you're ever in St. Louis, we'd love to show you around! Sincerely yours,
(Mrs.) Lorna Joseph

"Well, thank *you*, (Mrs.) Lorna Joseph," says Marian, pushing the folded paper back into the envelope and setting it down on top of the toilet lid. A little praise, a little heat…isn't it nice how everything is working out? And to think that there is a whole group of women waiting to show her around St. Louis! Marian begins to think of excuses to go to St. Louis. The centenary of the World's Fair? The arch? Barbecue?

She drinks a little more brandy.

The next letter is written on hotel stationery from the Miami Marriott but postmarked Los Angeles. It contains no salutation, and reads:

How dare you eggrandise this lesbien! "Lady" Charlotte was no lady and your as bad as her. I saw you on *Today* and it's a disgrace how you go around making out like this womans some kind of saint when all she did was fornicate with men she was'nt married to! You need to think about what your doing with your life. I am sending you some litrature because Jesus loves you and has a plan for you're life, and its not to write books about homosexuals.

It is signed *A Christian Women*. The inevitable brochure is attached with a paper clip. Its cover shows a painting of the Rapture: planes crashing into buildings, trains on fire, saintly bodies rising from their graves.

Marian puts it on the toilet seat, too.

In her new, albeit fragile, mood, this letter does not unduly distress her. One lesson she has learned is that any opinion expressed by a person who does not understand how to use an apostrophe may be disregarded with impunity. Marian sips her brandy and contemplates the lights of the city through her bathroom's tall, narrow window.

Next letter:

Dear Professor,

I write to tell you that my father's mother was Jane Wilcox, who was born in Chicago in 1923. My father thinks his mom's dad hailed from New York someplace, so I was wondering if you could write back to me and tell me where we fit in to the Wilcox family your book was about. My dad says you should look around the Jamestown area—that's where he thinks the family is from. I'm looking forward to hearing from you!

Sincerely yours,

Paul MacDonald

"Hire a genealogist, Mr. MacDonald," Marian says and sighs. "I'm a little busy right now."

She picks up the next letter.

It slips from its white envelope, a folded piece of paper that bears the heading "New York Public Library, Tremont Branch, Bronx," but the handwriting, belying such official stationery, is juvenile. Indeed, it slopes down to the right as it crosses the page, as if suffering from the lack of ruled lines.

Dear Professor,

I read your book about the woman who went to England and everything she did. I don't think I can understand what she had to be so happy about, because she was in prison. Didn't she mind being in prison? My mom's in prison and she doesn't like it and neither do I. I feel like I'm missing the point of your book, so I decided to write to you. I know you're probably too busy to answer me, but my address is 2111 Hughes Avenue, Bronx, New York 10457.

Yours very truly,

Soriah Neal

P.S. I'm eleven.

Oddly enough, the first thing Marian thinks is, *This girl understands the purpose of the apostrophe.*

The second thing she thinks is, *Why is an eleven-year-old reading my book?*

And then the last thing, before depression overwhelms her: *This is the saddest letter I have ever read.*

CHAPTER SIX

A New Rose

I N THE MORNING, Oliver eats his habitual breakfast of scrambled eggs at the Pink Teacup on Grove Street, and reads the *New York Times.*

In the Metro section there is an article about Bette Midler and her garden guerillas. The photograph shows the grinning diva wallowing in topsoil up in Harlem, surrounded by children and planting a dwarf apple tree. In the Arts section there is a review of a troupe of obese modern dancers, and Oliver gazes in wonder at the picture: bending bodies, their rolls of flesh defiantly bared, their faces grim. He looks at his watch, thinks of Marian asleep—sleeping it off, he hopes—and goes back to his paper. He is the only one in the restaurant just now, apart from Sam, the weekend waiter. Earlier, a groovy Village family had colonized the front table with their coloring books and newspapers and platters of food, and there was a tense young couple glumly eating their eggs before setting off on their unhappy day together. Oliver accepts a third cup of mediocre coffee and sits, turning the pages. He hopes Marian won't wait too long to call. It's a clear morning, blue and warm, and he would like to walk somewhere. South, Oliver decides. He never goes south. All the way to Bowling Green and—why not?—even beyond. He hasn't been on the Staten Island Ferry in years. He reads the review of a nineteenth-century courtesan's biography. This is one of several, hopeful, post–Lady Charlotte books he has noted. None have succeeded as Marian's has. He smiles with pride, puts away his paper, and pays his check.

Outside, he resists the urge to set out alone, to simply take off and begin the journey of his day. The point is to be with her, not merely to do what he wishes to do on his own, so Oliver dutifully retraces his steps to Commerce Street and enters his shop. Bell has arrived and is unloading from Twenty-eighth Street. There is a Jackson Pollock spatter of water across the dark wooden floorboards, from the doorway to the refrigerators. Oliver, pausing to survey the new blooms already arranged in their tin pails, notes to his satisfaction that Bell's taste, already naturally good, is improving.

"Howdy," he calls to the back of the shop. "Nice hydrangeas."

"I thought so," Bell's voice returns. "Never saw a purple like that on a hydrangea."

"You ought to get out more," says Oliver. Then he groans. "Jesus, Bell, who do you think's going to buy a black calla? How much did they cost?"

"You kidding?" He sticks his head out of the back room, his arms full of orange roses, and grins. "You ever heard of Halloween?"

"They look funereal," Oliver comments, eyeing them. The flowers are smooth, sinewy, downright scary. They give him the willies.

"I want to put some in the window." Bell sounds mischievous. He hauls the roses to the refrigerator and then sets a black urn on the worktable. The urn looks funereal, too. "You watch. It'll be like *Little Shop of Horrors* in here: *Say! What is that unusual plant!*"

Oliver sighs. "Fine. But let's not go overboard. Don't buy any more until we see how these do, okay?"

Bell shakes his head. "Why not decide you're gonna make black calla lilies the must-have flower for the nineties? Gotta think big, my friend."

"Why not gamble on your own time, my friend?"

It's a rusty routine, by now. They both put up their hands.

"Didn't expect to see you," says Bell, tying back his dreadlocks and preparing the urn. "Weren't you going to be away for the weekend?"

"Yes," Oliver agrees, trying for an offhand tone. "Small change in plans."

"She kick you out?" Bell asks. "I keep telling you, if you're serious about this girl you need to say so. Women are very insecure. They're not good at subtle—you have to spell it out."

Oliver marvels at how easily Bell can accomplish this authoritative posture. He feels as if he is a child on a stool in a kitchen, listening to Mommy. Actually, he is a year older than Bell.

"She didn't kick me out." Oliver sounds petulant. He sounds like an idiot. "We just changed our plans."

"Yeah," Bell says with a grin, plucking the first black calla from the tabletop, clipping its stem, feeding it through a skein of chicken wire inside the urn. "You think I haven't been there? It's like you got them coming at you from all sides when you just want to be having fun, but the minute you really fall for somebody, you're at the start of an obstacle course in the dark."

"Which is why you stick to the just having fun part," Oliver says dryly.

"Exactly, my friend."

Oliver has to admit, the lilies look good. Macabre, but sexy in their Edward Gorey container, ready to make mischief and exude superiority. He should listen to Bell more, it occurs to him. But not about Marian. Oliver has shared none of the salient details with his employee, who probably supposes that Oliver is in love with some gallery girl or waitress-slash-something. Bell has never—Oliver is quite sure—felt about any of his many girlfriends what Oliver feels for Marian.

"White Rose!" Bell says, answering the phone as the door opens to a trio of beautiful blond men. "That's not ringing a bell," Oliver hears him say. "It's possible someone else took the order. Can you let me have your name?"

One of the men is opening the cooler doors. Oliver, frowning, is about to step across the room when he hears Bell say, "I'm sorry, it was *going* to Klein or we're *billing* to Klein?"

Both, thinks Oliver, abandoning the three men, who are now pawing the hydrangeas, and rushing to Bell. "I'll take that," he says, reaching for the phone. "I know about that order. Go help those guys, okay?"

Bell hands over the phone, looking relieved.

"Hi, can I help you?" Oliver says, speaking, perhaps, a mite deeply. "Is this Mr. Ochstein?"

"This is Barton Ochstein," says Barton Ochstein. "Who am I speaking to?"

"I'm the owner," says Oliver, truthfully enough. "I got the order for roses. Deliver to...ah," he says, trying to remember the name of the fiancée, "Miss Klein?"

"On Friday," Barton says and harrumphs. "And they must arrive before dinner. White roses, yes? The card should say, *For dear Sophie, from Bart.* Should I spell that?"

"No need," Oliver says, writing it down. He is wondering why Barton, having gone to the effort of assigning this chore, is bothering to phone, himself. "I've already been given the address," he says. "And how would you like to handle payment?"

"Just send me the bill," he says shortly. "But there is another matter." Oliver frowns.

"The young lady who phoned you to place the order? Her name is Olivia."

Unsure of how to respond, Oliver merely nods. Then he says, "Okay."

"I would also like to have flowers sent to Olivia."

"Oh." Oliver actually blushes. "And what sort of flowers?"

"Whatever you're sending to Miss Klein, send the same. That should keep it simple."

"Olivia," he says, testing the name out loud. "Olivia what?"

"I don't know," Barton says dismissively, as if this particular bit of information is beneath his interest. "She works for Marian Kahn. I believe Marian Kahn is a client of yours."

"We know Dr. Kahn," Oliver says in some disbelief.

"Well then, you can find out. Only the flowers must be sent to Olivia at home, not at work. You will have to find out her home address. I don't have that."

Oliver takes a deep breath. "So—let me just make sure I understand, Mr. Ochstein—one arrangement of white roses, this Friday, to Miss Klein, and an identical arrangement to...Olivia. On the same date?"

"No need to wait till Friday on that one," he says. "You may proceed with that order immediately."

"All right," Oliver says meekly, his head spinning.

"And I want the card to say...are you ready?"

"Ready?" Oliver asks.

"Are you writing this down?"

"Oh," he says and nods, "yes, I'm ready."

"Darling Olivia, you are enchanting. I would love to see you again. Please phone me at..."

Oliver, breathless, scribbles down the numbers.

"With kindest regards, Barton Warburg Ochstein. That's W-A-R-B-U-R-G, not B-E-R-G."

"Warburg," Oliver confirms.

"That's all then," Barton says. "I've just given you my number, so phone me if you have any questions."

"I will," Oliver says, shaking his head in wonder, and Barton hangs up the phone without further comment.

Across the room, Bell is holding individual stems of hydrangea while the three men argue their relative merits. The two scenarios—simultaneous white rose arrangements to prospective wife and prospective conquest and hydrangea by committee—seem, for a moment, equally absurd. Oliver, abandoning the latter, takes the new order to his office in back and writes it down again, on an official order form, marking the Olivia request with an "O." He pins this to the bulletin board above his worktable. How he will handle the Olivia end of things he is not equipped to decide just now, but as the intended recipient of the illicit white roses, Oliver understands that he can do it privately, whatever it is, and that is no small relief.

"I'm going," Oliver says when the three men, their superior stems selected, depart.

Bell nods without looking up. "All under control."

Oliver fumbles with the key in his apartment door and goes upstairs. His heart quickens at the green light on his answering machine, blinking its own cardiac rhythm. Marian, he thinks, phoning about their date. He lunges for the button.

"Oh...you've gone out," her recorded voice says sadly. "Well, listen, sweetheart, here's the thing. I know you're going to be upset, but I actually had a pretty bad night and I think the best thing would be for me to just spare you my company right now. You won't believe me, but it's in your best interests, because I wouldn't spend the day with me either if I didn't have to. So what I'm going to do is head out to the beach and just be a misanthrope and try to at least get some work done."

Oliver, deflated with disappointment, shakes his head. He wants to alternately hug her and hit her.

"Oliver, please don't be mad. I feel terrible about this, but I'm absolutely convinced that if we spent the day together you'd hate me by the end of it, so I'm being selfish because I don't want that to happen. Look, I'm going to call you tonight, okay? I love you. Bye."

You love me, Oliver thinks. You just can't stand to be with me.

The phone rings, jarring him, and he snatches it up, though he knows it isn't her. How could it be her? She's already on the LIE, in flight from him.

"Hello?"

"Sweetheart?"

He inhales, then summons a buoyant "Hi!" It's his mother, the only other woman who calls him sweetheart.

"Is it a bad time? Are you doing something?"

Are you with someone? in other words.

"No, of course not. Just sitting around. What's up?"

"Oh, it's a pain, but Henry can't come to the ballet tonight, after all. He has to meet that woman he's representing, to do something about the trial."

"On Saturday night?" He regrets saying this instantly.

"The court date's in two weeks," she says, her voice careful and calm. "I guess they need the extra time."

"Of course," Oliver says, a little too heartily. "That makes sense."

"So he can't come with me. I've had the tickets for ages, and I thought I'd see if you were free. Are you? I know it's not much of a Saturday night. Your old mom…"

"That's right," Oliver laughs. "Twist the knife. Of course I'd love to. Why don't you come here first, for dinner?"

"No! Let me take you out."

He declines. "I've got something I was going to cook tonight, anyway. And I don't like those restaurants up around Lincoln Center."

"Well, if that's what you want. I'll come around six?"

They hang up. Oliver has not seen Caroline for nearly a month. This absence—as he knows perfectly well—is a hardship for her, and one for which their frequent phone conversations do not entirely compensate, but it hasn't been easy to be with his mother since meeting Marian. He thinks sadly now of the short ribs in their hopeful marinade, the frisée and box of orzo with which he had hoped to feed a lover, and an evening lost on the ballet (those tall, skinny girls with their washboard chests and impossible legs), and allows himself a moment of genuine self-pity.

Then, feeling chastened, he walks to his kitchen and opens the fridge.

The beef is soupy, gone gray in its wine bath, and smells of garlic. Oliver stands, drinking cranberry juice from the bottle, and considers. The day is his to be salvaged, and though his plans have been upended (and with them, he notes, his ambition to walk downtown), another use for the hours ahead now occurs to him. Oliver bends down and pulls out the fruit drawer: inside is a pile of little tin-foil sacks, each twisted at the end around a swelling the size of a walnut, each labeled with a tag.

He has never done this before.

He knows that he is supposed to be daunted, that roses resist the fumbling attentions of amateurs like himself, but the sight of his rose hips, chilled and—according to his notes—ready to germinate, elates him. The fact that failure is probable has not dampened his spirits, either last spring when he began his project or indeed today, when it strikes him as a good time to go forward.

Oliver takes his foil sacks to the kitchen table and retrieves from his desk a large black notebook, unopened since June. He is reassured to see that his notes are legible, their content clear, and is grateful that in this, at least, he has heeded not only the advice of his high school biology teacher (the disagreeable Boris Benedict, of prehistoric tenure) but also of Joe Murray, resident deity of Kent Roses in Connecticut, where much of Oliver's shop inventory is produced. Last spring, Joe responded to Oliver's wish to create a new rose with a kind of sarcastic grunt, but followed it with an offer of genuine advice. He listened, first, to Oliver's overblown description of the hoped-for rose (not knowing, but perhaps suspecting, that his young customer was newly in love), nodded with forbearance at the proposed "mother" (a pretty hybrid tea rose with five petals, called White Wings, already in bloom back on Commerce Street), and then took Oliver deep into the greenhouse to point out a trio of good paternal candidates. He showed Oliver how to collect the pollen sacs and stow them in baby food jars, then he dictated a road map for what came next. Scrawling frantically on a blank page in his Filofax, Oliver transcribed the rapid-fire, often anecdotal instructions about clipping off the stamens and pistils, applying the pollen, and harvesting the hips. It all smacked of the breeding barn and sounded inescapably obscene. The next day, when he phoned Marian, still in high excitement, she told him that he sounded like a master of ceremonies at an orgy.

All right—it was a rush, Oliver thinks now, recalling the morning not long after his visit to Kent that he decided the mother roses were ready. "Do early," his scrawled note read, and so he had risen at six and bounded upstairs to the roof without pausing to make coffee. The White Wings, six of them, procured from a rose nursery in Oregon, were nodding happily in the June sunshine. He had removed the petals from each bloom, then gingerly extracted the stamens, taking care not to injure the pistils they had surrounded. When, that afternoon, he had returned to the roof garden with great anticipation and peered through a magnifying glass at the pistils (and the dozen or so stigmas that constituted them), he could barely contain his elation.

On each stigma a sticky nectar had materialized.

"This is getting worse and worse," Marian teased, when he called her at her office.

"It's for you," he had said, a little wounded. "Remember, this rose is for you."

"Of course it is," Marian said, more kindly. "It's just that I can't really process words like 'sticky nectar' and 'stamen' and 'stigma' when I'm supposed to be thinking about Georgian economic trends in the port cities."

To this, Oliver made a suggestive suggestion and let her return to work. Then he got down to business.

Having retrieved the baby food jars from his refrigerator, Oliver brought them back to the roof and slowly began to apply the first of his three pollens to the stigmas of some of the prepared White Wings. He used a pipe cleaner for this operation—Joe Murray's favored implement—then immediately covered each inseminated bloom with a white paper bag, to prevent any bees or other insects from getting near them. When he was finished with the first of his baby food jars, he carefully labeled the completed plants with the name of the father, then repeated the process with the rest of the White Wings and the remaining two jars of pollen. It was painstaking work and took most of the afternoon. When it was completed, the rooftop garden bore strange fruit indeed: thorny green stalks capped with fluttering white bags.

Afterward, it was a matter of soil fertilization and patience, but Oliver was rewarded in late summer with the appearance of many rose hips, particularly on the White Wings he had crossed with White Bath, an old English rose that—and this, he knows, would please Marian no end—dated to the very period when Lady Charlotte was herself stooping to conquer England. To protect these precious hips from the birds and the tenacious Village squirrels, Oliver had again taken Joe Murray's advice and wrapped a small piece of tin foil around each, pinching it just beneath the neck. As they fell to the ground he collected them, labeled each with its parents' names, and placed them—still in their foil sacks—inside the refrigerator to stratify.

Now, taking a bowl of water to the kitchen table, Oliver attempts the fairly medieval-sounding method Joe has suggested to sort the most viable seeds. Using a razor blade, he carefully slits each hip, removes the seed, and drops it in the bowl.

The sterile ones float, and he throws them away.

The sinkers are fished out and sorted into their three paternal piles. Once again, Oliver notes, the White Bath crosses have trumped the competition, and he finds that fact strangely satisfying, as if he had long ago decided to root for this particular "bonk" (rose slang for cross, Joe had informed him, and wouldn't Marian love that?). Then he takes the good seeds downstairs to the shop and back into his office.

Oliver doesn't do much growing, either here or even at home in his mother's garden, but he has acquired a few specific materials—ordained by Joe Murray—in anticipation of this day. Now, clearing an area of his worktable, he assembles them: three seedling trays, Canadian sphagnum peat, medium vermiculite, and silicon sand, as well as captan to prevent mold. In a large bowl, he mixes together equal portions of the peat and the vermiculite, then fills the seedling trays and saturates them with water. He lays seven seeds, the products of his least fertile hybrid (Aimée Vibert, a Victorian English noisette) in the first tray, and spreads the twelve from his slightly more promising cross (with the old French Bourbon Boule de Neige, a favorite of Marian's) in the second. Twenty-five seeds from the White Bath cross fill the third, and Oliver labels each tray with care. Then he covers the seeds with three quarters of an inch of silicon sand and moistens the sand with captan. Placing the trays at one edge of his worktable, he switches on a four-foot HydroFarm fixture, which promptly floods them with fluorescent light. (On the wall above them, Barton Warburg Ochstein's double order of white roses is illuminated, too.)

And then, as so often in the world of flowers, there is nothing else to do but wait.

Oliver washes his hands and puts away the bags of soil, peat, and sand. From out in the shop's front area, the sound of conversation makes a gradual claim on Oliver's attention: Bell, laughing. Bell is always laughing. He is talking to a customer.

Oliver looks at his sandy trays beneath their bright light. What's in there? he thinks. Will they grow and then fail? Will they open into stubby, unlovely blooms? Will they be sound but not special? He knows enough about this spectacularly unlikely process not to hope for anything in particular—to be able to report an actual flower to Joe Murray would be an achievement his first time out—but he can't help himself. Before his eyes the bloom conjures itself: a rose so lovely that it silences him, a rose blindingly white and lushly full, as if entrusted with the passion of its creator. He believes in this possibility, because he has once seen it happen, up close. The White Rose—his White Rose—was named in tribute to that.

Bell speaks. Paper rustles. The front door opens to another greeting, and it occurs to Oliver that much of the day has slipped past him as he worked his fingers in the seeds, water, and dirt. He turns from his trays and rises, stretching, to discover that he is very hungry and it is nearly four. The shop area is not jammed—it is never jammed—but it is unquestionably full, and Oliver is embarrassed to think that he has not offered assistance to Bell. He offers it now, helping a short woman with a tight cap of gray hair to four bunches of yellow tulips and wrapping an unwieldy tangle of curly willow branches for two men in their twenties whose border collie accompanies them. When, quite by chance, he looks at the window display, he notes that the black calla lilies are no longer there.

"What happened to the callas?" Oliver asks.

"You kidding? Sold out by noon. I should have bought twice as many."

Oliver nods. "Yeah. What were you thinking?"

Bell harrumphs, good-humoredly.

When this group leaves, Oliver goes upstairs to begin dinner. Caroline, unlike her old friend, does not care for artichokes, so he leaves them for another day. He removes the ribs from their wine marinade and dries them, then sears them in oil as he chops onions and garlic. The hum of activity from downstairs dissipates, and the apartment darkens to early evening. After the meat is ready, he cooks the vegetables, some of the wine, a can of chopped tomatoes, and some chicken broth. Then he throws in Worcestershire sauce and a bit of rosemary. When it boils, he puts the seared ribs back in and leaves the whole thing simmering while he takes a bath.

From belowstairs come the sounds of the ending workday. Drawers scrape open as Bell attempts, in his imperfect manner, to put things away. A knock at the street door goes unanswered: it is after five. Oliver hears the refrigerator doors slide open and shut repeatedly as the last flowers are picked over and put back. He hopes Bell isn't throwing the weak ones away—Oliver likes to bring them upstairs as long as they'll last. He does not mind being surrounded by dying blooms.

The apartment begins to smell rich with cooking meat. Oliver closes his eyes. All day he has pushed Marian from his mind, but now she returns, and with her their lost possibilities for the hours past and now at hand. It is not that Oliver is sorry to see his mother, but the burden of what he can't tell Caroline—at Marian's request—feels heavy. He does not like having to hide from her these serious, wonderful things: the content of his happiness. He does not like having to lie, and having to remember his past lies, in order that the lies to come will not trip over them. He begins a fantasy, relaxed by the heat of the water and the sweet smell from the kitchen, of a sort of intervention, staged by himself and featuring Marian, Caroline, Marshall...even Henry Rosenthal, his stepfather. *We're going to sort this out right now!* (This is Oliver himself, strutting through Marian's living room with his hands on his hips.) *I don't care what the rest of you do, but I am marrying this woman!*

Oliver smiles.

Bell bangs on the apartment door, then opens it. "I'm going," he calls.

"Okay. See you Monday," Oliver shouts.

"Want to come?" Bell says. "There's a reading at KGB."

"No thanks. My mom's coming to dinner."

"The lovely Caroline..."

"Shut up, asshole," Oliver says, chivalrously.

Bell laughs from the bottom of the stairs. "Not my fault your mom's hot, my man."

"Good-bye, Bell."

Oliver hears first his own door shut, then, a moment later, the shop door with its heavy click. He sinks back in the bath, oddly depressed. It has suddenly occurred to him that a man his own age might desire his mother, even as he desires Marian, a notion that fills him with vague distress.

Oliver picks up his watch from the sink ledge. It is nearly six.

He hauls himself out of the bath and dries off. He closes the curtains in his bedroom before turning on the light, then dresses in khakis, a dark tweed jacket, and one of his father's ties. In the kitchen, Oliver removes the meat with a slotted spoon and places it on a tray, covered with foil, which then goes into the oven to keep warm. Then he begins reducing the cooking liquid over high heat and puts water on the stove for the orzo. He is just spinning dry the frisée when he hears Caroline's tap on the shop door and then hurries downstairs to meet her.

Caroline lights up through the window, her skin taut over regal cheekbones. He pulls back the door and lets her enfold him in her long arms, indulging her need.

"Sweetie," his mother says.

"Hi, Mom."

He brings her inside. Oliver is glad to see that she is letting her silver hair grow out a bit—he thought the buzz cut of last spring a little severe, but hadn't wanted to say anything. "You look great."

Her hand goes to her throat. "Henry gave me this."

It's a chunky silver necklace, silver like rough stones forged together, and it suits her. "Pretty."

"Thanks." She looks around. "How was today?"

"Oh, Bell's single-handedly starting a craze for black calla lilies."

Caroline makes a face. "How bizarre."

"There was a big urn of them in the window this morning, and another bucket in the fridge. All gone."

"Extraordinary. But it's Greenwich Village, I suppose."

"Come on, I'm cooking."

He brings her upstairs and gets her a glass of wine, opening the second bottle. "It smells so good," his mother says, taking the glass.

"Short ribs."

"Yummy. Though I'm sorry to put you to the work."

"No, it's fine. I was cooking, anyway."

"I didn't ruin a date or anything?" Caroline says, almost hopeful.

"No. Free and clear."

At this moment, as if to belie the words, Oliver's telephone rings. He dumps orzo into the boiling water and goes to answer it. "Hello?"

"Oliver." It is Marian. He is abruptly overcome with warmth.

"Hi."

She pauses. "Are you all right?"

"Yes. Hmm." He is thinking. This particular circumstance is occurring for the first time, and no code exists between them to accommodate it.

"You don't sound all right. Oliver, I'm really sorry about—"

"Mom?" Oliver says, suddenly and loudly. "Would you mind giving that a stir? You can use the wooden spoon."

Marian, on the other end of the phone line, collects herself. "Oh. Caroline's with you."

"Yeah," he says in relief.

"I didn't realize. We can't talk, then."

"No," he shakes his head. "But I'll get back to you."

"All right." But it isn't all right. The silence sits heavy on the line. Oliver watches his mother stir the orzo, tap the wooden spoon smartly against the pot's rim, and set it on the counter. She turns to him expectantly. "Oliver," he hears Marian say, "I love you. Good night."

"Yes, good-bye," he says, and puts down the phone.

"Who was it?" his mother says, naturally.

His head swims. "Oh, a client. Kamikaze bride. The wedding's next week and she wants four extra centerpieces."

"Why didn't she call the shop?" Caroline says, annoyed on his behalf.

"Oh, she has my home number, too. It's my fault, I probably gave her both. They get very frantic, these New York brides. It's like it's a big performance for them."

Caroline sits down at the kitchen table. "Well, I think that's very rude, calling someone at home on a Saturday night."

Oliver shrugs. "It's okay, Mom. Let's forget about it. I think we're about ready to eat."

He goes to the stove, tests the orzo, and drains it, then tosses it with oil and spoons it onto the plates. Oliver takes the platter from the oven and pours the sauce over the ribs. "Should have bought parsley," Oliver says.

"It smells great," his mother says ignoring him. "Did you want me to toss that salad?"

"Yeah, thanks."

Oliver, to his distress, thinks of Marian as he watches his mother eat. He wants to steal away downstairs and call her back on the shop phone, but he stays where he is. Caroline leans forward over her plate and makes sounds of appreciation. She is beautiful—a beautiful woman of a certain age. He finds, to his surprise, that she is more intrinsically beautiful than Marian, in almost every way: thinner, more finely drawn, her colors separate and alive. Sitting here, Oliver can easily glean what Bell has so delicately termed the hotness of his mother. Caroline, always lovely, is now a shimmer of elegance.

God, he thinks. Is this all it comes down to, in the end? A thing for older women?

"Sweetie, you're not eating," his mother observes.

Oliver takes a bite. The meal is a success.

Oliver can even remember the first time he thought his mother beautiful, on visiting day at Keewaydin Camp, circa 1982, when the cars had filled the parking lot, disgorging mother after mother: the gray and thick, the puffed and colorless. When his family's station wagon arrived—Oliver remembers now—and Caroline stepped out from behind the wheel, she was thin like a willow with pale yellow hair, and glittering in the Vermont sunlight. Oliver had run to her feeling select: he had no father, it was true, but he had this magical person with her arms open and her face alight, who drew every boy's attention away from his own parent.

The leers of a camp full of boys could not compensate for his mother's loneliness. Oliver understood that, even then, though she had not yet introduced him to Henry Rosenthal or to anyone else. Caroline had loved her marriage and family life, and her son already understood that what one loved, and lost, one sought to reclaim. He might have had her to himself, those years, but that passed.

Now, fifteen years later, Caroline had resumed the role of Greenwich wife, though with a husband whose higher profile brought her frequently to the city. Henry, who had a penchant for difficulty and loved to fight, preferably in public, handled a string of ugly divorce cases, most of which featured celebrity participants and vitriol all around. He loved to grapple and rant, and he would play the press without mercy for anyone. Oliver's teenage years had been dominated by the DiSanto case, with its sullen offspring and obscene assets. This was followed by the fighting Coneys and their labyrinthine real estate trusts (a marital dissolution that reverberated in aftershock lawsuits for years). The early nineties were consumed by the famous film director who ran off with his nearly ex-wife's sister, all three of whom were ultimately accused of the sexual abuse of the children, and after that Henry took on the Susskind divorce, a pitiable exercise in devastation culminating in the suicide of the thirteen-year-old whose custody was in dispute. (The day after the funeral, Henry filed a civil suit against the mother, on behalf of the father.)

Did Oliver love him? Of course not, but he saw his mother's contentment. Caroline warmed to her new marriage, and seemed to relish her emergence from suburbia. The Manhattan charity circuit was a homecoming for her, and not a few of the more prominent hostesses she now regularly encountered had been her classmates at Brearley or had taken riding lessons with her at the Claremont Stables. Henry took pleasure in the squeals that would sometimes follow his introduction of his new wife—"But of course I know Caroline! We were in the same bunk at Tripp Lake!"—and always in her beauty, hidden away for long years in widowhood and Greenwich. And yet, although she was meeting (and re-meeting) so many people in Henry's frenetic world, Caroline's circle of friends continued to diminish; Marian was only one of many who fell away as Caroline made her new life with a new marriage and a growing son. Her energy was divided between mothering Oliver and mothering Henry, endeavors requiring intense if different effort. She gleaned early on, for example, that the only way Henry could detach himself from work was to have an ocean inserted between himself and his clients, so Caroline plotted with his secretary to create firewalls of vacation time, during which she took him to Europe, Asia, South America. Once home again, she would lose him to the great world and have to content herself with glimpses at breakfast and late dinners, distracted embraces and rushed compliments as he passed through the house. She might have had another child, but didn't. She might have had a busy life of her own, but for some reason she didn't, at least until she joined the board of the New York City Ballet Guild. While Oliver lived at home, she perfected a presence that was attentive but unintrusive and took pains to construct a home life in which the three of them operated independently, but with generally benevolent overlap. When Oliver left for Providence, they mysteriously reverted to mother and son without reference to Henry. Oliver hardly saw his stepfather at all now, except on holidays and in the *New York Times*. In any case, Oliver had long since decided to think of his mother as happily married, mostly because he could not bear to do otherwise.

"How's Henry?" Oliver asks.

Caroline looks up. "Consumed. Of course."

"With what's her name?"

His mother nods. "It just goes on and on."

"But the trial's in two weeks, you said."

"Well," Caroline says and sighs, "unless the husband's lawyer asks for another continuance. Or Henry does." She shrugs. "One of them almost certainly will."

Oliver takes a sip of wine. "I don't understand that. I mean, it's been an age already. What's the point of dragging it out even more?"

Caroline rubs her forehead absently. "Well, right now she's got primary custody. And the longer she can hold the line, the better off she's going to be. Judges don't like to uproot kids."

"Possession being nine-tenths of the law," Oliver says grimly.

She shakes her head. "It's astonishing how some people behave. You have to remind yourself: these are people who stood up in front of their friends and said they loved each other!"

Oliver, despite himself, laughs. "It's a nasty business."

"Yes. Is there more orzo? I love the sauce."

He serves her another helping, then pours more wine. "Mom? Doesn't it make you cynical about marriage? I mean, it's none of my business."

It's when he says this that Oliver understands he is asking about her marriage, not marriage in general. Immediately, he wishes he could take it back, but Caroline is already looking contemplative.

"No, it's all right," she says, her voice quiet. "I think, to be honest, I have to say yes, but not because of what Henry does for a living, necessarily. I have my own experiences to draw from. Though both of my marriages have been good, they've been very different. So I have a sense of marriage as something that isn't necessarily sacred. It's just a box you put things in. How good it turns out to be is a matter of what you put in the box." She looks up at Oliver and smiles, suddenly embarrassed. "How profound."

"Yes," he says, relieved. "Profoundly profound."

"I should be hanging around with Bell," Caroline says. "He could translate my pearls of wisdom into poetry."

"Bell thinks you're beautiful," Oliver hears himself say.

Caroline smiles, shaking her head. "I knew there was a reason I liked that guy. At my age, you don't get that kind of compliment very often."

"*At your age,*" he says, disapprovingly. "What's the matter with—" He stops himself. He had been about to say, *with the two of you.*

There is a silence, more awkward than it should be.

"I mean—" he begins.

"Yes, yes," Caroline puts up an elegant hand, which bears an Elsa Peretti cuff of silver, "it's hard for you to get your head around. You're the kid, so I've always been older. But in my own mind I'm always younger. It's disconcerting to see myself in the mirror."

"But you're beautiful!" Oliver insists.

"Thanks, but it's a question of age. You know, last summer up in the Berkshires, at one of Farley's big weekends, we started talking about this."

Farley was Henry's partner, the Prenup Pasha. Between them, they had the state of matrimony covered, before and after.

"Not just people our age, either. There were a few kids in their twenties, and some couples in their thirties and forties. And an older couple, too—I think the man was sixty and the woman fifty-something. Anyway, we were talking about the feeling of age, you know? And we went around the table: how old do you think you are? Not that we didn't know how old we were, but the age that feels correct, you know, in your head. Do you understand?"

Oliver, who doesn't exactly, nods.

"The twenty-year-olds thought of themselves as adolescents. The thirty-year-olds thought of themselves as just out of college. The ones in their forties and fifties thought of themselves as a generation younger. Without fail. It's like a rule: your sense of self lags behind your actual age by a certain factor."

"And you think of yourself…," Oliver said, leading her, setting down his knife and fork.

"Oh, about the age I was when you were little, I suppose. Mid twenties. I'm always a little bit surprised to discover that I'm in my late forties, with a grown child."

"A grown child who's very fond of his mother," Oliver says, trying to be reassuring.

"Yes," she says and smiles at him. "That's some compensation."

"Some!"

Caroline does not bother to answer. "Though I wouldn't mind a daughter-in-law. A daughter-in-law would be nice."

"Mom," Oliver says.

"And you're not even dating. Maybe I can help."

You can't, he wants to say, but his goal is to block further conversation. He gets up and takes her plate and his own, then sets them down in the sink. "Want some coffee?"

"What are you afraid of?" Caroline asks. "Is it rejection? Because I can tell you, Oliver, this city is crawling with women who are not about to reject you. I say this in all modesty, given that you're my son."

"Thanks for the endorsement," he says. "I didn't really make dessert, but I have chocolates."

She sighs. "Well, I'd love a chocolate, but I'd also like to stay with this."

"I'm sorry," he says. This is both an observation and a dismissal.

He holds out the Burdick chocolates, snug in their wooden cigar box. Caroline picks out a white chocolate mousse. "I love these. Marian Kahn once gave me these."

Me too, he almost says.

"Do you remember her? We had dinner with her one evening last spring. She was with her husband."

"I remember," Oliver says. He purposely turns away, filling the coffee pot from the tap.

"Strange man. Very rich and very fierce. I wonder if small men are predisposed to be very fierce."

Oliver looks at her, puzzled.

"His family had nothing, you know. They came over after the war, I don't know where from. *Kahn*," she says and frowns. "That's German, right? It's hard to believe there were any Jews left in Germany after the war. Maybe they were from somewhere else. Anyway, Marshall got himself a scholarship to Brandeis, then Yale Law. Afterward, when he got to New York, he had no loyalties."

Oliver, despite himself, wants to hear more. Marian is not often forthcoming about Marshall. Oliver finishes preparing the coffee and takes his seat.

"What do you mean, no loyalties?"

"I mean, there were no family connections. There was no place ready for him—he made his own place. He didn't have to be careful of anyone's history or anyone's feelings." She smiles and shakes her head. "And he wasn't."

"You knew Marian first, right?" Oliver says. "Didn't you know her when you were a child?"

"Marian?" says Caroline. "God, yes! She's the oldest friend that I'm still in touch with. Well, not in very good touch, to be honest. We've been talking about a lunch date since that day in April, and it hasn't happened yet. But she's terribly busy. I think she's writing another Lady Charlotte book."

Oliver contemplates his wineglass.

"I remember her in ballet class—that's how far back we go. We met at Fokine, and our mothers knew each other."

Oliver can't help himself. "What was she like? I mean, was she a nice little girl?"

"Oh, I loved Marian. Her mother was so glamorous. We used to go and play with all her puffs and jewelry and perfume after she'd gone out. I always think of Mrs. Warburg when I hear the phrase 'society hostess.' She was the real thing—you get a copy of Emily Post from the 1950s, that was the Warburg apartment. Park and..." She pauses, considering,

"Eighty-first. And it had the most elegant dining room, with glorious Zuber paper and little crystal bowls full of nuts everywhere. Oh! And silver boxes of cigarettes on every table," Caroline says and laughs. "God forbid someone should have to walk across the room for a cigarette! She was on the board of the Jewish Museum and the Henry Street Settlement but, you know, her heart wasn't really in that. She tried for years to get herself on the board of the Whitney, but they wouldn't have her. It was a hard blow for someone like her," Caroline says and shakes her head. "There were some lines you just couldn't cross, even if you were a Warburg. Of course, she hated that Marian always had her face in a book. Mrs. Warburg believed that intelligence in a girl was wholly unnecessary, and ultimately detrimental. Later on, Marian and I ended up at Brearley together. Of course, Marian flew through Brearley."

Oliver, smiling, gets up to pour the coffee. "Are we taking sugar tonight? Or some chemical du jour?"

"Don't be fresh," says his mother. "Sugar is fine, if that's all you have. What's the time, by the way?"

"Quarter past seven. Plenty of time."

"We might have trouble finding a cab."

"We might take the subway, which goes right there."

"I'm not taking the subway, Oliver." This is a concession to city life that Caroline has never made, as Oliver knows perfectly well. He smiles.

"We'll go soon. Have another chocolate."

She does, then makes a face. "Oh! It's . . . I think there was pepper in that one."

"No doubt," he says. "They have some unusual flavors."

Marian, by way of example, favors the ones with clove.

"Anyway, Daddy and I were already in Greenwich when Marian brought Marshall out. It must have been . . . oh, I guess around seventy-three. They came down for dinner, from New Haven. Of course, she'd been at our wedding, but Daddy hadn't really talked with her until that dinner. Afterward, I remember he told me she was my only sensible friend." Caroline sighs. "Though, to be honest, that had more to do with the girls he didn't like than with Marian."

"What do you mean?" Oliver says. He reacts to anything that smacks of criticism when it comes to his father.

"Oh, just that the friends I went to college with were a bit silly for him. You know, we'd spent four years at Goucher sitting around eating ice cream in our pajamas—we didn't have that much to say for ourselves. Marian was doing a PhD at Yale. She was in a different stratosphere, intellectually."

Oliver carefully drinks his coffee, then carefully replaces the cup.

"Marshall was heading straight for New York, just as soon as he graduated from law school. He didn't mind that Marian was going to teach. He wasn't macho that way, which is actually saying something, or it was then. Mostly he was consumed by his own plans, I think. He couldn't wait to get established."

"But you and Dad didn't really become friends with the two of them. I mean, as another couple."

Caroline shakes her head. "No. It just never took. They went from New Haven to Manhattan, we already had you, and the next few years...well, I was pretty focused on what was happening at our end. She and I kept in touch, mostly by letter. I think they might have come out once or twice, for parties. I know they met Henry, after we were married. But it just settled into a fond-but-distant sort of thing. I was so thrilled for her when her book took off like it did!" She looks at Oliver. "You read her book, didn't you?"

"Yes. You gave it to me for Christmas last year."

She nods, remembering. "Don't you think we should go?"

Oliver agrees. He knows they should. Now, in a belated moment of insight, it occurs to him that this conversation may one day return to haunt him, that his mother may recall it with anger and that it will signify to her a betrayal. He does not know how he can both avoid this and have Marian, and the realization fills him with gloom.

"Leave the dishes," he tells her sadly.

"All right," his mother says. She walks to his bed to get her coat.

"So what's on at the ballet?" Oliver asks, watching her put it on.

"*Who Cares*," Caroline announces.

He shrugs, then reaches for her hand. "I guess you're right," he says.

CHAPTER SEVEN

Appetite

THE DAY IT BEGAN Oliver remembers as especially gray. Marian remembers the rain and the mist after, off—and she knows this would be pretentious were it not absolutely accurate—the cobblestones of his street. But then, it seemed the whole world was steaming.

It happened by coincidence that Marian and Marshall were getting out of a Sunday matinee at the Cherry Lane Theatre on Commerce Street just at the instant Caroline Rosenthal (previously Caroline Stern and née Caroline Lehmann) was leaving a shop called the White Rose, only a few yards ahead of them. Caroline turned to shut the door behind her, twisting on one foot, which was clothed in a smart Italian boot the color of sand, and stepped onto the sidewalk into the path of her oldest friend.

The boot is worth mentioning because it was the boot Marian saw first. She has a thing for boots, for shoes in general, though you wouldn't know it from her actual shoe collection. While most footwear enthusiasts go broad in their prospecting, filling their closets with variant pumps, flats, and heels, Marian's focus has always been on what she thinks of as the Ur-shoe, the shoe so versatile and so dependable and so flattering that it will never seem wrong. To locate an example of this Ur-shoe (which, to be clear, breaks down into the aforementioned categories of pump, flat, and heel, as well as boot) is a rush she has experienced only a few times: the deep brown T-straps with their gentle lift in a dank little shop near the Piazza della Signoria in Florence, the surprisingly sedate black flats in the punk den on the King's Road, the wildly expensive Prada boots she visited and visited before buying. When she finds an Ur-shoe, however, she sensibly purchases multiple pairs. Hence her closet contains a limited repertoire of proven entities, with boxed reinforcements in an auxiliary location.

The boots Caroline Stern was wearing attracted so much of Marian's attention (they were comfortable-looking, with a luxurious, well-tended glow) that she did not note the wearer until the wearer spoke her name, and with such warmth that Marian looked up in surprise.

"Caroline!"

"Caroline!" Marshall echoed. He had always spoken kindly of Caroline. He stepped forward to kiss her. Marian followed with a hug, pressing her friend's bony shoulders.

"What are you doing here? You look wonderful."

"Oh." Caroline touched her short hair with self-denigration. "That horrible salon in Greenwich. I don't know what I was thinking. Tell me it will grow."

"Of course it will grow," Marshall said and laughed. "I think you look great with short hair."

"You do," Marian assured her. "You had it short like this when you were a teenager. You were the only girl I knew who could carry off an Edie Sedgwick look."

Then Marian stopped. It had occurred to her that a woman in midlife with a short, short haircut is quite possibly a woman emerging from chemotherapy. But Caroline was glowing, happy. When Marian's own hair was this short, she had been bloated and pasty and clearly ill. "Are you well?" Marian said then, soberly.

"Oh, sure. I just came in to see Oliver. It's his shop," she said and nodded, over her shoulder. "You know? His shop?"

Marian looked. She saw the sign, a white slab of wood with the slender black writing of a Currier & Ives hostelry, and the window displaying a great black urn filled with peach, white, and the palest pink roses. The roses were wrapped in great swaths of elderberry branches, which trailed their droplets of black fruit down the sides of the urn. It was a still life, she thought. English, not Flemish, ripe enough to jump out of the window. But... Oliver? Wasn't Oliver still in college?

"Isn't Oliver in college?" Marian said.

"Oh," Caroline said, "I know, we've been bad. It's terrible we haven't seen each other in so long."

"Yes," Marian agreed. "Terrible. How long has it been?"

"Well, if you're thinking my son is still in college it must be a while."

"We went to Le Cirque for lunch. It was the old Le Cirque."

"At least a year," Marshall said authoritatively. He knew these things; they were important to him. "Old Le Cirque closed last year."

Caroline shook her head, but smiled so broadly her teeth seemed to gleam through the drizzle. "Terrible. Oliver graduated five years ago. This is his shop, the White Rose. Don't ask me about the name, I have no idea. But he's doing wonderfully here. Well, he was always so gifted with flowers. Did you see that little piece about him in *Elle Decor* last fall?"

"El what?" Marshall said.

"No!" Marian said. "How great."

"Yes. And he lives upstairs."

Marian looked up, instinctively. The house was two stories but squat, with a face of pink brick, easily nineteenth century. At the roofline a fringe of vegetation suggested a garden. As she looked, a light went off on the top floor.

"We're just going to dinner," Caroline said. "Will you come with us? Do you have plans?"

They didn't have plans, but years as Marshall's wife had trained

Marian to leave the response to him. Caroline might have escaped the censure he had directed at some of her other friends over the years, but Marshall was a man of unchallenged needs—the need, for example, to pursue that mythic Manhattan experience of the "quiet Sunday night at home." Dinner with her childhood friend and the friend's son, who owned a flower shop in Greenwich Village, might not conjure his best side, Marian was thinking, but Marshall had already taken Caroline's arm, and the two began walking, with Caroline's smart boots treading carefully on the uneven pavement. After an instant, Marian followed, grateful and excited in equal measures, though wondering if she and Caroline would be able to catch up properly with their audience of husband and son.

"We're going to Le Rouge," Caroline was saying. "Do you know it? No reason you should, but Oliver likes it. He sent me on ahead to get a table."

"Not very gentlemanly," Marshall commented, but with indulgence. He was talking to a mother, after all.

"A client called as we were leaving. He was unhappy about something. Oliver had to take the call."

"Roses not white enough?" Marshall said.

"I don't know," she said and laughed. "I guess we'll find out when we see him."

But they didn't see him, not for a while yet, and Marian nearly forgot him as they turned north up Bedford Street. Or was it west? Though she had lived in the city all her life the neighborhood was confusing to her, with streets taking off at odd angles, variously paved or cobblestoned, and while she thought them beautiful she also found herself unsettled at being off the grid of predictable Manhattan blocks. The sidewalk traffic was young and predominantly scruffy, and even the dogs were notably different from their uptown counterparts—larger, for one thing, and less readily distinguishable by breed. It struck her as remarkable that she could travel only a few miles from her ancestral home and feel such a foreigner, while Caroline, who had lived in the suburbs for years, seemed so acclimated. But Caroline was beautiful, Marian thought, had never not been beautiful, and beauty had a way of creating its own comfort zone. Strangely enough, Marian had never resented this about her.

Le Rouge was unremarkable in appearance, a narrow storefront with a nod toward bistro décor and aggressively red walls. They took a table for four against a banquette and Marian slid onto the seat, with Caroline beside her and the empty chair across the narrow table. Marshall took their coats to hang up in the back.

"You're looking great," said Caroline. "I've really missed you."

"Me too," Marian said. "I got your letter. I have it on my bulletin board in my office."

"Oh, I'm glad. I just loved the book. Actually, everyone I know loved the book. I've acquired real cachet in Greenwich from knowing you. I'm actually supposed to invite you to come speak at the library."

"Done," Marian said. "Just call me with a few dates. I'd love to come out and see your house. And Henry, of course. Maybe we'll both come."

"Both come where?" Marshall said, returning and taking up the wine list, which he immediately frowned at disapprovingly.

"To Greenwich. You remember Caroline's husband. Henry?"

"Of course," he said, though Marian knew he didn't.

"I've been reading about his case," Marian went on. "That woman he's representing sounds impossible."

This was a discreet intramarital cue: *We are talking about Henry Rosenthal, Marshall. Pay attention.* And he did. He looked up from the wine list and kept silent, waiting for more information.

"Oh, she is," Caroline said. "And he's something like her twelfth divorce attorney. She has a little problem accepting the reality of her situation."

"You mean that her husband wants a divorce?" said Marian.

"No, not that part. She's been divorced before, and she's very strong. It's about what she's entitled to. They had a watertight prenup, for one thing, but she's asking for twenty thousand a week to raise their daughter. And that's joint custody."

"How old's the daughter?" Marshall said, leaning back while a waiter poured water.

"Three," the women said, both at once.

"Three! What does she need, facials?"

Caroline laughed. "I believe shiatsu massage was mentioned in the petition."

"No!" Marian said.

"No what?" said the man who now stood behind the empty chair, and Marian first thought that he must be that overly familiar type of New York waiter, who insists on entering the conversation every time he approaches the table and then expects to be tipped like the old friend he is. But this man was wearing a jacket and jangling keys in his hand. He stood beside the chair opposite her, and looked expectantly at Caroline. Marian, to her own surprise, found herself averting her eyes.

"Sweetheart, look!" Caroline said. "I found Marian and Marshall on the street."

And Marian, even as she smiled, was frantically trying to affix the label "Oliver" to the man in front of her, who was not and yet was the gangly eleven-year-old she had last seen in a Greenwich backyard, huddling with a friend to avoid the adult company. In fact, there was nothing to link that child and this person—this man, she forced herself to think, because he was that—but the prima facie evidence that his mother was vouching for him.

"Hello there," said Marshall, rising. He and Oliver exchanged a robust handshake. "That's a very nice shop you have."

"Thank you," he said, turning to Marian, who began to get up.

"No," he said, "please. It's so nice to meet you."

Marian sat back down and watched, rather than felt, him take her hand. When he had released it, she immediately regretted not paying closer attention.

Oliver sat. He turned to his mother with a half smile. If he was disappointed with the turn his evening had taken, Marian thought, he was doing an excellent job of hiding it.

"So what did he want?" said Marshall. "The guy who called." This was precisely the sort of thing Marshall loved: conflict between people he didn't know.

Oliver looked quizzically at his mother.

"I was saying that the phone rang as we were leaving. You had an aggravated customer."

"Oh," said Oliver, nodding. "Yes. Though I don't think he's my customer anymore."

"Hard to please?" Marshall asked eagerly.

"Not so much that. Misinformed, I would say. Confused about the reality of flowers. The place of flowers in the world."

Whoa, Marian thought, fighting an urge to roll her eyes. A flower-philosopher! As if she didn't get enough academic pretension during the week. And then, quite suddenly, it occurred to her that she was trying not to like him.

"What's that supposed to mean?" Marshall said.

Oliver watched a waiter pour water into his glass, then he picked it up. "Mr. Mortensen was upset because his roses were dying. They were very beautiful roses. *Alba Maximas*. Sort of our shop's signature rose. I have them grown for us in Connecticut. And they were expensive." Oliver shrugged. "And they were dying."

"But you get that all the time, don't you?"

"Yes," Oliver said. "It's the most frequent complaint, despite the fact that we go out of our way to remind people to recut the stems and change the water every day. It's a big return on very little effort, which I'm sure this guy didn't make."

"Well, when did he buy the roses?" Caroline asked.

"Tuesday. They were cut Monday morning."

"But it's Sunday!" said Marian. "I mean, surely that's a reasonable time for a rose to last."

"It is," Oliver said and sipped his water. "But he doesn't see it that way. He sees it in terms of what he spent on a rose that looked perfect when he bought it, and how long it stayed that way. So we have a philosophical disagreement. From now on, he'll be investing in silk roses, or buying cheap flowers and expecting less of them." He sighed, but not unhappily. "He was a walk-in. Not to knock walk-ins. Sometimes it's kind of serendipitous, who happens to come down that street and happens to look in our window—that can be really nice. But for the most part, our customers are people who already know what we do."

"And what's that?" asked Marshall.

"Well, we're taking a position that celebrates the transience of the flower. Not that we don't prolong the bloom as long as we can, but we recognize that a flower's impermanence is part of its beauty."

Barely perceptibly, Marshall shook his head. He was thinking, Marian knew, that this was not a sound business plan.

"Was the man unpleasant?" Caroline asked with maternal concern.

"Yes," Oliver said. To signal the subject's closure, he opened his menu, but instead of looking at it, he looked at Marian with a directness that startled her. It was a look at once contemplative and blatantly hungry. It made Marian want to swallow. Then slap him.

"Marian wrote that book about Lady Charlotte Wilcox," Caroline said. "Remember? I gave it to you for Christmas."

He nodded. "I loved your book. What a character she was."

"That's so true," Marian said smoothly, with false camaraderie. She slipped easily into her professional mode, the tone and demeanor of the radio programs, the television shows she had done, smoothing over the imperfect preparation of each host with her own practiced conversational style. That she was good at this she had learned along the way, after too many otherwise insipid interviews had been salvaged by her quick returns. "I think her Americanness can't be underestimated as part of her success. Not many Americans made it to England in the late eighteenth century. To the end of her life in England people wanted to know her for that reason. She was a curiosity to them."

"It didn't seem to bother her," he said. "Did she enjoy the attention?"

"I think so," Marian smiled. "Self-effacement wasn't her style."

"Unlike yourself," he observed.

Marian, who had been glancing at her menu, for no reason she could readily identify and certainly not from hunger, looked up abruptly.

"I mean," said Oliver, "that you strike me as a very modest person, despite your accomplishments."

This was something no one had ever bothered to observe. Her husband had never called her modest. None of her friends had ever called her modest. Yet she *was* modest. Actually, she could be downright self-flagellating, another observation no one had ever bothered to make. She could not bring herself to respond, and the silence hung between them, finally broken by Marshall, who turned to Oliver and said, a mite heartily, "So what's good to eat? Your mother said you like this place."

Oliver shifted in his chair, and Marian watched without quite listening as Oliver offered some highlights. The menu was short, and looking it over, Marian thought there was nothing she could possibly eat, but when the waiter arrived she forced herself to order the salmon and watched with gratitude as wine was poured into her glass. *Careful*, she thought, tasting it. The situation was already precarious.

"Do you come down to the Village a lot?" Oliver asked, turning back to her.

"No, not very much. I ought to, it's so pretty here, but you know how it is. We all get into our routines."

"I live my life almost entirely between Fifty-sixth and Eighty-seventh on the East Side," announced Marshall. "Plus the theater district, okay. But almost everyone I know and everywhere I want to go's within walking distance. I never take cabs."

"It must be nice to be able to walk," Caroline said. "That is the drawback of the suburbs. You see anyone on foot in Greenwich who isn't wearing a jogging suit and you're immediately suspicious. *What's he doing there? Why isn't he driving?*"

"I'd hate that," Marian said. "I don't like driving. I don't think many Manhattan-bred people turn out to be confident drivers." She looked at Caroline. "Are you a good driver?"

Caroline set down her wineglass. "I am now. I wasn't for years.

Oliver's father used to follow me around in his own car, just to make sure I got where I was going."

"I never knew that," Oliver said.

She shrugged. "At the time I resented it, but I do understand now. I wasn't lousy enough for him to forbid me outright, but it worried him. I suppose you could think of it as very paternal and sexist, but the fact is, I really *was* a bad driver. And he thought he was taking care of me."

Marshall leaned back as a waiter set down his onion soup. "And did you ever need his help?"

She nodded, eyeing her salad. "Once. I was taking Oliver to a doctor's appointment. I must have been upset about something, and I went off the road. Not—I didn't veer off the road. I didn't hit anything, but I kind of fell off the pavement and couldn't get back on it. So I was pretty shaken, and then there was David. We just got in his car and went to the doctor's office, and he had the car towed back to the house. I couldn't drive for a few months after that." She looked across at Oliver. "Do you remember that?"

He nodded. "But sort of muddled. I remember driving off the road, but I remember Dad just being there. I didn't know he was in a different car."

Caroline smiled. "Well, anyway. Like I said, I'm a good driver now. I haven't gone off the road in twenty-two years."

"Glad to hear it," said Marshall, signaling the waiter. "Could we have another?" he said, lifting the wine bottle from its ice bucket.

Oliver turned from his mother to Marshall. "What took you out of the Upper East Side today, then?"

"Oh," he said, "we saw that play on your street. That restaurant play. What's it called?" he asked Marian.

"Fully Committed."

"Fully Committed," he repeated unnecessarily. "About the guy who works in the restaurant."

"Yes," said Oliver. "It's been running for months."

"Did you like it?" Caroline said.

"I did," Marian said. "Marshall not so much. It's difficult to get used to the actor doing so many different voices. I thought it was funny, and I'm sure it's quite accurate."

Oliver nodded. "My friend Bell says so. He used to work in a restaurant."

Ah, Marian thought. *He's gay.* Then: *Thank God.*

"He was a line cook at a restaurant that shall remain nameless. It's famous, and well within your stomping ground," Oliver told Marshall. "He said that each day began with generalized screaming and built to the chef's complete collapse. Bell actually loved the work. He's a very good cook. But he couldn't take the mania."

"He's a placid guy," Caroline agreed.

She must have made her peace with this, thought Marian.

"So he quit?" Marshall asked, trying to cut the melted cheese on his soup with the edge of his spoon.

"No," Oliver said and shook his head. "He got fired. The chef didn't like the way he was always talking to the plants."

They all stopped what they were doing and looked at him.

"I went down to a Nuyorican poetry slam last summer, and there was Bell. He read this poem. Well," Oliver said and laughed, "I'm not sure it was a poem, really. More like a rant. Or maybe a rap, I guess. Anyway, it was all about how he got fired for talking to the plants in the restaurant. The chef kept a rosemary bush, and there were a few other herbs in the summer, just to have on hand. Bell liked to take his breaks out in the back and talk to the plants. He said it relaxed him, and the plants seemed to like it."

The waiter arrived, made small talk, and set down their plates.

"So he got fired?" Marian said.

"Yeah. The chef was having one of his fits, and he told Bell to get out. He thought Bell was too happy, I guess." Oliver smiled. "Well, he is a little too happy. But the kitchen was just his day job, anyway. I mean his ego wasn't tied up in it, just his livelihood. He's a poet, and he's doing pretty well with that, but he got out of the MFA program at Columbia last year with the equivalent of a small country's national debt. So anyway, when I heard his poem, I thought that a guy who talks to plants was exactly the kind of person I'd been meaning to hire. It just hadn't occurred to me to put that in the job description, which may be why none of the assistants I had hired had been working out."

"What a motley crew," said his mother, shaking her head. "There was the guy who turned up stoned every day, and the Korean anti-Semite."

"Don't remind me," Oliver said and laughed.

"And that girl with the boyfriend who kept hanging around."

"Him I really didn't like. Poor girl."

"You wanted to save her," his mother said gravely.

Oliver nodded. "Wanted to. Didn't."

"Oliver, the guy knew where you lived. What could you do?"

Oliver turned to Marian. "Every time she talked to a male customer, the boyfriend had a fit. He was wound up so tight, everybody was tense when he was around, which was all the time. The whole shop was tense. The *flowers* were tense. The best you could hope for was that he'd fall under a train. I'm sorry, that sounds terrible."

He wasn't apologizing for what he felt, Marian noted. Only how it sounded.

"So one day she calls me from the highway. She's on her way to Seattle, on a bus. I said, 'Good for you!' And when the guy comes tearing around looking for her I said how furious I was at her, for quitting without notice, and he bought it and went away."

"You were fortunate," Marian said, picking at her salmon.

"Not as fortunate as she was. But anyway, that was another bad hire. I got lucky with Bell, even if I have to listen to him be happy all the time. And he's always trying to fix me up with his leftover girlfriends."

"Let him," said Oliver's mother. "I'm sure they're lovely."

"Then you are sadly misinformed," said her son, with a brief smile.

"Your Jewish mother would like to dance at your wedding," said Caroline, sighing.

"My Jewish mother will have to wait," Oliver said flatly. Then he turned to Marian.

Not gay, Marian thought, crushed, and everything her desperate assumption had held at bay these last minutes came surging back at her, the dam breaking everywhere at once. It felt like drowning. It felt like the spreading heat of an allergic attack, making her flush and closing her throat. She wanted to push her face into ice. He was still looking.

Now Marshall was telling, again, the story of how his partner of years and years had gone behind his back to force him out of the company they'd started and how he had learned of it (at the opera, of all places, between acts, in the Vilar Grand Tier restaurant, over-hearing some clueless underling from Goldman Sachs in the next booth) and again how he had gone to the partner the following week and confronted him, but not without first acquiring every share of stock he could readily locate and persuading the owners of others, which meant the confession of sins and the placation of not a few old foes over extraordinarily expensive wines, and then summoning the entire board to watch this traitor be escorted from the building, again, his friend! For years! And Caroline was murmuring and shaking her head as she ate, lifting her glass and setting it down. What was she eating? Marian, distracted by incidental curiosity, looked, saw, looked back to find Oliver still looking at her. He wasn't eating either.

"You're not eating," Marian observed.

"No." He agreed.

"Aren't you hungry?"

"Yes," he said simply.

"How awful," said Caroline. "I've never understood that. To some people, nothing matters but the money."

"I'm not like that," said Marshall, as if she'd implied otherwise. "I think it's very simple. Some people like to build. Some like to destroy. I'm a builder."

Even though the company he had built sometimes destroyed, thought Marian.

"It's very easy to tear things down, or to undermine a project. It's hard to make something out of nothing."

"You would have liked David," Caroline said suddenly, and now at last Oliver looked away from Marian and at his mother.

"I did like him," said Marshall. He looked at his wife, as if to ask, *I did like him, didn't I? Remind me.*

"Yes," Marian reassured him. "I remember how much you liked him. I'm so sorry we didn't all see more of one another. Greenwich felt a lot farther away, then, somehow."

"That was before we started driving five hours every Friday night to get to the East End," Marshall said. He told the waiter he was finished with his steak.

"Five hours!" Caroline said and laughed. "That's absurd. Is it worth it?"

"That's what we ask ourselves every week on the LIE," Marian said nervously. "You spend hours and hours trying to plot shortcuts, but there aren't any. Everyone's trying to squeeze through the eye of the needle out there. Once you hit Riverhead, it's just you and the rest of the financial, publishing, fashion, media, and art worlds, all attempting to buy the same tomato at the same roadside stand."

"Oh no!" Caroline said and shook her head. "I was out there years ago. It wasn't crowded at all. And the light!"

Marian nodded. "Yes, that's the problem. You finally crawl out of the car in the worst possible mood, and you're starving but every single restaurant is jam-packed, and the farm stands have been picked clean, and the line out the door of the Barefoot Contessa is an hour long, and you're ready to murder your spouse for not remembering to pack a lousy can of tunafish, and all you want to do is call the real estate agent. But then in the morning you wake up and you look out the window and there's . . . this *light*. This amazing, beautiful, watery, planetary light, and you think, Oh yeah. That's it. You'd go to the end of the earth, let alone Long Island, for light like that."

"And then," Marshall said, "your spouse goes out and brings you back a beautiful breakfast, which you and he consume in your garden, illuminated by the aforementioned light, and you relax all day and catch up on your reading and go for a walk and get together with your friends in the evening . . ."

"And try not to think about facing the LIE again," said Marian to Caroline.

"And that's why it's worth it," said Marshall, shaking his head (on everyone's behalf? Marian wondered) when the waiter asked if they wanted dessert. "You should come out with us some weekend," he said to Caroline. "You both should."

No, thought Marian.

"And Henry, of course."

"Well, that would be nice," said Caroline. Marian recognized the noncommittal tone of a woman who did not make plans for her husband without his consent. She looked at her watch. "I need to leave. I have my own drive, now." She got up. "Be right back."

Then Marshall, to Marian's horror, stood too. They walked away together, to the dark back of the restaurant, and parted left and right to the bathrooms, like square dancers separating at the end of a formation. Oliver was looking at her, still looking. The force of it was terrible. Marian closed her eyes.

"We're wasting time," said Oliver.

She touched her wineglass. There was no more wine.

"Why did you name your shop the White Rose?" she said, surprising herself. She was not aware of forming this question in her own thoughts, let alone having any real curiosity about it. So where had it come from?

"I'll tell you," he said quietly, "when I know you better."

"You must really love flowers," she said, absurdly, despising herself.

"Please," said Oliver.

From the edge of her vision, she felt the known vibration of her husband's stride: brown jacket, khaki pants, blue shirt, coming closer. She took a breath.

"Don't call me at home. Don't ever, ever contact me at home."

"I understand," he said.

And then Marshall was there, leaning over the table and reading the check. He drew bills from his wallet and flicked them onto the tablecloth. Oliver reached into his pocket.

"No, no," her husband said, waving his hand. "I'm delighted we ran into you both. It's my treat."

"Thank you. It was very nice to meet you."

"Oh, Marshall," Caroline said, returning, "that's not necessary."

"I've already done battle with your son," he laughed. "My treat. Such a pleasure." He kissed her on the cheek. Marian got to her feet, unsteadily.

"Marian." Caroline reached for her. "Now we've got to have a lunch. Just us. I'm going to call you next week."

"Yes," Marian stammered. "I want to."

"And I want to hear all about what you're doing now. I didn't even ask!"

"That's okay. More of the same. I have a chair in the history department at Columbia, since last year." She was saying this for Oliver, she realized. She was giving him information, betraying her husband, beginning an affair. By saying this.

"Oh, that's great! Miss Bakalar would be so proud of you!"

Miss Bakalar had been their fourth-grade teacher, an enemy of silliness in young ladies.

Marian smiled weakly. She held out her hand to Oliver, and he took it, but so briefly, as if he too were afraid of what the contact might produce. Even so, when he released it, she felt bereft.

They walked out into the evening, which was wet, with a river of forward-hunched pedestrians on Bleecker Street. Marian received a hug from Caroline, a sort of grip and release. Marian was in misery. She turned her face away from Oliver, to deprive herself of any more information. Marshall took her arm, above the elbow. She gripped her raincoat at the throat and they walked to Seventh Avenue, where they found a cab bound the wrong way. Marshall directed, and the driver bore this with equanimity. Marian sat, numb and dull, letting the city slip past in its motion and moisture, flying up, up the island along the luxurious corridor of Madison Avenue with its pointless boutiques, and then, at the last minute, across Eighty-seventh to their own apartment building. Hector opened the door.

Upstairs, she draped her wet coat over a dining-room chair and slipped off her shoes, staring at her bare feet. Marshall went into the bedroom. A moment later, she heard the bath begin to run. She turned and walked through the kitchen to her office, opened the door and looked at the blinking green light on her phone. She didn't listen to the messages. Already, she knew his word was good. Instead, Marian dialed the number of her other office, the small, crammed room she had inherited the year before, when the last possessor of her endowed chair had retired and she was on the cusp of her fame as the discoverer and interpreter of Lady Charlotte Wilcox. It rang four times and then clicked to life.

Three messages. The first, from Carter Hawes, about a senior distressed by her thesis grade. The second—ragged, gasping—from the student herself, asking for a meeting. The third from Oliver, still fresh. "It's me," he said. "When can I see you?"

CHAPTER EIGHT

Metaphysics

T HERE WERE MORE PHONE CALLS—four more, to be exact—
each in a voice increasingly straining not to be pitiful, each
more difficult for her to resist answering. Finally, with the air of
a last effort, he wrote a letter. This Marian received at her office, and
opened with a hand so eager that she got a paper cut on her thumb and
sat for the next, stunned moments, sucking it, like the very infant she felt
herself in sudden danger of becoming.

Actually, it wasn't a proper letter at all. It was a sort of list, a collection of information, on his shop stationery. And though she would
make a point of throwing it away, she first committed what it said to
memory.

Dear Marian,
There are some things I want you to know about me. I'm going to
tell them this way because I don't want you to wonder, or worse,
feel that you need to ask me. Though of course, you can ask if you
like, and I will answer. I will talk about anything with you.
   I am twenty-six years old.

Although this means that you are technically old enough to be my mother, I want to point out that you are not my mother. I am not remotely confused about this fact.

I love my mother, and I wouldn't willfully hurt her.

Although I've met your husband only once, I have no reason to dislike him, and I wouldn't willfully hurt him, either.

I am in love with you.

I am discreet. This is possibly the most important thing I want you to know. You will never have to wonder whom I'm talking to. I'm not talking to anyone.

I am aware of the fact that you are famous, or at least that literary counterpart to famous. If fame makes you happy, then I am happy for you, but otherwise it makes no difference to me.

I am not promiscuous. My most important relationship ended four years ago.

I am HIV negative.

I think about touching you. I think about it all the time. I want to do everything.

I am allergic to cats. I say this in case you have a cat. I'm sorry about it, because I have always liked cats.

I am in love with you.

Please, please.

Oliver

This was a Thursday in April, at about four in the afternoon.

Marian picked up the phone and dialed the number on the stationery.

It rang twice and he answered. "White Rose!"

"What is this?" she said angrily. "What are you trying to do?"

He took a minute to recover. "I think I've been pretty clear about that."

"Not clear enough," Marian said. "I want to ask you something."

"Ask."

She closed her eyes. "Is this some kind of mother thing? Are you looking for a mother?"

She heard an unmistakable wisp of laughter. Relieved laughter. Evidently, he had been expecting a much harder question.

"No," Oliver said. "I *am* looking for a father. But I don't think you're him."

"Is this a habit for you? Have you done this before? Gone around trying to seduce your mother's friends?"

"Oh no," Oliver said. "Not that I wouldn't have liked to seduce Mrs. Winograd, when I was fourteen. I had a very active fantasy life concerning Mrs. Winograd. But I never said a thing, I swear."

"Where is Mrs. Winograd now?" Marian said, astonished to find herself jealous.

"Greenwich, I guess. I don't think she's Mrs. Winograd anymore."

"No," Marian agreed, absurdly, as if she knew.

"Anyway, that was just physical," said Oliver.

"And this?" she said, her voice brittle, nearly hostile. She was, she discovered, gripping the phone so hard her fingers were beginning to hurt.

"Metaphysical."

Marian caught her breath. For a strange, strained moment, she felt the footsteps in the corridor outside, the sputtering jackhammer of a Con Ed crew on Amsterdam, even the Doppler-dissipation of a boom box retreating west alongside Saint Paul's Chapel, occur in synch with her own heartbeat, as if she were personally propelling the world on its way.

"All right," she heard herself say.

She hung up the phone, locked her office, went downstairs, and stepped outside into the cool spring afternoon. She walked unsteadily in the wake of the now receded boom box, west to Broadway through the campus, dispensing a wooden nod to a disheveled girl with a long black braid on the steps of Low Library, whom she vaguely recognized as a graduate student in her department. It took Marian less than a minute to find a taxi, less than eighteen to reach his door, his arms, his bed.

ACT II

CHAPTER NINE

Deliveries

BELL IS SICK. He phones at seven-thirty in the morning as Oliver is returning from the Pink Teacup, where he has spent a pleasant, steamy half hour recovering from Twenty-eighth Street. He is not sufficiently recovered, however, to greet this news with equanimity.

"It's not a great day to get sick," Oliver says, mashing the phone between shoulder and ear as he hauls the containers in from his parked van.

"Yeah, I said that to myself this morning, about four o'clock. It was between upchucks. Unfortunately, I didn't listen to myself, and here I am."

"Oh," Oliver says. "You mean really sick. Not metaphorically sick."

"I wouldn't waste a metaphor on you," Bell says, good-naturedly, given the circumstances. "'Scuse me."

Oliver hears a shuffle, then there is a brief moment of audible pain. The toilet flushes. "Bell?" Oliver says. "You okay?"

Bell, picking up the phone, grunts. "In other words, you don't need me today."

Oh, but he does, Oliver thinks. He has the delivery to Barton Ochstein's fiancée, plus there is a rehearsal dinner on Central Park West, plus restaurants all over downtown, not to mention that Friday is always the busiest day for walk-ins. He very much does need Bell today, but what can he do?

"Of course not," says Oliver. "Go to bed and stay there. Drink ginger ale."

"Mmm," Bell groans.

"No, seriously. It's good for your stomach. Where do you think you got it?"

"Academy of American Poets," Bell says.

"What?" says Oliver

"Langston Hughes tribute. Two of the people I went with got sick. The other one said he didn't trust the pâté."

Oliver shakes his head. "You got food poisoning at the Academy of American Poets' tribute to Langston Hughes? You don't think that's a little symbolic?"

"Yeah," Bell says miserably. "It's a conspiracy. Look, I have to go throw up now. Can we discuss this later?"

Of course, Oliver tells Bell, wishing him luck. Then he hangs up the phone and considers.

He will close in the afternoon. He will work now, make the arrangements, load everything up, and start his rounds. He doesn't like to lose the shop business, but there is no alternative. This is the downside of keeping the staff small, he supposes.

Resigned, Oliver goes to work. He quickly assembles the restaurant orders, working mainly with hardy, dramatic, and long-lasting stock. For the rehearsal dinner he fashions eight centerpieces of fat Prelude roses in crystal bowls the hostess has dropped off, each arrangement specified to the inch in height and of the precisely requested hue. As if to compensate for this display of anal retention, the hostess has also graciously commissioned a large arrangement for her entryway, to be determined entirely by Oliver, the only proviso being that it fit the vast Waterford punch bowl she has also provided, and into this Oliver crowds calla lilies in powdery white, carefully swirling the stems so that they may be seen through the prisms of the cut crystal. It is a stunning composition and will look extraordinarily expensive—which it will certainly be, but which, in fairness, is more or less what this particular hostess wants her guests to think as soon as they walk in the door. Then, so as not to give offense with his extravagance, Oliver prepares an offering of narcissus in one of his own vases, which he will include gratis. "I thought you might like something for the powder room," he'll say, and will hope that none of the guests are sufficiently knowledgeable about flowers and Greek mythology to take offense at his choice.

Then Oliver turns his attention to the dual Ochstein orders. If Barton has been sitting by the phone to learn whether Olivia liked his flowers, he must be disappointed—Olivia has as yet received no roses, and thus tendered no grateful thanks—but now Oliver has a small problem. He can't in good conscience charge Barton for a delivery to Olivia if no such delivery exists. On the other hand, he has no intention of allowing Olivia—and how protectively he already thinks of her!—to engage in a relationship of any kind with Barton. On the *other* other hand, if he does not charge Barton for an Olivia delivery, Barton will quite justly want to know why not, and what is the owner of the White Rose going to tell him?

Oliver decides that the solution, imperfect though it may be, is to assemble the arrangement, bill Barton Ochstein for it, and deliver it to someone else. To Marian, Oliver thinks. He will tell her the truth—he won't pretend to have sent the flowers himself—and they will laugh about it together. Marian, after all, is the only one in whom he can confide the circumstances, and the only one who will get the joke. In any case, he would have brought her roses today. He likes for Marian always to have his flowers near her. Having made this decision, he takes down the order form from his office wall and marks up the charges, noting the same price beneath the fiancée's—Sophie Klein's—name, and the "O" beside it. Then he sticks it back up on the corkboard, peers hopefully at his trays of dirt with their embedded roses (a few are just breaking the surface), and begins making up the two arrangements.

Ochstein's unintended gift to Marian will consist of hot red Royal Danes, swirled in a vase of cloudy Mexican glass. He inserts a card ("For Marian, with the compliments of Barton Ochstein, Esq." in case Marshall should see it) and turns his attention to Sophie Klein, whose taste in flowers he cannot know (but whose taste in men does not bode well for it). In the face of this void, Oliver makes a superior effort, comprising three dozen opulent white Iceberg roses in a squat container of frosted glass. Around this he wraps the slender black branches he buys on Twenty-eighth Street and soaks in water until they are pliant, and the effect is of a bird's nest with doves rising. It is not imaginative, but it is beyond reproach, and given the state of his information, it is the best choice he can make.

He is just wrapping the Klein vase with bubble wrap when the phone rings, and to his great chagrin Oliver finds himself once again fielding the inquiries of his eager customer, Barton Warburg Ochstein. Barton is not in a fine mood.

"I wish to speak with the owner," he begins, after identifying himself.

"Speaking," says Oliver. "I'm just putting the finishing touches on Miss Klein's white roses."

"Yes, yes," says Barton distractedly, "and did that other order go out?"

"Ah—" Oliver plays for time. His thoughts race.

"The roses to Olivia. I asked you to deliver—"

"Yes, Mr. Ochstein. But I'm afraid it's taken me some time to get in touch with her."

"I told you," Barton says with loud exasperation, "she works for Marian Kahn."

"Yes, but I didn't want to leave messages on Dr. Kahn's answering machine," Oliver explains. "I only reached her—Olivia—yesterday."

"Good," Barton says, regrouping. "Well then, you have her address. May I—"

"No," Oliver breaks in. "I mean, she didn't want the flowers delivered to her home. She said she lives in a bad neighborhood, and there's no doorman. There would be no way to leave them for her."

"Well, what are you going to do about that?" Barton demands, as if this is Oliver's problem. Oliver concentrates.

"She's arranged to pick them up here at the shop. I believe she's stopping by tomorrow."

Barton seems to consider this. "All right. Oh, and I didn't catch her last name. I suppose you have that information."

Does he? thinks Oliver. In fact, he has never gotten beyond "Olivia," much less given her a back story.

"Well?" Barton says testily.

Oliver clutches back to high school Latin.

"Nemo," he declares, then cringes, since that is far too obvious.

"N-E-M-O," Barton confirms, also confirming that it is not too obvious for him. "And I suppose she gave you a phone number? For you to contact her in the future?"

The future? thinks Oliver. Was he going to have to do this *again*?

"Uh…"

"Surely she doesn't want you to continue to contact her at her job."

"No," Oliver agrees, thinking furiously. "No. Well, yes, she gave me a phone number."

"And it is…?"

He nearly hangs up. What does Barton think he is? A procurer? Does $75 worth of roses entitle anyone to an unlisted number? Does the fact that Olivia has agreed to accept her flowers automatically mean that she welcomes his attentions? *Women are so put upon*, he thinks bitterly. *What shit we have to deal with.*

Then he dutifully recites the only number that comes readily to mind: his own. And Barton, his mission complete, puts down the phone without further niceties.

For a minute, Oliver just stands there, frantically reviewing the conversation, wondering if he has done the right things, given the right answers, chosen the right strategy. The phone number doesn't worry him. It rings upstairs only, not in the shop, and there's little danger anyone but himself will answer a call from Barton. Also, he has never gotten around to recording a greeting for his voicemail, so callers get the prefab, computerized voice instructing them to leave a message—no problem there. What concerns him is that he has now affirmed the reality of Olivia. He has fully named her, extended her existence. What are his intentions for her—mercenary? defensive?— and how does he plan to disentangle her—disentangle *himself*, thinks Oliver—from Barton's avid interest? And, worst of all, what would Marian say, if she knew?

Oliver shakes his head. It is, in any case, a conundrum for another afternoon. This afternoon, he has miles to go and promises to keep, and he is already pressed for time.

He wishes Bell were here to help with the Waterford bowl, which is unwieldy and nearly slips as Oliver edges down the front steps, but by two o'clock he has loaded the van with the centerpieces, the calla lilies, the restaurant commissions, the Ochstein roses. When everything has been wedged tightly into place, Oliver reluctantly puts the CLOSED sign in his window, locks the door, and heads off into the Friday traffic.

First, he drops off the restaurant orders, mostly in Clinton and Chelsea, one in the newly happening Lower East Side, only a few doors from the Tenement Museum. Then Oliver fights his way over to Ninth Avenue and creeps uptown to Central Park West, where he endures a catechism of muted hostility from the doorman and is finally allowed to park—briefly!—in the precious space they guard in front of the building.

"For Mrs. Holland," he says, again, this time for the super, who is glaring at him. Oliver sets down two of the centerpieces in the service elevator and goes back to the van. No one offers to help. When he arrives at the huge Waterford bowl, they watch him lower it to the pavement and lock the door, then carefully lift it again. Then he walks gingerly to the back of the lobby with the arrangement in his arms, and the super takes him up.

Mrs. Holland awaits, stick thin in jeans, a white silk shirt, and tiny shoes that look as if they have been formed from Persian carpets. Her dark hair is pulled back in a youthful ponytail, but she is too immaculate to seem truly young. "Ooh!" She claps her hands. "Didn't they come out beautifully! Now let's make sure they're the right height."

Has she forgotten that she specified the height? Oliver wonders. Or does she think he doesn't know how to measure?

With intense care, he brings her Waterford bowl into the kitchen, which is already humming with caterers and smelling distinctly of recently cooked foie gras, and sets it on the counter. Mrs. Holland is staring at it, undoubtedly running the numbers.

"I found them in the flower district this morning," he says with practiced admiration. "I've never seen such beautiful callas. They were in Costa Rica last night."

This has the desired effect. "Isn't that extraordinary!"

"They'll last a good long time, too," Oliver says. "Just please, every day, recut and change the water. You'll be amazed how long they stay this pretty."

"I will," says Mrs. Holland. (She means, of course, that her house-keeper will.) "Well, bring the centerpieces in," she says, eagerly now. "Let's try them out. And the bride just arrived. I want her to see them, too."

Oliver moves the last of the bowls from the elevator floor into the kitchen, then begins ferrying them through the apartment: kitchen, dining room, foyer, and into the living room, which is long and lined with tall windows. Through the windows, the autumn carpet of Central Park is visible, like a private holding. The room has rich red walls and serious art—he recognizes a Chagall over the mantelpiece, and a large Raphael Soyer portrait on the opposing wall—but its customary furniture has been banished to another location and replaced by eight round tables, already beautifully laid, and chairs cloaked in white muslin.

"Let's see!" the hostess says, with jarring excitement.

Oliver places the bowl and plucks a suspicious petal. He wonders if she is going to produce a ruler, or a paint chip.

"Perfect," she says.

"Oliver," says someone else.

He turns. Matilda is in the doorway, her face alight. This takes him a long moment to understand.

"Matilda," says Oliver. He walks over to her and kisses her on the cheek. Then, inevitably, he hugs her. Her hair is disconcertingly straight, disconcertingly blond. He is not clear on how this has been accomplished. There are diamonds in her earlobes, one of which scratches him as he steps back. "I take it you're the bride?"

"You know each other?" Mrs. Holland says in great confusion. The florist has just kissed her future daughter-in-law, and her understanding of societal strata has, accordingly, been uncomfortably shuffled.

"We were at Brown together," Matilda says, still looking at Oliver.

"You went to Brown?" the woman says to Oliver in palpable disbelief. Was it possible to go to Brown and wind up a florist?

"I'm so happy for you," Oliver improvises. "This is wonderful. It's Mrs. Holland's son, I take it."

"Davis," Matilda says and nods. "Thanks. We were in the training program at Morgan Stanley together."

"Are you still at Morgan?"

"Yes. I mean, no. Davis is being transferred to London. I stopped working last month. You know, to concentrate on the wedding. I'll think about going back sometime, but right now...you know."

"Well, that's great. And you're looking wonderful."

Mrs. Holland, if possible, is paying even closer attention.

Her future daughter-in-law blushes. "Thanks. The wedding's on Sunday. This is the rehearsal dinner."

"Yes, I know," he says. It is becoming too awkward to continue.

"I don't have a daughter," Mrs. Holland interjects with a new familiarity. "I'll never get to plan a wedding, so I've just subverted all my mother-of-the-bride frustrations into this."

"Well, it's going to be lovely," Oliver says smoothly. "Now, if everything seems all right to you, I've got to go." He offers his trump. "Oh, I've brought you some extra flowers, just as a gift. I thought...maybe for the powder room."

"How sweet!" Mrs. Holland lights up. "And what about the bill?"

"It's here." He takes the envelope from his jacket pocket. "It's been a pleasure. And," he turns to Matilda, who is now looking as uncomfortable as he feels, "I hope you'll have a wonderful night, and a wonderful wedding. And...," he shrugs, "well, all of it."

"Yes," she says. Then she kisses him on the cheek, one hand briefly touching his shoulder. "It was good to see you, Oliver."

Oliver leaves. He wonders what they will say once he's gone, back down the service elevator. He feels deflated, another hole punched in his day. He wants Marian, her smell and arms and murmurings. He wants to arrange flowers for his own rehearsal dinner and his own wedding and his own life with the woman he is in love with. He wants to not be alone when he sleeps and to not sit by himself at the Pink Teacup with the newspaper every single morning. He wants to phone her and talk to her whenever he wants, and not only when it is safe to do so. He does not understand why he can't have these things, what is the impediment to them. He does not understand why he has just brought flowers to one woman about to marry, and is soon to bring flowers to another woman about to marry, and yet he can't bring flowers to a woman who is about to marry him.

Though he can at least bring flowers to the woman he wishes would marry him, and so he does, across the transverse and up Park Avenue to her limestone building, where he double-parks and prepares, still morose, to unload the roses.

"Hiya," says the doorman. Hector. Oliver, aware of the delicacy, gives him a big smile.

"Nice to see you, Hector."

"You staying long?"

"No. Just dropping off a delivery." He extracts it from the packing material. The Royal Danes are luscious, verging red to orange. For some reason they make him even sadder, just now. He would give anything to hold Marian in some private place and be reassured, but hardens himself against it. He turns with the flowers in his arms, ready to hand them off to the doorman, and then he sees her across Park Avenue. She is wearing chinos, a turtleneck, an overcoat of brown wool, and her favorite black boots. She is carrying a heavy shopping bag from Eli's and holding one hand over her eyes to shield them from the glare of sunset as she moves west, in the direction of home and Oliver. She does not see him.

Another punch, another hole. Oliver feels himself break up a little, both at the relief of her appearance, and at the wound of it. Then, forgetting himself, he says to Hector, "There she is." Hector turns. He nods at the obvious. "I'll just give them to her," Oliver says.

Now Marian is coming down the street. With the building blocking the light, she has dropped her shading hand and sees first the van and then him. Uncertainly, she smiles. "For me?" she asks.

"Yes," he says formally. "They're from Barton Ochstein."

This is said for the benefit of Hector, who now retreats to his chair within the lobby.

"Actually, he doesn't know they're going to you. He thinks they're going to Olivia."

Marian looks puzzled.

"Olivia. Your transvestite assistant?"

"Oh no!" Her eyes widen. "Oliver, you're not serious."

"Utterly. He's been very insistent. More insistent about this order, by the way, than about the order to Sophie Klein. He wanted everything—phone number, address. And then I couldn't take his money and not deliver flowers, so I thought I'd deliver them to you. Not," he adds quickly, "that I wouldn't have brought you flowers in any case."

Marian smiles, and then, for a moment—not long enough—they stand in perfect accord. It is, he can't help but think, like that first time she came rushing to his door, when they stood just this way in the thankfully empty shop, each knowing everything that mattered about the other, until he was able to step away and lock the door and take her upstairs. Now the unease of his meeting with Matilda falls from him and he looks at Marian with open love and only his roses between them, and all he can wish is that they were not here, on the street, in public, with no upstairs except the one where she lives with her husband. Then Marian sets down her shopping bag and takes the roses from his hands.

"I had no idea my cousin had such good taste."

"He doesn't," says Oliver. "I miss you."

She nods. Her smile falters.

"Can I come upstairs?"

"Oh sweetheart," she shakes her head, "you can't. Marshall's there. We're going to the beach. I just got food," she nudges the shopping bag with her foot. "I'm sorry."

"Okay." But it isn't okay. With mortification, he realizes that he is in danger of crying.

"What does the card say?" Marian asks evenly.

"Oh…I made it out to you, from him. I didn't want you to have to explain Olivia to Marshall."

"That was smart." They look at each other. "Oliver…"

"Just tell me when I'm going to see you," he blurts out. "I don't want to get pathetic, I just want to know."

Marian nods. "I'll phone you on Monday. We'll plan something next week."

And the weekend stretches before him. And he wants to grab her.

"All right," Oliver says, instead.

"So where's Bell?" Marian asks. The crimson petals brush her chin. "Doesn't he usually make deliveries?"

"He got food poisoning. At the Academy of American Poets."

"You're kidding."

"No. At the Langston Hughes tribute. If you can believe that."

"Poor Bell." They look at each other. There is nothing either can think of to say. It can't be made better, at least not there, or then.

"Have a good weekend," Oliver finally says. "Bring my flowers."

"I will." She takes a step back. "So where are you off to now?"

He sighs. "Ninety-second and Fifth. I'm delivering flowers from Mr. Ochstein, Fiancé, as opposed to Mr. Ochstein, Man on the Make."

"Ooh," Marian says. "The Steiner mansion. Take notes. I want to hear all about it. And what are you bringing her?"

He looks into the van, as if he needs reminding. "White roses. Icebergs. It's hard to go wrong with white roses."

"True." Another silence. "Monday, then."

"Monday." He wants to kiss her but doesn't. She goes into the lobby of her building, holding the roses with one hand, the shopping bag in the other. Oliver edges into southbound traffic, then cuts over to Madison.

Madison is packed now, with packed cars, children in the backseats, shopping bags visible through the windows. Everyone is going to Westchester, Connecticut, the East End, upstate, somewhere that isn't Manhattan, inching toward the exodus by tunnel or bridge. The pace, and the air of anticipated escape, is not doing much to alleviate Oliver's mood, and he is grateful when he reaches Ninety-second and can turn left for the much-anticipated Steiner mansion. The edifice looms high at the corner, a limestone pile reminiscent of a French château and every inch the building a prominent German Jew might build to establish his toehold in turn-of-the-century Manhattan society. How might Julius Steiner react to the news that a descendant of those hordes (those unwashed hordes, who had swarmed the ports in their flight from the Steppes and jammed the Lower East Side) now lived in his home and used his newfangled indoor plumbing? Suddenly, the distance Oliver has just traveled, from the Tenement Museum to the Steiner mansion, seems weighted with history.

Oliver double-parks on Fifth and climbs the steps to the front door, bringing the roses with him. There he hunts for something resembling a doorbell and finds one, finally, against a Gothic iron grating. After a few minutes, he rings again.

A woman's voice comes from a speaker: "Yes?"

Oliver looks around. There is no one.

"I have a delivery," he says, loudly. "For Sophie Klein."

"Come to the service entrance, please," the voice says. It is not an unkind voice, but it is direct. It has an accent, Oliver notes. European.

"The service entrance?" He looks around and sees, finally, the camera trained on him from an overhang. It is attached to a speaker.

"Around the corner. On Ninety-first."

Oliver walks down the stairs. The white roses are heavy, the frosted glass vase heavy, his heart is heavy. Why has he chosen a profession that consigns him to the service entrance, anyway? And would it have killed the woman with the accent and the camera trained on him to open the door?

He has to descend from street level to reach the service entrance, and when he does he instinctively looks around for another camera, another speaker, which he quickly locates. He is too tired to smile at it. He wants to set down the flowers and go home.

Hoisting the vase into the crook of his left arm, Oliver rings a third time and waits.

No one comes.

Now he is angry. Now the flowers are heavier, the speaker is silent, and the streets are clogged with escaping cars. It will take him an hour to get home now, he thinks. He hates the woman with the accent, and Mrs. Holland for being so controlling and for having his ex-girlfriend as an almost daughter-in-law. He hates Marian for going away with her husband for the weekend, and he hates every family in every car they'll be packed in with on the Long Island Expressway. He hates the Academy of American Poets for serving bad pâté and he hates Bell for being dumb enough to eat it. Mostly, he hates himself for being so intractably sad.

The door is opened, but not by the middle-aged person he imagines attached to that speaker voice. This woman is young, around his own age, with a thick black braid that wags like a tail as she hauls open the door. She also has thick black eyebrows and very pale skin. She is wearing, bizarrely, a green silk skirt, scuffed beige shoes, and a brown plaid flannel shirt, which is buttoned up wrong. Involuntarily, Oliver stares at the buttons.

"You caught me," the girl says, breathing heavily. "I was just changing."

He gapes at her.

"It's almost sunset. So I'm late. Yes?"

"Do we know each other?" he says stupidly.

This shuts her up. And then, to Oliver's surprise, she blushes.

"I'm sorry. What was it you wanted? Are you coming to dinner? Why didn't you come to the front door?"

Now he is confused. "I rang at the front door. But someone told me to come to the service entrance. This is the service entrance, right?"

"Right. That was probably Frieda, and I don't know where she is. Can I help?"

He nods. "Look, can I set these down? They're for someone who lives here. Sophie Klein."

"I'm Sophie," says the girl, and Oliver nearly drops the flowers. "Hey! You need a hand?"

"Just show me where to put them," he says, and she points to a long kitchen table, one end of which has served in the recent preparation of dinner and still bears carrot tops and odd spice jars. There is a good smell in the kitchen, Oliver notices. He sets down the vase on the table's opposite end, which is clear, and she steps beside him and leans forward, smelling.

"Oh, they're beautiful."

"Thank you," Oliver says automatically.

"Are they yours?" She turns to him. Her braid flicks with the motion.

"My shop. Yes. The White Rose."

And at this Sophie Klein stands up straight. "You're kidding me. *The White Rose?*"

This is Oliver's cue to feel smug, he supposes, but he is inexplicably numb. "You've heard of us?" is what he can manage.

"No. I mean, yes. Look, do you know what the White Rose is?"

"Well...what?" He stands there, at sea. The fact is, he doesn't really understand the question. He knows what the White Rose is to him, but that is his own meaning, and private. Whatever else it is, he does not know. And she, evidently, does, which has him off balance.

"I'm writing my thesis on the White Rose. Look," she says, leaning in again to the flowers, this time with her hands, "can I ask who sent them to me?"

"Oh, your..." For some reason he can't say it. He can't say "fiancé." So he says, "Mr. Barton Ochstein." He points to the card, which has eluded her.

"Oh!" She laughs, delighted. "So that explains it. He saw the name and he knew how much I'd like that. That's so sweet of him." She smiles. "Thank you for bringing them."

"Yes, all right." But he can't, for some reason, go. "What did you mean? About your thesis."

She looks at him. The misalignment of her buttons makes a pucker, just below her breasts. He does not understand why this is of more than passing interest to him. She has amazingly dark eyes, with dark circles underneath them. She wears no jewelry, no makeup. Oliver is having trouble getting her to mesh with the reality of her house, and her wealth. Is she certain that she is Sophie Klein?

"I'm at Columbia," says Sophie. "In the history department. I'm writing my doctoral thesis on the White Rose."

"The White Rose," Oliver repeats.

"Hey, are you Jewish?"

Oliver stares at her. "Yeah. I mean, I'm not anything, belief-wise. But I'm Jewish."

"Typical," she says laughing. "New York Jews. Deny, deny, deny... admit."

"I grew up in Connecticut," he says, addled.

"Then you have no excuse!" Sophie goes to the stove, which takes up the better part of a wall and looks capable of cooking food to feed hundreds, and opens the oven door. She takes out a large roasting pan and places it on the stovetop, then begins to baste two chickens, surrounded by vegetables. More good smells. Oliver has not eaten since the Pink Teacup this morning, and his stomach contracts. "There was this group in Munich," says Sophie. "Not Jews. They were university students, and they called themselves the White Rose. Nobody knows why. One of them said it was after a Spanish novel he'd read, but he was being interrogated at the time, and possibly he was trying to protect someone else, or just misleading his torturers on principle. The students were caught distributing anti-Nazi pamphlets at the university, and they were beheaded." Oliver realizes that he is still staring at the food. Now he looks at Sophie. "That, since you asked, is the White Rose."

"I had no idea," he says, feeling weak.

"So I gather. Don't you think that's sad?"

He nods, but he's not altogether clear why it's sad. He would like to sit down. Actually, he would like to leave. But he does neither.

"Sad?"

"That you're Jewish and you don't know that? It's not like there were endless groups of Germans protesting the Nazis. There were a handful. These students called Hitler a mass murderer, and they died for it. We should know who they are."

Oliver nods. "You're right."

"Not that it's any of my business," says Sophie, shoving the pan back in the oven. "I'm sorry. I don't even know you."

"I'm Oliver," he hears himself say. "Oliver Stern."

"From Connecticut."

He smiles, a little sheepish. "Greenwich."

"How refined," she comments, in her flannel shirt. "Well, look. The flowers are gorgeous. And I love that they gave me a chance to be didactic, which is what grad students live for." She pauses. "I'm sorry I asked if you were here for dinner. I just thought maybe you worked for Kaplan Klein. My dad sometimes invites people home on Fridays. He doesn't always tell me. Sometimes he even forgets, till they show up."

"You do the cooking yourself?" says Oliver. He is thinking of this huge house, the huge amount of money that bought and inhabits it.

"It's a ritual," she says. The gap in her shirt puckers and goes slack. "Shabbos is about rituals. Not that you'd know, being a *not-belief-wise Jew*," she says lightly.

Oliver looks at her. It occurs to him that he has stayed too long, far too long, that his standing here is wrong. Then it occurs to him that he does not want to leave.

"You know, I hate to rush you," Sophie says, as if sensing his predicament, "but it's almost sundown. I gotta scoot."

He frowns. "Sundown."

"Yeah. Shabbos? Sundown?" She sighs. "You know about that part, right?"

"Oh," he says, dizzy. "Yes. Sundown." He turns stiffly and walks back to the service entrance. Then he stops. It comes to him that he has something else to say, but he is not sure what it is, so he opens his mouth and what comes out is, "You're getting married."

"Yup!" says Sophie.

"To Mr. Ochstein?"

"That's the one," she says. "Do you know Bart?"

"No." Oliver shakes his head. "Well, just through the flowers. We…uh…had a little chat. When he ordered them."

"He's upstairs now, if you want to meet him," says Sophie.

"No!" Oliver steps back. This information, at least, will get him out the door. He has no wish to see Barton Ochstein. He especially does not want to see Barton Ochstein in front of his intended—but already betrayed—bride. "I mean, that's okay. If he likes the flowers, I'll look forward to working with him again. Good-bye!"

"Good-bye," says Sophie, reaching ahead of him to hold back the door. "Hey, can I ask you something?"

He stops on the outside steps, almost reluctantly. He is near a getaway, but what he's escaping is still unclear to Oliver. "Sure," he says politely.

"If you didn't name your shop the White Rose after the White Rose, then why'd you name it that?"

Oliver looks at her. She is holding her braid between two fingers. It snakes from nape to breast and the fingers rest farther down. Near her navel, he thinks. Near the pucker of her shirt. One of the fingers holding the braid bears a diamond ring.

And this is where it gets strange, because Oliver does not plan to say what he says then. He does not plan to do anything to prolong this strange interview or this depressing afternoon, and certainly nothing to bring himself, once again, into the presence of Sophie Klein, with her black braid and her engagement ring and her puckered flannel shirt and her laughable fiancé. But when he speaks, it is to utter a phrase that is almost sacred to him.

Or should be, he will later think. *Or should be*.

"I'll tell you," says Oliver, "when I know you better."

CHAPTER TEN

An Observant Jew

I<small>N ACTUAL FACT</small>, chicken is not Sophie's strong suit. Roast chicken, the kind of roast chicken she is in the midst of preparing when a vase of white roses is delivered to her kitchen door, is comfortably within her repertoire, but then again, it's hard to screw up a chicken. You just buy a halfway decent bird, shove a handful of herbs under the skin, stick a lemon in the cavity, and coat the whole thing with salt and paprika—no culinary art required, and no extravagant praise accepted when the chicken lands, perfectly executed, on the dinner table. Sophie is far more gifted with what her father has charmingly termed "the shtetl cuts." Certainly, she has more affinity for them, but the truth goes well beyond that. The truth is that it moves her to contemplate those homely meats, the slabs of muscle worked to toughness in life and promising only toughness in afterlife. Looking at a brisket does something strange to her—it makes her float, Chagall-like, above the ocean, the lip of Europe, and east, east, to the other world of her history and dreams, and into those rude kitchens of the lost.

She tends not to make an issue of this.

In high school, Sophie took it upon herself to become a cook, an endeavor that Frieda first met with great satisfaction. Given that their chef at that time, an irritable Belgian named Armand, could be induced neither to provide instruction himself, nor to relinquish his domain to an outside instructor, Frieda conspired to schedule Sophie's lessons on Sundays, Armand's day off. The person Frieda selected was a sous-chef at the Quilted Giraffe, and he favored, not unreasonably, a classical curriculum, somewhat adapted to the tender years of his pupil, beginning with breaking eggs and making roux.

Sophie got restless.

"I want to make cholent," she said. "And do you know how to do tzimmes?"

The sous-chef did not.

Sophie soldiered on through béarnaise and béchamel. She learned to pound a supreme of chicken.

"Do you know the difference between prakas and holishkes?" Sophie wanted to know.

The sous-chef did not know the difference. He had never heard of either one.

She became a competent, if uninspired, handler of the chef's knife. She learned to peel asparagus stalks, though no one in her family could abide asparagus.

"Look," she said, in exasperation, "I don't care about pâté. I hate pâté. Can you teach me to make chopped chicken liver or not?"

Frieda, by this time, was on to her, and Sophie was forced to endure a strident lecture, complete with cringe-inducing descriptions of Frieda herself at Sophie's age, a paragon of all that was charming and lovely in a high-caste Jewish girl from Berlin. When Frieda had finished with her slovenly ward, Sophie slunk off downstairs, irritated and mortified in equal parts, but resigned to continue her forced march through the Cordon Bleu. Thus did she learn, with competence, the noble tradition of taking a lump of protein and doing various things to it in the name of cuisine. But she did not abandon her own particular calling.

Not everyone was like Frieda, who had entered the Klein family as a nursemaid and stayed on to become the brain, if not the heart, of the household, a kind of spinster consort to Mort and generally—in every way that mattered to her—the queen of all she surveyed. Some housekeepers were present only in the flesh (morosely ensconced at their kitchen tables, flicking the pages of the *Daily News* while dinner warmed up in the microwave), or so servile that Sophie wondered at their being able to command a shopping list, let alone a household. But when Sophie met Ruchel Zakar, who ran the lives of the Gotbaum family, she knew that she had discovered her mentor. The Gotbaum girls were at Dalton with Sophie, two fleshy creatures starved by their terrified mother. From Mrs. Gotbaum they received infusions of Tab, thin-sliced Pepperidge Farm bread, healthful bouillons of chicken and beef and the occasional treat of ice milk. The Gotbaums senior were often away from home, however, and when they were, their daughters were fed latkes and stuffed cabbage and great, melting hunks of brisket, slumbering beneath mountains of fried onions. Sophie, who struggled in ninth-grade math alongside the similarly unmathematical Samantha Gotbaum, had the good fortune to be present at a study session on one of these occasions, and in due course she offered herself to the bemused Ruchel Zakar as pupil, acolyte, and willing consumer of her knowledge and food.

"You are spending a lot of time at Gotbaum," Frieda observed.

Sophie shrugged. "She's bad at math, too."

"Exactly. Maybe better you should spend a lot of time with a person who is not bad at math, too."

In this opinion, Frieda was—as usual—perfectly correct. Sophie got a C in math that year, but in the Gotbaum kitchen she perfected mandelbrot, shaped balls of gefilte fish in the palms of her hands, and learned to braid challah more expertly than she braided her own hair. Given the underground element of these dishes chez Gotbaum, much of the food ended up going home with Sophie, where it had similarly to evade the attention of Armand, the ferocious Belgian, but was ultimately consumed by both Sophie and by her father. By eleventh grade, Sophie had the parallel repertoires of a *bubbe* and a post–Julia

Child Junior Leaguer, as well as a math SAT score sufficiently high (though only just) to get her into the college of her choice, which was Columbia.

Her family had not been religious, at least during her early child-hood. Mort, for his part, had gladly set aside the holy books after his bar mitzvah at Baith Israel-Anshei Emeth, and Felicia—Sophie's late mother—had been the daughter of parents who despised religion, their own not excepted. Their only concession on this subject—to cir-cumcise their child, should it prove to be male—had been a matter mostly of conventional wisdom pertaining to health issues, and was neatly sidestepped when the infant in question proved not to have a penis in the first place. Sophie had grown up quite happily in a house-hold without God and his chosen, and she spent a decade at Dalton before she learned the first thing about what she'd been missing. Too clever to be taken in by some evangelist Jew in the park, too resolutely modern to hear the siren song of the Hasidim, she met her ethnic transformation in an Amsterdam attic, courtesy of ninth-grade social studies and its elective unit on wars of the century.

Not that Sophie hadn't known. Of course she'd known—from her father's lost cousins, from the *New York Times* and its Holocaust obses-sions, not to mention from Frieda, who had actually been booked to sail on the *St. Louis* before the family found an earlier escape hatch. But this girl in the attic, Anne Frank, so like Sophie with her petty com-plaints and outsized longings, harried to her death with such focused determination, just shook Sophie awake. Once awake, she could not be asleep to it any longer.

Sophie was then fourteen years old, motherless and newly pubes-cent—her breasts, that year, had grown woefully large, and she spent much of her time regretting them—but she had somehow missed the surge of sexual interest that now consumed her friends. Sleepover dates and locker-room discussions became something of a torment as she learned to feign interest in the evolving codes of intergender interplay. Although her physical dimensions made her, by default, a participant in the relentless word-of-mouth currency of her school, she could not seem to drum up much interest in it, nor in the boys themselves, with their scurrying hands and breathy compliments. She was, it occurred to her, the opposite of oversexed, whatever that might be. (This concept was never discussed by her friends.) The whole grade was hurtling, lemminglike, over the cliff of virginity, while Sophie hunched her shoulders forward and wished they'd just leave her out of it. No one seemed interested in any other topic. Even in her social studies elective, the teacher permitted (lasciviously? she wondered) seemingly endless discussion of whether Anne Frank and Peter Van Pels had managed to consummate their awkward attraction.

And in the midst of all those hormones, the strutting boys and suffering girls, the Jewry of Europe became Sophie Klein's fervor. That summer, she read Martin Gilbert through her habitual summer internship at Kaplan Klein (not difficult to do, as her post was receptionist to some vacationing partner) and spread maps out across the long desk at which she was stationed. She immersed herself in the accounts, the rants, the litanies of disaster and grief, and then in the rationales, excuses, justifications, and theories, that cacophony of useless assaults on the problem of human evil. It was not a summer's project. Even in its infancy, she recognized the shape of a lifetime's obsession, and this she accepted, though it meant that she must, as Rabbi Greenberg had duly pointed out, live the remainder of her life in "the presence of... burning children." (Holocaust scholars, as she would learn, speak often of their inability to retain less cataclysmic interests. It's hard to downshift from genocide.)

For her own part, Sophie had not been in the habit of dwelling on her losses. She did not aspire to victimhood—quite to the contrary, Sophie had always been aware of her privileges. She came of age with one of the city's worst public policies, which released scores of mental patients onto the streets of Manhattan, and she grew as familiar with the homeless of Fifth Avenue as with its liveried doormen and Yorkshire terriers. Every Friday afternoon, as they drove between the Steiner mansion and the farm in Millbrook, her father—somewhat illogically—took a route that wound through Harlem to the George

Washington Bridge, and Sophie understood that half a mile from her oversized and beautifully furnished home were families crammed into primitive housing, on streets lacking both necessities and pleasures. This embarrassed her, and when her schoolmates fanned out along the traditional hunting grounds of Madison and Columbus Avenues, she found that she could not join in their pointless purchasing. (The fact that she never bought anything was interpreted by her friends as the cheapness of the filthy rich, something Sophie would be unaware of for years.)

Sophie's father, a good person as well as a good father, knew better than to dissuade her from her growing asceticism. Unlike many men of his generation, Mort Klein did not need to be told that his child trumped everything else. They had dinner together three or four nights a week and always on Fridays, spent their weekends generally without guests, and vacationed together twice a year—or once a year, depending on who was interpreting "vacation." Of these trips, one destination (selected by father) would generally feature a beach, a cove, and snorkeling, of which Mort Klein was very fond; the other (selected by daughter) would prove profoundly unrelaxing. After ninth grade, Sophie dragged her father to France (Drancy), Holland (Westerbork), Czechoslovakia (Terezin), and finally, when she felt able to withstand the experience, Poland. For the time being, she avoided Germany.

Conscious as Sophie was of this historical suffering (not to speak of her own local poverty), she wore her wealth uneasily, but she was also respectful of her father and would neither insult nor reject it outright. Mort had not been wealthy until the middle of his life, which perhaps explained the fact that money had few bitter overtones for him. The son of Polish immigrants—his father was a tailor until the loss of his sight—Mort Klein had won admission to Amherst despite the fact that the uncle who drove him to Massachusetts for his interview had had a racing form protruding from his jacket pocket, in full view of the startled admissions officer. Mort was the first in his family to attend college, the first to live in Manhattan, and—over the following decades—the first to acquire wealth, which he uncomplainingly siphoned back to the Kleins of Brooklyn. (A younger sister was sent to Skidmore. A home for his parents was purchased in West Palm Beach. A cousin's child with Tay-Sachs received private care until his death, and a memorial foundation for research was endowed in the boy's name. Temple Baith Israel-Anshei Emeth received a Torah scroll saved from a Czechoslovakian synagogue.)

Sophie at twenty-five is a slovenly graduate student with a black braid, a half-written thesis, a closet full of flannel shirts, and an apartment on Morningside Drive. Mort at twenty-five was a runner at Chase Bennet with a new license to trade (he had studied at night) and a yen to get on with it. With three friends he formed a brokerage firm from a combined sum north of two hundred thousand but south of three, and entered the 1960s on a tear. Everyone got rich, and the partners departed—one to publishing (he purchased a lauded but ailing literary magazine), one to restaurants (three, all French), the third to full-time philanthropy, with a sideline in Broadway producing—leaving Mort to make his play for Kaplan Brothers, a much larger brokerage firm on the verge of implosion. He named the new company Kaplan Klein, and with its operations streamlined, it surged ahead and began taking on ballast: securities, commercial credit, planning, insurance, a groaning board of financial services. The flag of Kaplan Klein was hoisted ever higher atop a growing heap of conquered companies, and every time he merged or acquired, Mort honed his corporation and redefined its points of weakness (he was not heartless, but he was not sentimental). Mort's original partners remained his board members and—more important—his friends. He commanded a chimera of businesses that served one hundred million customers in one hundred countries. He resided in one of the city's great mansions, and on a four-hundred-acre horse farm in Millbrook. He was a congregant of Temple Emanu-El, at least for two days each autumn. Once widowed, he never remarried. He was worth, by his own CFO's best estimate, $1.4 billion, a figure that he himself regarded with some measure of disbelief.

A person with that kind of money might make an assault on the social peak of his preference, but Mort Klein did not consider himself a social aspirant. Neither, however, was he enormously self-aware on this issue. His urges were not exactly vulgar—they merged, after all, with his intellectual interests—but they were not plain to him, as they were all too plain to others. To engage Mort Klein, for example, in a conversation on the subject of the first Jewish families of the city of New York—his abiding fascination—was to become painfully aware of how deeply he wished he himself had been born to such a family. Mort belonged to the temple founded by the German Jews ("our lady of Emanu-El," according to his daughter), made prodigious donations to the charities they created, and lived in their only remaining private home. He was routinely inaccessible to an untold number of applicants for his attention but would clear his schedule to have lunch with anyone named Loeb, Schiff, or Sachs. In some Manhattan circles, Mort had come to seem the tiniest bit ridiculous.

Those who followed such things found it perplexing that Mort had not begun to relinquish some of his involvement in Kaplan Klein, given his unrelenting schedule, his single child who appeared to show no interest in business, and the now unignorable rumors about his health. Sophie, one of the very few people privy to the relevant details, hadn't asked him to slow down (waste of breath), and no one else would dare. Mort lived for the riptide of adrenaline, flowing from all corners of the earth to the thirty-second floor of the Kaplan Klein building on West Street, where he chewed an unlit Cohiba cigar and made, all day, decisions that kept him feeling creative and robust, if not exactly young. In the pantheon of contemporary American tycoons, he was a little short on personality (there had been no up-from-the-streets autobiographies, no dubious girlfriends, no public pissing contests), an under-the-radar guy with a whole lot of money, a small circle of tested friends, and a kid he genuinely liked.

Sophie, who had, of course, already lost one parent, truly loved her father, so though her primary home was the small Morningside Heights apartment, her weekends were dedicated to Mort. Typically this meant that a black Lexus would appear in front of her building on a Friday afternoon so that she might be collected for the trip to Millbrook in time to finish her preparations for Shabbos, but sometimes a commitment would keep them in the city. The commitment was almost always Mort's, since Mort sat on the boards of many organizations, for which he was expected to donate lots of money and attend the overblown social functions that crowded the pages of the *New York Ascendant*: the Henry Street Settlement, the UJA Federation, and the New York Landmarks Conservancy. (These were of his own choosing.) He was also on the board of the Museum of Jewish Heritage, the Shoah Foundation, and the "I Have a Dream" Foundation. (These were of his daughter's choosing.) All told, Mort's board commitments preempted a handful of his weekends annually, but he did not complain, and for a very good reason. Left to herself, Mort knew, Sophie would take nearly uninterrupted refuge in her flannel shirts and the Nicholas Murray Butler Library at Columbia—most probably both—but if she were conscripted into service for a noble cause—being his escort for the Landmarks Conservancy Gala, or a fund-raising event for the Settlement House—Mort could experience the rare satisfaction of seeing her dressed in appropriate clothing and shaking hands with any number of potentially suitable men.

Past are the days he griped about her clothes and hair, or begged her to accept the Bloomingdale's credit card, or conspired with Frieda to do something about her shoe situation. Sophie cleaned up beautifully when she made an effort, which she did of her own volition every Friday night (one of the major reasons he consented to Shabbos dinner) and whenever he made a special point of asking. Before the Shoah Foundation benefit the previous spring, she had walked down to Nicole Miller and purchased a sleek black sheath, which had given him his first good look at her figure in years. She'd had her hair pinned up by someone who knew what he was doing, and Mort even detected a bit of lipstick (inexpertly applied, alas—but you can't have everything). Sophie looked spectacular, and Mort had for once not minded seeing their photograph in the Style section of the *Times* that Sunday.

After that night, he made sure that the various benefits and parties were on her calendar as well as his own.

Not that the boards weren't a pain. They were a pain, and in general Mort held himself to a personal limit of five years' tenure, the only exception being that of the Landmarks Conservancy, which fed his great passion for architectural preservation and gave him intense pleasure. The restoration of the Steiner mansion—which, forty years earlier, had been carved into eight apartments—had been an act of love (expensive love!), and the Millbrook horse farm featured a huge barn rescued from Warren, New Hampshire. For the past several years, Mort had offered the conservancy the use of his own homes for fund-raising purposes (a privilege he did not extend to the other organizations on whose boards he served, much to their consternation), and the Living Landmarks Gala had, accordingly, taken place in one of the city's last private ballrooms. Few of Mort's experiences had been sweeter than watching his exacting restoration come to life with historically accurate music and flowers and a crowd of appreciative guests. Few of Manhattan's social events—the Met's Costume Ball, say, or the annual Frick party—had acquired such a mystique, or inspired such a rush for tickets.

This weekend, however, it is not a board or a fund-raiser that keeps Mort Klein in the city. This weekend, the injunction to remain has come not from him at all but from Sophie, or rather from Barton Ochstein, who has for the second Friday in a row diverted father and daughter from their habitual weekend plans by traveling to Manhattan. The upheaval comes not from Barton's presence alone—since their meeting, Sophie has spent many of her weekend hours with Barton—but the novelty of his appearance in the city. Last Saturday was consumed by an interminable meeting with Farley Burkowitz ("the Prenup Pasha," Sophie has heard him called, and after her experience last weekend, she doesn't wonder why), but Barton has placed himself at Sophie's disposal this weekend, and she is full of plans: Barton has never seen her apartment or the Columbia campus, never taken her favorite walk in Riverside Park (from Ninety-sixth Street, heading south) or experienced the otherworldly pleasures of lox, capers, and warm bialys at Barney Greengrass on a Sunday morning.

More to the point, they have a meeting with the rabbi on Sunday.

Even so, Sophie's mind is elsewhere on the Friday of Barton's visit, and the shortened October afternoon finds her—of course, in Butler, of course, in a flannel shirt—immersed in the first White Rose leaflet, analyzing its use of Goethe's *The Awakening of Epimenides*, Act II, Scene 4, and appreciating the thrilling audacity of the group members in using the poet of Germany's soul against its demagogue:

SPIRITS:
Though he who has boldly risen from the abyss
Through an iron will and cunning
May conquer half the world,
Yet to the abyss he must return.
Already a terrible fear has seized him;
In vain he will resist!
And all who still stand with him
Must perish in his fall.

So the hours have slipped past her, until Sophie (with one of those rude reentries contemplative types are prone to) makes an agitated hunt for her watch (she tends to remove it in the library; it interferes with her writing), realizes that it's nearly four, which means that she can't possibly make the stop at her apartment she'd intended to, and so takes off at a run with her hastily crammed bag to find a taxi. There must be clothes to change into at home, at her father's house, she is frantically thinking. There are groceries delivered already, according to Frieda, and she has bought two loaves of challah, even now getting mashed in their plastic sack between the books and her right thigh. There are always cabs heading south on Broadway, slowing before the gates of the university in the expectation of someone like Sophie, running late. Shabbos afternoons are meant to be busy but calm—anticipatory, Sophie thinks, hurling herself onto the cracked plastic of the backseat and giving the driver her address. This afternoon promises to resemble Lucy Ricardo at the chocolate factory.

The taxi takes Ninety-sixth Street across the park, rounding the corners like a race car and hurling her against the door. Sophie closes her eyes, oddly content now that she is speeding toward her destination, mentally running through her list of preparations: the chickens first, then the cholent, the salad, the table, the candles, and she has to change clothes, of course, and it would be great to sneak in a shower—the truth is that she does not smell very good. How could she? She has been in the stuffy library for many hours, lost in the year 1942 and the city of Munich and the heroism of her namesake, Sophie Scholl, who would be seventy-seven years old this year had she not been executed at twenty-two. Sophie looks at her watch. There is still time for the chickens to cook, if she blasts them a bit first. And she needs to call Rabbi Franke to confirm the Sunday meeting—after the chickens, after the cholent, before the salad and shower.

When the taxi pulls up at the house, she catches, in the rearview mirror, the taxi driver's expression of distaste. Taxi drivers, in her experience, tend not to like the rich, who probably do not work as hard as they do. When Sophie was younger and oppressed by guilt, she had sometimes camouflaged her address by asking to be left in front of Mount Sinai Hospital, which might give the impression that she had a stricken relative (or was, herself, a stricken patient!) but actually left her only a short walk from the Steiner mansion. Now that she was older, she overtipped instead, as she does now, before slamming shut the taxi door and tearing up the stairs.

Frieda, psychic chatelaine, waits in the entryway.

"You are late."

"Thank you," Sophie says, letting her book bag crash to the parquet. "I'm aware of it."

"You are the one who wants to do this! You are the one who insists on doing everything before the sun goes down, like somebody superstitious in a fairy tale." Frieda folds her elegant arms, but it is not possible to look very fierce in pink cashmere, Sophie thinks.

"I know, thank you. I'm hurrying."

Frieda trails her down the stairs, light as a cat. "A chicken needs three hours!"

This from Frieda Schaube, who can barely cook pasta.

"Two. I'll blast them."

"Blast them!"

Sophie turns on two of the Wolf ovens and hauls open the Sub-Zero. The chickens, wrapped in brown paper from the Vinegar Factory, rest on the upper shelf with a large brisket. Sophie scoops everything up and pulls out the vegetable drawer for carrots and onions. "Where's the garlic? I asked for garlic!"

"In front of you," Frieda says, sulking.

Below street level, the windows let in only afternoon gloom. Sophie turns on all the lights and WQXR, which is unfortunately playing Wagner, and assaults her chickens with oil and herbs. The onions and carrots and garlic go in the pan. The pan goes into the oven.

"Is that what you're going to wear?" says Frieda.

Sophie smiles indulgently. With the chickens on their way, she is very nearly calm.

She dredges the brisket in flour and starts to brown it in a large copper pot, cutting up potatoes and more onions while it sputters. Frieda sniffs. "Another of your inedible stews?"

"It's called cholent, Frieda, as you know perfectly well."

"*Cholent.*" Into this word is infused all of the disdain a German Jew can express.

"You could help me, you know. You could set the table."

"No. You know how you want it. I don't know the rules."

"I'm not a stickler for rules," Sophie says and laughs, opening a can of navy beans over the brisket and pushing the cut carrots and potatoes from the chopping board into the pot. "As you know."

She puts the heavy pot on the stovetop, turns on the gas flame, and sighs.

Sophie's version of Shabbos would raise the hackles of any observant Jew, and with good reason. She has taken from the ritual those elements that are meaningful to her (and those, sometimes, for unorthodox meanings), even as she neatly, indifferently, excises many others. The fact that she can rush from her studies to prepare the Sabbath meal and perform the blessings over candles, wine, and bread, then spend the following day hammering out a contract in the office of the Prenup Pasha would be nonsensical, if one were not operating within Sophie's private litany of regulations. Both Frieda and Mort have abandoned the effort to learn these, though to Sophie they are simplicity itself.

She is an observant Jew who does not believe in God.

She is an observant Jew who believes in Jewishness, which is not precisely a holy concept but is a profound one.

Sophie respects and admires the Sabbath conceit of the island in time—the night and day consecrated to rest. (She would argue that she does precisely this when she drives into Rhinebeck with her father for lunch, or switches on an electric light to read a novel.) But the Sabbath also serves her in a more private manner, which is as remembrance. Immersed as she is in one of the great desolations of the century, Sophie has found that—in order to function—she must store up her grief or risk being overwhelmed by it, unable to function as a scholar, and probably as a human being. The Friday night rituals are her chance to discharge the grief accumulated during the week. They are her offering to the past, in honor of the suffering.

She has explained this, several times.

She has now given up trying to explain.

Frieda, relenting, goes to the fridge and retrieves the lettuce, which she pauses to glare at, then begins to wash. Picking over salad greens suits her exacting character, so Sophie leaves her to it and rushes upstairs for the briefest of showers. Her old room on the third floor is trapped in the aesthetic of her Dalton years: on the wall, a framed photograph of herself and her two closest friends (Roberta Sarnoff and Philippe Labatt), a Jackson Browne poster, a set of vintage Dickens, unread, alas. She drops her clothes on the bed, flicks dejectedly through her closet, removing a green skirt and a respectable white silk shirt, and finds a pair of beige shoes from eleventh grade—a bit tight, but she won't be walking anywhere. She is just stepping into the shower when Frieda raps on her door to say that Barton has arrived.

"I'll be right down!" Sophie calls, though clearly she will not. She steps under the stream, holding her braid out of the way and washing quickly, then closing her eyes for a luxuriant moment. The chicken is cooking, the fiancé is waiting... everything ought to be all right.

But I was going to call the rabbi, Sophie thinks.

She turns off the water and steps out, and faintly, there comes the sound of a doorbell from two flights below.

Delivery? thinks Sophie.

She dries off, pulls on a pair of stockings, zips the skirt. She is just fastening the straps of her shoes when the doorbell sounds again.

"Hey!" Sophie shouts, sticking her head around the door in a manner unlikely to meet Frieda's approval. "Anybody getting that?"

From below, she hears the sound of her father's voice. Then Barton's.

Where is Frieda, anyway?

The doorbell rings again.

Sophie goes back into the room. She is modestly clad from the waist down, naked from the waist up, and her first effort to button the silk blouse is hopeless. In exasperation, she throws her arms back into the flannel shirt and buttons frantically (and, alas, inexpertly), even as she hurtles down the stairs to the kitchen, where the afternoon light is nearly fled and the chickens roast on, oblivious, and a man waits for her at the door, with his arms full of white roses.

CHAPTER ELEVEN

The Song of Songs

Sophie," Barton Ochstein says, "your shirt is open."

Sophie looks down. Her shirt is indeed gaping open between the misaligned buttons, and she notes the white flash of abdomen visible. She sets down the vase of roses and straightens up. Instead of undoing the rogue button and refastening it, she grips the flannel shirt, closing the hole. Her fingers are cold against her skin.

"Oops," she says.

Her father and her fiancé look at her uncertainly.

"They're beautiful, Barton."

Barton glances at the flowers. Then he brightens. "Oh! Yes! Good," he says. "I'm so glad you like them. I took advice, you know. I asked around for the best flowers."

"Well, they're lovely. I don't think anyone's ever sent me white roses."

"From now on," says Barton grandly, "I'm going to send them every week. Every week until we're married, and every week after that."

"Barton," Sophie says and shakes her head. "You don't have to."

"I want to," he assures her. "It will give you pleasure. And I hope you noticed the name of the shop."

"Yes," she says, with enthusiasm. "It was so sweet of you. How did you find a flower shop called the White Rose?"

"The shop is called the White Rose?" says Mort Klein. He is in his work clothes, but with his tie loosened and his customary bourbon in hand. Both men, Sophie notes, are drinking bourbon, from identical Baccarat tumblers.

Barton turns to Sophie. "Through my cousin, Marian Warburg. I stopped in to see her last Friday night. I asked her, what is the best place in the city for flowers now, and she told me. She has exquisite taste," he says to Mort. "Like her mother. Exquisite."

"Mimi Warburg," Mort says. Since acquiring his prospective son-in-law, he has become fluent in the various branches of the Warburg family.

"We were having a drink in her apartment," says Barton. "I understand she teaches at Columbia. In your department," he tells Sophie.

"Really?" Sophie considers this information. "I don't know anyone named Marian Warburg."

"Ah. Well, it's strange she changed her name when she married, but she did. Her husband's name is Kahn."

Sophie feels her breath catch. "Are you serious? Marian Kahn is your cousin? Barton, why didn't you tell me?"

He shrugs. "I didn't think it was important."

"But"—in frustration she looks at her father—"Marian Kahn is incredible. She wrote a book two years ago about an American woman in the eighteenth century, and it just took off. I mean, *everybody* read it, not just historians. She's one of the best-known eighteenth-century scholars in the world!"

Two blank faces. Polite, engaged, but blank.

"I've never talked to her," says Sophie. "She has her own grad students to TA her sections, and I'm in my own little niche with the twentieth-century European history people. But I'd love to meet her."

"Then you shall," says Barton magnanimously. "I'll set it up for you. And of course she'll come to the wedding. I'm her only first cousin!"

"Sophie, is that dinner?" Mort says. "It smells delicious. But you might want to change," he says, rather pointedly.

"Oh, of course," she takes a step back, self-conscious again. "I'm sorry, I was getting dressed, and I kept hearing the doorbell, so I ran to get it. And there was this guy waiting outside the service entrance with the flowers."

"Well, I hope the delivery boy didn't see you like that." Mort is a bit sharp.

"He wasn't a delivery boy. I think he was the owner. Of course I had to ask him if he named his shop after the White Rose, but he'd never heard of them. Which is kind of a disgrace, don't you think?"

"I think it's almost dinnertime," says Mort. "Or doesn't it matter to you anymore that the sun is about to go down?"

"Okay!" she says. "I'm going. Where's Frieda?"

"She's just gone up to change," says her father.

From something elegant into something more elegant, thinks Sophie.

She leaves them and goes back upstairs, clutching her slightly odorous flannel shirt and feeling the rasp of her legs as they brush each other in their unaccustomed pantyhose. Dressing up falls short of torment for her, but she avoids it when she can. Of course, she would like to have been born effortlessly chic like Frieda, or with the purported exquisite taste of Marian Kahn and her Warburg mother, but for Sophie dressing up for pleasure died with her mother, and—Frieda's and her father's efforts notwithstanding—she cannot seem to revive it. All she can manage is to dress beyond obvious reproach: wearing clothing that matches and is without stains or other blatant flaws, satisfactory underclothes, and classic jewelry in moderation.

Sophie retrieves her silk blouse and undoes the buttons, then pulls the flannel shirt over her head and finds a clean bra in her old dresser. Fitting the bone buttons on the silk blouse into their slots makes Sophie think of the skin she had unwittingly revealed to the man in the kitchen, and now it strikes her that his awkwardness might be attributed to this unintended revelation. When a person embarrasses herself, she thinks defensively, fastening Felicia Litkowitz Klein's gray pearls around her neck, people are supposed to inform the embarrassing person of the fact, so that she doesn't go home and discover she's got salad in her teeth or an open fly. But if the person who sees the embarrassing thing doesn't really know the embarrassing person, he can't say so, because it's too awkward to say so, and this man in the kitchen didn't really know her. Which is why it is so odd—it comes to her now, as she takes the elastic off the end of her braid and eases it apart—that he said that strange thing, about how he would tell her why he named his shop the White Rose, but only when he knew her better.

But he won't know me better, Sophie thinks, because I am never going to see him again, and besides, I'm about to get married.

She brushes her hair, which, unbound, reaches the small of her back, and places matching barrettes behind each ear. Sophie's hair is near-black and thick, tending to waviness except that its weight pulls the waves straight. She is not very creative with it. By default, there is the braid: ropelike, lying neatly between her shoulder blades. On those rare occasions when she appears in public with her father, Sophie coils it in a low bun and pins it with the heavy black pins made for old-fashioned rollers. But on Sabbath evenings and in her own apartment, she tends to wear it loose and long, only occasionally with barrettes, to placate her father. "You look like one of Tevye's daughters!" Mort once told her, with affection, and Sophie—deflated, now, as she recalls it—thinks, *Yes, but which one?*

Chava, who falls passionately in love with a Christian?

Hodel, who falls passionately in love with an iconoclast?

Tzeitel, who falls passionately in love with a nice Jewish boy who is unfortunately not the nice Jewish boy her father wants her to marry?

Sophie has never fallen passionately in love with anyone. She is too Jewish to marry a Christian. She is too conventional to marry an iconoclast. And she is, in fact, within weeks of marrying precisely the man her father wants her to marry.

A young intelligent woman who reaches the age of twenty-five without ever having been in love will quite likely have subjected herself to thorough self-examination, and Sophie is not an exception. True, it was not difficult for her to feel superior to her Dalton friends with their histrionic romances, but by the first year of college it had begun to trouble Sophie that she had never felt remotely histrionic herself. Her romantic history has been one of contrived enthusiasms and falsified ardor, with sex serving as a pretense of intimacy. She has felt no hunger, no longing for the quick of another person. She has not experienced even one of those astonishing moments when two people own the desire between them and lunge for each other. Fortunate in so many ways, Sophie understands that she has not been gifted in this one, and as a result, over the years she has compiled a commonsensical list of her requirements in a partner and reached the following conclusions about herself:

That she is not a very sexual person.

That she is unlikely to experience, in the future, the kind of rapturous attachment she has not experienced in the past.

That she enjoys the company of men.

That she wants to be a mother, and fairly soon.

That apart from becoming a mother, which will of necessity alter everything about her life, she does not wish to alter anything about her life.

It may be because she is rich—very, very rich—that she can think this way, but Sophie has given up imagining her life without the cushion of wealth. Yes, she can afford to be a graduate student—even for the rest of her life—though she has no intention of doing so, and would not be doing so for a single day if she did not feel her work was useful. She can afford to have many children and raise them in one of the world's most expensive cities, without the financial input of their father, whoever he might turn out to be. She considers herself fortunate that such a suitable individual has come, first into her father's life and then into her own. She considers that the match has all of the virtues of an arrangement and—given that her own passions are not engaged elsewhere, nor engaged at all—none of its flaws.

That these pretty roses have appeared does not surprise her; Barton's manners are courtly. They make her feel cared for, and they remind her of wooing from another time. They suit her own formality. Barton may not be very vocal, nor at all physical—he had not even kissed her until they were engaged!—but his little gestures, the notes and the gifts, have been constant. After their first meeting he sent her a letter on stationery that bore a line drawing of the house he was restoring near Rhinebeck. It said that he thought she was a marvelous girl and was sure she had many more interesting things to do, but if she thought it might be amusing to attend a benefit at the Jewish Museum in two weeks' time, he would be delighted.

"How old is he?" she had asked her father.

"Not too old," he answered.

The following week, Mort received his diagnosis.

Sophie had phoned Barton soon after that, mainly to put him off, but she found herself accepting, lulled—she would later think—by his evident delight at hearing from her, and the almost anachronistic elegance of his manners. The event at the Jewish Museum? Nothing, really, only he was receiving a small honor. No, nothing special. He ought to do more, really, only he was so very involved with the restoration in Rhinebeck, just now. But his friends in the museum guild, they seemed quite determined to do this silly thing, and for such an inconsequential gesture on his part. A little matter of his donation of some Warburg family documents. He was a Warburg—had he mentioned?—on his mother's side.

In the end, Sophie and her father had both gone to the event that evening, walking the short distance from the Steiner mansion to the museum—itself a former Warburg residence—arm in arm. It was Mort's first social outing since the confirmation of his illness. He was not in pain, but he was unsteady, and Sophie felt him tighten his arm in hers as they climbed the stairs to the lobby. Immediately, Barton had loosened himself from a knot of people at the far end of the room and come surging over, shaking her father's hand, kissing Sophie on both cheeks. Barton took them through the crowd, alternately protecting them from some people and introducing them to others, making sure that they met the museum directors and his fellow honorees, bringing them to their seats at his table. Mort, Sophie remembered, had been elated to find himself placed beside a great-granddaughter of Jacob

Schiff. Sophie had been seated beside Barton. He was almost inex-
pressibly kind to them both, it seemed to her then. Not just entertain-
ing, not just ritualistically polite. It was as if he knew what they knew,
what they had been told only days earlier, and was so solicitous,
Sophie thought, seeing to Mort's comfort, making sure that she was
enjoying herself, which she found that she was. A kind man, she found
herself thinking, watching him as he stood beside her father's chair,
leaning forward to hear what Mort was saying, listening through the
noise of the crowd, one hand on Mort's shoulder. She could do a lot
worse.

Barton wasn't handsome, but he grew on her. He had good hair and
strong brown eyes. He was without objectionable features—warts or
moles, extra chins, that sort of thing—and unappealing personal
habits. He had surprisingly nice legs—thin but strong. He was unfail-
ingly interested in whatever she had to say. What's more, he struck her
as utterly a grownup, something she had not realized she was looking
for until she was faced with it. With him. She had never felt particularly young herself.

There was no passion, per se, but there had never been passion with
any of the men she had dated. Passion, Sophie suspected, was in
reserve for her children—they would be the loves of her life, and she
could not wait for them. This man seemed content enough with what
she was able to offer. She fell further and further into the relationship,
until they were spending part of each weekend together and going out
during the week in Manhattan. My life, she found herself thinking,
could always be this agreeable. And then he proposed.

When Sophie goes downstairs to the Sabbath dinner, the aroma of
her meal fills the kitchen. The chickens are brown and crackling, and
she leaves them in the oven to stay warm while she makes a salad dressing. In the dining room, she is touched to see that Frieda has indeed set
the table, and rather beautifully, with some of the old Audubon silver
and the simple china of her mother's trousseau, a sentimental favorite.
The challah has been placed on a platter and covered with a cloth, and
there is a bottle of Burgundy uncorked. The strictly correct moment of

eighteen minutes before sundown has passed, but there are still streaks of light in the sky: the spirit of the Sabbath will be honored.

Sophie walks to the parlor. Her new attire prompts the spoken approval of her father and fiancé, and Frieda's terse nod of sanction. She brings them into the dining room. Sophie places her father at the head of the table, Barton at his right, and Frieda next to herself, then goes to the candelabra on the ornate sideboard and lights the two candles: *zachor* (remember) and *shamor* (observe). She waves her hands over the flames and then covers her eyes to recite: *Barukh atah Adonai, Elohaynu, melekh ha-olam, asher kid'shanu b'mitzvotav, v'tzivanu, l'had'- lik neir shel Shabbat. Amen.*

"Good Shabbos," says her father.

"Good Shabbos," says Sophie, kissing him. She kisses Barton, too, and then Frieda, and sits down.

Mort gets to his feet, pours wine for them all and performs the Kiddush, holding his glass of wine before him. Then he lifts the challah and recites the Ha-Motzi, tearing pieces of the loaf and passing them out. The challah, from a bakery up near Columbia, is not very good.

"It's not very good," Sophie apologizes.

"It's very good," says Barton, agreeably.

"No, it's okay. I didn't make it. I was trying to finish something in the library today, and I didn't have time." She goes downstairs for the chicken and Frieda comes to fetch the salad bowl, into which she glares resentfully.

"Looks good," Sophie says.

Frieda scowls. "Not good. I had to throw out a lot. You can't trust them to send. You need to go, yourself."

"After I'm married," Sophie says with a smile.

"No. You won't."

Frieda leaves, trailed by her perpetual huff.

When Sophie returns to the dining room bearing her platter of chicken, Barton is telling her father that the upgrading of the plumbing at The Retreat has been unexpectedly delayed by the nonarrival of parts. This would be of little interest to Sophie, except that their rehearsal dinner is planned to take place at The Retreat.

"Will it be done in time?" she asks. There are seven weeks to go before the wedding.

Barton shakes his head. "I don't think I can count on it. Naturally, I'm disappointed. I was looking forward to hosting everyone."

"We'll have to find something else," Sophie says, cutting into her chicken, which falls apart, emitting a lemony fragrance. "What a shame."

"We can do it at the farm," her father says, pouring a second glass of wine for himself. "It's not a problem."

"It is, though," Sophie tells him. "We'll be setting up for the wedding the next day. It's only a small group for the rehearsal dinner, and we can't just throw them under that big tent. I think we need to go somewhere else. Maybe an inn?"

Her father sighs. Like Barton, he is reluctant to lose the prospect of admiring guests.

"I'll look around this week," says Barton. "There's that little place in Stanfordville. The Black Horse? They do a nice dinner. And is it too late to add someone to the wedding guest list?"

"Not at all," Sophie tells him. "Who is it?"

"That nice woman I met at Marian's last week." He turns to Mort. "She walked me over here, do you remember? She said hello to you at the door."

Mort considers. "I remember meeting her, but I don't remember her name."

"Valerie Annis," he says. "She's a close friend of Marian's. She writes some sort of social column. I thought it would be fun to have her."

"Are you kidding?" Sophie is horrified. "That woman's a scandal-monger!"

"No, no," he says, shaking his head. "No, you're quite wrong. She's a very close friend of Marian's."

"But she'll write about the wedding!" Sophie says in frustration. "I really wouldn't like that."

"It may not be avoidable," Mort says. "We have to acknowledge,

Sophie, that there is going to be interest in this wedding. After all, you're marrying into a very prominent family. The Warburg name alone will always attract attention."

"Surely no one is going to make an issue of that," she says.

"Oh, but I think you're wrong," Barton says. "These things may not be of much interest to you, but to many others they are. Not," he says to his prospective father-in-law, "that the marriage of your daughter would not attract attention for its own sake."

"All right, I accept that. But it doesn't mean we have to invite them in!" Sophie objects.

"Sophie!" Frieda says in her melodic tone of warning.

"Well, I certainly wouldn't invite Valerie as a *columnist*," Barton says. "Only as a guest. As Marian's friend. We did have such a nice discussion, you know. She was terribly interested in you, Sophie."

Sophie sets down her glass. "Oh? How so?"

"I told her how you're getting your degree at Columbia, and how close you and your father are. That's such a rare thing, today, isn't it? Anyway, she couldn't have been more charming. And I thought, wouldn't it be nice if I could invite someone else besides all of my stuffy friends. Of course, Marian is far too polite to ask me to invite her friend, though I know she'd be touched."

"Bart," Sophie says carefully, "even if you didn't invite her in her professional role, she'd probably feel she wasn't doing her job if she didn't write about it. Please, Bart. Afterward, if you want to see her socially, that's fine. But not at the wedding."

He looks grumpily at his plate. "She said she would like to write a story about me. About my house."

There is general silence in the face of this revelation. Sophie, alas, sees it all.

"That's very nice, Bart," she says, finally.

"Marvelous," Mort chimes in. "Be sure to tell her what you've gone through to match that paint in the hallway. People have no idea what a proper restoration entails. They think you call up Colonial Williamsburg and say, 'Send me the Federal Green!'"

"Yes," agrees Sophie, "but did you already mention the wedding? Inviting her to the wedding?"

His silence is his answer.

"Okay," Sophie says, thinking. "Just...we just won't send an invitation. You can blame it on me, if you want, later. And if she calls to ask, I'll blame myself. If we're lucky, she'll be gracious about it."

Though the Celebrant has never struck Sophie as particularly gracious about anything. Still, better she be vile and absent than vile and present.

"Okay, Barton?"

He nods his assent.

"Okay, Dad?"

"It's your wedding, Sophie."

"Yes?" she says, trying for humor. "Does that mean I get to exclude all of your businessmen?"

He scowls at her. This matter is a battle looming, despite ongoing attempts at preemptive diplomacy.

Barton asks for more chicken.

"And when am I going to see that dress?" Barton asks, gamely moving on.

She tells them all about the dress, which is white and drops straight to mid-calf in three sheets of satin, flattering to her chest (which is large) and her calves (which are small). Barton will see the dress at the wedding, and not before.

"You'll wear it with your mother's pearls?" Mort asks. Sophie's hand goes to her throat.

"Would you like that?" she says quietly, to Mort.

"It's a lovely idea," Frieda says. "And what are you going to do about your hair?" she asks.

Sophie raises an eyebrow. "Don't worry. No braid."

"I should hope not!" says Frieda.

"But I like your braid," Barton says. "You go on and wear a braid if you like."

"You will not!" Frieda sputters.

"Thank you, Barton," Sophie says. "But I'd like these two to be speaking to me on my wedding day, so I'll put it up. I'll *have* it put up," she corrects. In fact, she has already hired someone from the salon at Millbrook to come to the house on the morning of the wedding.

"What else?" says Mort, as Frieda places another piece of chicken on his plate. "What other crises?"

"No crises," Sophie says. "Though I did get an absurd estimate from the lady at Millbrook Floral. And I didn't even like what she wanted to do."

"What did she want to do?" Barton asks, helping himself to more cholent.

"She kept saying how it would almost be Christmas, so we should do everything in Christmas colors. She wanted poinsettias! I said, 'This is a Jewish wedding,' and she just went blank. You know: *What are the theme colors of a Jewish wedding?* And then the estimate came and it was insane. Fifteen thousand! I'd rather do without flowers. Or we'll just buy some plants and put them on the tables."

"We most certainly will not," Mort says. He turns to Barton. "My frugal daughter. Get used to her."

Barton laughs conspiratorially.

"Well, okay. What about the shop Barton ordered my roses from?"

Barton frowns. "But that's in the city."

Sophie, lifting her glass, shrugs. "So? They delivered here. They can deliver to Millbrook. He can't charge any more than fifteen thousand, can he? And I don't think he'd offer us poinsettias, even if he is a bad Jew."

All three of them stop eating and look at her.

Sophie is aware, quite suddenly, of her own right hand, nervously testing the buttons of her shirt, which are certainly, appropriately fastened, revealing nothing. Not that there is anything to reveal.

"He's what?" Mort says.

"Oh, it's nothing. We were just chatting."

"About how he is a bad Jew?" Frieda looks horrified.

"How did you even know he was Jewish?" her father asks. "The delivery boy?"

"No, not the delivery boy. The owner. I told you, the owner came himself."

"Good!" Barton says.

"Sophie, this is very inappropriate." Frieda is shaking her head in little arcs. "You should not speak to service people in such a personal way. You don't go questioning tradesmen on their personal thoughts."

"Yes, I'm sure you're right," Sophie says quickly, wanting to leave the subject. "I won't do it again. But can we go back to the flower problem? I'm going to ask him for an estimate. Okay?"

"A Jewish florist," Mort shakes his head. "Well, why not? It's in the Song of Songs, after all."

"What is?" says Sophie.

And her father closes his eyes and intones, from memory, from years before:

My beloved has gone down to his garden,
to the beds of spices,
to pasture his flock in the gardens,
and to gather lilies.
I am my beloved's and my beloved is mine;
he pastures his flock among the lilies.

"Daddy!" Sophie says. "That was beautiful."

"I accept your compliment," he says, "on behalf of King Solomon."

"I can't believe you remembered that!"

"Oh, your mother loved the Song of Songs," Mort says. "I used to read it to her. She would melt, every time! Very useful if we'd had a fight." He turns to Barton. "Remember that."

"Oh," Barton says, "it's not necessary. Sophie and I will not have fights."

And this is how it comes to her, in a wave, in a sinking wave, pitching her back, even as she sits there and smiles her agreement. Because Barton, her betrothed, is perfectly right: they will not have fights. She can no more see fighting with him than she can see turning to him in passion, and though it has never before seemed to her a loss—a terrible, irreparable loss—it seems so now. Theirs will be a life of geniality and avoidance of conflict, of deferring to each other's authority in front of the children and giving each other lots of space.

Which is surely what I want, thinks Sophie, who now finds herself—abruptly, astoundingly—on the point of tears. Surely I can't want someone who'll make me angry?

She turns in alarm to Mort, who is nodding.

"No father could ask for more," he says, fading before her eyes.

CHAPTER TWELVE

An Unlovely Daughter

O N A SATURDAY MORNING ONE WEEK LATER, Marian walks down Madison Avenue in a fog. She has left Marshall asleep, or near asleep, turning grumpy in their bed with a comment meant to be positive and hauling the duvet over his head. His bad mood is a remnant of the party she forced him to attend the night before at the home of her department head, Carter Hawes. The party is an annual event (and indeed is the only professional event at which she compels Marshall's attendance) featuring food catered by Columbia (bad) in an apartment provided by Columbia (enviable) and a cast of Columbians, who are—one and all—without the slightest interest in Marshall: his life, his times, his work. Invisibility is challenging for someone of her husband's temperament, Marian knows, and she would not ask it of him if Carter Hawes were not so irascibly susceptible to slights. It is simply the lesser of two ills to have a resentful husband than to have a department head smarting at the nonappearance of his media star's partner, and it is only once a year, as Marian had reminded him—both on the way uptown in the taxi and afterward at Nicola's (compensating him his earlier dinner). Hawes, a specialist in the English civil wars, had been unprepared to see one of his rank and file acquire actual late-twentieth-century American fame, and was known to have thrown tantrums in the office over the media requests for Marian still fielded by the department secretaries. Marian walks on eggshells around him, but not out of kindness. She does not like Carter Hawes. She does not like his wife, a former graduate student in linguistics who promptly dropped her own life to marry him and has had absolutely nothing to say, on any subject, in any of the conversations Marian has ever attempted with her. Marian does not like the department, which is not even occasionally joyful, like some of the other Columbia departments she has had contact with, but seems to run *only* on internal rivalries and petty schisms. But she likes her job, and this is one of its labors.

Marian's destination is Bloomingdale's, where she intends to distract herself, until her lunchtime appointment, with the purchase of a dress suitable for a December wedding. She looks forward to this task with as little pleasure as she anticipates the event itself, and walks to the store accompanied by a grim internal monologue on the general subject of herself.

In the days since her thwarted weekend with Oliver, Marian has felt her most profound wants grow in opposite directions. It pains her now to remember how skeptical she was at the inception of their affair, and her defensive and nearly constant disavowal of anything he said in praise of her or in devotion. Of course—she accepts this now—Oliver has always told her the truth. What he wants he has wanted from the start: to be living openly with her in a committed way. And what, she asks herself now, stepping aside to evade the Whitney visitors crowding a street display of fake Prada bags, is so terrible about that? Whatever friction exists between them comes almost entirely from herself. So what if she stopped resisting? Marian thinks, slowing automatically, respectfully, before the former storefront of the late and much lamented Books & Co., now home to a purveyor of sweaters. What if she were suddenly unencumbered by the need to punish herself for *every* moment of pleasure, *every* surge of happiness, even for the relatively innocuous interludes of mere companionship, all of which Oliver gives her? How would it feel to be actually *happy* with him, to allow him his own happiness without automatically dispatching the bad fairies to ruin everything? Oliver isn't just lovely and ardent, after all, he's smart. He's thoughtful. He is drawn to beauty, but not for selfish or hedonistic purposes. He has curiosity about almost everybody, but he likes being alone. If you could subtract the troublesome, unseemly bits—his being the son of her oldest friend, for example; her being married and old enough to be his mother—then they are actually wonderfully suited. What are we talking about, anyway? Marian thinks crossly. Great sex? Interesting conversation? Warm mutual affection? Even Jane Austen would be forced to approve of them. After all, what did Darcy and Elizabeth have that she and Oliver do not?

At Seventy-second, she stops and jabs at the red button that tells the light to change.

She waits.

The thing is, thinks Marian, shifting her weight at the curb, she actually is in a position to make a change in her life. A comprehensive change. If she wants it badly enough, she can actually do what Oliver has asked her to do, and survive the aftershocks. This is true for a variety of reasons:

Marian has no children.

Her husband of many years would recover, possibly very quickly.

She can afford to be a divorced woman, or married to a man with more precarious finances than herself.

I must be the most fortunately situated adulteress in history, thinks Marian.

The light turns green. She steps into the crosswalk.

For the first time since falling in love with Oliver, Marian permits herself the fantasy of walking with him, just walking with him openly, on Park Avenue, in Central Park, even into Carter Hawes's sprawling Riverside Drive apartment. She seats them at the front table at Nicola's, where her neighbors and her Brearley classmates and the aging friends of her parents would drift past to their dinners, and imagines herself introducing Oliver to these shocked matrons and their husbands. Marian could have that. She could withstand the amusement her altered circumstances would generate—older woman! younger man!—because she would have Oliver.

But for how long?

And this, of course, is the other direction in which her mind has traveled.

Reaching the opposite corner of the street, she pauses to look in the Ralph Lauren windows. It alleviates her mood to indulge her dislike of Ralph Lauren (which dates to his massacre of antique quilts, for skirts, in the 1970s), but she cannot sustain it for long and is soon walking south again, moving among the slender, blond women of the avenue: the shopping women, whose work is to pollinate these flower-boutiques with money and bring forth the nectar of their merchandise. There may be a reason, it occurs to Marian, watching a lynx-clad specimen paused at the doorway of Frette, that these shopping women do not age, a reason that has nothing to do with exercise or plastic surgery. They do not age because they are not permitted to enter the decrepit years in public; after their flush is past they depart and are replaced by women so closely resembling them in earlier years that, collectively, they maintain the illusion of stasis. Offstage, somewhere, Marian thinks—down a private Hamptons lane or in a grand Berkshires estate—the prior discards patiently wait out their golden years in meek compliance with the bargains they've made. Their children grow up, unknowing, with a tag-team of youthful, look-alike mothers, and their husbands underwrite the whole enterprise, compensated with the envy of their peers and the eternal twenty-nine-year-old in their beds. How much longer for this one? Marian wonders, passing the lynx woman as she enters Frette. And what happens if she refuses to go at her appointed hour?

Marian, as it happens, has never thought of herself as beautiful. Awkward daughters of acknowledged beauties do not long remain unclear on this issue, and Mimi Warburg—legendary hostess—was brutally honest when it came to her only child. Marian's ankles were held to be "good," and her eye color "fortunate." As to the rest, all was camouflage and acceptance of what could not be controlled. *Accepted*, Marian thinks, pausing to consider the windows of Barneys (already easing into holiday mode with cues of red and green). She *had* accepted it, all of it—the ordinariness of her appearance, the predisposition to feel lucky if anyone showed an interest in her—and the odd thing was that she had not resented this. Or she hadn't, at least, until a man came into her life and convinced her that she actually was beautiful. Before Oliver, she might have anticipated the years ahead as something subtle, a gentle walk down an elevation so gradual she would not feel the passage. Now she contemplates the loss of her looks with real fear, and wishes back her former plainness. Newly baptized as beautiful, all Marian feels is a kind of clutching against age.

Marshall, to his credit, has never made an issue of her looks. When he chose her, when he made his declaration of choice, years ago as they were walking across the town green in New Haven, Marian understood that he had chosen a companion mind, far more than an object of physical passion, and though this particular pairing might have seemed odd to some of Marian's more cerebral fellow students— Marshall being decidedly more clever than intellectual—it was not at all odd to Marian. (Her own parents had not been particularly well matched in mind and ran out of interesting conversation by the time Marian was old enough to listen for it.) Though Marshall had been spared the rarified and socially ambitious upbringing Marian had endured, and though he was in fact far too arriviste to have merited the regard of Mimi Warburg and her circle, he turned out to speak the language Marian herself had chosen to speak—about music and theater, the love of her city, its physical comforts, its literary institutions, its somber but nonbelieving Judaism. These were Marshall's predilections as well, though he had not inherited them as she had. Perhaps she respected him for that, too.

Marshall had always had an instinct for the deal, Marian thinks, turning east on Sixty-first. In the early years, his covetous enthusiasms for emerging companies would terrify her, tied as they were to great quantities of their shared wealth, but he had seldom made a misstep.

He upheld a personal, somewhat idiosyncratic, code of loyalty. He labored under the delusion that his subordinates were bound to him by respect, and that the directors of the companies he took over would willingly work under his new leadership once they saw that he meant only to make them—the conquered, himself, everybody!—even more successful. Marshall had never played very well with others, it was true, and yet he had been true to his word as far as Marian was concerned. Twenty years and they still had plenty to say to each other, and knew what not to say. That, too, is a kind of regard, thinks Marian.

By the time she reaches Bloomingdale's, the Saturday morning crowd has reached near-standstill at the escalators, and Marian, as familiar with the department store's floor plan as her own apartment's layout, opts to cross the cosmetics floor and catch the secondary escalators in the men's department. This requires the evasive movements of a running back to avoid the fragrance hawkers, but she can't avoid the miasma of scent entirely. Marian is holding up a hand to dissuade an eager representative of Bobbi Brown when she hears someone call her name above the din and lowers her guard long enough to receive a full facial blast.

"Thank you," Marian says, automatically.

"Marian!"

It is Valerie Annis, trim in urban black trousers and bright red boots.

"I'm so glad you're here! You're saving me a phone call," says Valerie.

"Valerie." Marian's greeting is perfunctory. "You're looking well."

"Oh, I'm in dreadful shape. I'm getting a facial at Arden later, but I came for some concealer. You know, you can't do the kind of work I do without seeing it all over your face the next day. *The Ascendant* should include a face-lift in the benefit plan. I keep telling Richard."

"You don't need a face-lift," Marian scolds. "You look great."

"No, but this is what I want to tell you," Valerie rushes on. "I'm doing a little piece on your cousin. He's such a sweetie. Do you know he invited me to his wedding?"

"He...what?" Marian is aghast. "You're going to the wedding?"

"Why not?" she says. "We got very chummy at your house that afternoon. And I walked him over to Mort Klein's place afterward. Of course I'd been to the house before," she adds.

"Really. I never have." Marian looks longingly into the men's department, where escape by escalator beckons.

"Well, I always go to the Living Landmarks party. They always invite me. It's so gorgeous the way they do it up. And Richard loves it when we get old money and new money into the same story." She stops herself and gives Marian a look. "I'm sorry, I forgot about your being a Warburg. You're very naughty not to have told me before. What are you, ashamed?"

Marian sighs. This is a variant of the what-kind-of-feminist-changes-her-name? reproach, another issue in which she has no great interest.

"I'm not ashamed. But we're pretty minor characters, you know. Most of the interesting stuff was already a few generations in the past by the time I was born."

Valerie regards her intently.

What does she want me to say? thinks Marian. *That I bang on the door of the Jewish Museum and say*, "Let me in! This used to be my house!"

"So have you met her?" Valerie says suddenly.

"Who?"

"The kid. You know, the girl your cousin's marrying."

Marian shakes her head. "No. I suppose I will at the wedding. You know, Valerie, Barton and I aren't especially close."

"But aren't you curious?" she says.

Yes, Marian nearly says, but she assembles a dignified smile, instead. "I'm sure she's lovely."

"It's just so classic," Valerie says. "I mean, Mort Klein practically wets himself whenever he gets to rub elbows with you people, and here's his daughter marrying into the clan."

Marian stares at her, amazed at the degree of tackiness a supposedly sophisticated chronicler of society can attain. "Yes, well...I need to leave, Valerie. I don't have much time. I have to find a dress."

"For the wedding?" Valerie says eagerly.

"Yes, actually."

"Well, I'll come, too. Then we can have lunch. My appointment's not till two."

"Oh..." Marian thinks frantically. "I wish I could, but I'm meeting someone. A student."

"Another student!" Valerie raises an eyebrow, plucked to within a hair of its life. "You were meeting a student the last time I saw you."

"Different student," Marian says firmly. "But it was nice seeing you. I suppose I'll see you at the wedding."

Valerie smiles, showing small, crowded teeth. "I can't wait."

I'm sure you can't, thinks Marian, stepping away, back into the cloud of scent.

How dumb is Barton? she thinks, grabbing the escalator handrail in the men's department. Isn't it enough that he's blatantly marrying for money? Does he have to haul out a megaphone to tell everyone? Doesn't he have the wit to see Valerie Annis for the user she is? Marian frets her way to the second floor, where packs of pubescent girls roam the racks and the music of the nanosecond blares at ear-splitting volume. One flight up, Marian leaves the escalator and begins, dejectedly, to look through the designer sections. She has not been here in several years, and everything strikes her as too colorful, too insubstantial. There are miniskirts trimmed in gold, and hot pink in abundance, astoundingly expensive dresses with chunks of fabric deliberately torn from them. All around Marian, the thin blond women of the avenue lift hangers and consider the clothes (which remain tethered to the racks by their anti-theft cords), then replace them and move on. Marian wanders, idly (guiltily) wishing for the kind of Bloomingdale's her mother enjoyed, with elegant, matronly dresses and servile staff. Something basic! she thinks. Something understated!

Something suitable for a forty-eight-year-old woman, neither white-blond nor rail-thin, forced to attend the marriage of a cousin she detests and a girl who, sight unseen, thoroughly baffles her.

Is that so much to ask?

Finally, in the back, light years from the enclaves of the most lauded designers, Marian finds something she can work with, an unexciting crepe de chine of almost black, with sleeves to the elbows, a square neckline, and a hem that hits just below the knee. The dress falls close to her body below the waist, without actually touching it—a neat trick, Marian thinks, and not unflattering—and the style is so classic that, trying it on in one of the grubby changing rooms, Marian experiences an uncomfortable jolt of recognition at the image.

"Hi, Mom," Marian hears herself say, very softly.

Her mother stares back.

Marian's mother died at fifty of cancer, retroactively diagnosed as uterine. Thirteen years later, by the time of Marian's own illness, what had once been so horrific as to be unmentionable was actually considered a "good" cancer, or so the entire staff at Sloan-Kettering had seemed at pains to assure her. That the illness meant the end of Marian's desire to become a mother herself was, naturally, a sad thing, but given the multitudes of the dying (including the terrible fifth floor, with its bald and swollen children), Marian understood that she should feel fortunate. On the day of her departure from the hospital, she had shared an elevator with a small girl and a nurse, and a third person—a fiddler dressed in a clown suit with a cracked plastic bulb over his nose. The fiddler played them down to the surgical floor with a jaunty tune, and the little girl gazed up at him with a ridiculous grin on her face. Marian, afraid to look at any of them while they were so confined, stepped out of the elevator to watch the small band disappear around a corner, then wept.

But you don't know! Marshall had said that night as she tried to describe the scene. *This could be part of a wonderful story, about how she was cured of cancer and went on to live a long, happy life!*

Yes, yes, Marian had nodded frantically. Because she was in pain still from her own surgery and this was making it worse, and because having said this to him she wanted not to say anything else, especially what she was really thinking and really mourning: that the girl in the elevator was her own girl, and they had lost each other forever to the accompaniment of that happy music and that horrifying clown.

My daughter, she thinks now, still looking at herself. Who wasn't.

Not that I was much of a daughter, myself, Marian tells herself, beginning to remove the dress. Her mother's disappointment had been so oppressive that Marian took flight from it as soon as she could leave. Of Mimi Warburg's own sorrows and shadings Marian was ignorant, because she had not asked when she might have asked. And now Marian wishes, wishes, that she knew what it had been like for Mimi at forty, and forty-five, and forty-eight, a once beautiful woman with an unlovely daughter, a disengaged husband, and a rapidly dispersing retinue of admirers. The sadness of that overwhelms Marian, and she remains for a moment in the drab safety of the dressing room, fully clothed and seated on the stool. Then she picks herself up, pays for the dress, and leaves Bloomingdale's by the men's department entrance.

Now the day is bright, the air crisp, the fog risen and gone. Across Third Avenue, outside the movie theaters, lines of teenagers snake in opposite directions. Marian crosses the street and walks east on Sixtieth, quelling her nerves by checking her watch, which only confirms that she is late. It occurs to Marian that she has not specified what she would be wearing, or given any other means of identifying herself, but in fact Marian identifies rather quickly the person she is meeting: a thick girl with cornrows and a dark blue parka, standing awkwardly alone beneath the canopy of Serendipity. Hers is not the only black face in front of the restaurant, but Marian knows it is the right one. The girl gives Marian a half smile as she approaches.

"Soriah?" says Marian.

The girl nods, squinting into the sun.

"I'm Dr. Kahn."

Soriah Neal frowns. "Doctor?"

"Or Professor. Or Marian, if you prefer."

"Okay," the girl says, though Marian is unclear about which she's agreed to.

"I made a reservation for lunch," Marian tells her. "I hope you're hungry."

Soriah nods again, and again offers the half smile. "It's crowded."

"Yes, this place has always been very popular. I used to come here when I was your age."

She gives Marian such a stunned look that Marian laughs. "Yes, it's true. I was actually eleven once. It was a very popular thing to do on Saturdays—go shopping at Bloomingdale's and then come here for lunch. That's why I thought you might enjoy it."

Marian leads Soriah inside, making her way through the adolescent girls wedged tightly into the narrow aisle between display cases. The maître d', an oily man in a Hawaiian shirt, smiles insincerely at her, and after some dissembling, leads Marian and the girl up the steep stairs to the second-floor dining room. Marian shrugs off her coat, sticks her Bloomingdale's shopping bag under the table, and awkwardly takes up the menu, an oversized broadsheet in a Victorian font. "Would you like to take your coat off, Soriah?"

"Okay," says the girl, and does.

"They have good hamburgers here. They have chili. And foot-long hot dogs."

Soriah looks lost. "What are you going to have?"

"Oh, I used to like the burgers. And the frozen hot chocolate. I haven't been here in years."

"Why not?" she asks, and Marian shrugs.

"I guess I haven't had any eleven-year-old girls to meet for lunch."

The girl smiles shyly at her menu. "Did you say frozen hot chocolate?" She looks up.

"It's sort of like chocolate slush. Trust me on this one. We'll order two."

The waiter takes their order. Marian plucks one of the thick breadsticks from a glass at the center of the table. Soriah looks avidly around, paying particular attention to one table in the corner, which is crowded with girls her own age. They wear braces on their already straight teeth, and diamond studs in their ears, and full Abercrombie & Fitch regalia on their boyish bodies. Soriah Neal wears dark blue jeans and a shiny white shirt that strains over her significant breasts. She is not wearing a bra, Marian notes, but seems to accommodate the problem by sitting with her shoulders hunched forward. Though Marian has been edgy all morning, it hadn't occurred to her that conversation would be *this* difficult. "You know," she says finally, "I don't think there are too many kids who've read my book. Can I ask how you came to read it?"

Soriah bites her lip and takes a gulp of water. "Well...I go to this program after school on Wednesdays. It's in the Francis Martin library?"

"Is that near your house?" says Marian.

"Pretty near. I have to get driven home afterward, though. My tutor...well, she's not really a tutor. I mean, I don't need a tutor. I do really well in school."

"That doesn't surprise me at all," Marian says.

"But her name is Professor Reynolds?"

Marian frowns. "Professor?"

"Yeah. She teaches at the college up there? Fordham College?"

Marian bites off the top of her breadstick and nods. "I know Fordham."

"On Wednesdays we go to the library and get a book. First we talk about the book we read last week, then we pick a new book. And I was reading about a woman who got kidnapped by the Indians? In Pennsylvania? And became like one of the Indians even though they killed her family?"

"Do you mean Mary Jemison? In the 1750s?"

"Yeah," Soriah says. "So we were talking about that, and she said—Professor Reynolds said—she knew another book about a girl whose family was attacked by Indians, almost the same year, but this girl escaped and had an amazing life. And it was your book."

"Yes," Marian says. Incredibly, she has not made this very basic and very interesting connection herself.

"That's how I read it. I'm sorry if I didn't say I like the book in my letter. I did like the book."

"No, no," Marian says, beginning to relax. "No, it's okay. Most people wouldn't write a letter about a book if it hadn't meant something to them. Even when I get letters from people who hate my book, I know they've gotten something out of it, or they wouldn't bother."

The waiter arrives and deposits two immense chocolate slushes before them, each topped with a mound of dense whipped cream and shavings of chocolate. Soriah stares at hers.

"Isn't this dessert?"

"It should be, but for some reason they serve them first here. If you want to wait till after, though, you can wait."

"Are you having yours now?" she asks hopefully.

Marian smiles. "I will if you will. I never had much willpower."

Soriah takes a careful sip. The slush is so thick it's hard to draw through the straw.

"I'll let you in on a secret technique," Marian tells her. "Use the spoon until it has a chance to melt a bit. Eat from the top, then you can use the straw to drink from the bottom."

The girl smiles, showing white teeth. She is really sort of pretty, thinks Marian. But she needs a bra.

"What other kinds of books do you read with Professor Reynolds?" Marian asks.

"Well, I like to read about people's lives. I like to read about scientists, because when I try to read about the science on its own I get confused, but when I read about the person who did the experiments, I understand it better. We read a book about Rosalind Franklin last month."

Marian looks at her. "Really? And you understood that?"

"Well, some of it. But before that I read the book about the double helix? That the man who discovered it wrote? And I didn't understand that. So Professor Reynolds said I should read the one about Rosalind Franklin, because she did a lot of the work that the man used when he discovered the double helix, but he didn't give her any credit."

"That's absolutely right," Marian says, mystified. "Your Professor Reynolds sounds like an amazing teacher."

"Yeah!" the girl says, animated at last. "If I didn't go see her, I wouldn't know what to read. I'd just be reading the books in the school library."

"What's the matter with the books in the school library?"

"Oh," she says, "I've read most of them. They're mostly about girls who like boys, or whatever. Or basketball. I don't like basketball."

"But," Marian says, "what about your teacher? Can't your teacher help you find books to read?"

Soriah rolls her eyes. "You know, there's so many kids, and half of them are always taking up her time because they can't sit still or whatever, or they can't read at all, and she's just rushing around all the time trying to keep everybody quiet. So the rest of us do our work in the class but when it's done there's nothing to do."

"Has your..." Marian is about to say "mother," but she remembers Soriah's letter. "Has anyone suggested that you move up to the next grade level? You might be more comfortable with older kids."

"Oh," she says, offhandedly, "I did that. I did it in first grade. And last year."

"So"—Marian calculates—"you're actually in seventh grade."

"Eighth," the girl corrects her. "I'm in eighth. I'm supposed to be in sixth, but they're, like, doing two plus two."

Soriah leans forward and sucks heavily on her straw.

Marian sits back as the burgers arrive. Soriah picks up the top bun and coats her hamburger with ketchup, then she takes a large bite. Marian, who is not very hungry, watches her eat.

"Soriah?" Marian says. "What's up with your mom?"

Soriah puts down her hamburger.

"I told you. In the letter."

"Yes, I know. But why is she in prison?"

"Drugs," says Soriah, matter-of-factly. "Why's anyone's mother in prison?"

"You have friends whose mothers are?" Marian asks, treading gently.

"Well, one. But I know a bunch where their mother's not, you know, in the house. So they live with their aunt or their granma, or whatever."

"Who do you live with? An aunt?" Marian self-consciously bites into her hamburger, so as not to seem too interested.

"My granma. But she's sick."

Marian sets this information aside, for now. She is trying to get clear on the mother, first.

"What was your mother's sentence, Soriah?"

The girl sighs. "Fifteen years. Nine years to go."

"Fifteen years! What was she convicted of?"

"I told you," she says, looking past Marian again to the chattering girls in the corner. "Drugs. They caught her with crack, but it was her boyfriend's. I mean, I'm not saying she didn't use it, but it was his, and they didn't believe her. Or they maybe did, but it's, like, a rule if you're caught, you have to get fifteen years."

"Mandatory sentencing," Marian confirms. "They thought it would make people stop using drugs if they knew they'd get those long sentences. But I don't think it's worked out that way."

Soriah goes back to work on her frozen hot chocolate. "Hey," she says, "you can drink it now."

Marian tries to smile. "Told you."

"It's good! It's better than an icee."

"So do you get to see your mom? Do you visit her?" says Marian, stirring her own drink with the straw.

"Well, I'm allowed, but my granma can't take me, so I have to wait for the social worker. Maybe every two months."

Marian nods. "That must be very hard."

The girl gives her a look, distracted or evasive. "Well, yeah. Because I miss her more when I see her, which is kind of strange. And she's sad to see me. I mean," she corrects herself quickly, "she wants to see me, but it makes her sad. Because there's no way she's getting out, you know?"

Marian does know. Though the mandatory drug sentencing guidelines have been roundly considered a failure, they remain entrenched.

"Why can't your grandmother take you?"

"Because," Soriah says, "she's sick. She's got to stay at home, because of the oxygen."

"Oxygen? She has emphysema?"

"No," the girl shakes her head. "Bronchitis. It's a little bit different. She has a home health, and she uses oxygen."

"Do you mean," Marian says, "that she can't leave your house at all?"

Soriah finishes her hamburger and nods with her mouth full. "Except with the home health. She likes to go sit outside."

"But who takes you to school? Who takes you to the library to see your tutor?"

"Oh," Soriah says, "Professor Reynolds picks me up at school and takes me home after."

"Who does the shopping and cooking?"

"Well, sometimes the home health. And sometimes me."

"But you're only eleven!" Marian says sharply. "You shouldn't have to do that!"

It is, Marian knows, even as she says it, a ridiculous thing to say. Of course Soriah Neal should not be doing the cooking and shopping for her grandmother and herself. Neither should she have a mother in jail nor be living alone with her chronically ill grandmother. Clearly, this girl is dangling above the maw of the foster care system. For all her promise, Marian thinks, she is within a filament of being lost.

"Soriah," she hears herself say.

The girl looks up from her slush.

"Can you tell me why you wrote me that letter? I know you said that you didn't really understand Charlotte Wilcox. Did you want me to tell you why I think she was the way she was?"

Soriah looks at her decimated frozen hot chocolate. "I talked about it with Professor Reynolds. I really liked the book until the part where she goes to jail, but after that I just didn't get it. I kept thinking about the little girls. I mean, I knew they weren't her actual daughters, but they were like her daughters. So wouldn't they have been sad that she was in jail? And how come she just kept being so happy when all these bad things happened?"

Marian sighs. Herein, after all, lies the crux of Lady Charlotte: the separation of personal happiness from outward good fortune. It is as baffling to Marian as it is to this eleven-year-old.

"You know," Marian starts, faltering, "I think it must go back to what happened to her, when she was so young, and she was attacked by the

Indians. It might have ruined her life, seeing her family destroyed like she did. But for some reason, Charlotte seemed to decide that she was not going to be sad about it, or let herself be sad about anything else that might happen to her. Maybe she thought that she'd already experienced the worst possible thing, and after getting through that she could survive anything else that life could throw at her. Like Mary Jemison, you know? She had a pretty good life with the Indians, didn't she?"

"Yeah," Soriah agrees. "She got married and had kids, and all. She didn't want to go back to the whites."

"And I think Charlotte just decided as a little girl that she would take whatever happiness was on offer, at any given moment of her life, whether it was with one of the richest families in England or in one of its poorest jails. If she had gotten too attached to the idea of happiness coming from wealth or status, she would have spent most of her life feeling that she'd lost her chance to be happy, but she never linked those ideas together." She fixes the girl with a smile. "You know what I think? I think if the rest of us could be more like her, we'd be happier, too."

Soriah, unconvinced, merely shrugs.

"But it isn't easy," Marian continues. "I mean, there are things in my life I'm sad about. There are things in your life I'm sure you're sad about. It's hard to just get up in the morning and say, *Everything's great! I'm going to go out and be happy all day!* But then again, if she could sit there in that awful jail and write letters about how good her life was, then surely we can look around for things that make us happy, too."

The girl nods, but distractedly, her eyes on the tabletop. The waiter comes to ask if they want dessert. Marian and Soriah look at each other. Marian rolls her eyes. "You're kidding!" Soriah says.

"After two frozen hot chocolates?" says Marian.

"You'd be amazed," the waiter says wearily, taking the plates away.

"I didn't think you'd answer," Soriah tells her.

"I'm sorry?"

"I didn't think you'd answer my letter. Professor Reynolds said I should write to you if I had a question. She said you probably were really busy, because you were a professor yourself, and she thought you probably get lots of letters about your book."

"It's true," agrees Marian.

"But there was always a chance, she said. So I did." The girl smiles suddenly. "I never met anyone who's written a book."

"Oh," Marian says, "I've got a feeling you'll meet lots."

For the first time since their meeting, Soriah looks elated. She beams, holding this slender illumination of possibility, and something inside Marian cracks open. She knows that none of it is her business, that a child with an incarcerated mother, evidently irrelevant father, incapacitated guardian, and inadequate teacher has nothing to do with her, is not her child, does not require the crossing of this boundary, but the transgression has already been made, and Marian knows that she will honor it. Perhaps it will all end badly, and pain her later, but now it is too late.

"Soriah?"

Still smiling, the girl nods.

"Do you have to go home right away?"

"Right now?" she asks. "No. Not really."

"Can you come to Bloomingdale's with me?"

Soriah cocks her head. "You buying me a present?"

"I'm buying you a bra," says Marian. She signals for the check.

CHAPTER THIRTEEN

The Flower Issue

SOPHIE OVERSLEEPS: flat on her stomach, her arms wrapped around the pillow, the blankets down around her ankles, where they habitually end each night. Her apartment building is a prewar pile that overlooks Harlem from the heights of Morningside Drive like a fortified castle, which, in a way, it is. Though he did not actively resist her intention to set up house near Columbia, Mort Klein set certain nonnegotiable conditions with regard to Sophie's proposed apartment. These included discernible police presence on the surrounding streets and twenty-four-hour security in the lobby. Sophie's apartment is a sky-blue perch on the uppermost floor, indifferently furnished and decorated. For a woman nurtured in a treasure house of Belle Epoque New York, Sophie is shockingly unconcerned by design. Her rooms are nouveau-IKEA, faithfully transplanted from Exit 13A off the New Jersey Turnpike to her four-room pad, with certain jarring notes of Mackenzie-Childs-ish excess left over from Roberta Sarnoff's first, premature trousseau (Roberta—engaged twice but married once—took her Columbia B-School degree straight to Princeton, where she is raising towheaded twin boys, throwing fund-raisers for McCarter Theater, and having a grand old time) and an amateur but beloved still life of irises by Felicia Litkowitz Klein. At least Sophie thinks they are irises.

She wakes with a start, freshly tense though lacking focus for her tension. It is Thursday, nearly ten, an outrageous time to be getting up, without even the excuse of a wild night behind her. (The night behind her, ordinary to the point of sheer forgetability, involved the library, a take-out falafel, a recorded tirade from Frieda on her answering machine—this pertaining to the omission of certain of her father's Kaplan Klein board members from the wedding list—and David Letterman.) Now she is groggy and low, reluctant to begin her day and wildly unhappy. Sophie retrieves the covers from her ankles and pulls them up over her head. She wallows for a good five minutes, during which time she tries to think of someone to phone, but each of the few who come to mind are rejected in turn. Frieda is not to be taken on without a certain clarity of mind. Her father is, at this hour, at the busy center of a busy universe. Sophie does not want to listen to Roberta bemoaning the dearth of good restaurants in Princeton, and while it may be shockingly late in New York, it is still early in Los Angeles, where Philippe Labatt has gone to be homosexual beyond the ken of his mother. Sophie does not want to call Barton.

So she drags herself up and makes coffee and drops her aged Dalton T-shirt atop the teetering mound of laundry at the bottom of her closet and puts on one of her many (but one of her few remaining clean) Olga minimizer bras, a green flannel shirt, and her last pair of laundered jeans, which feel undeniably snug at the waist. (The falafel, thinks Sophie, with regret—so fattening, so irresponsible with that expensive Vera Wang awaiting her. And it hadn't even tasted that good!) She drinks her coffee, which does revive her. Sophie then addresses the *New York Times* with her habitual scorecard of "That's good news..." or "That's bad news..." Today, surprisingly, the good news items on the front page (announcement of new cancer drug, unremarkable free election in Third World country, cautiously optimistic economic forecast) outnumber the bad (dismissal of lawsuit against manufacturer of assault rifles, intention of Jesse Helms to run for reelection), and Sophie tries to harness the resulting buoyant feeling for her personal use, but with limited success. Something is not right, she thinks, eyeing the most recent of Barton's now weekly flower deliveries: white roses again, and just as lovely as the ones last week, and the week before. Or they had been, when they came. The water, she notes, is now cloudy from lack of attention, and there is a definite air of fatigue about the flowers, as if they, too, had eaten unwisely and overslept. Sophie notices a petal tinged with brown, then plucks it away. She picks up one of Roberta's abandoned mugs (chipped), and holds it between her palms, absently blowing across the surface of her coffee. Something is not right. And it is not Frieda, nor the omissions from the wedding list (not quite accidental, though she will claim accident when she returns the call), nor the fattening effects of second-rate falafel, nor even the fact that she has grown undeniably apart from her two closest friends, to the point that she cannot phone them and merely whine the way good friends can.

Beyond this, Sophie does not wish to speculate.

Instead, she proceeds to do what she always does, which is gather her books and her keys and the bag of garbage from beneath the sink (a onetime infestation of mice has made her scrupulous in this practice) and her elderly leather Coach purse, and leave her apartment, bound first for the garbage chute and then for Butler, where another day in the company of Sophie Scholl, her chosen ghost, awaits her. Ordinarily this prospect is a meaningful, if not exactly cheery one, but by the time she reaches the library, Sophie is struggling to allay a sense of aversion. She has heard of this type of thing. It is the fear of any scholar: the sudden loss of passion, the craving for avoidance of what had yesterday seemed thrillingly obscure. But she is overreacting, she thinks as she begins to climb the stone steps. These moments happen. They are the equivalent of hitting the famous wall in a marathon and a necessary evil to any worthwhile pursuit. Besides, Sophie can't indulge such whims today. The wedding has already significantly disrupted her work, and the weeks ahead promise only increased distractions. Tomorrow she goes to Millbrook for the weekend, and she will stay on until Monday to meet with the caterer—that's four days lost—and next week is already peppered with once-in-a-lifetime, make-a-girl's-heart-race appointments. And she is within striking range of finishing her chapter on the first leaflet, a goal she fervently wishes to achieve before the wedding.

All the more reason to put her head down today, Sophie thinks, hauling open the heavy door. She has organized her thesis into chapters that correspond to the six leaflets of the White Rose. (There were seven, really, if you count the final one, retrieved in shreds from Hans Scholl's pocket at the time of his arrest, pieced and taped together by the Gestapo, and claiming that a German surrender would not be a surrender of the people but of a corrupt and in any case doomed political power. Sophie intends to add an epilogue on this embryonic leaflet, the movement's own epilogue.) She is using the pamphlets to deconstruct not only the group's ideological positions but its biographical information, burrowing into each of the members' lives—so German, so young and passionate—to try to answer what seems the most obvious and ultimate of her questions: not "Why did these few citizens rise in protest?" but "Why didn't it happen everywhere?"

The door closes behind her on creaking hinges. Sophie stops. In the vestibule before her are her thesis advisor, Chaim Bennis, and a woman in a long tweed skirt who stands, head cocked, pretending to listen to what he is saying. This woman, turning slightly, proves to be Marian Kahn. Sophie stands awkwardly, unwilling to pass them, terrified to be noticed by them, though she has had a call in to Chaim for two days and needs to reschedule their next meeting. Behind her the door continues to groan open and groan closed, with people parting around her and whooshing into the library. Within seconds Sophie regresses from competent grad student to uncool adolescent. Chaim natters on, oblivious, and Sophie notes the impatient jittering of Dr. Kahn's right foot in a soft leather boot with a little buckle at the ankle. The buckle glints as the foot taps, taps the marble floor. Sophie is riveted by this, by Professor Kahn's boot in general, really by all of Professor Kahn's clothes. They are precisely the sort of clothes

Sophie occasionally tells herself she would like to buy—beautiful and sort of basic and well made—except that when she does drag herself into a department store all she ever sees are flashy, insubstantial things made for women without breasts. Marian Kahn's skirt is deeply brown with flecks of red. Her black sweater is simplicity itself, but looks expensive. Where did she get that sweater? thinks Sophie. If I had ten sweaters like that, I would throw away my flannel shirts and be done with it.

This makes her think of Frieda, then of her father, then of the wedding, then of the reason she has to cancel her meeting with Chaim.

"Yes," says Marian Kahn. "I think you're right."

Chaim looks across the vestibule, noticing Sophie, who gapes back, mute. "Oh," he says. "You called me."

She nods. Marian Kahn turns, looking relieved, as if she might now flee.

"Do you know Professor Kahn?" he says.

Marian and Sophie look at each other. Marian nods, gracious and professional. Sophie's mouth is dry. It is her cue to rush forward, hand outstretched, and say she does not, but that they are about to be related by marriage, can you believe it? *All these years in the same department and now this coincidence, except that for most of those years she was only an undergraduate*, and *no reason Dr. Kahn should be aware of someone working in the twentieth century, but she is happy to meet, finally! And Bart has told her so much!* Et cetera.

She says none of these things. She is pathetic and only nods. Of course she knows Professor Kahn.

Professor Kahn, seizing her chance, says good-bye to them both, with an ego-stroking comment to Chaim about some departmental fire he has tamped, and a smooth "nice to have met you" for Sophie. Then she moves away and into the library proper, her beautiful skirt lifting behind her, her soft boots making soft sounds on the marble floor.

"You called me?" her advisor says, newly gruff.

Sophie, deflated, manages a nod. "I need to reschedule Monday. I'm going to be out of town."

"Fine," he says. He begins to turn away, not so much brusque as distracted.

"And the AHA took my paper. I heard last week."

This stops him. Chaim had primed her for failure. He had advised her to begin with a smaller conference, a more specialized conference, and not the mighty American Historical Association's annual summit. This, moreover, is her first attempt. And she isn't even on the job market yet.

"Well," says Chaim. "This is news."

Sophie nods. "Yes. I'm pleased."

"But your wedding. You won't have time to prepare."

"No, I'm all right. I'm going to do leaflet three. That chapter's already finished. I just have to pull an excerpt that meets the length guidelines."

He considers. A moment too long.

It occurs to Sophie that he is searching for something else, some other problem or impediment she hasn't thought of, and that he wants very much to find it but can't. Finally, he backs up against the door to the reading room, pushing it open. "Fine," says Chaim. "You coming in?"

Sophie looks past him. She can see the reading room with its long tables and glowing terminals, the undergraduates and grad students, a hive of sweat and concentration and pheromones and competition, all grindingly familiar. It is the scene of her year, and last year, and the last six years. She thinks of Marian Kahn, already in there, already at work, most likely, far off in her own chosen century. Sophie feels herself step back.

"No," she says.

Chaim turns without another word and leaves. Sophie is not even important enough to be considered odd.

She stands there for another moment, uncertain, the foot traffic parting around her. Someone actually walks into her and veers off without apology. It is incredibly hot in here, she thinks. Why does it need to be so hot? For the books?

Her Coach bag eats into her shoulder.

She steps out of the path of entering students and watches them blankly for a moment, and then she leaves the building and sits, bewildered, on one of the steps, gazing out across College Walk to the old statue of Alma Mater. Sanguine knowledge, Sophie thinks, looking her over. The great bronze woman sits in a chair reading a book and holding a scepter. There's supposed to be an owl hidden somewhere in the folds of her gown, and campus legend says that the first member of an incoming class to locate the thing is fated to become class valedictorian. It's hard to find, however, at least for Columbia students; schoolchildren apparently locate it instantly. Sophie, for her own part, has never looked, and she has no idea who her class's valedictorian was.

The symbolism here is not exactly obscure. The owl, Athena's familiar, represents wisdom. Sophie's own name means wisdom, too, a notion that has always struck her as bizarre, given that she does not feel remotely wise. Her knowledge is so specific, so bordered, and she has—it is humiliating to admit—a profound lack of interest in most everything else, allowing whole sections of the *New York Times* to go unread on a daily basis. She has no business representing her university and her field at a place like the AHA, Sophie thinks suddenly. She has no business even being called Sophie. What were they thinking when they named her? Perhaps she should change her name after the wedding. To Mrs. Barton Ochstein? And what does *Barton* mean?

It strikes Sophie then that she is under a kind of siege, that something is wending its way through her. And she does not know what to do about it, short of abstaining from human contact until it has safely passed. She does not want to discuss it, with anyone. Because she has been so fortunate, the notion of complaint offends her.

Sophie gets to her feet and slings her burdensome bag over her shoulder. College Walk, and the open plazas on either side, are crowded with kids, chattering, laboring beneath their own heavy book bags—all of them going somewhere important, or at least important to them.

Well, fine, she scolds herself. So you don't want to go to the library, one day out of your life—so what? People do it all the time, play hooky, see a movie in the middle of the day. New York is full of people seeing movies in the middle of the day! Isn't there a Woody Allen movie where people see a movie in the middle of the day?

Sophie has no desire to go to a movie. She can't bear not to accomplish something, not to salvage something.

You're a woman about to be married! Sophie thinks. There must be *something*.

Sophie frowns. There is indeed something. There is the flower issue, which she has allowed to idle, unattended, after making very opinionated pronouncements to her family. The woman from Millbrook Floral had indeed been dispatched the next day—and how much fun was that? Sophie thinks, remembering the icy silence coming from the phone—but she has done nothing about it since, and the wedding is now six weeks away. What kind of self-respecting Jewish bride is she, anyway?

She descends the steps, newly motivated. This is the problem for the day. This is the thing she will go to sleep tonight not having to do in the morning. Today. Right now. Taken care of. Done.

Of course she remembers the name of the shop, but she has no idea where it's located. Sophie walks west to Broadway, finds a phone booth near the 116th Street station, and thumbs the limp (and faintly malodorous) pages of the phone book to locate the listing: 22 Commerce Street, it says. But where is Commerce Street?

She puts a quarter into the phone and punches in the numbers. It has barely rung once when a man's voice says, "White Rose!"

Not the same man, Sophie immediately thinks.

"Where are you located?" says Sophie.

"Twenty-two Commerce Street," he says, hearty but distracted. Not the same man, she thinks again.

"Yes...but where is Commerce Street, exactly?"

"You know the Cherry Lane Theatre?" The man who isn't the same man says. "Off Bleecker?"

"Yeah," she lies. She knows where Bleecker is, more or less.

"We're right next door," he says, triumphant.

"Okay," says Sophie. "Thank you."

He hangs up. Sophie goes down into the subway and gets on the number 9, filled with purpose. She is hurtling down the island, her destination a street so obscure she has never even heard of it, despite the fact that she has lived her entire life within six miles of the place. Where else in the world can you say that? she thinks with a twisted kind of pride. And when she gets there she will make decisions and issue instructions and take care of things, or at least this one thing. *Oh, I took care of that*, she will say to Frieda or Barton or her father, whichever one of them asks first. *What else?*

The subway screeches and stops. She gets to her feet and leaves, blinking toward daylight. It is nearly noon.

Above ground, the streets fan out in a disjointed fashion. Twice she backtracks, unsure of which direction she is headed, then of which direction she is supposed to be headed. Bleecker, easily found, proves baffling after the first several blocks when it bends unexpectedly to the left, and after a few minutes Sophie steps into an art gallery to ask where the theater is, but unfortunately the woman sends her to the Minetta Lane Theatre, and when she arrives there she is forced to ask again for the Cherry Lane Theatre and then retrace her steps nearly all the way back, which leaves her overheated and annoyed. She is also hungry, but she is ignoring that fact for the present, stomping past restaurants and cafés in her pursuit of Commerce Street, the Cherry Lane Theatre (and why is the Cherry Lane Theatre on *Commerce* Street? Why is it not, then, the *Commerce Street Theatre*?) and the one particular flower shop, out of all the hundreds of flower shops in the city, that she has whimsically decided is the only one capable of providing flowers for her wedding.

By the time she finds the street, and the shop, her mood is so foul that she nearly refuses to enter, but there are white roses in the window, masses of them in a great black urn, more lovely even than the roses that arrived for her three weeks earlier, and have arrived every week since, and she takes a moment to simply look at them, and to think—for the first time in many months—of the mystery of her own White Rose and how it was named. Was it purity? The Virgin Mary?

The armies of York in their battle with Somerset? Or did one of those people, those heroes, those *kids*, simply think—in the midst of so much ugliness—of this lovely flower, and clutch at its beauty?

Sophie is so consumed by these thoughts that she nearly forgets her banal errand, and it is only the opening door of the shop that breaks her reverie. A man leans out—indeed, a different man—with very black skin and long Rasta dreadlocks. He is grinning so broadly she thinks for an instant that he must know her.

"Aw, come on," he laughs. "I won't bite you."

Sophie, somewhat abashed, climbs the steps and takes the door from his hand.

"I saw you skulking out there!" the man says. "Now don't be shy. Are you looking for something special?"

"Oh...no," she says, following him inside. "Well, not *something*. I'm looking for..." And she hesitates, because now she can't remember his name, though he said it in her kitchen, and more than once.

"Oliver?" the man suggests, and Sophie smiles in relief. Of course! Oliver!

"Is he here?" she says, looking around.

"No. But he should be, any minute. He had to go back to Fischer & Page. He needed more dahlias."

"Oh," Sophie says. "Well, I guess I can wait."

"I insist upon it!" the man says delightedly. "I'm Bell."

Sophie holds out her hand. "Sophie Klein."

He grins, holding it a little longer than necessary. "Sophie," Bell says, with feeling. "Well. I'm extremely glad to meet you. Does Oliver know you're coming?"

"Oh no," she says and shakes her head. "I guess I should have warned him."

"Don't be silly!" he says. "*You* don't need an appointment."

Instinctively, she takes offense at this. Certainly there are other children of other extremely rich parents who go about requesting special privileges, but she has never been one, and she does not like that Bell, whom she has only just met after all, would make such an assumption.

She considers that Oliver must have bragged to his employee about his standing order of flowers for Mort Klein's daughter. This is unsettling.

"Have a seat," says Bell. "Stay a while. You want some coffee?"

She wants lunch, Sophie thinks. And a bathroom. "No," she tells him. "Thanks."

"And tell me everything," he says, nudging aside some exotic-looking pink blooms and leaning forward across the table. "Because our friend Oliver hasn't said a word about you. Soul of discretion!"

Evidently untrue, thinks Sophie, letting her bag crash to the wooden floor. Not if his employee already knows who she is. She looks around. The refrigerator is filled with puffy blue hydrangeas. At least she thinks they are hydrangeas. "Are those hydrangeas?" Sophie asks.

"Spider chrysanthemum," Bell says, turning to look. "I take it you're not a flower person?"

"Not really," Sophie says.

"So where'd you meet up with Oliver, then?"

"Oh," she says brightly, "he brought me some roses. White roses. I don't know what kind. They were really beautiful."

Bell nods. His dreadlocks bounce against his shoulders. "Don't doubt it. Florally speaking he's a total fascist." He looks down at the flowers on the table and sighs. "Hey, I like flowers! I work in a flower shop, I look at them all day, I talk about them all day. But Oliver, he's hardwired for flowers. And what a snob! The guy won't even allow a carnation in the shop."

"What, not even on Saint Patrick's Day?" Sophie laughs, despite herself.

"*Especially* not on Saint Patrick's Day!" Bell says. "You should hear him. 'People get the flowers they deserve!' If somebody wants to go around wearing a spray-painted carnation, what more is there to say?" He shakes his head. "You sure you don't want that coffee?"

"Okay," she says. "Thanks. Milk and sugar, please."

He goes into a back room and returns with a mug for her. It steams invitingly and says ELLE DECOR in fat red letters.

"Thanks," says Sophie, taking it. "*Elle Decor*?"

"Yeah. They did a piece on the shop. Didn't he tell you?"

She shakes her head and sips. She is not a coffee aficionado, but this is heavenly.

"Really? I'm surprised. Oliver's not that modest, you know. Not about the shop, anyway." He peers at her. "Hey," he frowns suddenly. "Look, I'm not being a total asshole here, am I? I mean, it's you, right? The mystery woman?"

Sophie considers this question. Her first response is baffling disappointment. Then she is at least relieved that Oliver has not bragged about providing flowers to Mort Klein's daughter. Then, to her increasing distress, she feels deflated again. She sets her mug on the table between them. "Sorry," she says, "but I just came to talk about flowers. For my wedding."

Bell goes stiff. "Your wedding? As in ... your wedding to somebody who is not the person we've just been talking about?"

Sophie nods. "I've only ever met the guy once. Oliver, I mean."

Bell is covering his face with his hands. "Oh *man*," he says. "I'm ... look, I saw you outside and you said you were here to see Oliver ... I don't know, I was sure it was you. He's so damn mysterious! I mean, this guy's been off his head for months about some woman, but he never brings her when we go out, and he won't tell me a thing! She's got to be either married or a movie star."

"Maybe married *and* a movie star," Sophie says, still vaguely depressed. "Are you sure she even exists?"

"*Oh* yeah," he sighs. "Even if he didn't walk around with his head on another planet or race upstairs whenever his phone rings, you *know* when Oliver Stern walks out of here with the best flowers, it's got to be serious."

"I would say so," agrees Sophie, "but it's got nothing to do with me, I can promise you."

Bell shakes his head. "Look, let me make it up to you. Can I take you to dinner? I've got a friend who's sous-chef at Alison on Dominick. He can always get me in."

Sophie looks at him and bursts into laughter. "I'm *engaged. Remember?*"

"What's a little engagement between friends?" He raises an eyebrow. "You gotta eat, right?"

"Right. And thanks," says Sophie. "But—and I mean this sincerely—no thanks."

Behind her, the door opens and a waft of cold November air enters the room. Sophie turns to find Oliver stuck in the doorway, as if the new chill had iced him to the floorboards, and looking at the two of them with a kind of pained stupefaction.

"Asshole," Bell says, breaking this impasse. "I thought she was your girlfriend."

Oliver's eyes widen. "She's engaged," he says, baffled. "I mean, you're engaged, right?"

Sophie nods.

"So what are you doing here?"

"She's here about flowers. Asshole!" Bell grins. "Why else would she be here?"

"Stop calling me asshole," Oliver says tersely.

"For the *wedding*," Bell adds. And then, for emphasis, "Asshole."

"Gee," Sophie says, "it must be a load of fun to work here. You guys clearly get along great."

Oliver closes the door behind him. "I apologize. For him, too. I'm just surprised to see you here."

"Why? Those roses were beautiful. And the woman I was talking to in Millbrook wanted to charge me a fortune for poinsettias."

Oliver raises his eyebrows. "You want poinsettias? For your wedding?"

"No," Sophie says. "That's the point. She just assumed. You know, Christmas wedding equals poinsettias? Like I'm going to be dressed up in green fur with a sprig of holly in my hair? You know, not everyone in Millbrook's a WASP!"

"That's not what I heard," says Bell, laughing. "Tallyho central, am I right?"

"No!" Sophie says, peeved. "I mean, yeah, but not us. I just want a quiet wedding in the country, and the country happens to be Millbrook. And I don't want poinsettias!"

For the first time since entering the shop, Oliver smiles. "No, I see your point. We can't have that."

"So you'll do it?" she asks in thorough frustration.

"Well, we can talk about it," he says. "The thing is, I was just going to unload the van and then have lunch. I'd wait, but to tell you the truth, I'm really hungry. Would you mind coming with me? I'm only going around the corner to the Pink Teacup. We can talk there."

Sophie gets to her feet.

"Hey," says Bell, "just wait a minute. You won't go to Alison with me, but you'll go to the Pink Teacup with him?"

"Jesus," says Oliver. "You asked her *out*?"

"It's a business lunch!" says Sophie, who is nonetheless blushing.

"You thought she was my girlfriend so you asked her *out*?" Oliver demands.

"Only after she set me straight," Bell says merrily.

"Excuse me," interrupts Sophie, "do you mind if I use your bathroom?"

Still glaring at each other, both men raise their hands in unison and point.

Sophie leaves the room gratefully, certainly embarrassed but oddly excited, too, as if the two were truly at the point of blows on her behalf. She might as easily have taken offense, she thinks, shutting the door behind her. Given her day so far—the malaise, the awkward encounter with her thesis advisor and almost-relation, the inconvenience and exertion of her trawl through the West Village—a little offense might have been a logical progression, but Sophie is not offended. She feels...It takes her a moment to identify what she feels, and she settles finally on lighthearted. No, giddy. No no, she thinks, washing her hands in the tiny bathroom, just sidetracked. She had better pull herself together. Sophie eyes herself in the mirror, determined to be all chilly practicality when she emerges: *Bride on a mission! Upper East Side Jewish woman who wants it yesterday!*

The two of them have the front door open when she emerges. They are carrying in large plastic buckets of flowers: blue and white, red and orange. Bell lifts his bucket of dahlias onto the table. A blue light catches Sophie's eye as she passes back through the office, and she stops.

On a low table sit three long trays of dirt, each with an attached index card containing cryptic abbreviations. Two of the three trays look fairly dormant, with only an occasional flaccid seedling emerging from the dirt, but the third boasts several robust young plants. Sophie steps closer, peering at the card. "wb" it says. As in Warner Brothers? Or Yeats?

Above the trays, on a corkboard wall, her gaze finds something familiar, and this turns out to be her own name, and her own address, written up on a shop invoice. She spends a moment of guilty curiosity wondering how much Barton might have spent on her white roses, but as it turns out, the figures in the right hand column are too confusing for her to understand. There is a $75 charge, marked with the date of the Friday when the first roses arrived, and there are other notations—$75, $105, $85—marked with other, more recent dates. Too many dates, and too many notations of price. It doesn't make sense. She hasn't received that many deliveries, has she? Sophie frowns, counting back the weeks. Some of the charges are marked with an O in parentheses. Which means what? thinks Sophie. O for Ochstein? O for Oliver to deliver himself? Has Oliver been cheating Barton? Charging him for flowers that were never delivered?

When Sophie hears a noise nearby, she looks up to find Oliver looking on, somewhat nervously. "I'm sorry," Sophie says quickly. "I was just curious. I mean, about what you're planting."

"It's okay," says Oliver, though it doesn't look like it's at all okay with him. She sees him look past her—to the bulletin board, to the invoice—then force his own gaze away.

"Is it pot?" she says stupidly.

Oliver bursts out laughing. "No, it's not pot. It's a rose. I mean," he says shyly, "my extremely amateurish attempt at a rose."

Sophie looks down at the pale green plants. "I don't understand. What do you mean, your attempt? Is it hard to grow roses?"

"I'm not growing them," Oliver says. "I mean, of course I'm growing them, but what I'm trying to do is make a new rose."

This makes no sense to her at all. "What do you mean 'new'? Isn't every rose a new rose?"

"Yes, of course," he says, flustered. "But a new type. A new specimen. If you invent a new rose, you can name it."

"Is that why you're doing it? So you can name it?" Sophie asks, hearing—after the fact—how rude this sounds.

"No," Oliver shakes his head. "I'd like to be responsible for bringing something new and lovely into the world."

Sophie is just disciplined enough to prevent herself from saying what she nearly says next, which is that this is the sentiment most people attach to the prospect of having children. She herself would like to be responsible for bringing something new and lovely into the world, after all. She has just always thought in terms of people, not flowers.

"And what will you name it?" is what she says, instead.

"Lady Charlotte," Oliver says, standing over the slender plants. "Well, that's the working title, anyway."

Sophie looks at him. The artificial light makes him appear ghostly blue, his dark hair gleaming onyx. "Lady Charlotte?" she asks. "You mean like Lady Charlotte Wilcox?"

He starts. "I forgot you're a history student. You must have read that book."

"The book by Marian Kahn? Of course I read it. She's in my department!"

"Well," he says quietly, "that's a coincidence."

"Not that I know her, really. Actually, we were just introduced this morning."

Oliver says nothing.

"That book must have made a big impression on you if you want to name a rose after her."

"Yes," he says, nodding. "Let's go, okay?"

"No, wait!" Sophie says. "Tell me why they look so much healthier in this tray." She points to the central one of the three. "Why do they look so wimpy in the other two? Did you add something to the dirt in this one?"

"No," says Oliver, explaining the three father roses he has used to fertilize his mother rose, and how the White Bath cross is looking haler all the time. "Which is only appropriate," he says softly, "since it dates to the period when Lady Charlotte Wilcox was in England."

"You think she's watching over your efforts?" Sophie says with a smile.

"I hope so. I hope somebody is. I'd really like this to work."

"What if it doesn't?" she asks.

"If it doesn't, I'll try again next year. Maybe on a bigger scale. I'll try two mothers and more fathers."

"And you're going to do this in a tiny little room? You don't need a big greenhouse?"

Oliver shrugs. "A big greenhouse would be great, but what I've got is a tiny little room. If the rose is beautiful and it thrives and I can reproduce it, I'll be thrilled, but I'm not expecting to get lucky this quickly. Some people spend years trying to get a rose accepted by the ARS." He looks over at her, and saves her the effort. "ARS. The American Rose Society. They're the ones who decide whether your rose gets into the canon, so to speak. They register your name and the rose's name, if it does. They get bombarded by new roses every year, and they just pick a few, so it's a big honor. Which is what I care about, really, though a lot of the people do it for the money."

"There's money in roses?" Sophie asks.

"Oh, yeah. If you create a beautiful robust rose that's disease resist-ant and needs minimal care and grows in lots of different zones, and if you get a big commercial nursery to take it on, you can make a lot of money. But like I said, I'm not in it for the money."

"You're in it for the rose," says Sophie.

"Yes."

"A white rose," she observes.

"I hope it will be, yes. The parents are all white, but you never know."

"And you want it to be white because...?"

He looks at her. He will not repeat his mistake.

"I know," Sophie says, "you'll tell me when you know me better."

Oliver steps back, nearly out of the small room.

"Can we go?" he says.

They go, leaving a smirking Bell behind, sorting blue dahlias. They turn left on Bedford and then right on Grove and walk in awkward silence to the pink storefront near the end of the block.

"You come here often?" Sophie says as they walk in.

"Only about once a day," he says, walking purposefully to a table in the corner. His table, obviously. Sophie hauls her bag onto the banquette opposite him and takes a look around. Everything is pink, from the chairs and banquettes to the radiators to the menus. A montage of Martin Luther King Jr. photographs confronts her from the brick wall, opposite.

"Oliver." The lone waiter nods.

"Pete," says Oliver. "Can we get some coffee?" He turns to Sophie. "You want coffee?"

"Evidently," she tells him. Then, regretting this, she softens. "I mean, yes. Thank you." She takes up her pink menu. "I'm really hungry, too. I didn't eat breakfast."

"You're not doing that have-to-lose-twenty-pounds-before-the-wedding thing, I hope."

She looks up, distressed. "Do you think I need to lose twenty pounds?"

"No. Shit," says Oliver. "Look, I'm really not this much of a creep. You seem to bring out the worst in me."

"I never thought you were a creep," Sophie tells him. "Though you could have mentioned last time that my shirt was half unbuttoned. That was really fun, finding out after you'd left."

"I didn't notice," Oliver says, clearly lying. Sophie, annoyed, picks up her pink menu again. What is she doing here, halfway across the city, sitting down to lunch with a florist in a place where half the bill of fare appears to have once had cloven hooves?

"So what am I having for lunch?" she says.

Oliver smiles distractedly. "I tend to get the barbecued pork. I'm not a very good Jew."

"Yes, I think we've established that."

"But the hamburgers are fine. And you can always have breakfast. They serve it all day here."

"I've been known to eat pork," Sophie says, sitting back as her coffee arrives.

Oliver looks at her in surprise. "Really?"

"Really. Not everything in Jewish law is equally important, as far as I'm concerned. Identity is important, respecting the past is important, and not marrying someone named Muldoon is important. Observing the Sabbath is important. But I think some of the dietary laws had a lot to do with keeping healthy in the desert three thousand years ago. Besides, if God hadn't wanted Jews to be happy in the New World, he wouldn't have given us lobster Cantonese."

"Well said," Oliver laughs. "So will you be joining me in the pork barbecue?"

"I will not. A hamburger will be just fine."

"Okay. And then you have to try the sweet potato pie."

"Then I shall," she announces.

Oliver calls their order across the room. He retrieves a spiral notebook from his jacket pocket.

"When's the wedding?" he asks, flipping until he finds a blank page.

"December," says Sophie. "The sixteenth."

He looks up. "Cutting it a little close," he observes.

"Yes. Well, don't forget, I've wasted a couple of months on the poinsettia lady."

Oliver nods.

"Evening ceremony? Afternoon?"

"Evening. Ceremony is six o'clock. Then there's a dinner."

"And what's the venue?"

Her father's house, she explains. Under a tent out back. The house is on a hill, with great views, though they won't be able to see anything with the tent sides rolled down.

"Why not have it inside?" says Oliver. "How big is your party?"

Sophie sighs. "Either fifty or two hundred," she says. "Depending on who wins the guest list wars."

Oliver looks up.

"In other words, will we be inviting lots of people who have never laid eyes on me but are important to my dad? Or will we be limiting ourselves to people actually known to the bride and groom? Am I going to be married with friends and family members or is it going to be everyone my dad's ever done a deal with?"

He nods, uncertain. "I see. And who's going to win?"

"He is," says Sophie.

Oliver smirks as he writes, but not unkindly. "And why's that?"

"Because it would make him happier to win than it would make me unhappy to lose. Next question?"

Oliver is quiet for a minute, holding her gaze. Sophie is about to ask him if he is all right when he puts down his pad and sits back against his pink chair.

"Tell me about him," says Oliver.

"About Bart?" Sophie asks.

"No. Your dad. Tell me about your dad."

Sophie is instantly on guard. This is obviously not the first time she has been asked for personal information about her extremely wealthy father. In high school, the divorced moms of her classmates routinely cajoled her for insights, and in the years since then she has grown practiced at deflecting this kind of interest. For some reason, however, deflection eludes her now, and Sophie finds herself on the point of speech, of revelation. The words back up in her throat, heavy with love and impending, looming loss, roiling and roiling, trying to get voiced. In fact, the only thing holding her back is the uncomfortable prospect of tears.

"Why?" she says, buying time.

Oliver shakes his head. Sophie sees, for the first time, the little brown mole near his left ear. What a curious place for a mole, she thinks.

"It's just that you seem to really love him," Oliver finally offers.

"I do. I do really love him. Is that very unusual?"

"I don't know. I guess not. It's just that I don't remember my own dad very well, and all the time I was growing up I used to listen to my friends whining about their fathers. I really resented it. Of course, I never said anything. You know, it's not very cool to tell your adolescent friend that he ought to cherish his dad. I tell myself that if I still had my father I'd appreciate him the way you seem to appreciate yours. But who knows? Maybe I wouldn't."

Their food arrives. Sophie looks hungrily at the heap of steaming pork on Oliver's plate, then contemplates her own hamburger.

"What happened to your dad?" Sophie asks softly. She is thinking *abandonment? divorce?* though the indications are clearly otherwise.

"Car crash," Oliver says, setting down his coffee cup. "Drunk driver on the Merritt Parkway. Who walked away, I might add."

"I'm very sorry," she says, as if it has just happened.

"Yeah."

He starts to pick at his food.

"I don't remember my mother at all," she hears herself say.

Oliver puts down his fork and sighs.

"Was she sick?"

Sophie takes a bite of her hamburger and nods.

"Cancer?"

Another nod.

"Well, we're quite the pair," he observes, looking—really looking— at her, which Sophie can feel without glancing up. She concentrates very hard on her hamburger and focuses on the far wall, where Martin Luther King Jr. regards her with a purposeful expression.

"So can I ask you something?" Oliver says at last.

Still avoiding his gaze, Sophie shrugs.

"If you've already decided to give in to your dad about the wedding list, why are you bothering to fight about it?"

She chews on, tasting nothing, her appetite all but gone. She is perfectly capable of answering this question, but she does not want to hear herself say the reason, which is that if she were to give up concentrating on the details of the wedding, she would have to contemplate the marriage, and that prospect fills her with dismay.

"It's traditional" is what Sophie manages to say. "It's expected. But don't worry. I'll tell him soon."

"And you're telling me now," he observes.

"Yes. Right." She puts down her hamburger and takes a gulp of the now chilly coffee.

"Two hundred guests," he takes up his pad again.

"Sounds about right."

"And you've thought about the flowers?"

"Well, no," she says. "Just whatever you think. You decide."

He stares at her across the table. "*I* decide? Are you kidding me?"

She can manage only a facsimile of a smile.

"Miss Klein—"

"Oh, Sophie," says Sophie, wearily. "And it's Ms., anyway."

"*Sophie.* I've had brides who brought me paint chips to show me the exact color for their wedding flowers. I've had brides who insisted on their flowers' being organically produced, or from specific countries. I've had women tell me, to the *millimeter*, how long the petals were allowed to be."

"Good for them," she says angrily. "I really don't care that much."

"But you should." Oliver's voice is quiet. "I mean, maybe not to the millimeter, but you *should* care. The flowers you choose are a reflection of what's important in your life. This is your wedding. It should be beautiful and personal. It should be about the woman you are, and how you feel, and whom you love."

Sophie's breath catches. Her wedding isn't at all about those things, she knows, and it is terrible to know it and still go forward into her own future. It is terrible to think of the years, coming so soon, without her father, who looks ahead to this wedding with every happy thought she herself does not have, and only a genial, respectful blank of a man to replace him.

Naturally Sophie cannot say this. Not to herself, certainly not to someone she barely knows, no matter how incisively he looks at her and how patiently he waits for her response. No matter—and Sophie understands this suddenly—that he *is* waiting for the response, that he is actually, personally *concerned* with her response. She does not want Oliver to be concerned for her. It is not his business to be concerned. Besides, what makes him think he can speak to her this way?

"Maybe we're not all obsessed with flowers," Sophie says, with cruelty. "Maybe it just isn't that big a deal to some of us. Maybe a rose is just a rose, as far as normal people are concerned. Why don't you save your floral elitism for your own wedding, and just arrange some nice flowers for mine? I mean, isn't that your job?"

Of course, she instantly wants to take it back, but she can't, and in the brittle silence that follows, Sophie loses the thread of her own thoughts and simply stares at Oliver, at his stricken face and his gray eyes, which are staring back at her. The pain between them at this moment is more intimate than anything that has come before. It is also, incidentally, more intimate than anything she has shared with her fiancé. It is devastating.

"I'm sorry," Sophie says, breaking eye contact with her remaining will. "I have to go."

"Don't go," says Oliver.

She unzips her bag and claws for money. She puts a twenty on the table.

"That's too much," he says, getting to his feet. "Please don't go. I shouldn't have said anything personal to you. It's none of my business."

"Just call me with an estimate," Sophie tells him, hauling the bag onto her shoulder and moving. She will not look at the hand that reaches out to her. She will not let it touch her. She is already at the door, pushing off like a swimmer at the wall, wild to be far away.

CHAPTER FOURTEEN

A Prison Catechism

MARIAN GETS LOST, first in Harlem, searching for the Willis Avenue Bridge, then in the Bronx. Though it is morning, a lovely morning (brisk and cold and blue), she drives with moderate anxiety and with the nudging memory of certain scenes from *The Bonfire of the Vanities*, looking for signs of normalcy on the unfamiliar streets to reassure herself: bodega, mother with baby, pair of laughing men shaking hands as they meet. Even so, she is still lost.

By the time she pulls over to ask directions it is past eleven, but the woman pushing a grocery cart who comes to Marian's window says that Hughes Avenue is nearby, only four streets away. The woman, stooped and solid with electric red hair, speaks in the postwar accent of another Bronx; it is all Marian can do to ask if she is in fact the last Jew in the borough, and if so, then what is she still doing here? But having passed along the pertinent information the woman takes up her cart and resumes her course, and Marian eases her car back into traffic.

On Hughes, Marian drives a block before she realizes that she is moving away from her destination, executes a furtive U-turn, and pulls up alongside number 2111 without further incident. The building is modest and tidy, with an old limestone stoop fully populated by mothers and children—hardly surprising on a fair Saturday morning. There is no sign of a parking space, of course, so Marian takes her chances double-parking directly in front of the stoop, far less worried about a ticket than a theft, and hoping at least to avert one with such a large audience. She locks the vehicle with a chirp from her keychain, and gives an overly friendly smile to the women watching from the steps. Then she picks her way through them and goes inside.

Soriah's grandmother has a different last name, but the button beside it on the keypad fails to produce any audible sound. Not wanting to press repeatedly, she walks back outside and tells the assembled women that she is here to see Mrs. Nelson. "I'm not sure the buzzer is working," she adds, feebly.

"Sweetheart," says the massive woman on the top step, "you jus' go on up. You wait for that buzzer to work, you be here till the next century."

There is general amusement at this idea.

"Jus' push," the woman adds. "Go on."

Marian gives a tentative push. The door emits a meager click and swings open. Feeling it give beneath such a pathetic effort irritates her, but the lack of security in the building is not today's problem, she tells herself. Today's problem is enough for today.

The smell of bacon pervades the third-floor hallway, although there is no telling which of the dozen doors it originates behind. Number 26, near the end of the corridor, is gunmetal gray like the rest but bears an index card with a florid purple NELSON, taped above the security peephole. Marian presses the bell. From inside, she hears the unmistakable sounds of *The Price Is Right*.

A woman, small with a great ring of flesh around her middle, opens the door. She grins. "Come on!" she says, gesturing. "I'm Marisol. Soriah's waiting."

Soriah is indeed waiting, Marian sees, stepping inside. She is seated on the couch, half watching the television. Over her several meetings with the eleven-year-old, Marian has been struck by certain jarring dichotomies in the girl's character. Soriah possesses a truly nimble mind—capable of admirable concentration and elegant leaps of insight—but her deficiencies are significant. She has been completely untouched by music written before the year 1990, has never been to a museum, and does not understand why someone would want to sit in a dark theater watching other people move around and talk. She also suffers a lack of manners so appalling that only her innate sweetness redeems her.

"Soriah," Marisol says eagerly. "Your friend is here."

Soriah gets up and comes over to Marian. Awkwardly, they shake hands. She is, Marian notes, wearing one of her new bras.

"Is this your grandmother?" Marian says, indicating Marisol.

"Oh, no, no," the little woman laughs. "I'm the home health. *Gloria!*"

"Granma?" Soriah says at the same time.

"She probably in the bathroom," Marisol says, unconcerned. "She be out. This is nice, you know. Taking her."

"Oh, it's no problem," Marian says.

The apartment is small and clean, with a kitchen alcove off the room in which they stand and presumably a bedroom on the other side of the closed door. Oxygen tanks flank the couch like matching lamps, connected by plastic tubing, but there is otherwise little evidence of a chronically ill person living here. Neither has Soriah, who uses the couch as her bed, Marian knows, made much of an impact on the décor; the only things signifying her presence that Marian can see are the library copy of *Emma* on the armrest and the short stack of textbooks and notebooks on the floor beside the television. On top of the television, a photo in a plastic frame shows a grinning Soriah, but when Marian looks closer, the faded colors of the picture give its true subject away: Soriah's mother, seventies Afro and checked dress, à la Cindy Brady. The resemblance is strong, the grin identical. I don't suppose she's grinning now, Marian thinks.

The bedroom door opens, and Marisol ambles to the side of an elderly woman, who makes her way across the floor with a metal walker, her head down. Only when she has reached the couch and painfully descended does the woman look up and put out a hand.

"Hello," Marian says. "You must be Soriah's grandmother. I'm Marian Kahn."

"Thank you for taking her," the woman says simply. "It's very nice."

"Oh, I didn't have any plans," Marian says. This is not strictly true. When Soriah phoned her to say that her caseworker had cancelled their appointment, Marian had cancelled her own appointment, with Oliver. Marshall is in England (sweetening his two-day string of meetings in Birmingham with a weekend of London theater), and Marian had meant to compensate Oliver, at last, for their lost weekend. Even so, she did not hesitate to tell Soriah she was available. Not, Marian tells herself, because she is looking for a way out of her entanglement with Oliver, and certainly not because she views the day's expedition with anything but dread, but perhaps simply because the service she is now being asked to perform seems so much more straightforward than any of the other tasks currently facing her. Pick up a kid, take her somewhere, take her home... Isn't that blissfully uncomplicated? she thinks, considering the complex nature of her other commitments. Still, she had caused Oliver pain, and lied to him about why she was doing it, which had caused herself pain. All for a girl who still has one eye on *The Price Is Right*.

"Marisol," Mrs. Nelson says, pointing a bony finger. "You got the cookies? For Denise?"

"I got them," Marisol says. She retrieves, from the kitchen, a packet of Pepperidge Farm Mint Milanos.

"For Denise," says Soriah's grandmother. "It's her favorite cookies."

"All right," Marian says. "Soriah can take them in, right?"

"She's allowed. And Soriah, you mind your manners."

"Okay," says Soriah.

"You're very nice to do it," says Marisol, settling herself beside her charge on the couch and picking up a remote control. Marian gets the feeling that she is observing these two in their natural habitat. Marisol lifts the plastic tubing from one of the oxygen tanks and adjusts it beneath Mrs. Nelson's nose.

"I'm not sure what time we'll be back," says Marian.

"It's okay," the home health comments. "It's fine. You take your time."

"But—" They haven't asked her for her number, she thinks. They may not even know her name, really. Don't they want to take down her license plate, or her phone number? Aren't they concerned?

"It's okay," says Soriah, putting on her coat. She is used to being removed by strangers, it occurs to Marian. And the two women on the couch are used to witnessing it.

Marian says good-bye and goes downstairs with Soriah, emerging from the building's front door into the bright midday light. Two men are leaning against the front fender of the Volvo, but they shift without complaint when Marian unlocks her door. Soriah gets in the passenger seat.

"It's a nice car," she says.

"It's fine," Marian says. "I'm not that interested in cars, really. Fasten your seatbelt, Soriah."

"But you could have a really cool car if you want, right?"

"I don't know," Marian says, making her way down Hughes Avenue toward, she hopes, Route 87. "I guess so. What's a cool car?"

"Lexus," says Soriah. "Mercedes. Jaguar."

"Oh, I don't need a Jaguar. And I don't like Mercedeses. They used slave labor in the concentration camps. You know, during World War Two?"

Soriah frowns. "Yeah, but, that was like fifty years ago."

"Sure," says Marian, spotting a sign for the highway and merging left, "but if you have a choice of lots of different companies to buy a car from, why would you pick the one that participated in the enslavement of your own ethnic group?"

Marian can see Soriah turn to look at her. "Are you Jewish?" she says.

"Yes, I'm Jewish. My family was already here when the Nazis came to power."

"Do you, like, wear that little hat?" says Soriah.

It takes Marian a minute to decipher the meaning of this. "A yarmulke? No. Only men wear those. And besides, I'm not religious at all. I don't even really believe in God, but that doesn't make me any less Jewish."

Soriah shakes her head. "I don't get that."

"Well, look at it this way. I'm Jewish the same way you're black. Sorry, would you rather I said African-American?"

"I don't know," she says. "Whatever."

"Anything anyone's done to the Jews over the years, I kind of take personally. Like they did it to my great-great-great-great-grandmother. Which they probably did. Maybe it's the same way you feel about slavery. I mean, there may not be anyone alive in America today who owned a slave, but I can assure you, there are people walking around this country spending money that was earned by enslaving people. I think if I were an African-American, there might be a couple of products I wouldn't buy, on principle."

Soriah sighs. "That was so long ago."

"Not to a historian," Marian says. "To people like me, everything just happened, and we're all living in the aftermath." She accelerates onto 87, and moves into the center lane. "Besides, look at the two of us. We wouldn't be sitting here having this conversation if not for a slave trader."

Soriah turns in her seat to look at her.

"Well, think about it. You wrote to me because of a book I'd written. I wrote the book because of a person who lived a long time ago who had an interesting life. She had an interesting life because a very rich man in England paid for her to sail from America to Britain. And how do you think that rich man got to be so rich? Because he kidnapped Africans, transported them to America, and sold them into slavery."

"Okay," Soriah says with the beginning of a smile. "I get that. Well, that's something good that came from slavery, then."

Marian, touched, keeps her eyes on the road.

"Does your mom know you're coming?" Marian says.

"I guess so. The caseworker fixes it. She usually brings me, but she said one of her kids was sick or something." Soriah is quiet for a minute. "I probably shouldn't have called you. It's just…I didn't see my mom since August, and I thought, maybe, if you weren't busy, it would be okay."

"It *is* okay, Soriah. I told you last time, if you need something, ask me. I might not always be able to help out, but you never have to worry about calling."

"All right," the girl says with palpable embarrassment.

Marian drives. The route is happily clear and the river glints on her left. At Yonkers, she exits onto the Hutchinson Parkway and continues north on 684. She is surprised to realize how close it is, how many times she must have driven within a few miles of the prison, en route to Tanglewood or Canyon Ranch or—in the years before their rift— to visit Marshall's business partner, Robert Markowitz, in North Salem. The incongruity of Bedford Hills the correctional facility and Bedford Hills the sylvan, moneyed enclave is not lost on Marian as she exits the highway, passing first through the trim, prosperous town of Katonah and then skirting a synthetically bucolic golf course flanked by gargantuan new homes. Beside her, Soriah silently points out the prison entrance on Harris Road.

Marian parks in the visitors' area and locks her car, then she follows Soriah to a small, cement-block hut at the front gate. Inside, Marian produces a driver's license and Soriah, to Marian's surprise, withdraws a laminated card from her jeans pocket and hands it over.

"What's that?" Marian asks.

"My caseworker gave it to me. For when I come here."

The guard tells them both to remove their coats. He takes from Marian her heavy leather bag and meticulously unloads it onto his desk: wallet, reading glasses, bottle of Evian, and a great wad of files. As he moves through these objects, touching everything, he recites a prison catechism:

Who are you here to see?

We are here to see Denise Neal.

What is your relationship to Denise Neal?

This is her daughter. I'm not visiting. I've just brought her.

Are you carrying any of the following materials. Alcohol, prescription drugs, cell phones, beepers, weapons, or anything that might possibly be used as a weapon?

"Well, I have a cell phone," says Marian, pointing to the smart red leather case on the table, a gift from Marshall. The phone is taken and put on a shelf, as are the Pepperidge Farm cookies, which are not, after all, allowed.

Have you answered each and every one of these questions truthfully, and are you aware that failure to answer truthfully may result in criminal prosecution?

Marian has always been cowed by authority. "Yes, we have," she says, looking down at Soriah, but Soriah is impassive. Then both of them are scanned with a handheld sensor—a vaguely lewd and humiliating experience—and given stamps of invisible ink on the backs of their hands, as if they were entering a fun fair, or a party. After this, they are allowed to put their coats on again.

Just past the first guard, a second man, seated inside a glassed-in booth, opens the gate for them and they go through it to a small holding area where their new stamps are illuminated beneath a black light. Behind them, the gate closes, and for a moment they are trapped there, between locked doors, before a second gate is opened, and they are outside again. Marian, though she realizes that she is now actually within the prison, emerges from the small enclosure with relief. Soriah begins to walk up a long hill by a pathway bordered by dormant flower beds toward a building marked ADMINISTRATION, and Marian follows, hoisting her great bag. Inside the new building, they each sign a large logbook and have the stamps on their hands illuminated again. A guard, behind his glass partition, makes a phone call, and Marian understands that Soriah's mother is being summoned. He pushes a button under his desk and the gate before them slides open. Soriah leads the way through, then turns left past some vending machines to a bright waiting area, lit by windows all along one wall. At the far end of the room is a yellow door, marked with a NO UNAU-THORIZED ADMITTANCE sign. Soriah stands looking placidly at this door, which—Marian supposes—marks the way to where her mother is waiting. Almost immediately, it opens, and a woman in a gray guard uniform calls Soriah's name. Soriah goes without a backward glance.

Marian sits in one of the chairs and lets her bag fall to the floor. From parking lot to waiting room the transit has taken no more than fifteen minutes, but the effect is wearying, as is the realization that she is—for the first time in her life—inside a prison. The room is clean, and the view of the lawn through the wall of windows is pleasant, but nothing alleviates the sadness lingering here. Stacks of withered magazines teeter on one table in the corner, and Marian, by force of habit, gets up and goes to look. *Family Fun*, says the issue on the top of the pile. She returns to her seat.

Being caught without work is a circumstance Marian tries to avoid, a precaution responsible for the current weight of her leather bag. Today's burden is comprised of applications for two tenure track openings in her department. Given the glut of newly minted PhDs on the market, Columbia's ad in the *American Historical Review* has netted more than eight hundred CVs, the majority of them belonging to qualified applicants. Whittling down these applicants to a shortlist of serious contenders (each of whom will have to be interviewed at the AHA) is a task that will surely consume an unreasonable, painful proportion of her time over the next month, and of course she begrudges it. They're all fine, Marian thinks, flipping past a specialist in medieval fortification design, a postcolonialist with an interest in the Belgian Congo, an Americanist with a major work on the French and Indian Wars due out from Yale. It would be one thing if the department had an actual hole to fill, she thinks, shaking her head, and noting the fourth Marshall Scholar out of just the first ten CVs she has managed to get through. But the vacancies only exist because two new chairs have been endowed, creating openings at the other end of the tenure track. The hiring committee has the luxury of choosing whoever wows them most, which Marian knows is an enviable position to be in, but the wall of achievement and aspiration and urgency lurking behind the circumspect language of the cover letters (Isn't the New York native desperate to return from exile in Texas? Isn't the associate professor at Stanford married to a woman who teaches at NYU?) is already overwhelming. And she's still at the top of the pile.

Marian looks up. Across the room, seated before one of the windows, a woman with unnaturally red hair is hard at work on her own stack of papers. On a chair beside her, a little girl sits, looking directly at Marian. The girl's hands are politely clasped together, and her hair is tightly braided in cornrows. She looks about four, Marian thinks. Maybe five. She is dressed in good clothes: pretty green dress, pink tights, white sneakers. She has gold studs in her ears. The woman beside her is writing on a pad. The girl's face is perfectly expressionless, even when Marian attempts a smile. The woman beside her does not look up.

"Sheree?" someone says.

Marian turns to see the same corrections officer who took Soriah.

"Come on, honey. Your mama's waiting to see you."

The red-haired woman stops writing.

"Go on, Sheree," she says, not unkindly. "I'll wait here for you."

Sheree hops off the chair. She looks at Marian. Marian tries another smile, but she does not feel remotely like smiling, and the resulting grimace must not be very reassuring. The girl walks slowly to the door and disappears through it. The woman in the next chair has already gone back to her work.

"Uh, Marian?"

It's Soriah's voice. Marian turns in her seat.

"That was quick," she says, trying for a light tone.

"No, it's just—my mom was wondering if you'd come back and talk to her."

Marian goes still. The unexpectedness of this request has caught her completely by surprise, and she wants very badly to say no. But of course she can't say no. Soriah stands in the doorway, waiting, the gray uniform of the corrections officer just visible behind her. How close to this can I come? Marian thinks. To walk though this scuffed yellow door is to abandon all hope of detachment.

Marian gets to her feet.

Beyond the yellow door is a yellow corridor lined with library posters. Soriah leads her to a large open room, lined on one side with bookshelves and filled with low plastic tables. There are women in the room, and children running everywhere, crawling everywhere, being held. The place looks like a day care center, Marian thinks, looking around and trying to get her bearings. She has, she realizes, been expecting the kind of bleak setting she has seen in films and on television, where inmate and visitor face each other through glass and speak via telephone. There is no glass here, except for the windows, which admit white winter light. It is very nearly pleasant.

"So many kids!" she says wonderingly to the slim black woman standing a few feet to her right. Soriah has crossed to a far corner of the room and begun reading a picture book to three small girls, one of whom—Marian is glad to note—is the child from the waiting room, Sheree.

"Yes," the woman says. "We have about five hundred kids visit a month."

"It's a lot nicer than I expected," Marian admits. "I thought it would be terrible."

"It is terrible," says the woman. "Only, it's not as terrible as it could be. We work really hard for that."

Marian nods. "How long have you worked here?" she asks the woman, who has very short hair and is dressed in green.

"Ever since I got here. I'm Denise Neal," she says, holding out her hand. "I'm Soriah's mother."

Marian looks at her in shock. "I thought you worked here," she says finally, shaking Denise's hand.

"I do. I work in the children's center. It's my job."

"But I thought..."

"It's all right," Denise says flatly. "We can sit over here."

She crosses to one of the plastic tables, and the two women sit, uncomfortably. Marian, who doesn't know what to do with her legs, ends up in an awkward posture with her knees tightly together, like a matron at a suburban ladies' lunch, circa 1958. Soriah's mother watches a massive woman at the next table with a massive infant on her lap. The woman, ignoring the infant, is lecturing a teenaged boy, who predictably sulks. "Is the baby visiting?" asks Marian.

"No, he lives here. Babies can live here till they're eighteen months old. Then they have to go out."

"Oh. Well, I guess that's good," says Marian. "I mean, I guess it helps start a child off right to be with his mother. And they're too small to know they're..."

She stops, horribly embarrassed.

"Yeah. They know later, though," Denise says. "Somebody told me before I got here, it's always hardest on the kids. I didn't doubt it. Thank God for my ma, taking care of Soriah."

Your ma, thinks Marian, *can barely take care of herself.*

"Soriah's a great kid," Marian says, instead.

"Yeah. So. Can I ask? How did you meet my daughter?"

There is the faintest note of parental concern in the question. Denise looks directly at Marian, and Marian sees clearly now how pretty she is. She has even dark skin, a long, sinewy neck. She has hair cut quite close to her head, and very neat.

"Didn't she tell you?" Marian asks. "She sent me a letter. About a book I wrote."

"You wrote a book?" says Denise.

"Yes, but not a book for children. To tell you the truth, I was very surprised to get a letter from an eleven-year-old reader."

Denise nods. "Yeah. Soriah's smart. She's always reading."

"Not just smart," Marian leans forward across the plastic table. "She's curious. She reads to learn, not just for entertainment. And when she's done with a book, she doesn't just put it down. She asks questions about it. She wants to talk about it. She has—" Marian stops. She is aware, suddenly, of how this sounds, and how it is about to sound, but she can't stop herself. "Soriah has a really good mind. She could go to college. I mean, of course she could go to college. What I mean is, she really has to go."

Denise looks at her. "I went to college," she says quietly.

Marian, mortified, says nothing.

"I didn't graduate, but I went. Brooklyn College."

"Good school," says Marian.

"I was doing business administration. I did two years."

"You'll go back," Marian says, with an attempt at a reassuring tone.

"No. I'm trying to finish in here. They have a college program."
She stops, then says, "It was drugs, you know. I guess Soriah told you."

Marian nods. She doesn't trust herself to say anything out loud.

"I didn't hurt anybody. I want you to know that. But I had a habit,
I'm not denying it. What they found, though, it wasn't even mine. It
was something I was keeping for my boyfriend. He held someone up,
and when they came to search the house, they found it in my stuff. So
he got five years for holding someone up with a gun, and I got fifteen
for possession."

This is spoken tonelessly. Marian has been a reader of the *New York
Times* long enough to know that Denise's situation is far from unique.
Her story, in its basic parameters, very likely serves many Bedford Hills
inmates.

"You think she's okay?" asks Denise.

Marian turns to look at Soriah, far across the room. "I'm worried
her school isn't keeping up with her," she says. "Of course, it's none of
my business."

"What do you mean, not keeping up?"

"Nobody's pushing her at the school. And if somebody doesn't
push, they'll just leave her alone."

"But if she's doing okay," Denise says, "it's good they're leaving her
alone."

Marian shakes her head. "I don't think it's good. Look, she's a great
kid. I don't think you need to be worried about her."

Denise leans forward. "Why don't you help her with the school?
Why don't you tell them they should be teaching her better?"

Because I'm not her mother, Marian thinks, recoiling. *Because it has
nothing to do with me.* She is on the point of taking offense, but then,
abruptly, she sees something in Denise's face that is not an abdication
of responsibility, and not an imperviousness to her daughter's needs,

and not the narcissism of a mother who failed to reject both drugs and gun-wielding boyfriends the minute she gave birth to another human being. This is unfettered misery. And it is a supplication.

"I'm not getting out, you know," Denise says abruptly. "I don't know if Soriah told you that. She used to pretend I was going to get out and we were going back where we were living, but I'm not getting out. I've got nine more years, and that's it."

Marian nods.

"What you just said? About how she's reading to learn? There was a girl like that here, when I first came. Her mama's still in here, for killing her husband, because he beat her up. But this girl, she came to visit a lot. She was about six years old then. Her name was Samantha. You see that bookshelf?" Denise points to where Soriah is sitting. "She just sat herself down and read when she came here. She must have read every book. But the last time I saw her? She had on high heels and real tight pants, and she was wearing a shirt that looked like a bra. Her mama told me she was on the pill. And the mama was happy! She said, 'Samantha's not gonna get pregnant like I did.' But she's thirteen."

Marian, speechless, nods.

"I don't want that to happen to Soriah. I don't want her coming in here looking like that, you understand?"

Her tone hovers between desperation and command. Marian waits.

"When I first came here, Soriah used to say, 'Mama, let's play memories.' She wanted to talk about what she remembered, from when I took care of her. Now she doesn't ask that. I guess she doesn't like to remember that now."

"Maybe," Marian says carefully, "it just means she's thinking about the future, not the past."

Denise turns a pained face in the direction of her daughter. "I don't even know you," she says quietly. "I don't know anything about you. You got kids?"

Across the room, Soriah closes her book. She detaches herself from her audience and gets to her feet. "No kids," says Marian in a whisper, as if it were a secret. "I couldn't have them."

Denise nods. This, evidently, is explanation enough.

"Well, I want to thank you for everything you're doing for Soriah."

I'm not doing anything, Marian nearly says, but she doesn't, because it isn't true. Whatever her intentions—an hour ago, this morning, last month—they're all beside the point, and all that matters now is that she is part of the life of the woman seated across from her, because she is part of Soriah's life. This is the heart of the matter: *She has done. She is doing.* And, most significant: *She will do.* There isn't any point in saying otherwise. Instead, Marian offers her most gracious smile—a smile of social privilege and social obligation, a smile that might have earned the approval of even her mother, Mimi Warburg—and says, "You're welcome."

CHAPTER FIFTEEN

Insomnia

I T IS 3:28 IN THE MORNING, a fact made manifest to Oliver by the green glow of the numbers on Marian's bedside clock. Even so, even given the long concentration Oliver has brought to those numbers, he can't seem to get beyond their empirical reality to some kind of deeper meaning, such as a justification for his being awake in the middle of the night, beside Marian in a king-size bed, in a former stable, on a patch of outrageously expensive real estate at the eastern tip of Long Island. And then, in any case, it is 3:29 in the morning.

He is ill versed in insomnia. Sleep, for Oliver, has always come easily. If the odd truck or siren on Hudson Street should wake him, he merely turns over and falls again into sleep, letting it hold him until it is time for the flower market or the sun, whichever comes first. This aptitude is something Matilda once mentioned, he recalls now, as 3:30 clicks over and glows, sedately, from the far side of Marian's shoulder. In a fight once, ages ago, so long ago he can't remember its impetus or central theme, she had said, "You're so selfish, you sleep through everything," and he had been terrified that he might have told her, at some crushingly intimate moment, something he meant never to tell anyone, which was that he had once mostly slept through nearly dying, but in the end it turned out that she was talking about something else—about his sleeping beside her one night as she wept, loudly, hoping he would wake up and comfort her. And now he is the one hoping the sleeping person beside him will wake and comfort him.

Except that Oliver doesn't seem to want that, either. He lies stiffly, 3:31, 3:38, 3:50, watching Marian breathe, a crescent of white skin visible over the sheet at her shoulder, and he tries to recollect the sex, as if that will comfort him back to sleep and rid him of whatever irksome thing is hovering here. The sex took place only a couple of hours earlier, after all—and yet it baffles him that he cannot seem to remember anything about it. Except the fact that it happened here, in this bed, but that slip of remembrance may have been reconstructed from the smell they have left behind, which is still evident, which is usually a good smell, a smell he loves, but for some reason isn't just now.

Maybe it was simply unmemorable, Oliver thinks. And that's fine. The earth doesn't have to move every time. It isn't about the sex anyway, that's what he keeps telling her. Well, that's not precisely what he keeps telling her. What he keeps telling her is that it isn't about her looks, or her age, and it isn't! Normally he loves these trial domesticities, so rarely allowed, when they can act like the couple they might be, eating together and picking up the paper and talking and making the bed. But he is not loving this night, and he is not sure he wants to figure out why.

It is only Oliver's second time in the beach house, the first a midweek in July when she was so terrified of their being seen that they never left the property. Now it's early December and the Hamptons are deserted, with empty streets in the towns and plenty of parking for the few stores that remain open. Marian had been brave enough to take him to the hardware store to buy salt—a big deal, Oliver tells himself—and introduce him to her plumber, when they unexpectedly encountered him in the parking lot, without losing her composure. They even had dinner last night at Turtle's Crossing in Amagansett, where the only attention they attracted was reassuringly hostile—the kind of looks any townies might give any summer people who didn't know their place.

Maybe she is trying it on, thinks Oliver, so fully awake now that he can make out ocean sounds, half a mile away. Maybe she is actually beginning to imagine a life with him, with plumbers and the clerk at the hardware store, just possibly wondering what Mrs. Kahn is doing buying salt with a man half her age. Perhaps this trip is not the compensation he first imagined, for their thwarted weekend nearly two months ago, but an interlude with its face to the future. His future with Marian—the one he has been asking for, ever since the summer. But the thought does not lift him, and he can't bear that it does not.

Given that his mood now seems unshakable, Oliver makes an effort to pinpoint its beginning, and here, at any rate, he has some success. Before the sex but after returning from the restaurant. When he went upstairs to phone his answering machine at home.

Yes, that was it.

And yes, there had been yet another phone message from Barton Ochstein on the answering machine. And no, he no longer finds anything about Barton remotely funny, and wonders that he ever did.

Oliver closes his eyes. He is wired now, stiff with anxiety. He has not said a word to Marian about her cousin and his ardent attentions, not since that time in front of her building, delivering the first order of roses he assembled for the mythic Olivia. If she thinks, as she undoubtedly does, that Barton's suit has petered out, that is because Oliver has shielded her, and perhaps—he admits—himself. Barton has been anything but discouraged by Olivia's failure to respond to his gifts. In addition to the weekly deliveries to his putative fiancée's Morningside Heights apartment, Barton has continued to order arrangements for Olivia, growing increasingly flattering and specific in their accompanying cards, and Oliver has continued to charge Barton for his orders and also continued to deliver them to Marian, despite the fact that he has never yet been paid for a single stem. Oliver is no longer at all smug about his handling of the matter. How long will Barton be content to wait for his reluctant transvestite before saying something to Marian?

Or worse, bounding into the White Rose to demand actual physical contact with his elusive object of desire?

The phone calls madden Oliver. Naturally, he rues his decision to give out his own phone number. Over the past weeks, Barton's messages have progressed from formal greetings to something more familiar, more intimate, more pleading. And without the slightest reciprocation—without even the most formal thanks for his flowers! Olivia, thinks Oliver, has been chilly in the extreme to her suitor. Any other man would surely have gotten the message by now, but Barton seems to have convinced himself that Olivia is a coquette, toying with him before she reels him in. He dearly wants to be reeled.

Over the past weeks, Barton's pattern has established itself: a call to the shop confirming that Olivia has picked up her flowers, followed by a call to the apartment to flatter and cajole, followed—a few days later—by another call to the shop for a bigger and more flamboyant order, with a more explicit card. Plus hang-ups. Lots of hang-ups. Two of them, for example, when Oliver checked his answering machine last night. And then the message: "Hello, dear Olivia. This is Barton Ochstein. Did you love your dahlias? I'm coming into town at the end of the week. I know a sweet little restaurant in Chelsea, we could have a quiet dinner. Call me, dear."

Marian, if she knew, would be irate, and mostly—Oliver knows this—at him. Her cousin's impropriety aside, Oliver created this sorry scenario, Oliver took it upon himself to don Marian's clothes and saunter forth into the world as a latter-day Lord Satterfield. He had only wanted to make fun for them both, but now he is paying the piper. With every phone call and every flower Olivia has become more of a problem, more of a snare, and not just for himself and Barton but for Marian, too. And, he supposes, for Sophie Klein. Every one of them, he thinks, rolling stiffly onto his back, has a right to be furious with him.

Marian has always chided him for his playful side. Even as she laughed along, she cautioned him: he might easily make a mistake, and go too far, and harm them both. Now this silly trick would prove her right, Oliver thinks, closing his eyes. She would fail to understand how it had gotten away from him, week by week and flower by flower. She would not laugh with him now. She would find nothing at all amusing in the spectacle of Barton, on the eve of his nuptials, in avid pursuit of another woman, especially another woman he knows is no woman at all. Even speculation about her disapproval is more than Oliver can stand, but while he berates himself for having dug the hole in which he finds himself, the means to get out of his hole utterly elude him. He could try passing along a message from Olivia to Barton to cease his efforts, but he somehow doubts Barton would take that lying down. He could tell Barton that there is no Olivia, but that would leave the matter of the man dressed in woman's clothing in Marian Kahn's apartment on a Friday afternoon with her husband out of town. He could threaten to pass along certain details to Sophie Klein, but the memory of his personal remark to Sophie is still fresh, and she had been perfectly right to resent it. No matter how clear to him Sophie's imminent mistake may be, it has nothing to do with him. She has nothing to do with him. Oliver turns over in the bed again and opens his eyes.

Four-oh-three. Oliver looks bitterly at the numbers, then considers the bedroom window, which looks south to the ocean. It seems absurd that he has not seen the ocean on either of his trips here, but the beach does not appear to figure prominently in Marian's Hamptons life. The house, which once sheltered horses for a nearby estate, has a pool out back, so minimalist it registers as a kind of dark decoration in the lawn. The beach is for families and singles on the make, and a front lawn for a still loftier echelon of Hamptons houses. It might as well be an hour's drive away.

Oliver sits up. Suddenly, he is full of resentment that she has never taken him to see the ocean. Just because the beach isn't part of her routine, why has she never thought of him? Last summer they could have swum or lain in the sun like normal people, but she never suggested it. Last night they could have walked there in a few minutes and been back before the fire was out, but they didn't.

He is aware of his hands clenching fistfuls of goose-down comforter.

He does not know if he has ever before felt such a fog of ill will. Marian, undistressed, sleeps on.

Quietly, Oliver slips from the bed. He puts on his jeans, his sweater, and laces up his boots. He is going to see the ocean, right now. He will go quickly and stake his claim to it, and then return with his absence unnoted, which doesn't matter because he is not doing it to be cruel to her but to be kind to himself. He begins to move across the wood floor, which creaks.

Marian sleeps. She is—he pauses to note—very beautiful asleep, as not every beautiful woman is. In sleep, she abandons her self-conciousness and is merely herself, a woman of middle years with enough beauty, enough kindness, enough grace, and a superior mind. Watching her, Oliver finds her nearness almost unbearably poignant, and wants to wake her up to show her herself, but instead he walks quietly to the door and goes down the stairs.

It's different here from Marian's other home. The beautiful surfaces and rich colors of Park Avenue are not present in this house, which retains elements of its former life: massive beams overhead, wide planks underfoot, and a half door to the kitchen. There is a large log cabin quilt nailed to one wall and, opposite, a great fireplace composed of fieldstones, each individually chosen and placed—Marian has explained—by an ancient Sicilian. Oliver finds it strange that the house, so much closer to his own taste than the Park Avenue apartment is, feels far more foreign to him, but perhaps it is because this place is so much more an expression of Marian's intimate life with her husband. The New York apartment might be a home, even a primary home, but it accepts certain conventions of what an apartment on Park Avenue should look like, and so loses an element of individuality. This house, filled with Marshall's military art and Marian's books (all sorted by genre, then author, then publication date) and the fruits of their early, misguided (in Oliver's opinion) passion for Bauer Ringware, belongs to them. With the discomfort that attends this realization, Oliver opens the sliding glass door to the backyard and steps outside.

The night is hard with cold. It moves quickly through the woolen strands of Oliver's sweater, finding his skin, but he decides against going back for his coat. He walks fast to get warm, first going to the end of the cobblestone driveway and then turning along Hedges Lane. On either side the privet hedges are so high he can make out only the tips of the houses they nearly obscure, but he has glimpses from the driveways as he goes by: shingled "cottages" grown massive on steroids, and modern conflagrations of steel and glass. Oliver walks quickly, parallel to the ocean, which crashes some distance to the right. Then he slows in wonder. On his right a building of baffling immensity is being assembled. Oliver gapes at it, trying to discern its purpose. Surely not an office complex? he thinks. Surely not here? The zoning must be airtight around this particular patch of soil, with its ocean view and its private swath of beach far on the other side of the rising shell. It must be a house, he understands, but how can something so large be a house? There will be enough room within its projected walls for each member of the largest possible family to have a house of his or her own. Oliver shakes his head and steps back from the fence. The Hamptons, as far as he can tell, have been conjured out of equal parts potato field and pretension, and for all of Marian's rhapsodizing about the light, it is not light that mostly motivates the absent inhabitants of these houses. They don't come here to bathe in it, nor even in the waves he now once again hurries toward, but to be wealthy and exclusionary in the company of other wealthy and exclusionary people.

Not that he has anything against rich people. By the standards of most of the planet, after all, he himself has far in excess of his needs. What's more, a world suddenly deprived of the wealthy would sweep away most of his friends, nearly all of his relatives, the majority of his clientele, and, not incidentally, the woman he happens to be in love with. Yet there are the rich people he loves and the rich people who need to build châteaux for their weekend use, and something certainly distinguishes the two groups from each other. He will not bring himself to call it class (Oliver stubbornly participates in the mass fantasy that there is no class in America), though this is the position his mother would take, were she here to argue the issue with him. On the other hand, he knows it isn't really about money, either. People without resources can be astoundingly snobbish, while the wealthiest person he has ever met—the baffling heiress Klein—let him in at the service entrance wearing a half-buttoned flannel shirt.

The ocean is close now. Oliver turns right at the end of the lane and half-jogs toward it. By this point, he has entirely lost his desire to see the water. The cold assaults him through his inadequate clothing with an icy wind, but he resists turning around. This expedition is all goal now, all mindless attainment. Oliver is too depleted to be really angry. He will merely stamp his way across the sand and insert one boot in the first wave that approaches, then turn and run back the way he came. With luck, he won't remember any of it in the morning.

The road ends in a broken parking lot. Oliver steps onto the edge of the sand and his boot sinks. The effort of motion increases instantly. He can hear his breath in tandem with the waves. The night is unlovely, overcast and dull, the sand and water gray. He moves his arms in an exaggerated pump, like a power walker intent on the finish line, and crosses the beach by the briefest possible route. There is no pleasure for him, and—when the wet moment finally comes—not even any sense of accomplishment, but when he turns around, he is rewarded by the surreal skyline of houses, postmodern and glassy black, arrayed at the edge of the beach as far as the eye can see. No one is home, he understands. In all the Hamptons there is only himself and billions of dollars' worth of vacant real estate. It is the loneliest thing he has ever felt. And it is so cold.

Then, quite suddenly, he is not alone. Headlights flick to life in the distance, far down the road he now faces, coming nearer. Oliver stands uncertainly, and then with growing unease. The car, he now sees, is a police car.

The car stops. A man steps out on the passenger's side.

Oliver lifts a hand in tentative greeting, then walks toward him. "Good evening!" he hears himself call, with false heartiness. "Good morning?"

"May I see some ID?" the humorless cop says.

Oliver reflexively reaches for his back pocket, but there is nothing there. He has not thought to bring his wallet on this ridiculous excursion.

"I left it at the house," he says, hoping "the house" will, at least, establish his validity.

"What house, sir?" the man says. The "sir" is especially disconcerting. The guy is about Oliver's age, but huskier, with jowls.

"My...a friend's house. On Hedges Lane." He can't make out the man driving the car. There is a sheen on the windshield. "I couldn't sleep. I thought I'd walk to the ocean. I should have brought a coat!" he says, trying for humor. "My name's Oliver Stern."

The man leans over and speaks into the open door. Then he straightens again. "Let me have the name of your friend, and the address on Hedges Lane."

"It's...," Oliver begins. Then he stops. What would Marian want him to do in this situation? He thinks frantically. The idea that something might come of this, that any complications might ensue from these incredibly stupid circumstances, horrifies him. "Look," says Oliver, "I'm here for a few days with my friend. I'm willing to give you the information, but can I ask you to be discreet about it?"

The guy gives him an incredulous look. "This isn't a cocktail party. Give me the name and address."

So Oliver does, cringing. He can't remember Marian's number on Hedges Lane. Sixty-something? Ninety-something? "It's near where they're putting up that colossal house," he offers, trying to be conversational, but the cop only stares at him and then goes back to the car, and—he can just make out—to the small computer screen on the dashboard. Is it against the law to go for a walk in the Hamptons? Oliver thinks bitterly, arms crossed tightly over his chest. He hates it here. If they let him out, he promises never to return.

"Mr. Stern," the cop says, "I would like your own address. If you can remember that."

Oliver bites back his first response, then gives his address. He gives his telephone number, his social security number, his mother's maiden name. He is asked to wait while a phone call is made. A phone call to whom? The FBI? *His mother?*

"Please get in the car," the cop says, and Oliver stares.

"You're kidding. I was just walking!"

"Please get in," he repeats.

"But...Listen, I just came to see the ocean!"

"Hey!" A voice comes from across the car. Deeper voice. Older voice. Oliver instinctively stops. "Get in the car now."

"Look," he says desperately, "I'm not a criminal! I—" He stops, stunned to realize that he has been on the point of saying, *I went to Brown.* Then he is so ashamed of himself that he climbs into the car.

In the backseat there is a cloying smell, borderline offensive. Oliver sits stiffly, his hands on his thighs, trying not to think about what might happen next, how he is going to explain himself to Marian. Freedom Summer scenarios needle away at him, and it takes real effort to allay them: will some rash of beachfront break-ins be laid at his feet? Is there some even more nefarious crime wave under way in the Hamptons for which he has just volunteered himself as a suspect?

The two cops in the front seat murmur, their conversation indistinguishable. Oliver hears beeps from the computer console, static from the radio, and the sounds of the engine. Oliver feels ignored, as if they have moved on to other matters. He does not know how to respond to this, or what to think about his circumstances. He has never been in trouble before. Is he in trouble now?

The car moves. They back up and turn, driving away from the ocean. Neither of the two men in the front seat says a word to Oliver. They go up the road, then left on Hedges Lane. They slow as they near Marian's house, and then the police car turns in, driving over the familiar cobblestones. Oliver feels a surge of buoyancy, then, seeing Marian ahead in the doorway, wrapped in one of Marshall's heavy flannel robes with a phone in one hand, his buoyancy is replaced by abject humiliation. Are they going to deliver him and leave? Are they going to give him a talking to? Are they—oh God—going to give *her* a talking to?

Oliver closes his eyes. He would very nearly prefer arrest, he thinks, to Marian's expression, which—now that he is close enough to see it—is a piteous amalgamation of indignity and dejection.

The passenger-side cop opens his door and walks across the courtyard. Marian clutches her robe at the throat. She nods. She speaks too softly for her words to carry. She nods again. And then it is over. The men barely look at Oliver again as his door is opened and he scrambles out, and they drive off without either apology or explanation, as if he is no longer worth the effort of acknowledgment. Watching them go, Oliver feels his heart drum with rage.

"I was just going for a walk!" he shouts after the car. "Jesus fucking Christ!"

"Oliver," Marian hisses. "Don't do that. God, I hope there isn't going to be a report."

Forgetting that he has had the identical thought only minutes before, Oliver yells, "Well, so what, Marian? Maybe that's what we need. What *you* need."

He is standing outside the threshold. She stands just inside. Cold air rushes past them both into the living room.

"I hate this fucking place," he goes on. "How can you like it here? How can you relax in a place where you're Ted Bundy if you go for a walk?"

"Come inside," she says tersely. "Stop shouting."

"No, seriously. Tell me. What kind of people come all the way out here and never bother to go look at the shore? That doesn't strike you as strange?"

Marian seems to consider her response. "You'd better come in now," she says quietly. "Or you might find the door locked."

Oliver, suddenly deflated, looks at his own feet. "I couldn't sleep," he says, morosely, as if this admission ranks with the most shameful. "I didn't want to wake you up."

"I wish you had," she says, stepping back inside and holding open the door. Oliver, at last, walks past her and collapses on one of the couches. The room is gray with light from upstairs and from the kitchen. He is, without warning, exhausted. Finally.

"Oliver," Marian cries, as if the strain of the past half hour has just caught up with her, too, "what were you thinking?"

He shrugs.

"Did you do it to…Were you trying to push me?"

Oliver looks up. She is sitting across from him, stiff, her knees together. She is absolutely miserable.

"I don't know. I don't think so, but I can't rule it out."

Marian shakes her head. "Why didn't you say something if you were that unhappy? We could have talked about it."

"Talked about it! Are you kidding? We've done nothing but talk about it since we met. I've been straightforward with you from the first day, Marian. But here I am, all these months later, sleeping in somebody else's house. In somebody else's bed. With somebody else's *wife*."

"That may be all I can offer you," she says carefully. "I never suggested you had to be satisfied with it."

"Are *you* satisfied?" Even to his own ears, Oliver sounds unnecessarily harsh, almost punishing. "Is this enough for you?"

Marian looks at him. "This? You mean the twenty-year-marriage this? The beautiful home—*two* beautiful homes—this? The thriving career this?" She glares at him. He refuses to answer. "Which part of *this* am I supposed to find deficient, Oliver? I have a hell of a lot to be thankful for. Some might even think that having an affair with the son of my oldest friend is not the most appropriate way to show my gratitude!"

"Marian—"

"No! I know you don't like to hear this, but when you get to my age—"

"Jesus," says Oliver.

"When you get to my age"—she is gasping now, choking it out—"you see. How little people have. How hard their lives are. How much pain they get handed. And me! I've never gone hungry. I've never been without a home."

"Marian, what the hell are you talking about? Without a home?"

But she is off, galloping through parts unknown.

"I always had enough. I had teachers who appreciated what I could do, and a husband who let me do it."

"Let you!" he says scornfully.

"Which wasn't nothing when I was your age, Oliver!" Marian shouts. "And maybe it's never crossed your mind that I might not have been the ideal wife, either. Maybe there were things Marshall wanted that I couldn't give him, and he forgave me for that."

"Forgave you!" howls Oliver. "This is getting worse and worse! It wasn't his job to forgive you! It was his job to love you and be your partner."

She shakes her head. The light from the kitchen makes her cheeks glisten. Wet, he sees. She is crying.

"Not true," says Marian. "Well, true, but not entirely true. You're very young, you know."

"Fuck you!" he explodes, pushing off the couch and crossing the room so quickly that he arrives even before the awareness of what he has just done. An instant later, though, that arrives, too. "Oh," says Oliver helplessly, hovering above her. "Oh, no. Oh Marian, I'm so sorry."

"Don't be sorry," she says, her voice flat.

"I couldn't sleep," he says. Useless, pointless.

"No," agrees Marian, in a falsely bright tone of voice. "Well, I'm going to bed."

And she leaves him, wavering above the place she is no longer sitting, torn between dragging her back and letting her go but frankly too depleted to do either. Instead, he takes her place on the sofa and pulls a blanket from the armrest to cover himself, though he isn't really cold anymore, and sits, not feeling anything. At the top of the stairs, the bedroom light goes out.

CHAPTER SIXTEEN

The Diner That Time Forgot

IN THE MORNING, they are not angry with each other, or not outwardly angry, but they are careful—overly courteous, intent on not touching the bruises of the night just past. Marian makes coffee, Oliver goes to the Sagaponack General Store for the *Times*, and they sit at the kitchen table, reading and sipping and building a wall around what has happened, at least while they can.

Outside, the new day mirrors their shared mood: dank and chilly gray, promising no warmth. Marian retrieves a student's thesis chapter from her bag and begins to read, marking somberly with a fountain pen as she completes each page, her reading glasses slipping down her nose. Oliver itches to reach across the table and nudge them up, but she always beats him to it without once distracting herself from her reading. After the first several times he understands that she is not ignoring him; she has simply been absorbed by something else.

Oliver wishes he could follow her, if not to wherever she is then to some place of his own, some place equally absorbing. Instead, he is jittery, agitated, his unease unsourced and ambient. He wants to get up, stay still, start shouting, but there is no apparent object for his blame.

Besides, he has that vaguely ill feeling from having gone without sleep, and he does not trust himself to say anything right now. He turns the pages of the Real Estate section, the Sports section, trying to focus. Marian finishes her chapter and methodically retrieves another project, a draft of her paper for the AHA, and sets it on the table.

"When do you want to go back?" she says suddenly.

Oliver looks at her. "Weren't we...I thought we were staying another night."

"Oh," she says carefully. "I have a departmental meeting. I can't get out of it. I'm sure I said so."

"I don't remember that, Marian."

"I'm sorry. I'm sure I told you."

"But you didn't." He hates this. He hates the way he sounds. Why does he have to sound like this? "It isn't... Marian, I'm so sorry about last night."

"No, no," she shakes her head. "No, sweetheart, don't worry. I overreacted. I mean, *they* overreacted."

She says this, but she does not look at him. She looks past him, out the kitchen door, at the dormant garden.

"We need to vote on job candidates for next year. We're doing the interviews at the AHA. We have about fifty serious candidates for two jobs, and we need to get a shortlist, otherwise we'll never get out of the hotel room. So..."

He notices her left hand, not at rest. It tenses and releases, the knuckles emerging in peaks like a pianist's, the diamond of her engagement ring glinting in the overhead kitchen light. He wants to take that hand and stop it moving, but he seems incapable of making contact.

"We can leave whenever you like," Oliver hears himself say, and Marian nods and goes back to her paper. She does not leap to her feet and begin packing, tidying, setting things right for departure. She maintains a studied nonchalance, as if she were not really trying to get away from him, but of course she is, Oliver thinks. She is, she is. And this is all his fault!

Forty-five minutes later, she gets up, languid, unhurried. She puts the dishes in the dishwasher, the paper in the recycling bin, then sets about removing all traces of Oliver Stern from the house she shares with her husband. Sheets go in the washer, trash from the bathroom is brought to the kitchen, then bagged and carried outside, a copy of *The New Yorker* with his subscription label, thoughtlessly left on the coffee table, is thoughtfully placed in his bag. From the kitchen table, Oliver watches this subtle choreography with growing dismay, and when Marian emerges in fresh clothing, clothing for the journey, he understands that his inactivity is now officially detaining her. "I'll just get my things," he says sadly.

"No rush!" she says, with forced cheer.

They drive out on the uncharacteristically empty Route 27, passing the closed farm stands and the self-consciously retro motels, the garden centers with their stock wrapped in burlap and the sad-looking summer restaurants. Oliver sits stiffly in the passenger seat, staring out the window. Leaving the Hamptons, they head for Riverhead and the LIE, and when Oliver sees the first signs for the highway, hunger occurs to him. He is hungry. He would like to stop and eat. And perhaps, at the same time, talk. "I'm so hungry," he says, floating the concept. "Aren't you hungry?"

"Not really," says Marian.

"Well, I am. Really hungry. Can we stop?"

She looks briefly at him, trying—and failing—to hide her annoyance. Then she nods and turns off into Riverhead, driving slowly along Main Street and looking for something likely. "How about this?" she asks, meaning the diner.

"Great," says Oliver enthusiastically.

They pull in and get out of the car. The lot is nearly full—a good sign for the food but a bad one for seating, and indeed when they get inside there are seats available only at the counter, chrome-edged octagons with red leatherette tops. Marian takes one as Oliver hangs up their coats by the door.

"The diner that time forgot," she says when he returns. "What do you think?"

Oliver looks around. A half century of continuous grease seems to hang about the place. Still, it's cheery and loud, with photos of—Oliver supposes—local celebrities hung above the chrome-backed work area behind the counter. Marian reads the menu. When the waitress stops expectantly at their place, Marian asks for coffee and an omelet. Oliver just asks for coffee.

"I thought you were hungry," Marian reminds him.

"Hamburger, please," he says automatically, though he isn't really hungry; he's too sad to be hungry. Just desperate, thinks Oliver, avoiding Marian's eyes. But for what, exactly? "Tell me about your job candidates," he says. "Do you have any favorites?"

She sighs. "No. To tell you the truth, I haven't given it much thought. I went through the applications once, but nothing's jumped out at me."

"Why do you have to go to the meeting, then?"

"Because of Carter Hawes. My department head?" She prompts.

"Oh. Yes," Oliver says, briefly shamed that he hadn't known the name of her boss.

"Carter takes these things very seriously."

"Choosing which applicants to interview?"

"No," says Marian with a brief smile. "Who attends the meeting and who skips out."

"Ah."

Their coffees land with a little slosh before them. Oliver pours the overflow from his saucer back into the cup, and passes Marian the sugar.

"So I really need to be there. I'm sorry I forgot to mention it."

He looks up. She does not seem to realize what she has just said, how she has just contradicted herself. A wave of sadness comes over Oliver so swiftly that he is nearly unbalanced on his octagonal stool. It has ended. It is ending, right now, right here. But Marian cares for him too much to say so.

"Marian," he tries.

"You know," she rushes on, "it's a circus, the AHA. Everyone wants something—a job or a book contract or a recommendation. What happens to history in the midst of it all? And you'd be amazed how much plagiarism there is. Not the kind you can prove, necessarily—not text, but research. People help themselves to the work of other people, then rewrite the conclusions. They appointed a committee a few years back to look into it, and all they came up with was a statement about paying closer attention. Like we should all stop doing our own research in order to research other people's research?"

Oliver shakes his head. "I'm sorry," he says.

"On the other hand, everybody's desperate for jobs. The pressure to get hired is astounding. Fifty serious contenders—fifty *serious* contenders, that's not counting the people who merely have Ivy League degrees and three or four years teaching at the post-doc level—how are we supposed to pick a shortlist, let alone a single applicant? It's humbling, you know. If I were coming through now, I'd probably be thrilled with an adjunct position at a South Dakota community college. I'm not saying it's an excuse for plagiarism, though."

Marian stops. She looks, thinks Oliver, as if she has no idea what to say next. Then the arrival of her omelet saves her.

"This looks good," Marian says weakly, and begins to eat it with unconvincing enthusiasm.

Oliver watches her. She will not turn to him. He can't see her eyes. What color are her eyes? he thinks. In the future, how will he remember them?

The door of the diner opens, then closes. He imagines the miasma of grease disturbed by the puff of cold air. He removes the bun from his rapidly cooling hamburger and looks around for ketchup, though he cannot be said to truly want that, either. The ketchup is inches from Marian's right hand, and he is about to ask her for it when he sees that she is at last looking at him—eyes *brown*, he thinks fiercely. She's looking past him, really, but close enough. Oliver smiles in vague relief.

Then, quite abruptly, she is on her feet beside her stool. "Oliver," Marian says, "I need to leave. I don't feel well." She opens her purse. She takes her wallet out. She puts money on the table, a twenty-dollar bill, far too much, and moves away toward the door. Helpless, Oliver goes after her.

"Are you going to be sick?" he asks. "Don't you want to go to the bathroom?"

"No, no," Marian says, pulling her coat off the hanger by the door. In her haste it falls to the floor and he reaches down for it, fumbling against her own hand, which is also fumbling.

"What's happened?" he says. He holds the coat for her and she throws an arm into a sleeve and dives against the door.

"I'm fine, I just have to go. Can we go?"

"Well—" he starts to follow. She has her hand on the door, holding it open. She has her other hand on his sleeve. She is, Oliver realizes, actually pulling him outside.

"Wait, Marian," he says. "I need my coat."

She lets go with visible reluctance and stands on the top step, her eyes on him, waiting. Dimly, Oliver goes back and reaches up for his coat, and defiantly puts it on right where he stands. At the counter, the waitress is holding the twenty and looking at him. She seems reluctant to question the tip, in case he might change his mind, but he is too confused to explain himself to her. "Sorry!" he says. "Just remembered we were supposed to be somewhere else."

The waitress nods, relieved, and sticks the bill in her apron, then heads down the counter, away from him. Oliver watches her go to a booth in the back. And then he sees something.

"Oliver, come *on*," Marian says from the open door, but he does not come on. He moves back into the diner. His coat is on. There is a fine cord of amazing strength drawing him closer and closer to the booth at the end of the diner, which is in a town he has never visited before, where he knows no one, and this is why he cannot understand why he is approaching the person he is approaching, who is a person Oliver has always despised, in spite of the person's being married to Oliver's mother.

Perhaps Henry Rosenthal takes him for a waiter. Perhaps he is as impervious to the notion of running into someone who might know him in the Riverhead Diner as Oliver himself was, only moments ago.

Perhaps that is why Henry is here, with a woman clearly not Oliver's mother, just as Oliver himself is here with a woman he should not be seen with. So why is Oliver so stunned by his stepfather's audacity?

He is very close before Henry Rosenthal looks up, and the shock on his stepfather's face is gratifying, but not gratifying enough. No wound Oliver can inflict, nothing he can say will be gratifying enough. Words race through his head and depart. The woman detaches her hand from Henry's and puts it demurely in her lap, but she does not otherwise move.

"Well," Henry says, and Oliver hates, afresh, the nasal buzz of his stepfather's voice.

"Does she know?" Oliver hears himself say. He means his mother, but regrets the pronoun instantly. Without knowing the first thing about the woman seated before him, he does not want Henry to think he cares in the slightest about her.

"I think so," says Henry. "If I had to bet, I'd say yes."

"If you had to *bet*," Oliver says in sickened wonder.

"Your mother's very smart," Henry offers, as if in explanation.

The woman in the booth ducks out, swinging long, exquisite blond hair behind her. Even without looking at her directly, Oliver senses her extreme beauty. But his mother is beautiful, too, he thinks frantically. Henry should not be allowed to simply exchange one beautiful woman for a younger one. Henry should not be allowed access to oxygen.

"Were you going to tell her?" Oliver manages to say.

"Of course," Henry shrugs. "I care for your mother."

"Oh, *fuck you*," he says, for the second time in a handful of hours, and for the second time it comes out much louder than expected. In the next booth, hands freeze on the way to mouths. "If you cared for her, you wouldn't be here," Oliver hisses.

"The situation is complex," Henry says, offhandedly. "And I don't owe you an explanation, Oliver. Caroline, arguably, but not you."

"She's your *client*," Oliver observes. This fact has occurred to him and flown from his mouth in a single, fluid instant, propelled by outrage.

"True. It's not what anyone wanted."

"My God, you're such a hypocrite! You're whining to the press about how she deserves more money from her husband, and meanwhile you're screwing her."

"Hey!" Henry says sharply. He rises, as best he can from the cramped booth. Oliver, amazed, understands that he has insulted the honor of his stepfather's mistress. "I am in love with this woman," Henry pronounces. "I am going to marry this woman."

Oliver steps back. "Good," he spits. "Then I hope she gets her next divorce attorney to clean you out. I hate your fucking guts."

For a moment, Henry does not react. Then he sinks back onto the banquette, shaking his head. "I'm wounded," he says finally, laughing.

"I've never liked you," Oliver adds. This is actually for his own benefit. Loyalty to his mother has not permitted him to voice this for fifteen years, but he wants to get it on the record, and now seems like the last possible moment to do so. It does not have the desired effect, however. Henry's laugh broadens, then peters out in a chuckle.

"Well, you know, Oliver, I'm not going to take that personally. You wouldn't have liked any man screwing your mother who wasn't your father."

He steps back, stunned that someone thinks this of him and then stunned to realize that it's absolutely true. He wants to leave before the blond woman comes back. He does not want to see her again, to see how beautiful she is. "You tell her today," Oliver manages to say. "Or I tell her tomorrow."

Henry appears to consider this like the master negotiator he is, then he nods. "I agree," he says, with maddening gravity, and Oliver turns and rushes away, his face hot with rage. He bursts out through the door and stands for a moment, lost on the top step of the diner, until Marian calls his name from the window of her car. He stumbles forward and climbs inside, and they drive in leaden silence to the highway.

CHAPTER SEVENTEEN

Its Necessary End

A T THE BEST OF TIMES, it's a long trip; today, it feels interminable. The exit numbers diminish with wearying lethargy and the mood in Marian's Volvo stays intractably grim. Oliver feels by turns enraged and humiliated, alternately full of pity for his mother and disgusted with her for failing to recognize Henry's perfidy. He does not know whether he hopes his stepfather will indeed tell her tonight or not; he does not know whether he wants the privilege for himself or not; and he can barely hold one thought in his head before another comes crashing into it, like a pileup on an overcrowded highway.

The LIE is not, actually, overcrowded. The car moves swiftly enough but the exits still *tick*, *tick* slowly toward zero and the city, while Oliver fumes in the passenger seat and Marian drives in dour silence. They are nearly to Queens when she finally speaks.

"Poor Caroline" is what she says.

Oliver looks over at her. "She'll be rid of him."

"And that's good?" Marian asks.

"He's an asshole."

"To you," she says sadly. "But you're not the one married to him."

"I hate him," says Oliver.

Marian sighs. "I know."

The city's backbone slips into view. Marian gets in the lane for the Queens Midtown Tunnel.

"What are you going to do?" she says.

He looks at her as if she's insane. "Tell her. Of course."

"Oliver, don't."

"I will if he doesn't," he says bitterly. "I said he had to tell her tonight or I'd tell her tomorrow."

"I'm not sure that's wise. Right now," she adds, cutting him off. "While your feelings are so..."

He gives her a grace period, then he jumps in. "So?"

"I was going to say, 'emotional.' Not that there's anything wrong with being emotional, under the circumstances, but it might do Caroline more good if you cooled off a bit. Besides, you'll have to explain what you were doing in the Riverhead Diner."

Oliver frowns. This thought had not occurred to him. What if Henry tells Caroline about the encounter? Won't she get around to requesting the details eventually?

"I don't think he saw you," Oliver offers.

"No, I shot out of there pretty fast. I'm just sorry I didn't get you out, too."

"Why?" he says harshly. "Is it your responsibility to protect me? Or were you protecting *him*?"

Marian gives him a brief look. "I wasn't thinking of him. I couldn't care less about him. I was thinking of you. And not," she adds, with discernible hurt, "because it's my responsibility. Or are you confusing me with your mother again?"

It is an unfortunate slip. The temperature in the car drops again. All that restrains Oliver from shouting at her is his weariness, and the fact that they have just entered the tunnel, which is full of rapid, weaving traffic. He has also begun to be concerned about the question of their destination, an anxiety that leaps as Marian turns south on First Avenue.

"Where are you going?" he says tightly.

She frowns. "To Commerce Street."

"No!" Oliver says, with a force he hasn't expected. It has suddenly become clear to him that he does not want it to end this way, though he cannot yet examine the nature of "it": Their trip to the Hamptons? Their love affair? He does not want to be dropped off, left behind by her, at least not with this knot of tension between them. The notion that she might wish to be free of him, even for a short time, is terrifying. "I want to come with you," he says, straining not to whine.

"But I'm going to the office," she says deliberately. "For my meeting."

"I'll come with you."

"Oliver, that's... look, who knows how long it's going to go on? It might be hours!"

"Fine. I'll wait. We'll have dinner."

She bites her lower lip and turns right on Fifty-seventh. It is a noncommittal move.

"By then I'll just want to collapse," she says. "By then, *you'll* want to collapse!"

"No," he shakes his head. "It's fine. I'll hang out somewhere. I'll go have coffee."

"All afternoon?" She brakes for the light on Lexington and looks at him. "Oliver, look, let me take you home. I'll call you. We can meet for dinner somewhere if it's really important to you."

He shakes his head. "No, you won't call. Or you'll call me and say you're too tired. I'll come with you. I'll *wait*."

Marian glares, but not at him. She glares at the weaving bodies, moving in front of her car, even behind her car, pedestrians impervious to danger. "You're being stubborn," she tells Oliver. "I don't want to spend the afternoon worrying about you and feeling bad that you're sitting in some coffee shop waiting for me. It's going to be boring enough without that."

"Fine!" Oliver shouts. "The last thing I want to do is bore you."

"Oliver!"

The light turns green. He reaches back between them to his bag, on the floor behind her seat. It knocks her shoulder as he pulls it forward but he doesn't apologize.

"Just let me out. I wouldn't want to inconvenience you."

"Oliver, don't be stupid."

"There. On the corner," he says wildly, but she continues west, to Park. "Stop the car!" Oliver shouts.

"I'm driving you home."

He flings open the passenger door, jolting her to a stop. "Thanks for a lovely time," he tells her, with real cruelty, and steps out in the middle of Park Avenue, to the loud accompaniment of horns.

"Oliver, get back inside!" Marian says frantically.

He walks away, almost jauntily, holding his bag over his shoulder with a crooked finger, crossing Park to the island between its northbound and southbound lanes. The silver gray of her Volvo shoots past, westbound. He watches it as far as Madison, where it turns right, and when it does, every trace of his piggish contentment leaves him in a rush. He stands on the island, shivering a little in the air after the warm car, holding his bag in this ridiculous posture. He stands still.

Motion in the city is its own language, understood by natives, quickly learned by newcomers. There are not many legitimate reasons to stand, inert, on a Manhattan street, and the illegitimate ones—drunkenness, schizophrenia, criminal intent—are blaring signals to the justly cautious. Oliver thinks of this, dimly, as pedestrians stream past him in both directions, plainly giving him a wide berth, then again as the light switches and traffic runs north and south past his little island, but he can't somehow bring himself to move. *Isn't she coming back?* The question finally occurs to him. *Isn't Marian coming to get him?*

He calculates the time it would take from Madison, northbound, to a right turn on Fifty-eighth, and then a right turn southbound on Park. This is time long past by now, Oliver understands, but then, when you think about it, how can Marian stop for him when he stands like this, ridiculously, in the middle? He is prolonging this ordeal by his own ignorance. Should he cross the street to the sidewalk on the southbound side and wait there? Will she know he's gone that way and not the other way, to the northbound side? He turns experimentally to look at the other side. There is no silver Volvo on the northbound side. There is also no silver Volvo on the southbound side. Is she waiting for him on Madison?

And how could he have said that to her, about having a lovely time? What kind of asshole is he?

Unexpectedly, Oliver begins to cry. From the corner of one teary eye, he watches a mother snatch her little girl out of his path. In minutes he has devolved from citizen to untouchable, but he can't seem to stop falling apart. He wants Marian. He has to apologize right now. He has to get them back to where they were before...

But he has to keep going back, further and further, to find *before*.

Oliver waits for the green light. When it comes, he crosses Park and moves swiftly, in his city gait. He presses onto the crosstown bus, behind a clutch of pubescent girls hemmed in by Bloomingdale's bags, then leaps off at Broadway and rushes to the subway station at Columbus Circle. The wait for the number 9 is long and malodorous (two teenagers in down jackets and falling-down blue jeans share a gyro just down the platform), but when the train comes Oliver easily finds a seat. The intensity of his purpose, as the train flies north, feels good, though he has not yet brought his mind to bear on what he will say when he actually sees Marian, nor considered the possibility that she might not want him turning up in her office. All that matters, he tells himself with stubborn focus, is that he offer his apology and his love. Then he can leave her alone, for her meeting and the rest of her day. Just pull us back from the edge, he thinks. It's a modest goal, the only one he is capable of.

Oliver leaves the subway at 116th Street and walks east, moving swiftly through the Columbia campus, fairly confident of his destination. He has been here only once before, early in his affair with Marian (for a very memorable afternoon on the floor of her Fayerweather Hall office, while urgent students and aggravated colleagues knocked at the locked door), but he finds the building easily now and pulls open the door. He climbs the stairs, bucking the flow of students and dodging their ponderous backpacks. At the second-floor landing he turns right along the corridor to the faculty offices, walking past several open doors to the room at the end of the hall, where he finds Marian's door unaccountably shut. There is no answer to his knock. The unwelcome image of Marian and another man, rolling around on the carpet inside, assaults his imagination, and for a long moment he glares at the plastic rectangle on the pale wood door declaring her name and office hours. She isn't here, he reassures himself, calculating the travel time by car (considering weekday afternoon Manhattan traffic) compared to the rapid trip he himself has just made by bus and subway. He got here first, is all, and she is even now making her way from the university parking facility, or vainly searching for a parking space in the neighborhood. Or maybe—the idea strikes Oliver—she went home first, left her car there, changed her clothes before the meeting. Or maybe she is indeed on campus, but the meeting has already begun and Marian is there, not here. But where is there?

Oliver turns, retracing his steps to the department office beside the stairwell, an open area with several desks at which no one is sitting. He stands awkwardly at the periphery of the office, hoping someone will come to him. Minutes pass, though, before someone does, and he grows more anxious, waiting. He eyes Marian's likely colleagues, her possible students, feeling so detached from her, half-expecting her to turn the corner and see him and increasingly afraid of how she might react to the sight of him. It has just struck him that the best possible thing might be to go now, before he interacts with anyone here, when a woman catches his eye. "Help you?" she says. She is a young woman. Maybe a college student herself, Oliver thinks.

"I was looking for Marian Kahn," he says.

"Her office is down there," the woman says, pointing.

"I know. She's not there."

"Well then," the woman shrugs, setting down her stack of files on one of the desks. "She's not here."

"Yes, but... do you know where the meeting is?"

The woman looks up. She waits for more information.

"The meeting on the job applicants," he says, dropping his voice.

She frowns, her forehead deeply ridged. "Job applicants? Is that today?"

Before he can answer, she twists and shouts, "Lucy, is the AHA hiring committee meeting today?"

"Next week," says Lucy, from an adjacent office.

"Next week," the woman informs Oliver, unnecessarily. "Not today."

Oliver steps back, reeling, nearly tripping over his own bag. He is frantically trying to explain this to himself, to place it within the realm of the not-tragic, the not-irredeemable, but he can't. She isn't here. She isn't coming here at all. She is somewhere else, and she is staying there.

"Thanks," he manages to say, but barely.

"You can leave her a message," the woman says. "There's her box over there..."

But Oliver doesn't even look. He reaches down for his bag, grabbing it for dear life, and lurches toward the staircase. He is barely in control of his feet, barely in control of his face, and so horrendously sad that it actually hurts to think. The banister is clammy under his right hand. Gravity alone brings him back down the stairs. Then, before him, the entryway door opens, admitting the cold and a person who does not move out of the way. Irritated, Oliver looks up.

"Hello," the person says. "Oliver?"

Oliver nods. He is supposed to do more than nod. He is supposed to say, "Hello, Sophie." But this is quite beyond him, not least because he is suddenly, cataclysmically breathless, and not altogether sure where the floor is, and incidentally numb, especially in his hands. In fact, he is not even very sure that his hands are still attached to him except that, briefly looking down, he can see one of them still holding the bag, the bag of his long-ago sojourn in Marian's house and life.

"What are you doing here?" Sophie says. "Are you here to see me?"

Marian's eyes are brown, Oliver thinks. Sophie's eyes look black, her hair is black—*truly* black—the circles under her eyes are verging on black, themselves. She is wearing a flannel shirt again. The same as the first time? he wonders. In the kitchen? Automatically, he looks for the gap between the buttons, but it isn't there. He wants it to be there. He feels horribly gypped that it isn't there. It occurs to him that Sophie hasn't the slightest idea how lovely she is. And why should she? He hadn't the slightest idea himself, until just now.

"Are you all right?" Sophie says, with real concern.

"I don't think so," Oliver manages. It comes out hoarse, and barely audible.

"Are you lost?"

He shakes his head.

"Are you... Did you want to talk to me about the flowers? For the wedding?"

Oliver looks at her. He hasn't done the first thing about the flowers for her wedding. And now, just thinking about the flowers for her wedding fills him with abject misery. "I'm sorry," he hears himself say. "I feel terrible about what happened."

She frowns. Oliver notes the faintest of freckles on her skin. Those circles under her eyes—he hadn't seen them before. Maybe they weren't there before, or maybe he just hadn't noticed. But how could he not have noticed? He has missed so much, he thinks.

"You came all the way up here?" Sophie asks. "To apologize?"

"Yes!" Oliver says, with some relief, and truthfully enough. He has in fact come all the way up here to apologize, albeit not to her.

"Well, it's not necessary. I shouldn't have run out like that. I've actually been meaning to phone you, myself."

"You have?" he asks, astonished.

Sophie grins awkwardly. "Not that you haven't seen crazy brides before..."

"You are so beautiful," says Oliver.

They look at each other in shock.

"I won't take it back," he tells her.

Sophie nods. "All right."

"Don't ask me to," he adds, sounding very nearly angry.

"All *right*," she says.

The door opens. Someone pushes past them, up the stairs.

"Would you like to go somewhere? And talk?" says Sophie.

Oliver nods.

"My apartment is—"

"Yes," Oliver says, and walks past her, quickly, terrified to make contact. After the smallest hesitation, Sophie comes, too, then passes him to show the way, walking slightly ahead and not looking back. They cross Amsterdam and walk east on 118th, to Morningside Drive. He knows the address. He has written it himself, week after week, and taped it to a bowl or a vase of white roses, and given it to Bell for delivery, but he has never been here, himself. He follows Sophie inside the building, past the slumbering doorman, into the ornate, aged elevator. He won't meet her eyes, and neither of them says a thing.

There is exactly one thought in Oliver's head, and that is the remembered patch of revealed abdomen between the misaligned buttons of Sophie's flannel shirt. Whatever presents itself as an impediment to that patch of skin will have to be swept aside, he is thinking. Not because the hunger he feels is carnal—not merely that—but because he feels he is *supposed* to put his hand on her there, and then his mouth, and when he does these things he will understand why he is following Sophie Klein to her apartment, so full of longing that he wonders how he can survive the walk, and the wait, though it's measured in minutes, and then seconds. She is clattering her keys ahead of him in the narrow corridor. She is turning the key in the lock, then turning around to face him, her back to the open door, and then they are both inside.

He touches her face and her throat, the long thick plait of her hair. He touches her hand. It never occurs to Oliver that she does not want him to do these things. Sophie stands perfectly still, her breath shallow. "I want," he begins to say, but the object of his want escapes into redundancy. He wants everything: her hair, which is somehow unbound around them, and her breasts under his hands and her mouth, amazingly open, and at last, the white skin of her belly, which he goes down on his knees to press his cheek against. He is not confused about where he is, or whom he's with. Whatever disquieting thoughts occur to him—the fact that he is in love with Marian, for example, the fact that Sophie is engaged to Barton—he beats back and then returns to her, and to the amazement on her face. She holds him very tightly. "Sophie," Oliver says, kissing her throat and asking permission.

It afflicts him that another man might have touched her like this, but only until he is inside her. When he is inside her she looks at Oliver as she cannot possibly have looked at anyone, ever, ever, and he understands for the first time what it means to a woman to be, actually, penetrated by another person, and the privilege of that, and the joy of that, which is so much more than physical. Tenderness passes between them as they move, first slowly, then less slowly. Sophie pulls him against her, and he opens his eyes to watch until she stops and is very still. She is so lovely, he thinks. She breaks open his heart.

"Oh, don't cry," Sophie tells him, but he does. And then she does, too.

"I'm involved with someone," Oliver says, sobbing.

Sophie's fingers move in his hair. "What a coincidence. Me too."

Without stopping crying, he laughs. Then he asks her what they are going to do.

"I don't know," Sophie says.

They lie in some discomfort on the hard floor of her entryway, their clothes detached and strewn about them. Sophie's hair falls over Oliver's face like a veil. The afternoon light fades through Sophie's living-room windows, and the shadows edge up the hallway to where they are lying, and finally it is dark everywhere.

"My father's dying," says Sophie.

Oliver opens his eyes. He can't see a thing in the dark.

"Sophie," he says, "I'm sorry."

"He has hepatitis," she says. "We found out last winter. It was just after I met Bart."

Oliver's head is on her chest, rising and falling with her breath. "Yes."

"The crazy thing is, all this time I've refused to see the connection."

Oliver concentrates. Across the city, a siren whines. A thought occurs to him, but in a delayed, sluggish manner. "Isn't hepatitis…I mean, can't they cure that?" he says.

"Hepatitis A, they can cure. Hepatitis B. Unfortunately, our letter came up C."

"And that's…"

"Bad."

It's so cold now. The bare floor is cold. Oliver turns tightly toward her until his face, at least, is warm.

"How long…," Oliver begins to ask. "I mean, what are his doctors saying?"

"Oh," she says, "I don't think doctors tell you anymore. They didn't tell us, anyway. Maybe we just didn't ask. He was hospitalized last summer, then for a week in September. They keep switching the drugs, but it's sort of a diminishing return, you know?"

Oliver nods against her chest. She is, he realizes, both obstinate and wretchedly frail. Like himself. Which also, and just as suddenly, occurs to him.

"You lost your father," she says, matter-of-factly.

"Yes," he confirms.

"Did you get over it?" Sophie asks.

The unwelcome image of Henry Rosenthal shudders into his head. "No," he says.

"But you have your mother?" she asks, her voice cracking a bit.

Oliver lifts the hair from over his face. He can see her eyes. "Sophie," he tells her, "you won't be alone."

As if to prove this, the telephone rings. Sophie flinches.

"I don't have to get that," she says, unconvincingly, but when Barton Ochstein's booming voice begins to fill the apartment, she curses and scrambles to her feet. Oliver watches her move, naked, down the corridor. "I'm here," she cries, snatching up the phone.

Oliver sits, his back against the entryway wall. His sweater hangs on by one arm. His pants and shorts bunch stupidly at his ankles. He can hear Sophie, muttering agreements, giving nothing away. "Oh, no," she says, with false empathy. "Well, I'm sure that's fine. Okay. Okay. Yes, you too."

Oliver stands and pulls up his pants. He puts his other arm into the sweater and pulls it over his head. Then he walks down the corridor.

Sophie is sitting on a stool, next to the kitchen counter. Oliver's flowers—his, not Barton's—are on the counter, failing. One rose droops down to the butcher block, forlorn. The call is over, and Sophie leans forward, forearms together on the Formica surface. Her hair falls over her shoulder, nearly obscuring her breasts, her ribs, but oddly not her face. "That was Barton," she says, unnecessarily.

"I gathered."

"He doesn't want to have the rehearsal dinner at the inn after all," she says. "He managed to get his plumbing parts delivered. For the downstairs bathroom." She trails off. "At his house. So he wants to have the dinner there." Sophie pauses. "He's very proud of his house, you know. He likes people to see it."

"Sophie," Oliver says.

"I said it was fine. I don't really care about it one way or the other. And my father loves Bart's house."

"*Sophie,*" he says sharply. "What are you talking about?"

She looks up at him and frowns.

"My father . . . You should have seen him when he met Bart. When I started seeing him, my father was so thrilled."

Oliver shakes his head.

"It's . . . He thinks of Bart as someone who will keep me safe. Do you understand? Because he won't be here," Sophie says, stumbling over her words. "And he's right. I'll be safe. I don't feel anything." She laughs, a strained laugh. "How safe is that?"

"You can't marry him, Sophie."

"I realize that," she says. "But I can't not marry him, either."

Oliver is about to ask for an explanation, but he stops himself. He doesn't feel entitled to the question. Instead, he looks away from Sophie and takes in what he can see of the apartment: the view of the open sky over Morningside Park and Harlem beyond, a few paintings, a wall of bookshelves. Over the kitchen table is a framed poster bearing the black-and-white image of a woman's wide face, her dark hair parted far on the side of her head, with German text. It announces an exhibit, Oliver thinks, or perhaps an academic conference. He peers at the title, *Die Weiße Rose*, deciphering the language as best he can. Then he understands.

"Is that your white rose?" he asks Sophie.

She looks up and nods. "Yes. That's Sophie Scholl. She was a member of the group."

"I think you said...did they..." He can't quite make sense of the word, it's so medieval. "She was...beheaded?" Oliver asks.

Sophie nods. "All of them. They arrested them, interrogated them, tried them, and beheaded them. All in the space of a few days."

Oliver stares at the woman. She looks about fourteen.

"She was so brave," Sophie says. Her voice shakes. "She had everything to lose. She was a privileged member of Nazi society, and she risked it all. I, on the other hand, have nothing to lose, and I'm such a coward. I'm not even brave enough to do this one thing."

"You can ask for help," he tells her.

Sophie bites her lip. She sighs the way you sigh after tears: ragged and bereft. Then she looks at him.

"Will you help me?" says Sophie.

Oliver walks across the room to her, and she stands and faces him. She is almost his height, and much thinner than he had thought. Her hair, unbraided, comes down to her waist and shines in the dark. Standing so close to her, Oliver understands that all of his debts have been canceled, and all contracts dissolved, and that he has done nothing to merit that, nor bring it about, but that is not what stuns him most. What stuns him most is how this long and fraught day has hurtled to its necessary end, how its every twist and encounter has brought him here, to this room and this woman—and not just here, but peacefully here, because now, at last, he knows the thing that is wanted of him, and that he wants it, too.

ACT III

CHAPTER EIGHTEEN

The Magic Age

YOU CAN HURT ME.

    Just before noon on Monday, Marian walks down Park to Fifty-seventh. As she turns east to cross the wide avenue, she is hit by a glare of sunlight and shuts her eyes tightly. But it isn't really the light, or not only that. In fact, she has been dreading this moment all the way here, all thirty blocks of the way, and yet, of the many other routes she might have taken, she still chose this one. For this purpose, she thinks now. For the specific pain it promises. Well, all right then. And she opens her eyes, and looks.

Just there. The traffic island, in the middle of the avenue: the precise last place she saw Oliver. She saw him in her rearview mirror as she drove off, furious and not at all sorry—at least, not sorry then—because he had stormed out of her car and her life and their love affair. Gone. So gone that she can barely remember, now, how he looked, standing there with his weekend bag and his petulant, childish—yes, *childish*!—expression.

You can hurt me, she thinks again, her hands deep in the pockets of her heavy coat. Those words, they've been haunting her all morning, dogging her down Park Avenue. Two months ago she had let those words ruin an entire weekend she had planned to spend with Oliver. One of the few weekends, she now knew, that she would ever have with him. Why the words should have come back to her today has been a mystery until this very moment, but now, looking across the traffic at that small perch of cement, she understands. She could hurt him, yes. She was capable of it, yes, and he had given permission for it, yes. But here, exactly here, was where she had finally done it.

Marian clenches her hands inside her pockets. Only in the past couple of days has winter finally beset Manhattan, first one brittle frost and then a curtain of icy rain. Not that she hasn't felt cold for weeks, she thinks, and jittery, and certainly distraught. Because once the cushion of her rage had passed, that afternoon (and it passed so quickly, she had barely made it home in time), all the rest of her repertoire of caustic emotions had rushed in to fill the void: raw pain, blaring regret, every hoarded self-recrimination of the past six months. Those had been bad days, their only blessing that Marshall was not due back from his trip until the following week. She had unplugged all the phones, not so much to keep Oliver from getting through as to keep herself from calling him. This was good, she had concluded, somewhere in the middle of that rotten time. This was good. The affair had ended, as of course it had to be ended, from the start. Maybe, moreover, it was the best of all their possible endings: angry but at least fast, nasty but at least clean. And best of all, Oliver thought he was the one who had ended it.

Still, she sighs, looking across the moving traffic; some irrational woman in her head is disappointed, because Oliver is not, actually, still on that traffic island right now, just as she left him, two long unhappy weeks ago. Wilted to the spot in sadness, perhaps? Stubbornly waiting for her to pick him up? Sitting cross-legged atop his weekend bag with a baffled, all-is-forgiven expression? Oh don't be so dramatic, she tells herself. There is no one on the traffic island, as it happens, or only a copper-haired woman on a cell phone, waiting for the light to change. The light changes.

You can hurt me, Marian thinks, walking forward, eyes straight ahead. She had done just that. She walks through the space he occupied, and then she keeps walking.

Ten minutes later, Marian steps into P.J. Clarke's and takes off her coat, waiting for her eyes to adjust to the darkness. The long-fabled bar is full of men drinking their lunch, and she steps carefully between bodies toward the restaurant. She is late, but not very late, and when she gives her name to the maître d', he nods curtly and turns, gesturing over his shoulder. Marian follows, carrying her coat, fighting her apprehension.

Caroline sits near the back of the restaurant, her menu open on the red-checked tablecloth. She looks very thin—nearly gaunt, thinks Marian—but she is also lovely. Her short hair is cut in the same style as last spring—the last time they were together, and memorable to Marian for so much more than their chance encounter—but it is now peppered with gray. Caroline looks up and waves, and when Marian reaches her, Caroline gets to her feet and offers not the kiss Marian expects, but a real hug. Marian, after the smallest pause, hugs back.

"How are you?" Marian says as they sit.

"Actually, I'm all right," says Caroline. "I know I'm not supposed to be, but the amazing thing is, I am." She smiles, shaking her head. "That's your cue to tell me I'm in denial, or something."

"Wouldn't dream of it," Marian says. "If you feel all right I won't argue with you."

"I wish everybody else felt that way," she says. The waiter comes and stands by the table. Without a word, he conveys the hostility of service traditional to P.J. Clarke's. "Shall we have a drink?" says Caroline.

"Oh, why not. A *real* drink. No wimpy wine."

"A sidecar!" says Caroline, with delight. "Remember?"

"How could I forget? Two sidecars, please."

The waiter, with a grimace, goes away.

"When I was seventeen, one of the waiters here had me in tears," Marian says.

"You took it personally."

"Yup," she says. "I always did, whenever anyone behaved badly. Now I couldn't care less."

Caroline laughs. "An advantage of getting on in years. Right?"

"Well, there ought to be a few."

Marian looks over at the next table. A four-top of generously proportioned men in suspenders are cutting into thick steaks.

"Time stands still," she observes.

"Oh, I don't know," says Caroline. "I was sort of thinking of a steak, myself."

"Good. I know they say you can't be too thin, but you look too thin."

Caroline looks up. "It hasn't been a walk in the park. It's been a hard time, if not exactly a shock. But I've had a chance to think about what I want to do now, and I've discovered that there *are* things I want. Once you know what you want, everything sort of brightens up, you know?"

"You get to go and get it."

"Precisely. Ooh, good."

Their drinks arrive. They are bright orange, electric with Cointreau and cognac.

"To your mom," says Caroline, lifting hers. "She would be horrified."

"Yes! Imagine! Women, in P. J. Clarke's!"

"Dining alone!" Caroline adds.

"But we're not alone, we're together." Marian sips. The drink is heavenly and absolutely lethal. "Oh my God. Wasn't this restaurant in *The Lost Weekend*? Now I know why." She smiles appreciatively at her glass. "It's a good thing I canceled my office hours this afternoon. Please tell me you're not driving home."

Caroline shakes her head. "I'm not driving home. I'm staying in town. I have an appointment with a broker tomorrow at nine."

Marian looks at her. "You're moving back. Is that what that means?"

"That's what it means," says Caroline. "When you live in Greenwich for thirty years and still tell people you're from New York, it's really time. Don't you think?"

Marian nods. It takes her a moment to work through the anxiety this announcement produces, but once she does, Marian is happy. The waiter materializes, silent and expectant. "Do you know what you want?"

"Um...shell steak. Rare, please," says Caroline.

"I'll have the spinach salad."

He takes their menus and goes away.

"He ought to have one of these," Caroline says, laughing and lifting her glass.

"Have you told...your son?" says Marian.

"Oliver," Caroline says, actually reminding her of his name. "Yes. He's happy about it. Well, I think he's happy about it. He's a bit obscure these days. He's certainly thrilled that Henry's gone, though of course he's concerned for me."

"Of course," Marian mutters.

"When I told him Henry was seeing someone, he was so angry. I think he was angrier than I was."

Marian, who does not trust herself to say the right thing, merely nods.

"But he's never been...forgiving of Henry, you know? He lost his father at exactly the wrong moment for that."

Marian carefully sips her drink. "You mean, he idolized David."

"He was old enough to have memories of him, but not old enough to see his flaws. Henry would have had to be superhuman to satisfy him. Not that Henry didn't try. He used to take Oliver to the Met, but it was pointless. Oliver hates music. He once took him to a ranch in Wyoming. They even played in a father-son tennis league one summer. After a while, I think Henry just kind of cut his losses."

Their waiter stands beside them, waiting to be acknowledged. The two women lean back in their seats. Marian makes a point of not looking at him. "Two more sidecars, please," she says as he sets her salad down with a *thwack*.

"Mmm," says Caroline. "Red meat. I love it."

"Good. Eat it. You need it."

Caroline picks up one of the thick steak knives and cuts.

"You said it wasn't a shock," says Marian. "Did you know he was seeing someone?"

Caroline nods. "Well, I knew he was gone all the time. And I knew he was with her. But she's got the highest profile of any client he's ever had, so it didn't seem out of order. Then in September we ran into her at a benefit, and when I met her I thought there might be a problem."

"Because of how they behaved?" Marian asks.

"No. They were very good, both of them. It was how she behaved with every other man that night. There were ten of us at the table, and every single one of the men was sitting up straight and holding his stomach in. She's just one of those women..." Caroline trails off. She cuts another piece of her steak.

"Those women?" Marian prompts.

"Those women. You know, they're not even all beautiful, though this one is, of course. But you're not on the radar with them unless you have a Y chromosome. They'll talk to you, they'll stand a few feet away and look you in the eye, but they won't see you. You almost can't blame them—it's like they're missing the rod or the cone they'd need for you to be visible. But with a man they just come alive. Men *adore* them. Men just drop their lives to get a woman like that. I mean, isn't that more or less what her husband said?"

"The one she's divorcing?"

"Yeah," says Caroline. "I read this in the *Ascendant*. He met her at some political fund-raiser, and of course she made a beeline for him. He's worth—what?—a hundred million? He said she just made him *feel* great, the way she *looked* at him, the way she *talked* to him. Do you know how to do that?"

"Nope," Marian says.

"No. And neither do I. So anyway, it was out with his old wife and in with her."

Marian sets down her glass. "Okay. Then what went wrong?"

"What went wrong," says Caroline, "is that the husband made the mistake of thinking his new wife would then stop making *other* men feel great, and she didn't. I don't know," Caroline shrugs. "Maybe she couldn't. So now there's the little problem of the hundred million and the iron maiden prenup and the four-year-old daughter who vitally needs shiatsu massages and a Louis Quinze escritoire for her playroom."

"You know," Marian says pointedly, "you don't seem very angry, Caroline."

Caroline looks up. "Trust me. I'm angry. I'm angry that he made it through all the hard parts, like raising a kid who wasn't his and watching his wife become middle-aged, and *this* is where he loses it. And I'm furious at him for making me a stereotype. But I'm conserving my energy for myself."

"Bravo," Marian says.

"No, really."

"Yes. Really. I think you're great."

Caroline deflects the compliment. "When it occurred to me that I could sell the house and move back, you know how I felt? I felt like the sky was splitting open and light was just pouring through. I should have done it years ago, when Oliver went to college, but we were just very stuck in there. Or I was. Well, I thought we both were."

"What will you do when you get here?" says Marian, immediately worrying that the question might offend Caroline, but she doesn't appear offended.

"Not sure. Well, I'll do more with the Ballet Guild, I suppose. As for the rest, I'll probably volunteer. Maybe dust off my social work degree."

"Right!" Marian says. "I forgot you went to Hunter."

"And never practiced," Caroline says. "Isn't that terrible?"

"No," Marian says evenly, "that was life happening to you. That was getting married and moving out of the city and having a child."

Caroline shrugs. "I could have gone back to it, but things never seemed to settle down. First I was going to start work when Oliver went to school, but then David was killed. And then Oliver was sick, and I just couldn't."

Marian goes slightly numb. She takes a careful sip of her drink and says, "Oliver was sick?"

"He had leukemia," says Caroline, looking up. "You didn't know that?"

Marian shakes her head slowly, willing her face to be still.

"The year David died. Actually, we found out just before the accident. It went on for about a year." She suddenly frowns. "I never told you this?"

"No," Marian says.

"Well, they treated him with Cytoxan, which was pretty new then. We were extremely lucky," she says.

"This was in Greenwich?"

"No. Sloan-Kettering. I took an apartment near the hospital."

"You never called me," she says, stricken. "I would have come right away."

"Oh," Caroline says sadly, "I know, Marian. But I had a sort of bunker mentality at the time. Even David's death—I couldn't think about it then, even though it had just happened. I couldn't think about it, really, for years. I was in Cancer World, with Oliver. You know?"

Marian, who does, actually, know, shakes her head anyway.

"Cancer World. Hospital World. The only people you talk to are people who are in it with you. You hate everyone else," she says. "You especially hate everyone whose child doesn't have cancer. It's an extraordinary thing, because it cuts across all the boundaries. You suddenly have everything in common with the Dominican housecleaner whose kid has a brain tumor and nothing in common with people you grew up with. You know," she says, considering, "I probably should have called you."

"I wish you had," Marian says, still fighting. All of these months with Oliver, and he never...he never told her. Well, to be fair, she never told him, either. What a thing to have had in common.

"But he recovered," says Caroline. "He missed starting second grade with his age group, but they skipped him up later, so that was fine. He never talks about it now."

"Oh no?"

She shakes her head. "But it's in there. I mean, if you could open up Oliver's head and look inside, you'd see Cancer. Right there next to Dad and Roses." She pauses and considers her empty glass. "You should get to know him. He's a wonderful person. I think I'd feel that way even if I weren't his mother. Well," she says and laughs, "maybe not."

Marian swallows and says nothing. Oliver is indeed a wonderful person, a nuanced person, sharp and kind, like his mother, also—like his mother—generous and loyal and loving.

"When I'm living here, you'll get to know him better," Caroline says.

"Okay," Marian manages.

"I'm looking on the Upper East Side tomorrow. But I'd go to the West Side. I'd go to Murray Hill. Or even the Village. So long as I'm here."

Their waiter comes. He doesn't ask. He just takes the plates away.

"I didn't realize you loved the city so much," says Marian.

"I didn't either. But you know, I think it's really more about me than it is about Manhattan. When I started thinking about the rest of my life, it occurred to me that I wanted to be old in the place I'd been young. Maybe it's something everyone feels. I feel it."

"I feel it, too," Marian says. "Now that you point it out."

"Good. We were young together. Let's be old together."

"Good!" Marian says. "But do we have to start right now? Or can we wait a few years?"

"We can wait. It isn't going anywhere."

They defiantly order dessert. Caroline asks what Marian is working on, and Marian describes the Lady Charlotte pillow book, now nearly completed, "which is basically just an excuse to send me on another tour," she says wryly. "But after that we're doing her novels," says Marion. "And that really will be worthwhile. One of them's quite good. Well, if you remember that the novel was a brand-new art form when she wrote it."

"It must be a great feeling to have brought her back like that," Caroline says.

"Oh, she brought herself back. She reached out of her grave and tapped me on the shoulder. At the Beinecke, no less! She has a habit of getting her way, in death as in life," Marian says. "Hey, I wonder if she was one of *those* women. You think?"

"Nah. All those letters to her girlfriend back in America? And don't forget, she raised two little girls. I think she was an equal-opportunity appreciator. With an emphasis on opportunity!"

Marian nods happily. In the years since her book's publication, it has pleased her most to know that women of her own generation have related to Charlotte Wilcox. Perhaps they have had the most to learn from her, she thinks. The waiter brings their cheesecake and coffee. A minute later, he is back.

"Hello, ladies!"

Marian looks up. It is not their waiter at all. Under the circumstances, she wishes it were.

"Oh, hello, Valerie."

Valerie Annis looks pointedly at Caroline.

"This is my friend, Caroline...," Marian begins to say.

Here, though, is a crucial point. Rosenthal is hardly an uncommon name, but *Caroline Rosenthal* will surely bring Valerie up to speed. Only days earlier, after all, Henry Rosenthal had declared undying love for his famous client on Page Six of the *Post*. *Caroline Stern*, she is about to say, but the name that emerges from her throat, in the end, is *Lehmann*. She has taken her friend all the way back to childhood.

"Hello, Caroline," Valerie says, brightly enough. She is wearing the same taupe pantsuit currently hanging in the window at Armani. "I'll join you. But I just have a minute."

And she does, loudly dragging a chair from the next table. Caroline registers a flicker of alarm. The use of her maiden name has warned her.

"Valerie writes the party column for the *New York Ascendant*, Caroline."

"Oh. Yes, I know it," says Caroline with a practiced smile. "That must be a fun job."

"Absolutely untrue!" Valerie cries. "People don't understand!"

"I didn't see you in the restaurant," Marian says.

"Oh, I was in the first dining room." She says *first* as if she meant *better*. "I watched you come in. I had lunch with Farley Burkowitz. Now there's a guy who shouldn't drink at lunch."

Across the table, Caroline sits very still.

"I don't think I've met him," Marian says, treading on dangerous ground and thinking frantically of a way to change the subject.

"No? They call him the Prenup Pasha! I was trying to find out about the deal he made for your cousin and Sophie Klein, but all he wants to talk about is his partner and that woman."

Marian nods glumly.

"I had that story first! Did you know? They came up to me at the Met benefit last week, and I put it right in my column. But what can you do? We're a weekly, the *Post* comes out every day. It's one of those bitter pills a journalist has to swallow."

Journalist! thinks Marian.

"What do you do, Caroline?" Valerie says sweetly.

"Oh, I'm just visiting," Caroline says pointedly. "From Connecticut."

"Well. That's nice." She turns back to Marian. "I've just done a big piece on your cousin, you know. I was up to the house."

"Oh, really? I haven't seen the issue yet. I've never been to the house. Is it nice?"

Valerie looks scandalized. "Are you kidding? He's putting an absolute fortune into it."

A fortune of Mort Klein's money, thinks Marian.

"Well, I expect I'll see it this weekend sometime. Perhaps he'll have guests over."

"Rehearsal dinner," Valerie says.

Marian frowns. "Really? I don't think so. It's at some inn."

Valerie smiles the smile of a woman who has more recent information. "You didn't hear? It's been moved. Barton decided the house was ready. Well," she says soothingly, "I'm sure you'll get the information eventually."

"I'm sure." Marian nods wearily. She prefers the topic of Barton and his unfathomable bride to that of Henry Rosenthal's love life, but thinking about her cousin still depresses her. She is not looking forward to the wedding. "What does your profile say?"

"The usual swill," Valerie says. She takes up Marian's unused fork and jabs a bite out of her cheesecake. "Longtime bachelor finally meets the right woman. And the house, of course. Richard loves those decrepit old houses. I said to him, I said, 'Richard, if you want me to go all the way up to goddamn Millbrook to look at some falling-down house, you'd better get me a driver.' How am I supposed to hobble through a building site and get back in time to cover the Met benefit?" She pauses, then looks, with exaggerated politeness, at Caroline. "The Metropolitan Opera. They had their annual benefit last week."

"*Really*," says Caroline.

"And the whole time, he's going on and on about the plumbing and the floorboards. My God, as if any sane person gives a fuck about what the original inhabitants did with their shit. And when he's not talking about that, it's all about the great and powerful Warburgs." She pauses, mid-chew, to look coolly at Marian, seemingly pondering whether or not this last comment requires an apology, then evidently deciding it does not. Marian is determined not to react, not to prolong. As a diversionary tactic, she stares at the corner of Valerie's mouth, where a tiny nugget of cheesecake has lodged itself in a bright pink crease of lipstick.

"Well," Marian says. "I suppose I'll see you at the wedding, Valerie."

"You won't," Valerie says. Savagely, she spears another bite of cheesecake. "I'm not going."

"You're . . . but why not? You seemed to be looking forward to it."

"Because your cousin seems to have forgotten that he invited me. I phoned to see how he liked the article, and when I happened to mention that my invitation hadn't arrived, he got very flustered. Out of his hands, he told me. Of course, he had made the request, but the bride . . ." Valerie shakes her head briskly. "I've had to cancel my reservation at the Black Horse," she says bitterly. Then she looks frankly at Marian. "It's generally a bad idea to renege on invitations, don't you think?"

"It's not good manners," Marian agrees, with care.

"To tell you the truth, I wish I'd known he was going to behave this way *before* I turned in my piece. I might have given it a different . . ." Valerie purses her thin lips. Then smiles. "Tone."

"Well, I'm sure you won't be missing much," Marian says, selfishly delighted to have escaped the added punishment of a weekend with Valerie Annis. "Big weddings aren't usually any fun, especially when you don't really know the couple well. I'm sure you'll find something much more interesting to write about."

"Oh," Valerie says, laughing unexpectedly, "I'm going to write about it."

Marian glances, frowning, at Caroline. She is frowning, too.

"But, didn't you say you're not going?"

"I don't need to go. I'm doing a big piece for Friday about the new social climbing. Your cousin's wedding makes it timely, doesn't it? I don't need to be there, under the tent, eating off the solid gold dishes, to point that out, do I?"

"Social climbing?" Caroline says.

"Sure. As far as I'm concerned, Mort Klein and your cousin have done a deal right out of Edith Wharton. What?" she says, sardonically, taking in Marian's horrified expression. "Some guy with an old name and a falling-down house just happens to get engaged to a borscht belt heiress? It's a coincidence, right?"

Marian, speechless, only stares.

"This is an old-fashioned story," Valerie says. "That's all. I mean, here we are at the end of the twentieth century, you know? Nothing changes."

"Valerie," Marian says, managing at last to find her voice, "don't write that. I understand that you're angry. You have a right to be angry. But please."

Valerie's eyes widen. "Don't be silly!" she says, with exaggerated reassurance. "This has nothing to do with *me*. It's not *personal*, Marian. It's a *story*, and I'm a *journalist*."

"I'm sure there are very genuine feelings between Barton and his fiancée," Marian says desperately. "Look, he may be conceited and rude and all those things you said, but he isn't worth it. He's harmless."

"Marian," Valerie says, with palpable dislike, "you're such a good egg."

Marian hears Caroline's long exhalation: fury and amazement. Her friend's silence, thinks Marian, is a triumph of grown-up restraint.

Valerie rises to her feet and puts on her camel's hair coat. "Well, I have to get back to my office," she announces. "I have a phone interview with a cultural anthropologist from NYU at two-thirty. Unless," she says evenly, "*you'd* like to give me a quote, Marian? How do you feel, as a Warburg, watching someone like Mort Klein marry into your family? Hmm?" She waits hopefully. "Well, never mind. I have plenty of material, I think. And people always come out of the woodwork when you're working on something big like this." She turns to Caroline. "Um…" Valerie frowns, trying to remember Caroline's name. "It was nice to meet you. Have a safe trip back to New Jersey."

"Connecticut," says Caroline.

Both of them wait until Valerie is safely gone from the room.

"She is some piece of work," Caroline says, in wonder. "Thanks for not blowing my cover."

"Oh, that's all you need, to have Valerie Annis write about how you're drowning your sorrows in sidecars and cheesecake."

"*She* ate the cheesecake," Caroline observes.

"True." Marian tries to catch their waiter's attention, for the check. "And poor Barton. Not that it wasn't asinine, uninviting her to the wedding like that. He should have known Valerie wouldn't take that lying down."

"He said it was the bride's idea," Caroline reminds her.

"Even so. Though I can see her point. I mean, who'd want a gossip columnist at her wedding?"

"You know," Caroline says, thoughtfully, "I always thought Barton was gay. He was in Freddie's confirmation class, remember? At Temple Emanu-El?"

Marian nods. "I forgot that," says Marian. Caroline's younger brother and Barton are, she now recalls, the same age.

"I was surprised when I heard he was getting married," says Caroline.

"That makes two of us."

"I mean, I'm not exactly fond of Barton, but I'd be so sorry for him if I thought this was actually some kind of arrangement. You know, for the money."

"Well, you're a better person than I am, Caroline, because I'm not sorry for him at all. I disapprove of Valerie's tactics, but I probably share her theory about this wedding. I think that's exactly what it is. The family name may not mean much to me, but it certainly does to Barton, and according to him, it certainly does to the prospective father-in-law. I do feel bad for the girl, though. I mean, unless she really loves him, and that's pretty hard to imagine."

"But what's in it for her if she doesn't really love him?" Caroline says. "She must care for him."

Marian sighs. "What do you think I should do?" she asks. "Should I warn them about Valerie?"

Caroline considers this, then shakes her head. "You can't stop it. Why add any more stress to the next few days? I'm sure they're under enough pressure, getting everything ready. And anyway, the Kleins are probably used to having horrible things written about them. You don't make as much money as Mort Klein's made without attracting the envy of strangers."

Marian nods. "I think you're right. About Klein, too. You need a tough skin to be that successful."

"As I'm sure you've discovered, yourself," says Caroline kindly. "I admire you, Marian. You wear your own tough skin very well, I think. Very gracefully."

Marian looks up. Ever ungifted at accepting compliments, she finds herself awkwardly touched, and grateful. "Thank you," she says, meaning it.

"I remember thinking that last spring," Caroline tells her. "You remember that day we ran into each other in front of Oliver's shop?"

Marian nods. She does remember that day.

"I thought something had changed about you. Or not a change, exactly, but that you'd sort of grown into yourself."

"Grown into myself," Marian laughs, deflecting.

"I mean, you know how every woman is supposed to have a magic age when she's never more lovely? Lillian Hellman said that, didn't she?"

"A woman not known for truth telling," Marian comments, but still smiles.

"No, but she was right about that. Every woman does have her magic age, and when I saw you that day I thought it must be yours. Maybe your book was part of it. Maybe the success it had, and your pride about what you'd accomplished. That's all right. What I'm talking about, it's not the same thing as vanity. I remember thinking..." She stops. "This is going to sound bad."

"Tell me," Marian says.

"I remember thinking, I'm glad she wasn't an especially pretty girl, and I'm glad she wasn't a cute college coed, because if she had been, she wouldn't have this, now." Caroline looks up at her. "I was so happy to see you, Marian."

The check lands between them on its china plate. Both women reach for it.

"Let me," Marian says. "I'm a rich author."

"Let *me*. I'm a rich divorcée."

They both laugh.

"You know," Caroline says, "I think she has to love him. I mean Barton. Who are we to say? You can never tell why people get together. Or stay together. Can you? Or even split up, I guess. It's all a mystery..." She throws up her hands and smiles. "Great wisdom, right? From the fountain of age."

Marian, her throat suddenly tight, can only nod.

"Only first, do no harm. That's my philosophy," says Caroline.

She gives a girlish grin, and suddenly Marian can see Caroline in all her magic ages, all at once: the child Caroline in her ballet leotard, and in her velvet dress, and then the young woman Caroline in her smart violet Pucci shift, and then the settled, matron Caroline that afternoon in Greenwich, with eleven-year-old Oliver out in the backyard. She sees Caroline at forty-eight, with her fabulous cheekbones and graying hair, and then she sees Caroline of the future, thinner still and frailer, but also lovely, still lovely, walking on Fifth Avenue with her old friend, which for the briefest moment makes Marian want to cry with happiness. But she doesn't. Instead, she reaches for Caroline's hand across the table and squeezes it. "Welcome home," she says.

CHAPTER NINETEEN

Transformations

JUST AFTER ONE P.M. ON MONDAY, Oliver sits by the phone, knowing it is about to ring, but then when it does ring the sound of it shocks him anyway. The normal shop noises downstairs of opening doors and footfalls on the old floorboards, of paper being ripped from the roll and the refrigerator door opening with a suck— they are nearly surreal in contrast with that ringing phone. Oliver forces himself to breathe, reaches for the phone, and says, with genuine breathlessness, "Hello?"

"Olivia!" says Barton, with obvious pleasure. "I'm delighted you called. I must tell you, I'd about given up."

"I'm sorry!" Oliver says. "I'm sorry for that. I was...confused."

"My dear," says Barton. "That is the last thing I wanted. I thought we had a real rapport. I wanted to see you again. Simple as can be. Now tell me, did you love your flowers? They were far from inexpensive, I can tell you."

Or would have been, thinks Oliver, if you'd ever get around to paying for them.

"They were beautiful, Mr. Ochstein."

"Barton! I insist upon that."

"Barton. I would have…thanked you before now, but Dr. Kahn is your cousin. I don't think she would like…"

Oliver waits optimistically for Barton to jump in, but he does not.

"I don't think she would like the idea of our seeing each other, Barton."

"Oh now," he says dismissively, "she needn't know. We hardly move in common circles," he says with a chuckle.

"Oh. Is that so? I thought…don't you have many friends in common?"

"Not really. I doubt *my* friends would appeal to Marian," says Barton meaningfully. "She's a fairly staid person, you know."

She is not! Oliver thinks, instinctively leaping to Marian's defense. But just what is Barton talking about here? Rent boys on Gansevoort Street? Dungeons in Tribeca?

"I think you would like my friends," Barton continues. "They tend to have open minds. They would appreciate a young person like yourself. They would appreciate all your qualities."

"I would like to meet them," Oliver says carefully. "But first, I would like to see you, alone. I mean, if you still want to. I'd like to meet soon!"

It had better be soon. The wedding, after all, is just days away.

"Well, I'm a bit tied up for the next couple of weeks," says Barton. "How about after the holidays? I would love to come see you in town. I'd make a special trip."

"No," says Oliver stubbornly. "Barton, do you really want to see me?"

There is silence on the other end of the phone. Oliver panics.

"Barton, don't you understand how hard this was for me? To phone you? I can't wait until after the holidays!" Oliver says, with quite genuine desperation. "I thought you felt the same way. I mean, all those beautiful flowers!"

In the continuing silence, Oliver's anxiety grows.

"Barton?"

"Just thinking," says Barton.

"This Saturday?" Oliver suggests, coyly.

"Saturday's bad," Barton says, understandably enough, given that Saturday is his wedding day.

"Well, what about tomorrow? What about today?" Oliver asks, then regrets it. Today would be problematic. With Marian's wardrobe off limits, he hasn't a thing to wear.

"No, no," Barton thinks aloud. "I'm afraid I have a lot on my plate up here just now. I have…some people are coming in to see me at the weekend. I really can't make it into town."

"I'll come up there if you're not coming to town. I can come to where you live! All right?"

There is another pause. Oliver waits like a dread-filled angler. But then comes a twitch upon the thread.

"That would be splendid. If you are really willing to come all this way…"

"I am willing!" cries Oliver, his mind racing. "I'll come to you. You said Saturday was bad. What about Friday?"

Friday is the rehearsal dinner.

"Unfortunately, no. Those people are arriving on Friday. Perhaps…Thursday?"

Oliver considers. Millbrook on Thursday is both temporally and geographically closer to the wedding than Manhattan on Wednesday, but he will have to work with what's available. "Thursday, then. I'll come to your house."

"No!" Barton says firmly. "Not here. It's in a state. Construction," he says lamely. "Why not…I know a little inn, not far from here. Very private and very…"

Discreet? thinks Oliver.

"Just the place for a little quiet time together. Does that sound pleasant?"

"Oh yes," says Oliver, his thoughts racing. "What's it called?"

"The Black Horse. In Stanfordville. No one will be there on Thursday night, I'm sure."

Oliver wonders if "no one" means, literally, no one, or only none of the wedding guests, due to assemble there over the following days.

"Barton," he says, "that would be wonderful. And you'll book the room."

"No! No!" Barton says quickly. "That is, Olivia, it would probably be best if you booked the room. Use your name, not mine, if you would. Naturally I'll reimburse you…"

Oliver sighs. "I'll book the room. And I'll meet you there at…?"

"Six on Thursday. And Olivia?"

"Yes, Barton."

"It's a rather restrained sort of place. You know. In case you were wondering how to dress…"

Oliver, pointedly, does not respond.

"Not that your taste is anything but refined," Barton says, solicitously. "I hope I haven't offended you."

"I'm not offended," says Oliver, who actually is, on Olivia's behalf. "Thursday at six, then. The Black Horse in Stanfordville. I'll book the room. You won't forget?"

"I am already looking forward to it!" says Barton warmly.

Oliver hangs up the phone. For a moment he can only stare at it, adrenaline and anxiety coursing through him. He should feel more mercenary, it occurs to him. After all, he does not like Barton, and it appalls him that Barton is conducting an affair on the eve of his marriage—at least until he remembers that Sophie is doing precisely the same thing—but there will be no sense of triumph in these proceedings, and absolutely no merriment. The game may be afoot—and it may, moreover, be his own game—but he feels far from playful now.

Oliver leans forward in his chair, folding his arms on the table's wooden surface and resting his head there. He is exhausted from thinking and planning and then second-guessing every single thing he has thought and planned. He feels depleted from lack of sleep, due not just to the late and fervent nights with Sophie but also to his near-constant elation and also to his near-constant sadness. The elation is for Sophie, the sadness for Marian.

Everywhere in his life is the absence of Marian. It isn't merely that he misses her or that he bitterly regrets the harm he has caused her, and the further harm he will cause when she finds out about Sophie. It's that, in spite of everything that has passed between them, she is the one person he most wants to tell, and talk to, about what has happened to him. More than anyone else—more than Bell, or even his mother—she is the one he wants to know this astounding fact, which is that he has suddenly and without warning discovered the woman he is supposed to be with, whom he cherishes, and who has swept away all others—herself included. Without Marian to talk to, it's almost as if Oliver can't commit himself to an opinion about any of this, still less think his way through what he needs to do, and what he needs to do will require much from him.

Oliver sits up in his chair. He picks up the phone again and calls information for the number in Stanfordville, New York. Barton is correct that "no one" will be in residence at the Black Horse Inn on Thursday night. The helpful young man who takes his name—who takes the name of Olivia Nemo—volunteers that they are quite empty that night. "In fact," he adds, "I've just had a cancellation for the weekend, if you'd care to stay on. We're fully booked otherwise. A wedding."

"Oh, that's all right," says Oliver. "One night is enough."

The call ends. Oliver sits, brooding.

It's as if the crumbs he has trailed behind him through the forest have all disappeared. He doesn't know where he is, or how he got here; he doesn't understand how, only two weeks earlier, he woke up one morning in Marian's house and went to sleep that night in Sophie's bed, his hands entangled in her hair, his life entangled in her life. Fallen in love, but not out of love—that's how it feels—as if he has been caught in one of those time-lapse photographs, jumping from one point to another and occupying the place he started from, the place he finished at, and every place in between. Why shouldn't he have this happiness, this feeling of completion? Every time he touches Sophie he is more sure. Every time he hears her voice it is both more familiar and more welcome. Most strange of all is that the uncertainty surrounding them—the blatantly unfinished business of her wedding and the grief Oliver nurses about Marian—seems not to have penetrated what is taking shape between them. Of course, of course, Sophie should have ended her engagement months ago, weeks ago, and at the very least, days ago, but Oliver isn't even very angry about her failure to do so, because while her passivity in this matter is certainly frustrating, he understands its cause.

The difficulty, thinks Oliver, getting up at last from his chair and taking his jacket from the closet, is not between Barton and Sophie at all; it is between Sophie and her father. Mort, for reasons Oliver himself can't readily grasp, has a genuine attachment to Barton and obviously believes that he has brought his daughter to the brink of a good marriage. It's her reluctance to hurt him, and not her fiancé, that stops Sophie from acting on her own feelings—or lack of feelings, Oliver thinks, putting his wallet in his breast pocket. She is trapped, quite simply, by her love.

That Oliver—thanks to a bizarre and fairly embarrassing turn of events—happens to know something about Barton that Barton's prospective bride and father-in-law evidently do not, would under other circumstances be irrelevant, but it isn't irrelevant now. This information has become necessary. And in any case, time is now too short to wait for Sophie to suddenly rally and seize control of the situation. When she asked for his help, her problem became his own, and a matter of honor, even while it serves his own ends. He is far from sure that what he intends to do—that the plan on which he has finally settled, after all his exhaustive machinations—will even work, but it has to work, he decides. He can't bring himself to think of what its failure would mean.

The plan isn't so much a strategy as a destination: a room, with three people in it. Oliver knows now when and where the room is—he has just booked it—and he knows who the people are: Barton and Mort, who must reach an understanding together to cancel the wedding, taking the decision out of Sophie's hands and relieving her of its responsibility. The third person is Olivia, whose existence was once a frivolity, but no more. Having now arranged for the meeting of Barton and Olivia in this particular room, at this particular time, Oliver turns his attention to Mort. Getting Mort there is the remaining problem he needs to solve, and soon. But not right now. Right now there is an even more pressing task waiting for him, and he is too afraid of it to keep putting it off.

It's nearly two o'clock now, and downstairs Bell is undoubtedly watching the clock. He has an interview this afternoon at a midtown law firm for an Amy Lowell travel grant, an appointment for which he has borrowed Oliver's only suit. A dreadlocked poet of Jamaican extraction is probably the last person Lowell could have imagined traveling in her name, but Oliver knows how badly Bell wants this. He's never been to Europe or Asia, anywhere, really. Oliver has given him the afternoon off, and it's almost time for him to head uptown.

He puts on his jacket and goes downstairs. Bell, as predicted, is shifting nervously in the unfamiliar suit, standing in the middle of the room, as if he's afraid to get his clothes dirty.

"Hey, that looks good," Oliver says. "You feeling fine?"

"Feel like shit," says Bell.

"You want my advice? Tell them you need to see Greece. Tell them you need to drink from the well of Western civilization."

"Colonial swine," says Bell.

"Precisely," Oliver smiles. "That's the point. Take it from me as a white, privileged, Ivy League–educated, heterosexual male."

"You forgot Jewish," Bell observes.

"I did not forget. I merely de-emphasized. Look, why don't you just go? I'll take it from here."

"No, that's okay," Bell says and shakes his head. His dreadlocks shift against his shoulders. "I can stay till three."

Oliver smiles. "Bell. Go away," he instructs. "All is well here. I will see you in the morning."

Bell emits a nervous sigh. "I'll go. Okay." He goes into the office and returns with his own coat, which he carefully puts on. Then he leaves.

Oliver steps over to the window and stands behind one of the urns, which he and Bell packed that morning with Boule de Neige. Silently, he watches Bell walk past the theater, the restaurant nestled in the crook of the street, and on to Barrow, where he turns the corner and disappears. The street is empty now. The afternoon is passing. There is nothing else to wait for.

Oliver puts the CLOSED sign in the window, turns off the lights, and leaves, walking in the opposite direction, toward Seventh Avenue. He feels prickly and false, as if he is already in disguise and fearing detection, as if anyone might tell, from looking at him, where he is going, what he is doing, which of course they cannot. He goes to Bleecker and looks around for a minute, a stranger in his own neighborhood, only vaguely clear on what he is looking for and how to find it. Then he walks south.

There is a vintage clothing store on the corner of Great Jones, five long racks of old jeans and leather jackets with a few moldering hostess gowns from the sixties hung in a back corner. Useless. There is a women's boutique on the next block, all wisps of dresses suspended by sequined straps. The saleswoman smiles at him, thinking—Oliver supposes—that he must be shopping for a girlfriend. He flicks through a few things, nervously, not really seeing them, then looks with interest at a short black dress, briefly trying to imagine it on Sophie's body. He has no idea what Sophie would look like in such an item. Marian— yes. Marian likes clothing, likes to put it on, likes to take it off. Marian's clothing makes you forget to pay attention to it; you see only her, and how it makes her look. Whatever she knows about dressing, it's something Sophie hasn't begun to learn, Oliver thinks. Sophie's instinct seems to be for coverage, but he doesn't really understand why. Her body is lovely to him, curved and shallow, her skin creamy, everything warm and soft. She has broad shoulders and a large chest, yet her lower half tapers to something sinewy and trim. There is a wholeness about her you don't appreciate unless she is naked, thinks Oliver, with all her lines and surfaces revealed. Then, when she dresses, her beauty somehow abandons her.

Oliver looks at the dress in his hands, and shakes his head.

The dress is too skimpy for Sophie. She would never wear it. Neither would Marian. Neither would Olivia.

Oliver leaves the shop and keeps walking. What he needs is the sort of clothing Marian might wear. Olivia, after all, was born in Marian's clothes, and they are the clothes Barton imagines her in. He needs to find the kind of clothing Marian would buy for herself, if she happened to be shopping for herself on Bleecker Street. Which she would never do, Oliver thinks.

Just before Sixth Avenue, he finds a store that carries more sedate things: tweed slacks and silk shirts, skirts that cover the upper leg. This is promising. He goes in and takes a green skirt off the rack and holds it against his hips. It looks microscopic, a doll garment. He hunts for the label: size 2. What size is he? There are no helpful measurements for the waist and inseam. There *is* no inseam. So how is he supposed to know?

Oliver looks up. On the other side of the room, two women about his own age are staring at him. He feels his face go hot. He looks at the floor. He does not even like the skirt. Does he need to like the skirt? He has never thought about whether he likes his own clothes, really.

He barely manages to get the skirt back on its hanger.

Oliver moves down the wall of clothes, lightly trailing one hand along the chrome hooks of the hangers. He is too mortified to leave, to walk past them to the door. His hand touches a silk blouse the color of mayonnaise. Marian would wear that, he thinks. He wishes Marian were here to guide him, and the notion is so absurd he actually smiles.

"Can I help?" says the salesgirl, a tiny thing in a tiny black skirt. She has come up behind him and stands with one red-clawed hand on a bony hip. Her hair is so short it's a cap.

"My girlfriend," Oliver says haltingly. "I wanted to buy her some things."

"And she's about your size? I saw you holding that up," says the girl, nodding down the rack.

"Oh," Oliver says. "Yes. My size. But a girl."

She gives him a baffled look.

"I need a whole outfit. You know. A skirt and...top. Maybe a sweater. And some shoes, too."

"We don't sell shoes," says the girl.

This brings him up short. It's been nearly impossible to do this once. He's supposed to go to a different store and do it again?

"So what's her style?"

Oliver, bewildered, says nothing.

"What kind of clothes does she wear? Does she go out clubbing? Is she, like, a sorority girl, or what?"

"She's...a student," he says. "She goes to school."

"This isn't The Gap," says the girl.

"No, I know. Just, something nice. To wear...to meet my parents," Oliver hears himself say. "I want her to wear something nice."

He sounds, it occurs to him, like his own mother, circa the late 1980s.

The girl starts pulling things out: a tartan sweater, a black long-sleeved item that sort of crosses itself over the chest, black pants. He couldn't possibly wear any of this stuff.

"No," he tells her, starting to sweat.

She takes a hanger off the rack on the opposite side of the room: a black dress, long sleeved, with a high neck, and a hem at the knee. Maximum coverage. Modest, ideal for meeting potential in-laws. For a moment, his heart leaps, and then he pictures himself wearing it, and he is only Oliver Stern, ridiculous in a black dress. What is he thinking? What is he thinking? There is no fucking way he can do this.

"I have to go," he says quickly, and he dives for the door.

Outside, there is the first hint of evening, a diminishment of winter light. The encroaching darkness alarms him. He needs to begin this so that he can finish it. He can't go back to his home until he does.

Oliver begins to walk again, but this time in the opposite direction, northwest on Bleecker. It takes him a moment to realize both that he knows where he is going and that his failure to go there first was a willful evasion. When he reaches Christopher he turns left, his head down, trying to conjure the normality of his everyday walks in this neighborhood—his own, after all. Christopher Street might be holy ground to a generation of gay men, but it's just another street in his orbit. Doesn't he shop at the Duane Reade at Christopher and Seventh? Doesn't he buy his Cabernet Sauvignon at Christopher Wines? *I am a child of the Village. No less than the trees and the stars. I have a right to be here*, Oliver tells himself

Right next to the wine store, the display of leather men in the window of Transformations looks just as it always has, but for the sprigs of holly protruding from the mannequins' black chaps. Oliver does not pause, looking being—in a sense—worse than entering. He pushes open the door and charges in. A slender blond man looks up from his laptop at the counter.

"Hello," he says amiably.

"I'm not gay," says Oliver. "I mean...sorry."

"I'm sorry, too," says the man, bemused. "That is a great loss, I'm sure. But on the other hand, why should you be?"

Oliver frowns. "Because...isn't this..." Oliver gestures, words having failed him.

"Look," the man says, not unkindly, "are you a customer or a tourist? Because I can recommend a few good books if there isn't a chance in hell you're going to buy anything."

"I'm not a tourist," Oliver says, with some offense. "I live on Commerce Street."

The blond man raises an eyebrow. The eyebrow, Oliver notices, is brown. He's wearing a blond wig.

"I mean," he says, "I definitely need to buy something. I need help."

The man folds down his laptop.

"But I just...I know this is a store for drag queens. And that's great. I've got nothing against drag queens. I'm just not a drag queen."

"Shocking news," the blond man says. "And here I had you pegged for Wigstock."

"I'm...I need..." Oliver falters. "I have to buy some clothes. I mean, not clothes for a man. I have to get..."

The man puts up a hand. "Please. This is hurting me. You can stop."

Oliver stops.

"Drag queens. Yes," he says. "Downstairs. Everything from Joan Crawford to Bette Midler at the baths. Leather in the back room. But everything else is just for your garden variety cross-dresser. Suburbia to Wall Street. Suitable for parents' night at the middle school. Nothing Faerie Queen. Nothing *offensive* to your very *heterosexual* requirements, I promise."

"But I just said—"

"Cross-dressing," the man says, rolling his eyes. "Look, here's a cram sheet: drag queen equals gay, cross-dresser equals straight. Straight?" he repeats, taking in Oliver's confusion. "As in, *I like to wear the dress, the tasteful pumps, and the understated jewelry, whenever my wife takes the kids to visit her folks in Iowa? By the time she gets back I'm so revved up I practically have to make my move in the SUV. Yes?*"

Dumbly, Oliver nods. "Okay. I didn't know that."

"Sit down," he says, pointing to a chair. "And my name is Jan."

Oliver sits. He wonders if he is obligated to give his name, too.

"Your first time, I take it?"

First and last, Oliver wants to say. But it isn't his first time. And it won't be his last.

"It's a long story," he tells Jan. "I sort of did it by accident once. Now I need to do it again. I need to be this...person."

"You liked it, in other words," Jan observes, and Oliver is about to object: No, of course he hadn't liked it. Then he remembers: the flirting with Barton, the sweet, strange seduction, of and by Marian, on the couch in her living room. He had liked that. But it was too complicated to explain.

"Yes," he says.

Jan smiles, showing small, even teeth. "Fine." He gets up. He is a small man, with narrow shoulders. He is wearing a silk shirt, unbuttoned to just above the navel, showing a hairless, honey-toned torso, and jeans. "So tell me all about her."

"About...?" says Oliver. He is sweating now and wants to take off his jacket, but he is afraid to do it. Taking off his jacket means he is staying, which means he is actually doing this.

"This person you mentioned. Tell me about her. Then we'll figure out her wardrobe."

Oliver takes a breath. "She's a graduate student. She's..."

A gay man, he has been about to say. *A straight woman*. He can barely keep it all clear anymore.

"She's a very nice girl."

"I'm sure," Jan drawls. "Does she go out or stay in?"

"She goes out," Oliver says. "I mean, not nightclubs. But she needs to be able to walk down the street. Just... not flashy, okay?"

"I got it," says Jan. "Tweed, cashmere, no stilettos, am I warm?"

Very warm, Oliver considers, thinking about Marian's clothing. He nods.

"So let's go shopping."

It takes nearly an hour, most of it spent in the dressing room. After allowing Oliver to choose a wig nearly indistinguishable from Marian's and wordlessly handing him a boxed item that proves to be a bra with separate breastlike fillers, Jan directs Oliver to the dressing room at the back of the store and shifts into a Zen-like shopping zone from which he both procures and rejects, evaluating each combination of garments with either a "yes" or a "no." In short order, Jan confers approval on a red boatneck cashmere sweater, a beige button-down silk shirt not unlike the one he himself is wearing, a brown skirt that zips up the side and falls to Oliver's knees. He brings two pairs of tights, rejects one of them, rejects the other, and goes back for a third, which satisfies him. He produces a gold necklace and takes it away, to Oliver's relief. He brings shoes that are too tight, shoes that are too loose, and, finally, shoes that do not hurt too much, do not look too wrong, and with heels that are not too high. "Nice legs," Jan observes.

Oliver, lost in his own reflection, only nods.

The astounding thing, he thinks, is that she really is here, even more present than the first time. Olivia—Marian's devoted research assistant and the object of Barton's dogged attentions—has taken on her own freight of character in the dressing room at Transformations, with every small decision contributing to the person she has become.

Oliver sees her now. She is not pretty, exactly, but she is sweet, and a little shy, and also very determined to have what she deserves. She is...alluring, Oliver decides, scrutinizing her in a guy way. Not the girl you notice the first time you sweep the room, in other words, but the one you wake up wondering about five days later.

Looking at himself in the mirror, from the front, the side, the front again, is a queasy, out-of-body experience. Oliver's instinct is to avert his eyes, but at the same time, he can't seem to look away. He forces himself to take several deep breaths, and meets his own gaze.

"Hello, Olivia," Oliver says, experimentally.

"Hello," Olivia says.

Jan returns, his arms full. "You need a coat," he says briskly. "You can't wear this with your jacket. You need a purse."

"No purse," says Oliver, snapping out of it.

"Don't be silly. Nice girl like you wouldn't go out without a purse."

Oliver lets him choose a purse. He lets Jan show him how to hold it. He lets Jan pick a coat, camel's hair.

"You could use a little makeup," Jan observes. "You have pretty good skin, but makeup never hurts."

"No makeup," says Oliver, and this time he holds his ground.

"Whatever," Jan puts up his hands. "Okay, that's one outfit. How about some evening wear?"

Oliver gets out his wallet. "This is fine, thank you. You want to ring it all up and I'll get changed?"

"Get changed?" Jan asks. "What for? You look great. I'll throw your other clothes in a shopping bag."

"No, no," he shakes his head. "I couldn't."

"Don't be silly. You said she has to be able to walk down a street. If a man can't walk down Christopher Street in drag, where can he, pray tell?"

Oliver smiles, but he shakes his head.

"Look, you live on Commerce, right? What is that, like, three minutes? If you can't walk home from here, why have you wasted your time with all this?"

Oliver considers. Jan is, of course, perfectly correct. Three minutes. And when will he ever have the nerve to practice again?

"All right," Oliver says. He pays, using his Visa card, and stands looking between the two leather-clad mannequins at the now darkening street as Jan totals the bill. Outside is an unknown country.

"I'm here on Tuesdays and Fridays," Jan says. "In case you don't want to start over again with somebody else, next time."

"Thank you," says Oliver, meaning it.

"You look beautiful," Jan says, appraising him. "I mean it about your legs. Don't hide them."

"Okay," Oliver stammers. "I'll try." He takes the bag of his clothes, his own safe clothes, and goes outside.

The wind seems to rush at him, nudging him off balance. Every step is a separately strange experience. The hose rub between his thighs. There is an odd flutter of skirt against his knees. His feet pinch. *Why do women wear heels?* Oliver thinks crossly. It is not *natural* to walk on tiptoe. He stops, only feet from the beginning of his journey, and looks at himself in the window reflection of Christopher Wines, against a display of Chardonnays. *That* is why they wear heels, thinks Oliver, noting the rounded calf and narrow, nearly graceful angle of his ankle. Nice legs. Marian had said that to him, too. She'd said he had nicer legs than hers, when was that? The first time he had shown them, really, in Olivia's clothes. He squints at his legs now. He lifts one, just slightly, and admires it, and then movement from inside the shop makes him look up. A young man is watching him from inside. Oliver's heart thrashes as he recognizes his admirer. *The Violet Pen*, he reaches. *The Violet Pencil, wasn't that it?* The man frowns at him. Oliver looks away so fast he totters on his heels, then pulls his new coat tight at the throat and walks off down the street, carefully, one foot deliberately in front of the other. With each step, one knee and then the other makes its appearance through the slit of his open coat.

Oliver watches his knees, watches the pavement under them. He lets himself believe that it is fascinating to observe this, but the truth is that he is terrified to look up, to see anyone seeing him. This is a level of physical self-consciousness he has not experienced since adolescence, thinks Oliver, crossing Bleecker with attention to the ground. Someone nudges him, an invisible body of great height, and Oliver looks up, involuntarily, into ardent eyes. A man in an orange down vest, baldheaded, a stranger. "Sorry," the man says, standing his ground.

Oliver hurries away.

At Bedford, he turns left, and, leaving the busier thoroughfare, he actually slows down. The street is nearly empty, and with the light rapidly fading, the few people he does share the sidewalk with are focused on their own business. Oliver feels...not safe, precisely, but—easier. Still, he forces himself to linger before every other shop, feeling himself shift his weight and stand, examining the merchandise. Oliver idles before a restaurant—Le Rouge. He pretends to read the menu, then, slowly, he unclenches his coat and lets it fall open. The earth does not stop turning. He puts his hands on his hips.

"We're open," a waiter says, opening the door and smiling at him. "Like to come in?" He has a thick French accent, almost a stage-French accent.

"Oh," Oliver says. Looking past the man, into the restaurant's dim interior, he can make out the table where he once, an eternity ago, sat with Marian. "No, but another time."

The guy nods. He wears thick silver earrings, like jacks, in both ears. He grins, not just with warmth, but with heat. "Any time," he tells Oliver. "Ask for me. My name is Valéry."

Valéry, thinks Oliver. Like *Valerie*.

Then he smiles.

"Thank you!" Oliver says, and walks off down Bedford.

On the next block, Oliver walks briskly to the smoke shop and enters, so focused now that he has nearly blocked out the reality of his altered appearance. They know him here, or do in his normal guise. He comes in for emergency milk, the *Daily News* whenever there is some scandal too undignified for the *Times* to cover, Häagen-Dazs from the freezer in the back, but never for what he is purchasing today. There is one copy of the *Ascendant* left in the rack. Oliver puts it on the counter and fishes out cash from his new purse. He does not look at the man behind the counter, a Sikh in a red topknotted turban. He does not wonder if the man sees him, knows him. He grabs his paper and goes, anxious to get home, gleeful at this new idea. It's all going to work, he thinks, turning down Commerce, which is empty of people. He holds his coat closed with one hand and fishes in his pocket with the other for his keys. With each step, his plan crystallizes. He sees how to do this. He knows precisely how to get Mort Klein to the Black Horse Inn on Thursday night.

He opens the shop door and shuts it behind him. Then he goes upstairs.

It is after five o'clock now. She may not be there. She may be home, preparing for some party, or meeting someone for a drink, spreading some nasty rumor or other. He opens the salmon-colored newspaper on his kitchen table and turns on the light. He skims her hateful column, noting a gushed reference to Henry Rosenthal and his lovely new girlfriend, then finds her profile of Barton Ochstein, bachelor bridegroom, Warburg, preservationist, on the verge of marrying his fortune. It's a fawning piece of writing, culminating in a gleeful *See you all at the wedding!* but Oliver knows that Valerie Annis won't be seeing anyone at the wedding. Sophie absolutely forbade it. The Celebrant would not be pleased about that, thinks Oliver. The Celebrant would not be unwilling to embarrass a man who'd embarrassed her.

At last, in the second section of the paper, he finds the phone number on the bottom of the page and dials. The next edition of the paper comes out on Friday. Olivia's assignation with Barton is to take place on Thursday. It can work. It can absolutely work. He won't think about the alternative.

"*Ascendant!*" chirps a voice, female.

"I would like to speak to Valerie Annis," says Oliver, enunciating with care. "My name is Olivia."

CHAPTER TWENTY

Another Woman

AT JUST BEFORE THREE P.M. ON MONDAY, Sophie stands on a raised, circular pedestal, carpeted in beige, being tugged and pinned and glared at with varying degrees of impatience by three women.

"Hold up your arm a little bit," says Suki, one of the whippet-thin women Vera Wang has hired in an effort to make her customers feel gargantuan.

Sophie raises her arm. The illusion sleeve puckers at her armpit.

"You lost weight," says the seamstress, with discernible aggravation.

"*Sophie*," says Frieda, who is sitting on an upholstered ottoman in the corner of the dressing room, her aristocratic legs crossed at the ankle.

"Sorry," Sophie says, automatically.

"I need to take in more," says the seamstress, and she pins. Sophie holds up her arm, idly looking at herself in the mirror.

The pucker under her arm is not the only pucker in evidence. The dress has gone from sleek at its first fitting to baggy this afternoon. She would not want to marry Oliver in this dress, Sophie thinks. Actually, she would not want to marry anyone in this dress.

"I don't think we're finished," says Suki sadly.

"No," Sophie agrees.

"I think we need one more. Wednesday?"

"What?" says Sophie.

"For a *fitting*," Frieda says. "Yes," she says, taking it upon herself to answer. "We come back on Wednesday. It must be ready the next morning, though. We are leaving for the wedding on Thursday."

"Fine. And bring your undergarments when you come," Suki says, tapping a note into her Palm Pilot.

"My what?" Sophie says, rousing herself.

"Well, you're not going to wear that bra," Suki says with a mincing shake of her exquisite head. She looks up, worried. "Are you?"

Sophie shrugs. "I hadn't really thought about it."

There is general awe at this remark.

"You know," says Suki, "there is a very good lingerie shop. Near Bloomingdale's?" she says deliberately, as though Sophie, lifelong New Yorker that she is, might not know where that is.

"I know where Bloomingdale's is," says Sophie.

"I have their card. I think you should go right now. Let them fit you. Tell them you're wearing strapless with illusion sleeves."

"Oh, I can't go right now," she says vaguely, though there's nothing pressing right now. There is no work. There is no Oliver. Her only occupation, all this week, is to prepare for a wedding.

"Why not?" says Frieda shrilly, and Sophie shrugs again, making the seamstress actually grunt in frustration.

"I have my paper. Remember? To get ready for the conference?"

"You have this wedding. Remember? To get ready for being married?"

"Fine," Sophie says.

Frieda and Suki exchange a look.

When the first arm is done, Sophie lifts the other arm. No one speaks but the seamstress, asking for more pins, then chalk. Sophie is thrilled when she finally gets the dress off her body. She has to resist an urge to kick it as she steps from its fallen circle.

"Are you coming?" Sophie asks Frieda when she emerges from the dressing room, clad—out of deference to Vera Wang and to Frieda—in a black suit.

"*Nein*. Let me take your veil home. I think you can buy a bra without me."

"*Really*," Sophie says, allowing the tiniest smile. "Why, thank you, Frieda. I appreciate the vote of confidence."

"Besides, today I need to fight with the caterer."

"Oh. Well, have fun."

"And your father canceled his dinner. I will need to order something for him."

"What's going on?" asks Sophie, concerned.

"Nothing terrible, I think. Just saving his energy."

"I could come have dinner with him," Sophie says, holding open the door. Frieda passes through. She is carrying the large Vera Wang shopping bag, laden with Sophie's deftly packed veil.

"No," Frieda says and shakes her head. Her expensively maintained copper hair shines in the afternoon light. "You buy your bra, and after that go home and do your work. Maybe then, by the weekend, you can begin to act like a bride. Really, Sophie. All of this effort."

"All right," she says sadly, and they walk north to the corner together. "Give him my love," she calls, watching Frieda until she crosses Seventy-ninth. Then Sophie turns east to Park and begins to walk downtown.

It's a chilly day, and Sophie keeps her hands in her pockets, one of them fingering the business card Suki handed to her. The lingerie shop is not, as it turns out, unknown to her: a block or two south of Bloomingdale's on Lexington, run—at least, in the past—by a crotchety Russian woman who determined bra size by gazing balefully at her customer's chest and then called out the correct numbers and letters. Sophie had gone there once... when was it? In high school, she thinks, when she failed the self-serve test of Bloomingdale's own chaotic lingerie department. How many bras has she bought, and worn, and washed to death, since then?

She stops at a red light and reaches down to pat a bichon frise.

"Pretty dog," Sophie observes to its owner, a brittle old lady in mink, though she does not think the dog is at all pretty. The woman smiles, gratified, her powdered skin shockingly white around the mouth. Standing beside her on the street corner, two schoolboys in Collegiate blazers puff at cigarettes.

The light turns green.

At the end of the block, Sophie suddenly sees Marian Kahn, walking in her direction. They will cross paths and it occurs to Sophie that she really ought to say something this time—to her colleague, to her almost-relation-by-marriage—but she can think of nothing to say, and Marian Kahn looks distracted, as if she really does not want to be wrested from her thoughts. *Dr. Kahn!* Sophie rehearses, nonetheless. *It's me, Sophie Klein. Barton's fiancée? Chaim Bennis's graduate student? We met? We're going to meet?*

We pass, thinks Sophie, as they do, Marian walking briskly north, with an idle half-smile on her face. Does she live near here? thinks Sophie. On Park? Had Bart said that? Sophie turns and watches Marian go. Marian moves confidently through the crowds and up Lenox Hill, now lined with its December evergreens.

Where is Oliver? thinks Sophie, suddenly. She thinks this all the time now.

Oliver is in his shop. Oliver is on Twenty-eighth Street. Oliver is at the Pink Teacup. Oliver is sitting at my kitchen table, watching me cook. Oliver is in my bed.

Right now, Oliver is downtown, on Commerce Street, selling flowers, even as she walks to a lingerie shop to buy a bra for the purpose of marrying someone who isn't Oliver.

Which is completely, completely wrong, it seems to her.

In front of the Regency Hotel, Sophie pauses, extracting the card from her pocket and peering at it. The futility of her errand overwhelms her, and she finds herself shaking her head, like a street schizophrenic.

"Taxi, miss?" says the doorman.

"Oh, no," she shakes her head. "I'm not a guest here."

He nods and she walks on.

But this is when it occurs to her that she does want a taxi. She wants to go where Oliver is, which is downtown, and she wants to go there fast. Because though only two days have passed, because though he said, only this morning, on the phone, that he is working on the problem that is her life, that everything would be all right, she needs to see him again, and to hear that again. She needs to. She turns north to look for a taxi, and there, right in front of the hotel, a taxi is switching on his light.

Sophie races back. "Is it all right?" she asks the same doorman, breathless, her hand already on the door. "I'm not a guest."

"You told me," he says and laughs. "Go on. There's no one waiting."

"Thank you!" she says and climbs inside.

The driver looks back.

"Greenwich Village, please," she chirps.

He swings into traffic. Park Avenue is clogged with angry cars, all carping in the language of Harpo Marx. Sophie thinks of Oliver. She thinks of the small of Oliver's back, which fits perfectly the curve of her cheek. She thinks of the sound he makes when he comes, and then of the sound he makes her make, which is not a sound she has ever made before. She thinks of Oliver's smell, and is astonished to find that she can conjure it precisely, as if he were right here in the cab beside her. The cars are not moving. Where is everyone going? Sophie thinks crossly.

"Where is everyone going?" she asks the driver.

"Oh, it's like this all the time here," he says reassuringly. "You live here, you get used to it. Where you visiting from?"

He takes her for a tourist, Sophie understands. And why not? Wasn't she picked up in front of a hotel?

"Uh...Millbrook. New York."

"Where is that?" he says, turning west on Fifty-seventh. "Upstate?"

"Yeah. Horse country."

"Racetracks?"

"Kind of," she says, thinking of Saratoga.

"So is it business or vacation?" He honks at a FreshDirect truck. The two drivers promptly give each other the finger.

"Oh...," Sophie says. Then she remembers. "I'm getting married. I'm getting ready for my wedding."

"Yeah? Congratulations."

"The flowers," Sophie says, warming to her theme. "A shop in the Village is doing the flowers for my wedding. The flowers are going to be so beautiful."

She closes her eyes and thinks of Oliver's flowers, and as the wedding itself fades, the flowers seem to come forward in glorious focus. She can smell them here, mixed with the remembered Oliver-smell. She is in love, she thinks. This is what it smells like to be in love.

"So, where in Greenwich Village?" the driver asks.

"Commerce Street, please," says Sophie.

"Excuse me?"

"Commerce Street?"

She sighs.

"Seventh Avenue, then. Where it hits Bleecker."

"Right."

When he pulls over, Sophie puts bills through the little plastic window and gets out, quickened with longing. It's a magic thing, chemical, and she rushes on, turning right on Grove past the Pink Teacup, which she reflexively glances into, but he isn't there, because he is home, only a block away, waiting for her, though he doesn't know it yet. *I am a woman who is having an affair,* she thinks in amazement, *only days before her wedding.* An hour ago, she was trying on a bridal gown. Now she's here and happy and can barely remember the name of her fiancé.

Barton, she thinks, with effort, but even this fails to puncture her elation.

Then she rounds the corner onto Commerce Street.

The shop windows are dark, which makes no sense. It's afternoon, and someone should be here, Bell if not Oliver. She looks upstairs, to Oliver's apartment, and there too the lights are out.

Sophie shakes her head. She stoically climbs the stone steps to the shop door and reads—deliberately, as if she were quite dense—the small sign in the window, which says CLOSED.

Then she knocks anyway, and listens to the sound bounce off the walls inside.

She does not know what to do with herself.

The street, of course, is empty. The street is nearly always empty, unless the little theater is letting out. There's a restaurant just past it, where Commerce bends and veers into Barrow, but nobody seems to be there, either. Idly Sophie wanders down to the Cherry Lane, and attempts to read the reviews of the current offering, then walks past to examine the posted menu on the restaurant, but nothing really registers, and besides, the restaurant is closed, and besides that, she isn't hungry.

Actually, Sophie hasn't been hungry for a while. Since the day Oliver came to find her at Columbia, her appetites have moved in a different—for her unprecedented—direction. Not that she has stopped eating. Only a few nights ago she was here, up in Oliver's apartment, making pot roast and kugel (Oliver had shown himself to be shockingly ignorant of kugel) and eating both with relish, but every morning she has been lighter, more lithe, more loved, more astounded at what her body has done, and now it looks as if Oliver's long-ago comment about brides who drop twenty pounds before the wedding might actually have proved prescient. But of course, there isn't to be a wedding. Oliver has promised her. And besides, she doesn't have the right bra.

Sophie looks at her watch. The street is darkening, and not a single person has appeared since her arrival. This must be the stillest place in the city, she thinks, reluctantly retracing her steps toward Bedford, and passing in front of the shop once more. There are white roses in the windows massed in matching black urns, looking voluptuous and confident. Before knowing Oliver, Sophie had never thought much about flowers, even, despite her own historical preoccupations, about white roses, but now she has come to regard a flower in the room as a participant in her mood. Barton's white roses, for example, which had arrived every week, she had heartlessly allowed to wilt. Or the new white roses, in a white vase on her little kitchen table, which Oliver had carried over her threshold two nights before: instantly the most beautiful thing in her home. Or the astonishing moment she woke up, one morning last week, in Oliver's bed on Commerce Street, with his mouth over her breast and his hands coiled in her hair and the dark pink calla lilies, in an ironstone jug on the bedside table, at which she had stared in wonder for as long as she could keep her eyes open. Whatever happens, thinks Sophie, walking fast, there will now have to be flowers.

At the corner, she turns right on Bedford, pausing to read the historical marker on a skinny townhouse—Edna St. Vincent Millay's, it turns out, in 1923—then walks past to a smoke shop where she buys herself a Styrofoam cup of anemic coffee and a copy of the *Ascendant*, the last but one in the rack. Armed with these props, Sophie goes back and sits—not in front of the shop itself, but farther down, nearly opposite the theater, under a handy streetlight, on the steps of a brownstone that looks uninhabited. It's dark now, but at least it isn't cold, Sophie thinks, peeling off a corner of her cup's plastic lid and taking a first sip, which promptly scalds the roof of her mouth. She opens the coral colored pages of the paper, skimming the accounts of a recent real estate war, the battle for control of a Broadway producers' consortium. She is looking for the article about Bart, of which he is very proud, and most of which he has already read to her over the phone, but before she finds it she is sidetracked by the Celebrant column, featuring a caricature of its author, Valerie Annis, and a photograph of Oliver's grinning stepfather, Henry Rosenthal, with his new girlfriend. Sophie, reading the couple's fervent quotes of happiness, is selfishly glad that Henry Rosenthal is departing Oliver's life at the very moment she herself is entering it, thereby relieving her of the need to be polite to such an odious man. The girlfriend, in the throes of her own absurd divorce—twenty thousand a week in child support! Sophie marvels—is shown in another picture with her nearly ex-husband, CEO of an entertainment-information conglomerate. They look happy, too, thinks Sophie.

Then, at the bottom of the column, she finds herself mentioned as the almost-bride of "Barton Warburg Ochstein (see profile, page 14)"

—which is odd in itself, thinks Sophie, because Barton's middle name isn't Warburg but Samuel—but that's only the first of several mistakes in the text, some of them quite worrying. There's her own description as a Columbia "undergraduate," a "reclusive heiress," and the likely inheritor of three billion dollars (which isn't only off by roughly 50 percent but is not, in any case, a point Sophie wishes to see in print). There's the description of her impending wedding as "the event of the season in party-obsessed Millbrook" (*Really?* thinks Sophie dryly), and finally, there is the Celebrant's rather chilling sign-off, "*See you all at the wedding!*"

Oh no you won't, thinks Sophie, enraged (and quite forgetting—for the moment—that there isn't going to be a wedding). No invitation had been sent to Valerie Annis. Hence Valerie Annis had no cause to think she was in a position to *See you all at the wedding!*

There comes, from up the street, the click of a woman's heels on the pavement. Sophie, registering this, does not look up at first—a woman in heels, after all, is not the person she is waiting for—but the novelty of an actual human presence on Commerce Street eventually gets the better of her. She wrests herself from the distorted Sophie of the Celebrant's column and peers over the top of the paper. A woman is indeed coming down from Bedford Street, teetering a little on her heels, wearing a coat she holds together at the throat. She has dark hair to her shoulders and walks with her head down, as if unwilling to take her eyes off the pavement, and she moves hurriedly, nearly skipping as she reaches the center of the street. From beneath her arm, a pink newspaper peeks out. Sophie assumes she's headed for the restaurant—a manager, perhaps? or the hostess?—but then, to her great surprise, the woman slows in front of the White Rose, and stops. Sophie puts down her paper entirely. The woman climbs the steps, reaches into her coat pocket, and extracts a key. The key fits the door. The woman goes inside. A moment later, Sophie, devastated, watches the light in Oliver's apartment switch on.

I'm involved with someone, he told her.

He told her, right away, on the floor of her apartment, with their clothes everywhere around them. And what had she said? Sophie concentrates. *What a coincidence. Me too.*

She is about to be married, for Christ's sake! And Oliver is already involved with someone. Who is up there now, Sophie thinks, biting her lip. Who has her own key, which is something Sophie herself does not. *Because if I had one,* thinks Sophie bitterly, *I wouldn't be sitting out in the cold with a cup of lousy, scalding coffee.*

He may help her. He may even want her. But he is involved with someone, which he told her, and she can't say he didn't. She can't even be angry, except at herself. Which she is. Oh, she certainly is. Her face is hot in the cool evening air, and her eyes burn with imminent tears, and she has never, never felt so lonely in her life as on this dark, forgotten little street.

But she does not indulge these thoughts for more than a moment, at least in public. And when her moment has passed, Sophie gets to her feet, empties her Styrofoam cup onto the pavement, and walks west to Hudson Street to find a taxi home.

CHAPTER TWENTY-ONE

A Good Person,
If Not a Good Wife

MARIAN'S HAPPY MOOD lasts just as long as it takes her to walk home, moving among the fur-clad and satisfied citizens of Park Avenue. Christmas is afoot now, and the city's stubborn insistence on referring to this season as the Holidays cannot negate the omnipresence of mistletoe and fir. A large electric menorah has been erected on the traffic island at Park and Sixty-first, and Marian turns to look at it as she passes before the Regency Hotel. The menorah is a good ten feet tall, and towers above the bodies crossing beneath it, but it diminishes when set in scale with the great line of Christmas trees, stretching all the way up to Spanish Harlem. The trees have always appeared at this time of year, for as long as Marian can recall. She saw them from the window of her childhood bedroom, on Eighty-first Street, little bouquets of color making their own string of lights along the center of Park Avenue. Marian remembers the great cross of lighted windows left behind each night in the Pan Am building at the avenue's southern end, and thinking of them now, she even turns to glance back in the direction she's come, as if they might still be there. But of course there has not been a cross at the southern end of Park Avenue for many years. There has not, come to think of it, been a Pan Am building for many years, either.

"Hello, Hector," Marian says, smiling, as she reaches her lobby. She unwinds the scarf from her neck. "Getting chilly."

"Yes. Gonna be snow," Hector says agreeably.

They ride up in accustomed and not uncomfortable silence. Marian watches the numbers flash by and thinks ahead to the good and the bad of her anticipated afternoon: a hot bath (good) and the abbreviated pile of thirty-one shortlisted applicants for the Columbia job openings, their thinned ranks considerably offset by their bulked-up dossiers (bad). Perhaps she will have the bath first and then address the stack in a calm and focused mood. Perhaps she will do her work first and have the reward of her bath after. Or maybe she should just take the dossiers into the bath with her and be done with it. *Who's to know the difference?* Marian thinks, almost gaily.

But all gaiety dissipates when she goes to collect the files in her office and notes her answering machine light, which is fluttering with waiting messages.

Oliver, is her first thought, but Oliver, in all these months, has never broken his word—when he needed to speak with her, he phoned the office. Moreover, he has not contacted her since their disastrous return to the city. The message counter reads fourteen. With a groan, Marian takes off her heavy coat and drapes it on the chair. Then she finds a piece of paper and sits down at her desk.

Number one. "Hi. Um, Marian? This is Soriah." Then nothing. And more nothing. Then, "Well, all right. I guess I'll call again."

Soriah, writes Marian on her pad. No phone number.

Number two. The silence of someone listening.

Number three. More silence.

Number four. "Oh, Dr. Kahn? It's Betty Evans with the Rhinebeck Historical Society. Just wanted to touch base with you about Thursday? We'd like to invite you to stay the night at the Beekman Arms as our guest. A few of us would be very glad to take you to dinner. It's a nice inn, if you don't know it, and good food. Anyway, if you'd call me to confirm the lecture at two, I'll give you directions, my number is..."

Marian writes down the number. The Rhinebeck Historical Society has been asking her to come for nearly a year. Though she's glad to use the excuse of Bart's wedding to cross at least one outstanding obligation off her list, Marian has no intention of spending an evening trapped with historical society ladies at the Beekman Arms, no matter how good the food is. She had planned on driving back to the city after the lecture, but now it occurs to her that she might just remain in the area, book a hotel and stay on for the rehearsal dinner the following night. Then she can get a good night's sleep and rest up a bit before Marshall arrives and the dreaded ordeal of her cousin's wedding festivities begins. *Book room—Millbrook*, she writes on her pad, thinking how stupid she's been to leave this so late. With the many wedding guests, surely everything will be booked. Only... didn't Valerie say that she had canceled a room? Marian concentrates, her pen tapping the page, but she can't remember the name of the inn.

Number five. "Um, Marian?" Silence. "Okay."

Number six, and number seven, again and again, Soriah. As Marian listens she becomes not frustrated, but very, very worried.

Number twelve. "This is Soriah. I don't know the number here. I'll call you again."

The number here? thinks Marian. She reaches across the desk to her Rolodex and flips to the card bearing Soriah's name, then dials her telephone number. There is no answer.

A homebound invalid and a paid attendant in two small rooms, and no one answers the phone? Marian draws a box around the name *Soriah*.

Number thirteen. "Ah, hello Mrs. Kahn. My name is Frieda Schaube," says a voice, clipped and formal and strongly accented. "I am calling on behalf of Mr. Mortimer Klein and Miss Sophie Klein. I am telephoning everyone invited to the rehearsal dinner on Friday night to inform them that the location of the dinner has been changed. The dinner will now be held at The Retreat, and not at the Black Horse Inn, as originally planned."

Aha! thinks Marian. *The Black Horse Inn!* She writes it on her pad.

"Time remains seven P.M. Dress code will remain black tie. Should you need directions, you may telephone me here in the city, or in Millbrook from Thursday," Frieda Schaube says, helpfully giving the numbers.

Number fourteen. "Oh…it's Soriah. Okay."

Marian snatches up the phone and calls the apartment on Hughes Avenue again, though she knows it's pointless. Scenarios race through her brain, less and less likely, more and more ominous: they are visiting a neighbor, they are at a doctor's appointment, they are sitting outside (to take in the pleasant December afternoon?).

Something's happened, thinks Marian, hanging up. She stares at the phone.

To distract herself, and to delay her next attempt to phone the apartment, Marian calls information for the number of the Black Horse Inn in Millbrook and dials the number. "I'm driving up for a wedding this weekend," she tells the man who answers. "The Ochstein, um…" She frowns, momentarily losing the name of Barton's fiancée. "Klein?"

"Oh sure," he says amiably. "We've got a load of people coming in for that on Friday. We were going to do the rehearsal dinner, too, but that's been moved."

"So I understand. That's too bad," she says politely. "I understand you have wonderful food."

"Oh we do!" he confirms with pleasure.

"Well anyway, I'm coming up a bit early. On Thursday night?" Marian says. "I was hoping I could get a room for the whole weekend. I really shouldn't have left it this late. You must be full."

"Yes," he agrees. "Have been for weeks, but the gods must like you because someone canceled this morning. I can give you her room. It's a suite on the second floor. Very pretty."

"Perfect," Marian says.

"And Thursday's no problem. Wide open, just you and one other guest. Hang on, let me get my book," he says. Marian waits, drawing another box around the word *Soriah* on her pad.

"Here it is," the man says. "Now, let's start with your name."

She tells him her name. She tells him her address and her phone number and her platinum card number, then she jots down the directions from Rhinebeck, which seem very involved. After hanging up, she immediately calls Soriah again.

Five rings, six rings. Marian starts to hang up.

"'ello?" says a curious voice.

"Oh!" Marian almost shouts. "Mrs. Nelson?"

"Mrs. Nelson not here."

"Oh. Well, who is this please? I'm looking for Soriah."

"Soriah not here. It's Marisol. I'm the—"

"Yes!" Marian cries in relief. "Hello, Marisol. It's Marian Kahn. We met last month? I came to take Soriah to see her mother?"

There is a pause. How many people come to visit, anyway? Marian thinks.

"I remember, yes. Soriah not here."

"Do you know when she'll be back?" says Marian.

"Uh-uh. The caseworker come and take her. Mrs. Nelson had to go in the hospital. She have a stroke."

So, thinks Marian.

"That's terrible. How is she?"

"I don't know. I just here to get my things."

I'll bet, Marian thinks. All those afternoons watching TV on the couch. I don't suppose you've even been to visit.

"But...what hospital is she at? And how do I get in touch with Soriah?"

She can almost see the home health aide roll her eyes. "I don't know. I guess the caseworker."

"But who is the caseworker?" Marian says, courtesy failing her at last. "Do you have a number? Do you have a *name*?"

"I don't know. She the usual one who comes. Wait a minute."

Then there is a little clatter as the phone lands on a surface, and Marian can make out the faint sounds of rummaging. At last, Marisol returns and says, "I find the card. It's Hilda. Last name is Rodriguez. Okay? And the number?"

She recites it. Marian writes it down.

"Marisol? When did this happen? When did Mrs. Nelson have her stroke?"

"Uh…" She stops to think. "I guess last Wednesday. She took a sleep but she don't wake up. I call the ambulance."

Bully for you, thinks Marian.

"Thank you, Marisol."

"Okay," she says, and hangs up the phone.

And just help yourself to anything you want in the apartment, Marian thinks, still holding the receiver.

She puts down the phone, and picks it up again immediately to dial Hilda Rodriguez, but the extension is outdated and the system hangs up on her after a maddening sequence of clicks and rings and silences. Marian opens her desk drawer and takes out her phone book, but the directory gives only the number for Children's Services in Manhattan, and Hilda Rodriguez's number has a 718 prefix. She phones the Manhattan office anyway and asks for the office overseeing cases in the Bronx, and so begins another odyssey through the city bureaucracy and its fiendish phone system. When at last she is rewarded with the voicemail of a person who says her name is Hilda Rodriguez, Marian—relieved to have reached her goal but dubious about the efficacy of the voicemail system—leaves a polite but insistent request to be called. Then, without further apparent options, she hangs up again and sits staring at the phone.

Soriah. No.

The grandmother. No.

The home health care aide. No.

The caseworker. Not yet.

Who else is there? A teacher she could call? Marian doesn't even know the name of Soriah's school. A neighbor who might know where she's been taken? Not a clue. Would it be worth trying to make contact with Denise at Bedford Hills?

Then Marian remembers the professor from Fordham, who takes Soriah to the library—the woman who gave her the Lady Charlotte book and encouraged her to write to Marian. Named...Marian concentrates, and finally it comes to her: Reynolds. Professor Reynolds. At Fordham. She clutches the phone, gets the general number for the university, calls it, and asks for Professor Reynolds. There are three of them. A female professor Reynolds, she tells the man she is speaking to. There are two of them: English and Slavic Languages. "English," says Marian, guessing.

She is transferred to the English department.

"May I speak to Professor Reynolds, please?"

"One moment."

No, thinks Marian, breathing rapidly. It can't be this simple. She's teaching, she's with a student and not picking up the phone, she can't just be there.

"Carol Reynolds," a woman says.

"Oh! Hello, this is Marian Kahn. Professor Reynolds?"

"Well, this is an honor."

"Thanks...ah...I'm phoning you about Soriah Neal."

The woman pauses. Marian can hear her sigh. "Yes, of course. It's awful, isn't it? Not a huge surprise, but still."

"But what exactly happened? Do you know?"

"I don't know anything more current than Thursday. I usually pick Soriah up at school on Wednesdays and we go to the library, but she wasn't in school when I got there last week. I called the caseworker's number, and she told me about Mrs. Nelson. I don't think she's regained consciousness, so no one is very optimistic."

"But where is Soriah?" asks Marian. "Is she staying with friends?"

She asks this, but she knows the answer. What friends, after all?

"No. She's been placed in foster care. The caseworker wouldn't tell me where, because I'm not a family member. I mean, the whole system is completely inhumane."

"But have they been bringing her to see her grandmother in the hospital?" Marian asks urgently.

"I really have no idea. You should call and ask."

"I have," Marian says. "I'm waiting for a call back."

There is a pause as both women have the same thought: *Right*.

"What's going to happen to her?" Marian asks. "Who will take care of her?"

"It might work out all right," the woman says. "It might be a great placement. She might even end up in a better school."

"Unlikely," Marian says caustically. "What a waste."

"Yes," Professor Reynolds says. "I've been tearing my hair out since Thursday. That poor kid. She can't catch a break, you know? And so much promise."

"Look," says Marian with sudden desperate inspiration, "couldn't you... I don't know, let her stay with you for a while? Until this is over?" Until *what* is over? she thinks, even as she says it. "Couldn't you... Do you have room to keep her?"

There is silence on the phone, but not the silence of hostility. Not the silence of consideration, either. The woman on the other end of the phone, thinks Marian, is merely formulating her response.

"Dr. Kahn—"

"Marian. Please."

"All right. Marian. I think Soriah is terrific, and I would do a great deal to help her. I *have* done a great deal to help her, and I don't begrudge the time at all, because she's been such a rewarding kid to deal with. But my life is complicated. I've got three small children of my own, and a hellish commute. I live in Princeton, you know."

"I didn't know," says Marian, her heart sinking. She doesn't know anything about this woman, who has, after all, done far more for Soriah than she herself has done. And who is Marian, anyway, to ask such a thing?

"I couldn't take it on," says Professor Reynolds. "Not because I don't care, but the red tape would do me in. Besides, my husband would absolutely refuse. I wish I could say otherwise, but I can't. I just can't."

"I understand," Marian says. "I'm sorry for even mentioning it. I'm just upset."

"It's okay. I'm upset, too."

They sit in silent communion for a moment.

"Well, it was nice talking to you, anyway," Professor Reynolds says at last. "Soriah was so thrilled you answered her letter. And she loved your book, you know. So did I," she says, with a small, embarrassed laugh. "Did I say that?"

"No. Thanks."

"Look," the woman says suddenly, "we can't fix it, you know? It's too big to fix. It never gets fixed. We just...I don't know...we do what we can."

"I know," Marian says. "Well, thank you. It was nice...meeting you."

"You too. Good-bye," she says sadly, and hangs up the phone.

Marian hangs up her own phone. She feels numb. She can't remember what she is supposed to be doing now, and she hopes it isn't very important.

I don't know the number here, Soriah had said.

The phone rings.

"Soriah?" Marian says, snatching it up.

"This is Hilda Rodriguez," a woman says, brusquely. "Returning your call."

"Oh good! Thank you for calling me back so quickly. I really appreciate that!" Marian, to her own ears, is sounding hysterical. She swallows and tries again. "I phoned about Soriah Neal. I just heard what happened to her grandmother."

"Soriah Neal...," says Hilda Rodriguez.

"You just put her in foster care?" Marian reminds her in disbelief.

"Yes, I'm getting the file. Bear with me."

"I'm sorry!" Marian cries. And waits.

"The grandmother died this morning," the woman says, offhandedly.

Marian closes her eyes, hearing only the sound of her own breath. "That's terrible," she manages to say, at last.

"Now what can I do for you?"

"I just…I've gotten to know Soriah this fall. I wondered if there was anything I could do."

"I don't know," the woman says mildly. "*Is* there anything you could do?"

"I…," Marian sputters, ashamed and irritated in equal parts, "could I get in touch with her?"

"Are you a family member?" asks Hilda Rodriguez.

"No, I'm not."

"I'm sorry, I can't give out her contact information if you're not a relative."

"I'm a friend."

"I'm sorry," she says.

Marian bites her lip.

"What's going to happen to Soriah now? Will she stay with this foster family, or what?"

"I really have no idea," the woman says. "We'll see how it works out. Sometimes you need a few tries to find the right place."

"But…," Marian says and takes a breath, "Ms. Rodriguez, I don't know if you're aware of this, but Soriah is very gifted. Academically. She needs a good school, and she needs stability, so she can continue to do her work. She's far ahead of her grade level, you know."

There is a pause. "I don't have anything about that in the file," she says finally.

"But it's true. I'm a college professor. I've been working with her. So has a professor from Fordham."

"Well, I can assure you, she'll be in school, Mrs. Kahn," the woman says, clearly offended. "Going into foster care doesn't mean getting taken out of school."

"No, I know, it's just…this girl is really special."

There is a groan from the other end of the phone. The unspoken rebuke—*They're all special*—passes between them.

"Ms. Rodriguez?" Marian says, "I've been thinking of trying to get Soriah into a better school. Maybe here in Manhattan."

She has? thinks Marian. *She has been thinking of getting Soriah into a better school in Manhattan? Since when?*

"Yes?" is the noncommittal reply.

"I was wondering...," but words fail her here, and it takes a moment for Marian to discover what it is that she wants to say. "I was wondering, couldn't she stay with me for a while?"

The question falls like a great weight. Marian closes her eyes. *I said that,* thinks Marian. *I heard myself.*

"You're not a relative, you said," says Hilda Rodriguez.

"No. Not a relative," Marian agrees.

"Well, are you a foster parent registered with Children's Services?"

"No!" Marian says in alarm.

"Well, then..."

But, she wants to say, *I'm rich! I live on Park Avenue! Don't you understand what I'm offering?*

"I don't see how I can help you, Mrs. Kahn."

"Wait!" says Marian. "How do you get to be a foster parent? Do you have to get a license or something?"

It can't be much, thinks Marian frantically. Like a driver's license. A wedding license. You show your birth certificate and have a blood test. How big a deal can it be? Aren't they desperate for people? Aren't they always saying so?

"Yes," Hilda Rodriguez says, "there is a licensing process. There is a training program and there are evaluations, leading to a license. Foster parenting is a paid service, you know."

"Oh," Marian insists, "I don't need the money."

She doesn't *want* the money, she thinks, and in consideration of that, won't they just let her take the girl?

"Well, you'd still need to undergo the training and evaluation, Mrs. Kahn. I'm sure you appreciate that." There is silence. Then she seems to relent. "Look, Mrs. Kahn, I know you're trying to do something for Soriah. It's all any of us is trying to do. Sometimes we get overwhelmed, is all. I mean, I've got eighty-six active cases right now. I don't want to discourage you if you're serious about taking her to live with you. Are you serious?"

Are you serious? This is precisely what Marshall will say—will shout—when she tells him. She has not said very much to Marshall about her young friend from the Bronx. She has not, for instance, mentioned Soriah's incarcerated mother, nor her own recent trip to Bedford Hills prison. And she has never hinted at the possibility of bringing this, or indeed any, child into their home, even years ago, when the idea of it might not have struck him as quite so absurd. So is she serious now?

"I am," she tells Hilda Rodriguez. "I would like to find out more."

The world does not stop. The walls do not come crashing in. Marian sits, waiting, but oddly peaceful after all.

"Okay," the woman says. "I'm going to have Gloria Hernandez call you, from foster care. She'll set you up with an orientation session and then, if you want to go forward, we'll start on the home study and a background check. Let me...right, I've got your number here. Okay, Mrs. Kahn. Give me a call if anything comes up."

If I change my mind, in other words, Marian thinks.

"Thank you, Ms. Rodriguez."

After they have hung up, Marian remains in her chair, looking at the ceiling of her office. It is painted a warm rust color and studded with inset lights that rise and fall on a dimmer switch. Her desk is an antique, English, bought from Sotheby's in the eighties, and Marian has always appreciated its bowlegs and well-used pine surfaces. She will have to move it now, she thinks, perhaps to the little alcove near the master bath. She will have to move the low chaise that takes up most of the rest of the space, to where she has no idea. And the stacks of books, the wig that got her through the months she was bald from chemotherapy and mourning the children she would never have, and the boxes and boxes of Lady Charlotte letters filling the room's little closet, jammed in behind its shuttered accordion doors—she will have to get rid of it all.

The rest of the room is not as dark as the ceiling, but it's a somber red. Something must be done about it, thinks Marian, vaguely considering: yellow, blue. A child with a newly dead grandmother and an imprisoned mother should not be expected to live with such sad colors. And something must be done about the light, because there isn't enough light, really. A lamp on the wall over the bed is needed. This room, her office, typical of the maids' quarters in this type of New York apartment, is not large, but it has been large enough for her. And it will be large enough for Soriah.

She thinks of her friends. Will they whisper that childlessness has finally caught up with her? Will the few who know about her cancer shake their heads knowingly? Will the others be critical—another career-obsessed woman who forgot to have children, and now look what she's done? What will Caroline Lehmann, her oldest friend, make of Soriah Neal? What will Oliver Stern, her oldest friend's son, her lover, make of Marian for taking her in, a girl he has never even heard her mention?

Marian closes her eyes. *I want this*, she thinks. *I have been a good person, if not a good wife. I have not asked for many things.*

When she opens her eyes, she is surprised to find herself utterly calm.

I can't fix it, Marian thinks. *It's too big to fix. But I can do this.*

She reaches, again, for the telephone, and presses the buttons.

"Mr. Kahn's office," says Jennie Phillips, his assistant.

"Hi, Jennie. This is Marian. How are you?"

"Oh, Mrs. Kahn. It's nice to speak with you."

"Tell me something," Marian says evenly, "what does Marshall's afternoon look like?"

"Ooh, let's see," says Jennie. "Not too bad. He'll be out of here by six, I think."

"Is there anything absolutely crucial?" she asks.

This question does not compute, and Jennie is silent. Marian imagines the bafflement on her sharp little face.

"Ah..."

"Anything that can't be rescheduled?"

"Rescheduled?" Jennie asks. "For when?"

"I'm coming down," Marian says. "I want you to cancel whatever you can. I'll be there in half an hour, and I need some time with him. If you can't cancel his appointments, try to put them off till after five. Okay?" she says, trying for a cheery lilt.

"Is everything all right, Mrs. Kahn?"

"Oh, fine," she says. "And tell him that, would you? That everything's fine. I'm on my way."

"But—" the tiny voice erupts. Marian puts down the phone and picks up her coat, and then she is through the door, closing it behind her.

CHAPTER TWENTY-TWO

Aubergine Time

O N THURSDAY AFTERNOON, after a solo lunch in a corner
of the Beekman Arms's dim tavern restaurant—and she does
have to admit that the food is excellent—Marian addresses
the ladies (and token gentleman) of the Rhinebeck Historical Society
in a paneled room off the reception area. In the two years she has been
giving some version of this talk, she has come to note a pattern of
strained proximity in her audience, a historical version of celebrity
name-dropping, in which Charlotte Wilcox's latter-day admirers
attempt to persuade Marian that they have crossed spiritual if not
physical paths with their heroine. Someone hails from Brund, Derbyshire, home of the Forter family. Someone's ancestor was a thief,
incarcerated in one of the London prisons. A man once visited
Northumberland House while on a walking tour of the border country. A young woman, who had detoured into a master's degree in
women's studies before deciding to go to law school, had actually read
Helena and Hariette in the rare book library at Stanford.

Marian finds these encounters pleasant, if not precisely enthralling.
For someone working in the past, it is always invigorating to see people

look backward and measure their own experiences against the long-ago experiences of others. In Rhinebeck, moreover, the members of the local historical society have an actual claim on Charlotte Wilcox—who after all began and ended her life on this general patch of earth, and whose bones lie buried not five miles to the north—and their interest in her is as affectionate as it is proprietary. Several members of this group, Marian is touched to learn, have taken it upon themselves to care for Charlotte's grave in Rhinecliff, even writing and printing a pamphlet for visitors with a map of the site, including other graves of interest in the churchyard. "We did it ourselves," says Betty Evans, the president of the group and the author—she informs Marian—of two pamphlets about the Roosevelt estate up the road. "We started to notice cars parked by the roadside. They were tramping over everything looking for the grave. We thought, Well, it's good they're coming, but let's make it easier for them and try to point them to some other interesting people."

"I hope it hasn't caused too much trouble," says Marian.

"Oh, not at all! Come for the past but stay for the present—that's what we say around here," she chortles. "Anyway, it's wonderful for us. The chamber of commerce ought to give you a citation."

"It's my pleasure," Marian says graciously. "After all, I enjoyed the time I spent in Rhinebeck doing research. Wish I'd stayed at this inn," she says. "You were right about the food."

"New York chef," comments the token man, in a tone that implies this is not necessarily a good thing.

"It was finding those letters that really made her come alive for me," Marian says. "Before that, I felt like I was following a ghost, but when I read those letters, I heard her voice...It was an amazing feeling."

"Still," the man goes on, homing in on his true theme, "I was hoping you'd delve more deeply into Alice Farwell's family. It's quite an illustrious family in its own right, you know."

"I didn't know," Marian says politely. Charlotte's correspondent of so many years, who faithfully preserved her precious letters and gave her friend a home at the end, had not gotten much of Marian's attention, it was true. But after four hundred pages of dense historical biography, Marian had been anxious not to add more heft to her book.

"Well, her daughter married into the Wharton family. And her granddaughter married into the Danvers family. Henry Wharton Danvers was her great-grandson. You've heard of him, I assume?"

Marian, who has just gone numb, nods her head. "Henry Wharton Danvers? Who built The Retreat?"

The man positively glows. "Yes, precisely. He was my own ancestor, actually."

"That's amazing," Marian says, floored and shaking her head. She does not care that he is, of course, misinterpreting her response, that he thinks it's his own direct link to the Lady Charlotte story that has Marian so obviously awestruck. Let him think as much, Marian decides, as the man goes on to tell her all about his own myriad accomplishments as self-published chronicler of the Millbrook Hunt and a fly fisherman of national stature. She nods, careful to keep her gaze steady on his face, her thoughts wandering far. Oddly enough, what preoccupies her most is regret at not having made more of her connection to *Barton*, of all people. Might some remnant of the Farwell family have remained at The Retreat? And could she have found it? Were there descendants of Alice Farwell who might have had their own inherited stories about Alice and her lifelong friend? Marian had spent the past two years making light of her readers' attempts at narcissistic connection with Lady Charlotte Wilcox. Was it possible that she was now grasping at her own?

When the alleged descendant of Alice Farwell and Henry Wharton Danvers has at last exhausted his litany of claims, Marian finally is able to begin disentangling herself from the group in the Beekman Arms. It is nearly four, and she has begun to feel that heaviness in her legs and arms, a signal of weariness. Between today's lecture and the coming weekend's ordeal, she can only hope for a wedge of sleep and privacy, and she thinks ahead to the romantically named Black Horse Inn with longing. But first there is the matter of finding the place—which, given the complexity of her driving directions, threatens not to be straightforward.

Marian thanks Betty Evans for her hospitality, and the chronicler of the Millbrook Hunt for making her day, and retrieves her car from the parking lot behind the inn. The light is beginning to sink, and there is the faintest hint of pink at the wintry edges of the sky. With one hand, she scans the radio for NPR and finally finds a station playing Mahler, but the Mahler is too lush, too soothing, so Marian cracks a window to let in the cold air, and it rushes through the interior. She has not driven the car since that day with Oliver, and she is struck by the bittersweet thought that her last remnants of him—of his breath, of miscellaneous, left-behind filaments—are thus being scattered away. She will call him when she gets back to the city, Marian thinks, to say all of those end-things she wants to say, and that she loves him, which will be better over the telephone, anyway. Marian can't see him yet. She's in too much danger for that. But there is no good in this silence between them, especially now, with Caroline coming home, and the certainty of their meeting in the future. What Marian will do is find the precise, internal location of her sadness about Oliver, and fix it to the spot with stones, like a cairn at a roadside. The sadness—she will know it's there, but she will not visit it to peek between the rocks or listen to see if it's stirring. It is over. With love, absolutely, but over.

Marian turns east along the rural roads, passing great estates with grazing horses and baronial entrance gates. At Rock City she pulls over to get gas and asks the attendant if he knows the way to Stanfordville, but he's never heard of the place. The Black Horse Inn? she tries, but this, too, draws a blank. Marian squints at her scribbled directions. "What about Bangall?" she asks, and that, finally, draws a glimmer of recognition.

"Hey, Bill?" the attendant says, evidently to his boss. "Which way to Bangall?"

The boss comes over, examines Marian's directions, pronounces them useless, and begins a litany of rights and straights, including a description of a big oak tree where she is meant to make a "hard, sharp left. Like, a hairpin turn, yeah?"

Marian nods dully. She pays for the gas and sets out, resigned.

Ten miles and forty minutes later, she finally reaches the crossroad of Stanfordville and sees, at last, the sign for the Black Horse Inn. It's a little place, but it has about it an air of purposeful obscurity and serious wealth, from the impeccably landscaped parking area behind the building to the heavy wooden door she opens, stepping into a pretty, wood-paneled parlor. There is a rack of boots, walking sticks, and hats in one corner, an open bar on the opposite wall, and a good smell coming from somewhere. "Hello?" Marian calls, setting down her bag on the stone floor and shutting the door behind her.

"Yes!" someone says. "Just coming!"

He comes, a wiry man with receding blond hair, holding an open red ledger.

"Hello there!" He reaches immediately for her bag. Marian recognizes his voice.

"I made it," she says. "I think we spoke on the phone."

"Yes, probably. And you are either Ms. Kahn or Ms. Nemo."

"Kahn," Marian says. "But that's funny."

He looks up from his ledger.

"Just…Nemo. That means 'nobody,' doesn't it? In Latin?"

"Does it?" The man smiles. "Well, it's just you and Nobody tonight, though as I said, we'll be full of wedding guests tomorrow. You're here for the wedding, I think you mentioned."

"The groom is my cousin," Marian says. She looks upstairs, hungry for her bed.

He leads her up the wide stairs onto a landing furnished as a parlor. There are doors on either side, and he opens one for her, showing her into a small sitting room with a fireplace. Marian looks around, silently crediting Valerie Annis for her good taste. The only things standing between herself and utter contentment, she thinks, are a hot bath and a good nap.

When she's alone, she sets down her bag and unpacks the toiletries, opening the taps on the long, claw-footed bathtub and turning down the bed. She carefully hangs up her dress from Bloomingdale's in the wardrobe and takes down the inn's white bathrobe from a hanger—Frette, she notes with guilty pleasure—and gets out of her clothes.

The bathroom is full of lavender-scented steam. Marian puts up her hair. She stops the water and is about to step into the tub when something in the bathroom window catches her eye, and she steps close to look. It is not afternoon any longer, but it isn't yet night. Marian smiles. That thing is happening outside, that sudden flush of color, so imponderably rich it seems to saturate the world. She wants to hold up her hands and catch it, but it's so fast, she can never be quick enough, and then it's gone and the evening floods in to replace it. Aubergine Time, thinks Marian, jubilant. Then she climbs into the bath and lets the hot water close over her.

CHAPTER TWENTY-THREE

Awake, But Not Awake

WEDDING CENTRAL, Sophie thinks, walking into the kitchen of their Millbrook house and nodding grimly at Frieda, entrenched since the day before in full command mode. The long wooden counter is strewn with yellow legal pads, one of which is being slowly leaked over by a great chrome urn of coffee. The party urn, brought out only for large functions, like her father's historical society meetings, or a wedding.

"No, no," says Frieda unkindly. "I did not say that. I did not say four to park the cars. I said *enough* to park the cars. There are two hundred and eight guests expected."

Lacking the physical object of her scorn, Frieda narrows her eyes at Sophie.

"No, I do not think so either. Yes. Twelve. Good. And by four o'clock sharp on Saturday, please."

Crisply, she puts down the phone, then crisply picks it up.

"Four men! Idiots."

"Hi, Frieda," says Sophie.

"Your dress is upstairs," Frieda says, dialing.

Sophie pours coffee for her father. She stirs in his low-fat milk and Equal, staring dimly out the window over the winter vineyard and the field where the horses are grazing. She can't see Win, her own horse, but that doesn't surprise her; Win tends to favor the shelter at the far end of the barn. The horse Barton rides when he visits is standing at the fence, nose to the ground. Barton is a fine rider, which means a great deal in Millbrook. She wonders if Oliver can ride. Oddly, it has never come up between them. Like so much else, Sophie thinks, stirring.

"Yes," Frieda says. "I am holding for Mr. Weil. No, thank you, I need to speak with him personally."

Mr. Weil, Sophie thinks. The cake guy? No. Millbrook Spirits.

"Well, tell him it is Miss Schaube calling. About the Klein wedding. Yes."

Hostile silence.

"Oh, a small matter of five missing cases. Yes, that is what I said. Missing!"

Sophie closes her eyes. Surreal. Unreal. Or what is that thing people always say? That thing. That whine. *It was a nightmare.* They mean: a missed bus, a lost reservation at the restaurant, a canceled plane at the airport. Only once has Sophie ever heard someone use the expression and felt it was earned, it was necessary. A mother on the news one night, describing the sick, elastic feeling of turning around in the supermarket and finding her child not there, the hours that followed, the not knowing. *It was a nightmare.* Awake but not awake, functional but not really alive. *This,* Sophie thinks, her spoon clattering against the coffee mug, *is a nightmare.*

"That will be cold," Frieda says. "It is for your father?"

"Oh." She nods. "Yes. Sorry."

"And that woman called about your hair. She would like to speak with you before Saturday. You need to phone."

"All right."

"You want to tell me something?" Frieda says.

Sophie stops. The coffee mug in her hand is indeed cooling.

"Something?" Sophie says.

"Why are we doing all of this?" Frieda says bluntly. "You are not happy about this. This is not a happy wedding."

"No, it's fine," Sophie says, automatically.

"Fine. Is fine good enough? You would want your own daughter to be 'fine' two days before her marriage?"

Sophie looks at her, mildly stunned. There, secreted in the typically blunt and quite accurate observation, is the nearest Frieda has ever come to admitting a maternal sentiment for her. Sophie's instinct is to cross the room and hug her. But this passes.

"Frieda, I know it will work out," she says instead.

"What? What will work out?"

"Barton has never lied to me," she hears herself say, as if this were the issue at hand, and not the fact that she doesn't love Barton, she loves Oliver, who loves someone else.

"Your father would not want this, if he thought you were not happy," Frieda says curtly.

"I know that. Look, everything's okay. I just have that pre-wedding thing. Just...jitters. There's no problem."

Frieda stares at her. Then—mercifully, without signaling any more disapproval—she picks up the phone again, punches numbers on the keypad, and begins berating the rental agency for having sent the wrong covers for the chairs.

Sophie leaves the room with her cooling cup, her spirits as dull and hard as the stone floor she walks over. The farm has been as much her father's passion as the New York house, and as faithfully restored. Unlike the Steiner mansion, though, this home had spent its entire three-hundred-year existence in the smug cocoon of the non-Jewish elite, and while Jews had inevitably penetrated the Millbrook colony (one had even been admitted into the vaunted Millbrook Golf & Tennis Club way back in 1970), a brief frisson of regret had nonetheless flowed throughout the town when one of its great architectural prizes had passed—twenty years earlier—into the hands of the Chosen. The house Mort moved into then, and brought back to its origins soon after, had been the home of Dutch farmers and English younger sons, gilded members of the Astor 400 and impoverished, downwardly mobile WASPs, thinks Sophie, passing the great staircase and moving into the beamed living room, where her father is sitting before an absolutely searing fire. But never a Jew. Till Mort.

"Wow," says Sophie, handing him the mug. "Hot enough for you?"

"Actually, no," Mort says, making a face. "What did you do with this coffee? Bring it by way of the Gulag?"

She sits down on the couch, taking up the Home section and effortfully starting to read an article about a house specially built from recycled materials. As if, she thinks, willing it, the day were ordinary, the wedding unconceived.

"Where's Frieda?" Mort says, sipping his coffee and grimacing.

"In the kitchen. I mean the command center. Doing what she does best."

"And why aren't you there with her? Don't you have a hundred things to do?"

Sophie considers this question. Actually, she can't think of a thing she needs to do, other than hit her marks and say her lines. And pretend to be happy. She is saving her strength for that.

"Frieda's good at this, Dad. You know that. She likes to expose incompetence."

"Oh, I know *that*," says Mort. "Are we seeing Bart tonight?"

Sophie shakes her head.

"No? Wasn't he coming to dinner?"

"He was. But he canceled. He said he had too much to do at The Retreat. For tomorrow night."

"Ah," Mort says. "That's going to be splendid. So much more personal than a hotel."

"Inn," Sophie corrects.

"Still a hotel. The Retreat is going to be your home. It means more to have your family and Bart's family meet in your home."

Sophie, fighting tears, nods. She looks determinedly at the fire. Then, composed, she looks at Mort. And he actually *is* crying.

"Daddy," she says, surprised.

"No, I was just thinking how much she would have loved this."

Sophie says nothing. She knows who "she" is. They don't often talk about "she."

"You're going to wear the pearls? With your dress?"

She flinches. Her mother's pearls aren't even here. They're at home. At her childhood home, that is, in her old room. They're in an old Leon Uris hardcover fitted to hide jewelry. ("Burglars," said Frieda, who gave it to her, "are not book-minded.") Sophie has forgotten them. Her mother's pearls, for her own wedding. She is a terrible daughter. And she loves him so much, Sophie thinks. "Daddy...," she begins. "Dad, I need to tell you something."

"It doesn't really matter," Mort puts up his hand. "It's a fashion thing, is that it?"

"No, that isn't it."

"I'm too sentimental. And you know, I don't even believe that stuff. *There in spirit*. There is no spirit. You know that, right?"

Soundlessly, Sophie nods.

"We're alive, then we're not alive. No in-betweens. Yes?"

"Yes," she says, one hand at her throat, as if the forgotten pearls were there.

"It's just that she would have loved Bart, too. She would have loved so many things about him. She loved men who acted like gentlemen." He chuckles. "I wasn't much of one, myself."

"That's not true!" Sophie says, defending her living father to her dead mother.

"Oh, it was true. Back then it was true. I married up, no question."

He looks at her.

"My God, she loved you."

All semblance of control evaporates, and Sophie bursts into tears.

"Hey!" her father says.

"Sophie!"

She turns, blubbering. Frieda stands at the edge of the room, phone in hand.

"I'm okay," Sophie says mechanically. "Is that for me?"

"No," Frieda says, looking at Mort. "For you." She covers the phone with her hand. "I am not quite sure how best to handle it."

This statement, from Frieda, might be considered tantamount to Einstein expressing uncertainty about the theory of relativity. Sophie abruptly forgets why she is crying. "Who is it?" says Mort.

"It's that woman from the *Ascendant*," Frieda says.

"She's not invited," says Sophie.

"Yes, but I don't think she's calling about that. She says it's in reference to a story about Barton, for tomorrow's edition."

Sophie frowns. "She just *wrote* a story about Bart."

"She said to me," Frieda announces, with hostility just tempered by confusion, "that Mr. Klein will be very unhappy if he is prevented from commenting on the story, and I will want to put him on the phone."

All three of them contemplate this notion in silence. Then Mort stands up. "All right," he says, holding out his hand. Frieda hands the phone to him and he puts it up to his ear. "This is Mort Klein," he says.

Sophie watches him. He does not move, but his face begins to tighten.

"No," he says curtly. "Absolutely not."

Frieda, for once, looks unsure of herself. This is just novel enough to distract Sophie, but only for a second.

"That is an absurd and extremely offensive assertion," Mort says. "Whoever is feeding you such an obvious falsehood can't possibly be a legitimate source."

Sophie can hear the sound of her own breathing, open-mouthed and fast.

"Dad?" she says.

Mort puts up a hand.

"Does Richard Stevenson know you're preparing to publish such a libelous and unsubstantiated rumor? Do I need to phone him right now?"

He doesn't look good, Sophie thinks. She hates that he looks like this.

"Yes, of course I'm saying it. Other than that, I wouldn't dream of commenting. Now I need to end this conversation. I need to telephone your employer." With a punch of his thumb he disconnects the call and then throws the phone onto the couch. All three of them stare at it.

"Daddy," Sophie says, mystified. "What was it?"

"Frieda," he says, "would you run and find me Richard Stevenson's phone number? New York and also Sag Harbor."

Frieda takes the phone and walks briskly away.

"Daddy?"

"You're not to worry about it," Mort says with false nonchalance. "I'm not convinced she's writing anything at all. She's probably just offended not to be invited to your wedding, after claiming in her column she'd be here."

"Writing what, Dad?" Sophie says. "What did she say?"

"You're not to worry about it," he says again, more sternly. "It's just lies."

"About me?" Sophie asks, frantic.

"No," he says, his tone softening. "It's not about you. It's something about Barton. Something obviously untrue. There's some lowlife who smells money, trying to get himself in the paper. That's all it is, sweetheart. I'm going to call Stevenson and see if I can nip this in the bud. Good," he says, "here is Frieda."

But Frieda, who has indeed returned and with the phone still in hand, is not wearing her usual expression of disapproving command. She is merely disapproving, and she looks at Sophie.

"Your florist is on the phone. For some reason, we are not permitted to phone him back in a few minutes."

Mort looks at Sophie. Sophie looks at the phone in Frieda's hand.

"I don't know why he won't let me handle it. I told him I am in charge." She speaks loudly enough to be heard on the other end of the line.

"I'll take it," Sophie says, getting to her feet.

"Why he can't talk to me I don't understand. He says he will speak only to the bride. I told him, the bride is busy."

"It's *okay*, Frieda."

Frieda gives Sophie the phone, then goes to sit beside Mort. They are both watching her. "It's...about the flowers," she says lamely. The phone is warm in her palm, she notes. Oliver is in the phone. "I'll go...I'll go take it in the kitchen."

"Keep it short," her father says. "I need to phone Richard Stevenson."

"Okay." Sophie nods. She turns and walks back to the kitchen, the Oliver phone in her hand. She does not know what to say to him.

"Sophie?" she hears, from the farthest distance.

She puts the phone to her ear.

"Sophie?"

"I'm here," Sophie says.

"Sophie, I've been trying to reach you for days."

Days, she thinks, calculating. Tuesday, Wednesday, Thursday. That's accurate. There was a message Tuesday night, two on Wednesday, one just this morning. She heard it as she lay in bed, in her apartment.

"Sophie?"

"I saw her," Sophie hears herself say. "I was at the shop on Monday. I saw her. Your...the woman you're involved with."

His silence tells her she isn't wrong.

"Sophie..."

"No!" she says brightly. "I'm not mad. You told me. I mean, you were honest."

"Sophie, listen, that's...I wanted..." His voice trails off.

"Things are pretty busy here. With the wedding," she says evenly.

"No! Sophie, listen to me, it's going to be all right."

She nods, as if he can see her. "Thank you for...everything, Oliver. I mean it. And I'm glad you called, because...I mean, about the flowers. Maybe, under the circumstances, I should let Millbrook Floral do this." She hears herself actually laugh, a strained, strange sound. "Maybe they have enough poinsettias left."

"*Sophie...,*" she hears him say.

"And Oliver, I'm sorry to be abrupt, but we've got kind of a crisis going on here, so I need the phone."

"Jesus Christ, Sophie. Will you *listen* to me?"

It is the aural equivalent of a slap. She grips the phone, staring down at the legal pad on the table in front of her.

"Sophie," says Oliver, "I wish...I wish so much that you hadn't seen that. But you did, and it means I'm going to have to tell you some things I didn't want to tell you." He pauses. She can hear him breathe. "Not right now, though. That's not why I'm phoning you. This is about the call you just got. From Valerie Annis."

Sophie stiffens. She can feel rage surging through her, shooting to her extremities. "How do you know about that?" Her voice comes out hissing. "Oliver, did you have something to do with that? Did you give her this number?"

"Don't worry about Valerie," Oliver says. "In a few hours she won't have a source."

"*What?*" Sophie says, still furious but now unsteady, too.

"Sophie," she hears him say, "do you trust me?"

Then the anger just leaves, gone the way it came, in a flash of heat, and she finds herself sitting there at her own kitchen table with a white plastic phone mashed to her ear, listening for his voice. She trusts him. She doesn't want to, particularly, but she does. There seems to be no helping that.

"Oliver?" Sophie says. "Is this for me?"

"Yes," says Oliver. "For you."

She nods to the legal pad, the kitchen table. "Okay."

"Go back to where your father is. Tell him you've just gotten off the phone with Barton, and Barton wants to meet with him. It's very urgent."

She frowns at the legal pad. "Barton's at home. He's setting things up for the rehearsal dinner tomorrow night."

"No. He won't be at home. At six-fifteen he'll be in the Cavalier Suite at the Black Horse Inn, in Stanfordville."

She shakes her head, horribly confused. "No, it isn't there. It was going to be there, but he moved it."

"Don't worry about any of that," Oliver says. "Just say it all back to me."

And she does, surprising herself with the flat, efficient way it comes out. *Barton wants to see him. Urgent. Six-fifteen. The Black Horse Inn. Cavalier Suite.*

"One more thing, Sophie. The timing is really important. He has to get here after six-fifteen, not before."

It's the "here" that wakes her up. Maybe the thought of what she doesn't know. Maybe just the notion that he isn't so far away, as far as she'd imagined. "Oliver?" Sophie says. "Where are you calling from?"

He says nothing, but she can hear him there, wherever he is.

"Are you...somewhere close?"

"I love you," he tells her, and then the line clicks shut.

CHAPTER TWENTY-FOUR

Two Lovely Women

OLIVER SITS BY THE PHONE, his head between his knees. For hours, his most pressing physical wish has been to throw up whatever lingers of his lunch at the Millbrook Diner. (STOP! TIME TO EAT! said a sign over the clock on the diner's storefront, and Oliver, who had arrived hours in advance of his own schedule, unfortunately did just that.) Relief not forthcoming, he sits this way in his chair, listening to his own shallow breathing and willing the minutes to pass. It's 5:30. Not long before it begins. Not long, he fervently hopes, until it ends.

The inn is so private and lovely—every bit as "restrained" as Barton suggested—that he almost regrets bringing such a sordid pantomime to its elegant rooms. It looks, thinks Oliver, like somebody's private country home, but so opulently maintained that it's ready at all times in case twenty- or thirty-odd dear friends happened by, needing haven. Those friends might be elsewhere on this particular night, but unfortunately the inn is not quite so vacant as the man who took his reservation had indicated a few days before. Across the landing, with its long comfortable couch and stately chairs, a tasseled DO NOT DISTURB sign hangs from a gilded doorknob. One other traveler, then. Not ideal, but better than an inn full of wedding guests. *Just stay where you are*, Oliver silently instructs the occupant. *Whoever you are, whatever you might hear, it's none of your concern.*

Oliver wipes his forehead with the back of his hand and takes a final look around. The Cavalier Suite is not large, but it suits his needs perfectly. The sitting room has green striped silk on the walls, and green ticking on the armchairs flanking the fire, and even a pretty good still life above the mantelpiece. He takes a moment to assess his own still life, on the low table before him: two champagne flutes with a swallow left in each, the bottle emptied (down the sink, despite temptation) and on its side, a decimated box of Godiva chocolates. *Too obvious?* he worries suddenly. *Too patent?* Even so, this is a Norman Rockwell tableau compared to what lies behind the bedroom door, an installation worthy of the Whitney Biennial. With its once pristine sheets twisted to the ground, the bed is strewn with evidence of a variety of unwholesome acts. There are smudges of lipstick, patches of rubbed-in Vaseline, a leather belt studded with very scary metal points draped across the pillows and even a black riding crop Oliver plucked, in a moment of opportunistic improvisation, from the inn's own stand of whips and boots just inside the front door. On the bedside table lies a half-squeezed tube of K-Y jelly, an unsubtle product placement. Reviewing it all now, his nausea returns. Oliver leans forward again and closes his eyes.

The point, he thinks, trying to reassure himself, is that once he goes into the bathroom and changes into his clothes—into Olivia's clothes—there should be no trace of himself, of Oliver Stern, in sight. The only reality here must be the reality of Olivia and Barton and the hours they have evidently just spent, in these rooms, in each other's affectionate company. It is a reality of visual evidence: a billboard declaration to Mort Klein that the favored almost-son-in-law has been withholding certain critical facets of his character. This room—and the bedroom, of course—are the world Oliver has made, for the purpose of his purpose, and after the purpose has been served, the created world will dissolve before his eyes. If he is fortunate, thinks Oliver,

Mort will stay just long enough to verify the content of Valerie Annis's phone call. If he is very, very fortunate, Mort will not linger long on Barton's correspondent, a young person of uncertain gender in a red cashmere sweater and a beige skirt. Then, after it's over, after they have all fled, Oliver will put on his jeans and boots and sweater, make a final phone call to Valerie Annis, and disappear back into his own life. His life, he can only hope, with Sophie.

Five forty-five. Oliver's head is pounding. He is falling behind, unable to think through the necessary plot points, the rehearsed material, losing the traction of his motivation. He understands, vaguely, that he should be ready by now, dressed already, his own clothes safely stashed in the under-sink cupboard in the bathroom, but he is having trouble getting up out of his chair, and it may no longer be possible to blame the Millbrook Diner. So, as a catalyst, he tries to summon back the thin ribbon of pleasure that attended Olivia's first appearance, the moment he left Marian's tiny office and walked, alive with anticipation, through her kitchen and dining room to the waiting audience of Barton Ochstein. He thinks of his walk through the Village, and the reflected Olivia in the window of Christopher Wines, in the stare of that tall man who purposely brushed against him in the crosswalk, in the warm interest of Valéry, the waiter.

Then he remembers Sophie, who was there, too.

Oliver shakes his head quickly. He can't think about that now. He can't let himself fall into self-recrimination, or wonder how he managed to miss her on that small and familiar street when he should have been paying attention. He can't worry about how he will explain Olivia to Sophie. He has to concentrate on now. Barton is en route to see Olivia, and Mort is en route to see Barton. Oliver gets one chance to do this right.

But even as he thinks this, it's too late. Outside, a car crunches heavily on the gravel behind the inn, followed by the smart slap of a car door. Barton is here, Oliver thinks. He claws at his wrist, pulling back his sweater and fumbling with his watch: 5:48. Barton is early, and Olivia is late. Oliver jolts to his feet, rigid with panic. He hates Barton for being early, for his eagerness, though this is no one's fault but

Oliver's own. He stands in sick paralysis, listening. *At least*, he thinks, *the wig*. He can get to the wig if he moves now, but he still doesn't move. The inn's back door groans open, then shut. The stairs begin to creak. He will never forgive himself, Oliver thinks. He takes a pointless step, then stops again. The wooden floorboards are creaking, an atonal chamber piece. Someone comes to the door, and knocks.

Barton.

And Oliver is merely standing still, a man in man's clothing.

"I'm not quite ready, Barton!" he manages to say. "Can you wait just a minute?"

"Oliver?"

The voice knocks all other sound from the air. Oliver stares at the door. That must be wrong, he thinks. The nausea, the nerves. So why can't he move?

"Oliver, is it you?" She calls again, and this, at last, brings him reeling across the room. He takes hold of the doorknob, opens the door, and gazes at her, stricken. Sophie looks back at him. She appears pale and horribly tired, her hair pinned up at the back of her head, but without precision, so the coil of hair is off center and fraying, threatening disintegration. Oliver, too stunned to gather the meaning of her appearance, focuses instead on this detail. "I wasn't sure," she says, finally. "I thought you might be here, but I also thought I might be coming to see Bart."

"He's late," Oliver says, unsteady on his feet. "Sophie, you have to leave."

She gives him a look of dull forbearance. "No, not if Bart's on his way. I need to talk to him."

"You don't understand!" Oliver says, and his voice comes out so strained and harsh, he flinches. "He's not coming to see you. Or me. He's…meeting someone."

Sophie looks past him, and then, helplessly, he watches her take in the room: the champagne glasses and chocolates, the mercifully closed bedroom door…and then the open bathroom door, through which Olivia's clothes are clearly visible; they hang from a towel hook, the heels placed modestly together, beneath them on the tile floor. Olivia's wig sits waiting on the closed toilet seat. Oliver can almost hear the combination lock of her comprehension, clicking open. "That was you," Sophie says in wonder. "On Commerce Street."

He shakes his head, but it's pointless. He can't even look her in the eye. And in any case, another car is driving onto the gravel of the parking lot.

Oliver pulls her inside, and shuts the door behind her. "I'm sorry," he tells her. "I'm so sorry. I told you I would take care of this."

"I shouldn't have asked," she says simply. "It was my responsibility. It was wrong of me to ask."

"It wasn't wrong," Oliver insists as the heavy inn door opens downstairs. "I wanted to. And I had...a plan," he says stupidly. "It's all going wrong. But I didn't want you to have to see anything."

Sophie nods, as if, Oliver thinks, she is actually following the disorderly progression of his logic. From downstairs comes the murmur of voices: Barton, being directed to Olivia Nemo's suite.

"I've told my father," Sophie says quietly. "Now I'm going to tell Bart. Is that him?"

Oliver tries to glean the meaning of this, but the noises are distracting him—whining wood and human effort: *Barton Ochstein sounds upon the stair*. Undoubtedly Barton, now. That he could have taken Sophie's step for this heavy, eager tread seems thoroughly absurd.

"Oh-Liv-Vee-Yah," Barton sings, *tap-tapping* with a knuckle.

Sophie seems to go still, intent on the sound.

"Is there a young lady at home?" Barton calls, sounding for all the world like a man who is *not* two days from his own wedding. They both stand where they are, listening.

Tap-tap.

"Will you...," Oliver whispers, feebly, "could you wait in the bathroom?"

She kisses him. It is not a passionate kiss, but resolute and lightning quick, on Oliver's open mouth. "No," says Sophie, and she walks to the door and opens it.

Oliver can't see what she sees. He sees the open door, and Sophie's face in profile, the great knot of hair teetering at her nape. He sees her expression, not fond or angry or bereaved, but finally blank, as if she were looking not at her faithless fiancé but at some stranger on the subway. She has one hand on the doorknob still, and Oliver stares at it, riveted by the new information that she is no longer wearing her engagement ring. There is utter silence from the landing.

"Barton," Sophie says at last, "I think you should come in."

She steps back and he follows her, stumbling into the room, leaving the door ajar behind him. He is holding flowers, of course. Red carnations, commonest of the common, four days old and wrapped in… yes, cellophane. Barton notices Oliver and looks at him with incomprehension, then goes back to Sophie.

"Well," he begins, gamely. "This is a surprise."

"So I gather," Sophie says. "Look, I suggest we skip over the part about what we're all doing here and go right to the content."

Barton frowns. "Content," he considers, perplexed.

"I want you to know," she says, "that I bear you absolutely no ill will. I mean that, Barton."

"Sophie!" Barton snaps to attention. "Please, don't say anything more."

"There isn't much more to say," she tells him. "But this is the important part. I've decided not to marry you, Bart. I'm very sorry, but I don't think I'd be happy as your wife. And actually, I don't really think I'm what you're looking for, either."

"Sophie, now listen," Barton counters anxiously. "This is all—"

"You're a kind man. I appreciate that. And my father has very warm feelings for you. I hope you'll want to see him, still. He would like that, Bart."

Oliver watches her, stunned and moved. She seems to ascend in place as she speaks. She is, it comes to him, magnificent.

"Sophie!" Barton says sharply. "This is…someone called me to say…my…I have a cousin. Olivia. She is here for the wedding," Barton announces. "I was coming over to see her. This is not at all what you evidently have decided it is."

"*Bullshit,*" Oliver says, but under his breath, as if, having abdicated his role, he is reluctant to reenter the drama.

Barton seems to really notice Oliver this time. At first, he doesn't hold Oliver's eyes, but then, almost immediately, his gaze flickers back. Then back again. Then he begins to glare. "Who are you?" he says, finally. "Sophie, who is this?"

"It doesn't matter," she says, shaking her head and sounding tired. "It isn't about him, really."

"About…" Barton trails off. "Why is this man here?"

Sophie looks at Oliver. She seems, for a long moment, to need reminding about why he is here.

"He's here," she says, "because I love him. And…" Then, unaccountably, she smiles. "Also, he's doing the flowers."

"Flowers?" Barton says. "You." He lifts the carnations in accusation. "Tell me your name."

"You know my name," Oliver says.

"He does?" says Sophie.

"You've known it for months. Tell her."

"I've never seen him before," Barton announces, desperation edging his voice. "Sophie, this is preposterous. A trick has been played on us, and we should joke about it. I have a good sense of humor about these things, you know. That's one thing you know about me," he says heartily, managing even to produce a short laugh. "There's no need to take it all so seriously. Let's go downstairs and talk about this, right now. You know how fond of you I am."

"I do know," she says kindly. "But I'm not going to do that."

"Sophie," Barton says, more angrily, "this…person…clearly is taking advantage of you. I never want to see that happen to someone I care about."

"Tell her my name," Oliver says to him, enraged. "Tell her about all the phone calls you made to me, and all the invitations. And the flowers you've sent. Hundreds of dollars' worth of flowers. *Which you've never paid for!*" he can't resist adding. "Talk about taking advantage!"

Barton, with sudden understanding, begins to shake his head, frantically. "Utterly untrue!" Barton tells Sophie.

"Utterly true," Oliver says bitterly.

"You're a deceitful...!" Barton bellows. A deceitful what, he doesn't say.

"You know him?" Sophie asks Oliver quietly.

"Oh, sure," Oliver nods. "He's the kind of guy who stops on his way to a romantic assignation to pick up *carnations*, all wrapped up in cellophane and tied with a red ribbon. What else is there to know?"

Sophie turns to face Oliver. "I don't think it's fair to hold that against him," she says. "Not everyone's as invested in the beauty of flowers as you are."

Barton, dazed, regards the carnations he carries. "This is...," he says feebly. "This is...not for..." He draws himself up, recovering from his outrage. "An...*assignation*, Sophie. I was merely stopping here to see my cousin Olivia. Then I was on my way to the farm. This bouquet was intended for *you*, Sophie."

"Bouquet," Oliver says in disgust. "Naturally. *Bouquet!*"

"You know"—Sophie shakes her head—"some people *like* carnations."

"Impossible," Oliver states with repelled authority. "No one *likes* carnations. They're inherently despicable." He stops, a matter of great significance now occurring to him. "You don't...like carnations. Do you?"

She gives this sober consideration and duly locates her answer. "No," she sighs.

"No?" Barton asks, baffled.

"I'm afraid not," she tells him. "It was a nice thought, though."

"It was bullshit," Oliver says. "There's no cousin Olivia. He only has one cousin. And her name isn't Olivia, is it, Barton?"

"You seem to know quite a bit about my cousin," Barton says menacingly.

"I know you made a pass at her assistant, right under her nose. I know you couldn't care less about her. I know she'd be horrified if she knew what you've been up to."

"Are you talking," says Sophie, struggling to follow, "about Marian Kahn?"

"Marian *Warburg*," Barton says, pausing amid the general absurdity to assert his preferred nomenclature.

"Marian *Kahn*!" Oliver shouts. "Jesus, you don't know the first thing about her, do you? You pay all this lip service to your family name, but you don't give a damn about your real family." Then he can feel, in some detached way, Sophie's cool hand at his wrist, and the bitterness slips from him. He is here after all, with Sophie, who is here with him. The rest is noise. "I have nothing against you," he says. "I only wish..."

But he stops. His wishes are not for the likes of Barton.

"Sophie," Barton says. "I really think this matter is for us to discuss. Alone. Whatever this person has told you, there are genuine feelings between us."

"There are," Sophie agrees. "But they're not enough. Please, Bart. Let's just finish it now."

"I—" Barton begins, already disagreeing, but then all three of them fall silent. There is a disturbance just outside: the displacement of air, a sound on the landing. Then the door opens wide, swinging into the room and against the wall, where it silently stops. Oliver looks up. What he sees makes him want to disappear.

Marian stands in the doorway, her face drawn and sad, and his first thought—before the disbelief and the humiliation and the wave of deepest regret—is that she looks so young. Like a girl, younger even than himself, wrapped up in a white bathrobe with her hair loose to her shoulders and her feet bare, as if she has just been awakened, which—Oliver now understands—she undoubtedly has been. Behind the DO NOT DISTURB sign, all this time. But how?

"Marian," Oliver asks quietly, "how can you be here?"

She looks at all three of them, then only at him. "I came for the wedding," she says simply. "I was sleeping. But then I heard someone call my name." She seems to consider this, almost languidly. "Was it you, Oliver?"

"*Oliver!*" Barton says, outraged.

"Oliver?" Sophie says, her hand now heavy on his wrist.

Oliver shakes his head, speechless and bereft. "Marian," he hears himself say, "this is Sophie."

"I know who she is," Marian says. She comes into the room, her eyes on Sophie, her hand offered. It slips from inside the thick robe: a fragile wrist, long fingers, unpolished nails. She takes Sophie's hand. Oliver can only look at her. He can't recall ever having loved her as deeply as now, when he can see so clearly what he has already lost. She is very lovely. They both are: lovely women, women he loves. He is so ashamed he can barely stand.

"It's a good thing you've come, Marian," Barton says, rebounding. "I don't think you have any idea what your friend here has been up to."

She turns from Sophie, but reluctantly. Along the way, Oliver watches her notice everything else: the women's clothing in the bathroom, the champagne flutes. By the time her gaze rests on Barton, nothing has eluded her.

"Does it really matter?" she asks her cousin. "I think we all end up in the same place."

"Of course it matters!" he sputters, clenching his carnations.

"Barton," Marian says, sighing, "isn't it time for you to leave?"

"No, no,"—he shakes his head—"no, it's all a mistake. Really, Sophie, we've been horribly abused tonight. A terrible thing has been done."

"Barton," Marian says wearily.

"I reject this!" he cries. "I find this behavior reprehensible."

"Barton," Marian says, her voice sharp, "you are not listening. You need to know when a thing is over." And she looks, unavoidably, but for the briefest instant, at Oliver. "It's over now."

"Sophie," says Barton, pointlessly.

"I'm sorry, Barton," says Sophie.

At last he goes, taking his horrible flowers away with him, clomping loudly down the stairs. For a moment, no one speaks.

Sophie's hand isn't on his arm any longer, Oliver notes. He has failed to mark its departure, or even its absence, until now. What does that mean? he wonders. Who is with him? Who loves him?

"I take it the wedding is off," Marian says at last.

"It's off," says Sophie. "I'm so sorry."

"Don't be sorry." She gives a faint smile. "I had to be in Rhinebeck today, anyway."

"No," Sophie stumbles. "I didn't mean that."

"Don't be sorry," says Marian. Then she looks at Oliver. Then she goes, shutting the door behind her.

Sophie drifts away from him. She crosses the small room and sits, facing the fireplace, almost disappearing into the wings of the armchair. He has no idea what to say to her, or whether there is any point in explaining, or even what his explanation might be, and so he stands pointlessly, pondering and then discarding the few ideas he has. The fact that he is about to lose everything is abundantly clear to him. All that's left are details.

When he finally steps closer, when he finally gathers enough courage to crouch down beside her, he can see that her eyes are closed. From first one, then the other, single tears emerge and descend. She looks, he thinks, as bereft as that other day, the day he understood that he loved her, the day she asked for his help.

"That day at Columbia," Sophie says, jolting suddenly into his thoughts. "You weren't there to see me at all, were you?"

Oliver considers. "I think I was," he says. "I just didn't know I was." She shakes her head.

"I'm sorry," Oliver says, reaching for her. "I don't know what to say. It wasn't a casual thing. I really loved her."

"You don't owe me anything," Sophie says, biting her lip. "You never lied to me. You told me you were involved with someone. And even before you told me, Bell told me, so I knew. If I convinced myself otherwise, it's entirely my fault."

"No!" says Oliver, grabbing for her hand.

"I want you to know that I don't expect anything from you. You helped me, out of kindness. As a friend."

"No, no!" Oliver says. "I mean, yes, as a friend. And I am your friend. But I did it for myself, too, not only out of kindness. Because of what I want for myself."

"And what do you want, Oliver?" says Sophie. "Now would be a good moment to tell me."

But now is the moment he hears, from across the landing, the unmistakable creak of the old floorboards, and a door shutting. Marian is there, and he needs to say something to her.

"I'll be right back," he tells Sophie.

Outside, the landing is empty. The DO NOT DISTURB sign swings gently on the door handle on the opposite room. Oliver tears down the stairs, but he doesn't find her in the foyer, or in the lounge. Only the tap of a heel on stone draws him to the back door, where she stands, her suitcase at her heel, shrugging on her coat.

"Marian, wait," Oliver calls, and she stops where she is.

At first, he can only look at her. When he finally speaks, it's to state the obvious.

"You're leaving."

"I'm going to drive back to the city," she says quietly. "I don't really feel like spending the night here."

"Marian," Oliver says desperately, "I didn't mean for this to happen. I didn't…I didn't decide to fall in love with someone else. I couldn't control it."

"I know that," Marian says, impassively. "But I need to go, Oliver."

And they stand again in their mutual sadness.

"I don't regret it," Marian suddenly says, looking surprised at her own emotion. "I wish I'd spent less time worrying about everything and more time just appreciating you."

"I felt appreciated," says Oliver. "I know you loved me."

She nods. She has one hand on the door. The other holds closed the lapels of her coat.

"I think," he says, "I'll always feel some of it."

"All right," she agrees. "Me too."

"And you'll know I do, if we see each other. Even if I don't say so."

"Okay," Marian nods. "Good-bye, sweetheart."

He rushes to her: one step, two steps. It takes forever to get there. Then it takes forever to let her go.

"She's very pretty," Marian says, her face slick with tears.

"Marian," says Oliver, who is also crying, "you're so good."

Then, to his great surprise, she laughs. A genuine laugh.

"The last person who said that to me was Valerie Annis," she says, shaking her head. "Isn't that funny?" Marian picks up her suitcase. "Now go back upstairs," she tells him, and opens the door, and goes outside.

But he can't do that yet. Long minutes will pass before he can do what she says.

CHAPTER TWENTY-FIVE

Here Saw Nothing to Regret

AT FIRST, Marian drives in silence and without thought. Retracing her route through the labyrinthine thoroughfares of Dutchess County takes a happily large portion of her attention. The roads are empty, blessedly empty. In silence Marian locates her landmarks, finding her way back, reversing herself: the big white birch tree, the great nouveau mansion with the name she'd thought was twee, only a few hours earlier, the house with the big dog who'd come charging down the driveway to bark at her when she'd slowed in indecision before making her turn. The dog isn't there any longer.

But after she drives through Rhinebeck, it gets harder. She knows the way from here, and she finds it more difficult to hold at bay the things she has seen, and said, and the room, and the other people in the room: Oliver and Barton and the girl—Sophie. Mostly Marian thinks about Sophie, and the thought of her is far more painful than an abstract notion of a person Oliver might one day love.

So when Marian reaches the stoplight where she needs to turn right for the Kingston-Rhinecliff bridge, she is perhaps especially vulnerable to a road sign she might otherwise have missed, and when she sees that sign, idling behind a Land Rover with Connecticut plates, Marian makes not a decision, really, but a gesture, and turns left, and drives south. She is sure of where she's going, but not at all sure why.

In Rhinecliff, she drives through the little village and winds up the hill to the church, leaving her Volvo by the roadside. True to Betty Evans's word, there is indeed an enclosed wooden case of pamphlets, offering guidance to the grave and the brief biographies of other, less celebrated inhabitants of the cemetery, and Marian carefully folds one into her coat pocket before slinging her bag over her shoulder and beginning the walk uphill. This is the third visit she's made to the Rhinecliff Reformed Church. The first was during her initial research trip to Rhinebeck, when she had come looking for accounts of the 1757 Fort William Henry massacre, and some clue as to who had cared for the child, Charlotte Wilcox, after the death of her family, and found, instead (in the local history archives of the Rhinebeck Public Library, in a moldering box marked "Miscellaneous 1750–1850, Farwell"), seventeen precious letters from Charlotte herself. Marian had returned one year later, when her purpose had been to record a description of the grave for her book. The first time, it had taken a half hour of searching, pulling away the overgrowth and peering at the faded stones, before she had found Charlotte's gravestone, unvisited for two centuries. The second time, she forgot the location, so the search had taken nearly as long. But this time Marian follows an actual path among the markers, the earth underfoot worn bare and the winter grass flattened on either side. The path takes her directly to the corner of the churchyard, where she can look through an iron railing down onto the little town and the train station, and even the wide Hudson, lit by a pearl-gray moon. The grave seems, somehow, crisper than she remembers, and it occurs to her to wonder just what Betty Evans and her colleagues have done to care for the site. Is it possible that someone has reset the slender blocks of granite that form a border for the grave, or cleaned the etched words on the stone? She bends forward to read it, even though there isn't really enough light for that, and even though she knows the inscription by heart.

IN MEMORY OF CHARLOTTE WILCOX
WHO DIED APRIL 17TH, 1802
IN THE 55TH YEAR OF HER AGE
CALMLY SHE LOOKED ON EITHER LIFE, AND HERE
SAW NOTHING TO REGRET; NOTHING THERE TO FEAR

ALSO HER HUSBAND, THOMAS WILCOX
BORN IRELAND, DIED JUNE 14TH, 1804
AGED 38 YEARS

This is no longer a forgotten or neglected place. Marian, looking down, sees that the earth at her feet is covered with small tributes, mostly stones carried here and placed carefully on the spot, as in the Jewish custom, but also odd trinkets, seashells, a reproduction of the drawing by Thomas Wilcox, the sole image of Charlotte, carefully laminated and propped against the gravestone. There are bits of tape left on the stone itself, and a forgotten pencil—the remnants, thinks Marian, of attempts to make rubbings of Charlotte's marker—and a stack of flowers in various stages of demise, wrapped in their cellophane cones and tied with fading ribbons. There are even two or three handwritten notes, which Marian refrains from reading, but it's all overwhelming to her, and for a moment she looks out over the graveyard, over the still overgrown and unvisited memorials, and allows herself the faintest pride.

Because I did this, Marian thinks. With work, and with care. I did this.

Except, of course, that she hadn't. It was always Charlotte, Marian thinks, who was not just an adventuress or a woman of letters, and was not a heroine because she chewed men up or even because she had touched and reported on every stratum of English society. The bearers of these flowers and the authors of these notes had come to honor her because of what they had learned from her story, which was not a lesson restricted to Charlotte's time or place. And a good thing too, Marian tells herself, or I couldn't have learned it myself:

> When I was twenty, I had work I loved.
>
> When I was twenty-two, I had a husband I loved.
>
> When I was thirty-six, I had a chance to stay alive.
>
> When I was forty-five, I had a book, that I wrote, that changed everything.
>
> When I was forty-eight, the very age a woman is supposed to become invisible, there was a man who actually saw me.

Marian wipes her face with her hands.

And now, Marian thinks, there is this girl, who is not my daughter, and will never be my daughter, but who might need something that I might be able to give her. And that's a gift.

She looks across at the other graves, filling the space between Charlotte's stone and the abandoned Rhinecliff Reformed Church. Alice Farwell is here, too, somewhere, and possibly also her daughter, who began life as a Farwell and ended it as a Wharton, giving birth to a future Danvers along the way. Some of these flowers and notes are due Alice as well, thinks Marian, for keeping those letters, for holding out the promise of friendship across an ocean and a lifetime, either of which must have felt prohibitively distant. Alice Farwell, thinks Marian, was a historian before her time, and a great woman, and this hilltop is a fitting place for both of them, a fortunate berth for eternity with the glittering Hudson below and the trains, coming in from the city. *And so lovely*, Marian thinks, looking west to the moonlit Catskills, but she is already distracted, now: the bridge, the thruway, the newly liberated weekend. She walks back along the tidy path and climbs into her Volvo, turning up the heat and turning on the radio. Schumann's "Frauenliebe und Leben" floods the car. Marian smiles: not inappropriate, after all. Then she starts the engine and heads for home.

CHAPTER TWENTY-SIX

The White Rose

WHEN OLIVER FINALLY RETURNS TO THE ROOM, he waits in the doorway for a minute, as if for permission to enter. Sophie, though clearly aware of him, does not speak, and her silence is not gentle.

"I thought what you said to Barton was wonderful," he tells her at last, both because it is true and because he needs to say something. "You were…I thought you were very brave."

"Oh, very." Sophie's voice is caustic. "Put me right up there with Sophie Scholl."

"It took courage," he says. "You were gracious, but you were clear. I thought you were amazing."

"Amazing would have been telling him last week," Sophie says. "Or better yet, last month. And sparing us all…this," she says, gesturing around the room.

"I wanted to spare you this," he says, growing afraid. He walks over to the chair, and then, finding no graceful way to sit beside her, he sits on the floor at her feet. He is too frightened to touch her. The idea of losing her, too, is nearly unbearable. "Sophie," he says, "I'm not going to burden you with the details, but I promise you, this wasn't a scam. I mean, not just a scam. Barton was very, very interested in that girl. In...the person he thought I was. He has been for months."

"I don't want to think about Barton," she says and turns her head. "I don't have to now, and I don't want to. I want you to tell me something else."

Oliver nods, waiting.

"I know it's none of my business, but how long did it go on? With her."

"It is your business. Since last spring."

Sophie absorbs this information.

"And when did it end?"

The answer to this does not come as easily. Finally he tells her: "Five minutes ago."

He takes her hand between his hands. Sophie doesn't move but she doesn't resist. "Do you need to go back to the house?" he says.

Sophie nods. "I do. It's going to be a scene over there. We've got two hundred people to head off at the pass, before Saturday."

"All right," he says, resigned, but Sophie is shaking her head.

"No," she settles back a bit in the armchair and turns to him. "I have a little time. And Frieda is already working on it. She'll be in her element. She loves a crisis, especially one I've caused." She considers. "You haven't met Frieda, have you?"

"Only on the phone," he tells her. "And when she told me to bring your roses to the service entrance."

"Oh," Sophie says with some embarrassment. "I'm sorry."

"I'm not sorry. How would I have met you, otherwise? How would I have been able to see you half undressed, with a big hole between the buttons of your shirt?"

Sophie leans forward in the armchair and swats him. "You said you couldn't see anything!"

"I lied," he says. "I won't lie to you again."

She looks at him. She smiles. Then Oliver feels it all fall away: the strain, the wondering how it will end. But there is another thing.

"Sophie," Oliver says, "there's something I have to tell you."

She smiles at him and pushes her hair behind her ears. "If it's that you like to wear women's clothes, I already know that."

"No, it's not that. I didn't like it. Much, anyway. But it isn't about that."

"Then it must be about why you named your shop the White Rose," she says. "That is, if you know me well enough yet."

Oliver nods. "I do. I mean, I think I will. But it's not that, either. Well, that's not true. It's part of the same story, what I need to tell you. Not a story," he shakes his head. "I mean," he rolls his eyes. *I am making a mess*, he thinks. "Not a made-up story. It's something that happened. In the past."

"Well, you've come to the right place," Sophie says, looking only slightly more worried. "As a historian, I'm partial to stories about things that happened in the past. How far back in the past?"

Oliver closes his eyes. "I was six years old. So twenty years ago."

Now, at last, Sophie seems to understand that he is serious, and she must be serious, too. "All right, Oliver," Sophie says. "You can tell me."

But he doesn't, for another minute, and when he speaks again it's only in frustration. "I don't know how to do this," Oliver says, shaking his head. "I've never done this."

She doesn't say anything, and she doesn't touch him. She just waits.

"I got sick when I was six. I had leukemia. Now," Oliver says hurriedly, "I'm not trying to be dramatic, or whine about it. There's no suspense about this, okay? You know how the story comes out. I mean, it's twenty years later. I'm here, right?"

"Right," Sophie agrees, but her voice is uncertain.

"And I'm not saying it was so horrible, I suffered so much, blah, blah, and I nearly died, because I don't remember it like that. And if I did nearly die I didn't know it at the time. Actually," Oliver looks at her, "what I remember about it all is...almost nothing. Which is *incredible*. Don't you think? Because I read the file when I was older. When I was twelve. I found it in my mother's desk and I read the whole thing. I don't remember the drugs or my hair falling out. I don't remember having a spinal tap. Is that incredible?" Oliver says. "I mean, a spinal tap? How could all that have happened to me and I can't remember?"

"Maybe you were protecting yourself," Sophie suggests. "You... detached, I guess. For self-preservation. But you said *nearly* nothing. You do remember something."

"Right. Yes," Oliver nods. "I remember...waking up in my bed, in the hospital. I don't remember lying in bed awake or falling asleep, only...waking up. It was like being trapped inside the same moment, over and over—waking up, then waking up again. Except it wasn't always exactly the same. When I woke up, I might see something, or hear something someone was saying, but then I would wake up again. It just kept on like that, for weeks and months."

Oliver sits on the floor still, facing away from her, his hands interlaced, and Sophie can see—eerily white in the growing darkness—the knuckles of his hands, tensing and tensing. She reaches down to touch them, but they don't stop. She touches his hair, his face, but he doesn't seem to respond to that, either. "It sounds kind of merciful, actually," she tells him. "If I had a very sick child, I'd hope he could experience it like that."

"I suppose," Oliver says. "Yes, I can see that. Though it's been hard in retrospect, like I can't really believe any of it actually took place. But," he says concentrating, "there was something that happened once."

"When you woke up," she prompts him, after a minute.

"Something I saw. I was lying on my side in the bed, and I opened my eyes. And someone had put a flower on the table next to my bed."

"A white rose?" guesses Sophie.

"Yes. I didn't know anything about flowers, but I knew it was a rose. I saw it was white. It was so big. It seemed bigger than me, but I couldn't have been thinking clearly. And I remember, just...staring at it. I remember seeing every part of it. It was so...It was a *living* flower. Does that sound crazy? Bright white, like it was almost glowing. The petals looked like they were wet, like someone had just cut the rose in the rain and rushed to the hospital to bring it to me. It was in a plastic cup. You know, a hospital cup. I just looked at it as long as I could, and then I must have fallen asleep."

Sophie waits. "It had to have been beautiful," she finally says, "if you remember it so well."

Oliver nods. "It was. Then I woke up again, and I remember, I felt excited to see the rose there. But this time it wasn't as big. It was sort of... flagging." He shakes his head. "I know this sounds ridiculous."

"It doesn't," says Sophie.

"It had some brown at the tips of the petals. And it was smaller than I remembered."

"Okay. And the next time?"

"Smaller. But I could sit up in bed. So maybe I just felt bigger. And the stalk looked thinner. And the leaves were getting limp."

"It was dying, in other words."

"Yes. Exactly. But the thing is," Oliver says, "that's when I started to get better. And this is the point where I start remembering more things, you know, which is strange. Isn't that strange? I don't remember being sick, but I remember getting better? I remember sitting up and eating. I ate an orange. I remember going to the playroom upstairs with my mother. I remember going in the elevator in my wheelchair. There was an aquarium, and a Ping-Pong table. But the rose died. And the funny thing is, I don't think I was even that sad about it. I watched it get so withered and brown. I didn't touch it. And then one day I woke up and it was gone. Somebody had finally thrown it away."

"But you were cured," says Sophie.

"Well, in remission," Oliver tells her. "Nobody said cure, at the time. The drug they used was still pretty new. I don't think anybody felt very confident about predicting the outcome, though after twenty years I think we're allowed to call it a cure. So I left the hospital, went home, went back to school. I got to grow up and be healthy. And all I knew about having had leukemia was the waking up and the rose."

It's dark in the room now. There is light from under the bathroom door, light from under the bedroom door, light from under the door to the landing. But it's still so dark, Oliver can barely see Sophie. Which is good, he thinks, because it means she can barely see him.

"Sometimes," says Oliver, "I think that's the rose I'm trying to make. The new rose. You know."

"The Lady Charlotte rose," Sophie says.

"Yes. That's the rose in my head. I never saw it again. I *want* to see it again. I want..." He stops, suddenly shy. "I want to say thank you. Is that nuts?"

"I don't think it's nuts," says Sophie.

"Maybe that rose wasn't even real. Maybe I made it up. Or it was a delusion, or something. From the drugs. And if it hadn't been a rose, it would have been something else."

"But to you it was a rose," she confirms.

"Yes. My white rose."

He stops. He closes his eyes.

"I might not be able to have kids," Oliver says softly.

He can hear her breathe. He can hear the old walls of the inn, the air in those walls, humming. "You might not be," Sophie says.

"No," his voice cracks.

"Because of the leukemia."

"No. Because of one of the drugs. Cytoxan. I read the release form in my file about not being able to have children. I've read some other studies, too."

"But you don't know for sure?" Sophie says.

"No."

"All right," says Sophie, after a moment. "Now you've told me."

"I know you want them," Oliver says, distraught.

"I want them," she agrees. "Do you?"

"I want them," Oliver starts to cry again. "I really do. For years I pretended I didn't. I even broke up with my girlfriend from college because I couldn't tell her. I said I didn't want to have children. But I do. I don't know what to do."

"All right," she tells him. "It's all right."

"I'm sorry, Sophie."

"*Oliver.*" And she gets off the chair and sits down, beside him, on the floor. She takes his head in her hands and makes him look at her, though it's too dark to really look. "I love you," she tells him. "I want this. I want you."

Oliver, like something switched off, stops crying. "Really?"

"We don't know what will happen. We don't even know if there's a problem."

He nods, terrified.

"I'm a brave woman," she reminds him. "You said so."

"I did," Oliver agrees. "You are."

"What you told me, what you're afraid of," says Sophie, "that's not where we end. It's where we begin." She smiles. "You see?"

"Yes," he says, because he does. And that's a gift, of course, like anything of real value, even if he will never know precisely whom to thank. He holds her and holds her, and laughs out loud, and says, "Then let's begin."

ACKNOWLEDGMENTS

I must, by all means, express my most heartfelt thanks to Richard
Strauss and Hugo Von Hofmannsthal for the gift of *Der Rosenkavalier*.
That a work so intuitive about women's experience was created
entirely by men is an ongoing source of wonder to me. If I wore a hat,
I would tip it.

I thank Michael Davis of Elan Flowers in Manhattan and Stephen
Scanniello, eminent rosarian, for teaching me more about flowers in
general and roses in particular than I had any right to pretend I knew.
Penelope Coker Hall told me all about life in Millbrook and Corinne
Linardic, MD, helped me with medical research. Charlotte Wilcox's
epitaph was ruthlessly stolen from *Epitaphs to Remember: Remarkable
Inscriptions from New England Gravestones* by Janet Greene. The chapter about Bedford Hills owes much to Jean Harris's book *They Always
Call Us Ladies*, and even more to the incomparable Hettie Jones, who
helped me get it right, or at least right-ish. I am, as ever, grateful to
Deborah Michel, goddess of plot, for her incisive reading and great
friendship. I thank Pam Bernstein for the purloining of her Hamptons
home (and so much more), Joan Hamburg for the benefit of her experiences, and the Bread Loaf School of English for serving as my virtual
artists' colony, these past years.

Thank you, thank you, Suzanne Gluck, for all of the enthusiasm
and support you brought to this novel, and thank you, Jonathan Burn-
ham, for giving it such a good home.

READING GROUP GUIDE

Introduction

"We're taking a position that celebrates the transience of the flower. Not that we don't prolong the bloom as long as we can, but we recognize that a flower's impermanence is part of its beauty."

A sweeping tale of love and deception, wealth and beauty, obligation and desire, *The White Rose* is as seductive a story as the flower for which it's named.

Marian Kahn, a forty-eight-year-old professor of history at Columbia University, is in the midst of an affair with a man twenty-two years her junior. Although Oliver's wish for commitment is genuine, Marian knows the day will come when they must part ways. She will never leave her marriage, no matter how passionately she feels for Oliver, and she doubts his own devotion can last.

Then Oliver commits a spontaneous and seemingly harmless act, setting in motion a series of unforeseeable events that lead him to Sophie Klein.

A graduate student in history and an idiosyncratic heiress, Sophie is engaged to Marian's pompous cousin, Bart. Oliver's deception eventually builds to a startling confrontation, bringing harsh truths to light and forcing Marian, Oliver, and Sophie to each evaluate what they're seeking from life—and to learn that love, like even the most beautiful of blooms, is often transient.

With *The White Rose*, which was inspired by Richard Strauss's opera *Der Rosenkavalier*, Jean Hanff Korelitz has crafted both a thought-provoking treatise on social mores and a compelling page-turner.

A Conversation with Jean Hanff Korelitz

Q: When did you first see the opera *Der Rosenkavalier*? What was it about the story that inspired you to put a new twist on it for *The White Rose*? Are you an opera devotee?

A: Despite having been dragged to many operas over the years, I have never been a devotee of the art form (much to the disappointment of my mother, who adores opera and did the dragging), but when I first saw *Der Rosenkavalier* in London in 1983, I had an extraordinarily powerful reaction to it. Perhaps that had something to do with the fact that I'd just been dropped by a man I was in love with in favor of a woman twice my age, or perhaps, even then, I identified strongly with the character of the Marschallin, who knows her young lover will one day leave her for a woman his own age. In the twenty years that followed my first viewing of the opera, as I myself progressed from ingénue to woman-of-a-certain-age, those impressions grew even more powerful. I admired the goodness and decency of the three major characters, and honored their efforts to do the right thing, even as they struggled with their own, very human flaws.

Q: What appealed to you about setting the book in contemporary Manhattan versus another time and place?

A: I think much writing (and, I suppose, much other art) can begin with a *what if* question. What if *Der Rosenkavalier* were happening not in 18th century Vienna, among aristocrats, but in late 20th century Manhattan, in the upper middle class Jewish setting I myself grew up in? I have a great deal of personal nostalgia embedded in this novel, and feel much tenderness for these characters, even as I occasionally poke fun at them.

Q: In the Acknowledgements sections you state in regard to *Der Rosenkavalier*: "That a work so intuitive about women's experience was created entirely by men is an ongoing source of wonder to me." What does *The White Rose* say about women's experience?

A: It seems to be part of our received wisdom that only women can truly illuminate what it means to be female. (This derives, in part, from the feminist literary criticism that was part of my own education.) I'm as much in thrall to that notion as anyone else, so much so that I'm always surprised when I come across a Madame Bovary, a Portia, or a Marschallin. I must give credit where it's due. Every time I see Der Rosenkavalier or reread the libretto, I understand that Richard Strauss and his librettist, Hugo von Hofmannsthal, did not just portray the Marschallin's circumstances, they truly understood what she was enduring. Almost exactly one hundred years after the fact, I salute their great accomplishment.

Q: Both Marian and Sophie have devoted themselves to studying history. Is history something that interests you? Do you enjoy the research aspect of writing?

A: I always want to know what happened, how we got here, and whether we've learned anything along the way. Even so, I despise the research, itself. (If I didn't, I'd be locked up in an ivory tower by now, studying some obscure thing or other.) When I wrote my first novel, *A Jury of Her Peers*, I used to write up to the very sentence in which I needed a question answered, then figure out the answer to the question, and I've pretty much stuck by that strategy ever since. For this novel, I had to learn about 18th century England, rose breeding, foster care in New York City, cancer drugs from the 1980s and how flower dealers secure their inventory. Some of that was fun, and some was drudgery. I'm grateful to people who knew far more than I did about so many things, and were willing to talk to me.

Q: *The White Rose* is essentially a story within a story. Why did you choose to share in detail the story of Charlotte Wilcox's life rather than merely allude to her? What does it add to the narrative?

A: I think Charlotte is a woman for all times because the thing she has learned—how to snatch personal happiness from the jaws of misfortune—is something we all need to learn, no matter when or where we are living, no matter how outwardly fortunate and unfortunate we may be. Marian understands that she has been no less a beneficiary of Charlotte's example than Charlotte's legion of fans, and that learning from her subject has enabled her to make peace with her own choices.

Q: Is Charlotte Wilcox an actual historical figure? If not, did you base her on anyone in particular?

A: Charlotte is fictional, but she is very (and I mean *very*) loosely inspired by Charlotte Lennox, (c.1727–1804), who was born in the

American colonies and spent her adult life in Britain. The author of several novels, most notably *The Female Quixote* (1752), and once celebrated by Samuel Johnson as a superior woman of letters, she nonetheless died in poverty and obscurity.

Q: Do you have a favorite scene in the book?

A: I do have a favorite scene. Twice during the course of the novel, we get to experience a long day in Oliver's life, a day full of distressing experiences for him. At the end of each of these two days, he will encounter Sophie, and both times she will handily deprive him of whatever equilibrium he retains. Which of these is my favorite scene? Guess.

Q: Your two previous novels, *The Sabbathday River* and *A Jury of Her Peers*, are both thrillers. Why did you depart from that style of writing to pen *The White Rose*? Although this book is not a "thriller," in what ways is it suspenseful?

A: I have a strong capacity for self-delusion, and to this day I maintain that *A Jury of Her Peers* was a Greek tragedy masquerading as a courtroom thriller and that *The Sabbathday River* was a literary novel in which Nathanial Hawthorne ran amok through a bizarre true-life Irish case of infanticide. After two such flights of fancy, it was something of a relief to write a novel whose genre the critics and I could agree on. I always took great care with my writing, whether describing a courtroom scene or a moment of intense self-discovery a character was experiencing. By the same token, it was always necessary for me that my novels had a strong story (I have personally flung aside any number of beautifully written books in which *nothing happened*.) The books I love to read are beautifully written, and never stop surprising me. I have always tried to write books like that, and I will continue to try.

Q: How did the process of writing this book differ from that of *The Sabbathday River* and *A Jury of Her Peers*?

A: It was not so different. As with *The Sabbathday River*, I had a template (in the case of that novel it was Hawthorne's *The Scarlet Letter*), and the challenge was to let the unfolding story escape that template. Characters arise from and depart from their prototypes, and new characters and situations impose themselves where no precedents exist in the source material. It's fascinating for me to see how the end result is true to its initial inspiration, and how it departs. Certainly, fans of *Der Rosenkavalier* can amuse themselves by finding the parallels between the opera and *The White Rose* (Valerie Annis, for one less obvious example, is a conflation of the two scandalmongers, Valzacchi and Annina), but there are characters in the novel that would probably have made Strauss reach for his smelling salts. (What, for example, would he have made of Jan, Oliver's helpful guide in the world of cross-dressing?)

Q: There are references in *The White Rose* to Jane Austen and Anne Frank. What writers do you admire? What books have been memorable ones for you?

A: I have loved so many novels, by so many novelists, but like any other writer I carry with me at all times my personal pantheon of books. Here are a few that come readily to mind. They are—be warned— an eclectic bunch: Jane Austen's *Pride and Prejudice*; Chaim Potok's *My Name Is Asher Lev*, Marilyn Robinson's *Housekeeping*, Frederick Forsythe's *The Odessa File* (I warned you. But if you love a breathtaking, thought providing thriller, read it and see why.), and the Irish novelist Molly Keane's brilliant late novels, *Good Behavior* and *Time After Time*. Oh, and one more: *What a Carve Up*, a comic tour de force by the young British novelist Jonathan Coe. (It was published in the US as *The Winshaw Legacy*, I can't think why.)

Questions for Discussion

1. From the opening page to the closing scene, white roses appear throughout the story. How does the symbolism of the white rose factor into the novel? What do they mean to Oliver in particular?

2. *The White Rose* opens with a scene told from Marian's perspective, making her the first character the reader gets to know. Yet by the time the novel comes to a close, the emphasis has shifted to Oliver. Why do you think the author chose to do this? Is *The White Rose* more one character's story than another?

3. Oliver is twenty-two years Marian's junior. In one instance he says to her, "I'd marry you today if I could. I have no problem with the age thing, you know I don't. I only mention it because I don't want to ignore that it's problematic for you." Why is the difference in their ages more of an issue for Marian than it is for Oliver?

4. Discuss marriage as it's presented in the novel, including Sophie's reasons for agreeing to marry Bart and why Marian refuses to end her marriage to Marshall.

5. How does Oliver's impulsive decision to masquerade as "Olivia" alter the events in the story? Why does he continue with the deception and especially to such an elaborate extent? Were you surprised by Marian's passionate response to Oliver when he was dressed in her clothing?

6. When Marian first reads the letter from Soriah she sets it aside, and there is no indication that she intends to take further action. Were you surprised to then learn she had arranged to meet Soriah and the resulting relationship that develops? What compels Marian to take on Soriah as a foster child?

7. Twice Sophia has the chance to introduce herself to Marian—in the history department at Columbia University and on the street near Bloomingdales. Why does she let both opportunities go by without saying anything? What holds her back?

10. *The White Rose* is a re-imagining of the Strauss opera *Der Rosenkavalier*, which is about a man who must choose between two lovers—an older woman and one nearer his own age. Does knowing this give you a different perspective on the story? In what ways?

11. Religion is a pervasive theme in the book. How do Marian, Oliver, and Sophie each view their Jewish heritage? In what ways do they draw on and/or deny the Jewish religion and its role in their lives?

12. The novelist and critic Edmund White said that in *The White Rose* Jean Hanff Korelitz "manages to talk about the gripping topics of our day, including race, wealth, aging, and our historical legacy." How does each of these topics play out in the storyline?

NOTICE TO BOOK GROUPS

Jean Hanff Korelitz is very happy to meet with or talk (by speaker phone) with groups who are reading *The White Rose*. To arrange an appointment, please send an e-mail to SGasst@wma.com with "Forward to Jean Hanff Korelitz" in the subject line.